Tales of
WONDER, HO
inc

The girl who ma...

The sorcerer who was too good at sorcery . . .

The alien who conquered Las Vegas . . .

The 12th-century city that appears
once a year in downtown Chicago.

Discover seventeen
WONDERFUL AND CAPTIVATING
stories by:

Eric Lustbader ⋆ Edward Bryant ⋆ Tad Williams
Katherine Dunn ⋆ Peter S. Beagle ⋆ Anne McCaffrey
Greg Bear ⋆ George Guthridge ⋆ Robert Silverberg
Robyn Carr ⋆ Kevin J. Anderson ⋆ Charles de Lint
Karen Joy Fowler ⋆ Steve Rasnic Tem ⋆ Neil Gaiman
Janet Berliner ⋆ David Copperfield

Illustrations by Cathie Bleck

Books from David Copperfield and Janet Berliner

David Copperfield's Tales of the Impossible
David Copperfield's Beyond Imagination

Published by HarperPrism

DAVID COPPERFIELD'S

Beyond Imagination

CREATED AND EDITED BY
David Copperfield and Janet Berliner

PREFACE BY
Raymond E. Feist

HarperPrism
A Division of HarperCollinsPublishers

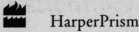

HarperPrism

A Division of HarperCollinsPublishers
10 East 53rd Street, New York, N.Y. 10022-5299

Copyright © 1996 by David Copperfield's Disappearing, Inc., Janet Berliner Gluckman, and Martin H. Greenberg
All rights reserved. No part of this book may be used or reproduced in any manner whatsoever without written permission of the publisher, except in the case of brief quotations embodied in critical articles and reviews. For information address HarperCollins*Publishers,*
10 East 53rd Street, New York, N.Y. 10022-5299.

Individual story copyrights appear on pages 475–76.

ISBN 0-06-105493-3

A hardcover edition of this book was published in 1996 by HarperPrism, a division of HarperCollins*Publishers.*

HarperCollins®, 📖®, and HarperPrism®
are trademarks of HarperCollins*Publishers* Inc.

Cover photograph by Herb Ritts
Interior illustrations by Cathie Bleck

First printing: September 1997

Printed in the United States of America

Visit HarperPrism on the World Wide Web at
http://www.harpercollins.com

❖ 10 9 8 7 6 5 4 3 2 1

Contents

Acknowledgments

ONCE AGAIN, THE EDITORS WISH to thank both Harpers—Laurie Harper of Sebastian Agency and HarperPrism—for their support and enthusiasm. Also "Cowboy Bob," Robert L. Fleck, and John Douglas, without both of whom this volume might never have seen the light of day. We wish to thank Vicki Krone, Christy Johnson, and Dee Anne Dimmick for their assistance, and Al Rettig, even if he still doesn't know why.

As always, David Copperfield wishes to send his special thanks to his parents, Hy and Rebecca, and to Claudia for being Claudia; and to Janet Berliner for all of her hard work.

Janet Berliner wishes to extend her personal appreciation to Martin H. Greenberg, to her mother, Thea Cowan, her greetings to her daughter, Stefanie Gluckman, and maximum gratitude to Laurie Harper and Bob Fleck, who *do* know why.

Preface

DAVID COPPERFIELD FOOLS PEOPLE, but the people he fools don't mind. In fact, they enjoy it a great deal. "Honest con man," is an oxymoron, given that a confidence man is one who gives a false impression of honesty. David gives a genuine impression of honesty, because he is an honest performer, and therein lies one of the secrets to his astonishing talent as a stage illusionist.

I had the opportunity to meet David after one of his shows. Following a demanding performance, he met several of us involved in this book, and we chatted briefly. I observed the following about him: David Copperfield is a charming, funny, smart, warm, and humble man.

His mother and father stood close by while he chatted with visitors, and it was apparent to me this is a close family; his folks are as proud of him as parents could possibly be, and he is obviously devoted to them. This is a nice boy from New Jersey made good by any objective measure. We are then left with the question, "How did this nice kid from New Jersey arrive at such tremendous success by spending most of his waking hours fooling people?"

The answer is simple: that is what stage illusionists do. They fool people.

If stage illusionists and magicians are "honest con men," then writers of fiction are "paid liars." We deal in stories of events that never happened. We make things up and, like David, if we do it right, people are entertained. Great stage illusions are like great storytelling, and they have many elements in common: narration, plot, style, and execution.

But foremost of these common elements is what in literature class they call "the willing suspension of disbelief." If you're reading a fantasy story and the author states that a character snapped his fingers and flew, you believe the character did so. Despite your real-world certainty that people can't snap their fingers and fly, you accept the event within the context of the story. When you see David Copperfield fly above the stage during his show, you may have that same real-world certainty that people can't do this, but for the duration of David's flight, you are a believer. You see him fly, and you believe that he's flying.

How he flies is beside the point. Technology or magic, science or mystic art, real or illusion, the *how* isn't as important as the *effect*. The impact of the illusion on the audience creates a result. And if the art is great, if the performance is adroit and the illusion well conceived, if the execution of the feat is flawless, then that result is delight and wonder.

Wonder is an integral part of both fantasy literature and great stage illusions, and nowhere is this as apparent as in David's performance. At every level he works his wonder, from start to finish, at the simplest illusions and the most complex.

Isaac Newton once stated, "If I see farther than other men it is because I stand on the shoulders of giants." Mozart followed Bach, and both prepared the way for Beethoven. Leonardo da Vinci preceded Michelangelo. Jules Verne, H.G. Wells, and J.R.R. Tolkien forerun the authors in this volume. And Robert-Houdin, Harry Houdini, and others came before David Copperfield. All established traditions we follow as we struggle to climb upon their shoulders so we may reach new heights.

This awareness of the past, the history and traditions of the art form, is necessary for innovation. David understands that history and tradition. He is clearly a student of the art, for his act encompasses the traditional as well as the innovative.

David does sleight of hand: he performs legerdemain with cards; takes a ring from an audience member and materializes it somewhere else. These are time-honored, traditional, theatrical "magic." They require dexterity, concentration, hours of repetitive practice, and only look effortless if tremendous effort has gone into rehearsal. Then there are the great illusions, the innovative performances that leave the audience in openmouthed, wide-eyed amazement. David accomplishes both with equal attention to detail, style, and verve. Nothing is overlooked or thrown away. At no point does he ever condescend to his art; he is an honest performer and respects his audience, and himself, too much.

Among illusionists and magicians, David Copperfield is unique. He is singular in the combination of showmanship, execution, and personality he brings to his performances. He mixes traditional "close-up magic"—the card, coin, and other sleight of hand we remember from our childhoods— with brilliantly realized heart-stopping illusions that can only be termed "events," and he does so with equal ease. No other illusionist I've seen possesses his intuitive equilibrium, between the familiar and the new, romance and the prosaic, humor and danger.

Warm and friendly banter with the audience only heightens the drama when David performs his more lethal illusions. And they are, indeed, potentially lethal, because anything fashioned by the hand of man is potentially flawed. David risks injury, even death, at times, and this cannot be understated: much of what David does, seemingly without effort, is *extremely* dangerous. When David chooses illusions, he tests his personal limits. He doesn't stay within "secure" boundaries. Harry Houdini escaped from inside a safe bound with chains a hundred years ago, but he never did it in two and one-half minutes from inside an imploding building, surrounded by eyewitnesses, to appear moments later between a silk covering and a steel plate.

If I would point to the one thing in David's magic that leaves me the most in awe, it is the execution. The incredible attention to detail and critical requirements of timing are almost impossible to explain to those uninitiated to the demands of live performance. The man is the consummate professional; his sense of showmanship is unsurpassed.

I am not an expert on stage illusions, but since my stepfather first showed me card tricks when I was eight, I have wanted to know "How did he do that?" I might not be able to explain the nuances of any given illusion, but I believe I could tell you in general terms how a particular illusion is achieved. I won't, because it is up to each of us to learn the secrets, and because I respect what they do too much to possibly give offense. Suffice it to say that I am not ignorant of what goes into great theatrical illusions. I say this only to stress the following: David does *very* difficult things so smoothly and with such apparent ease that it borders on the unbelievable.

Everything he does requires flawless execution. This demands a level of commitment to art that few in the theatrical community today understand, let alone practice. David Copperfield is not only the best I've ever seen at what he does, he may very well be the best illusionist ever.

Lastly, there is the element of David the person. David appears on stage, and the audience sees who he is. There is no "persona" up there on stage, no part written by a playwright, just David, the nice kid from New Jersey, putting on a show. The show is alive, funny, sexy, dramatic, and compelling, because David is all of these things. Unlike other performers, who establish a barrier at the proscenium edge and keep the audience on the other side, David reaches across that boundary and gathers the audience to himself. His stage has a thrust platform that has steps leading down into the audience. He embraces them, and they return that embrace. There is no pretense evident. If the warmth and enthusiasm he shares with his audience is counterfeit, then David Copperfield is not only the finest illusionist who ever lived, he is one of the world's greatest actors.

When I saw David's show, I was down front. Next to me sat a boy, perhaps ten years old. Several times when I glanced over at him, he was sitting in rapt awe. David's performance transported him, bringing him to the edge of tears at times, from nearly overwhelming joy. Then I would glance backwards and look at the faces of the adults in the audience. The expressions were the same. Can you remember the last time you felt that way?

David touches the child in us all because he has never lost touch with the child inside himself. This is the single most important element of his honesty, I suspect, as it is a rare child who is capable of being false. He shares his childlike enthusiasm for what he does, and we are infected by it, caught up in it, and, in the end, experience the joy of it.

It was in those moments I understood just what a rare performer David Copperfield is. For while many entertain, few reach beyond entertaining to touch the emotions. And this is what makes art.

David Copperfield is an artist. He has proven this in his own arena. Not satisfied with that, he has written a story for this volume where you will encounter other artists, some of the better writers of our day, who in their own way do with words what David does on stage. They spin tales that range from the humorous to the terrifying, and each asks you to believe in wonders.

They are here because, like David, they represent a unique attempt at capturing magic in a moment of time, and at presenting it to the reader with the showmanship, execution, and personality David brings to the stage.

I am pleased and honored to have been asked to write this preface, for it is both an august company and a compelling project. The stories are about illusions, and illusions are the siblings of dreams.

Writers of fantasy dream, and those dreams take on substance in the mind of the reader, else we would never have visited the Emerald City of Oz, seen Mars through the eyes of Burroughs or Bradbury, braved the darkness with Lovecraft and King. We would never have flown above the clouds like David Copperfield, carried away on the words of those other giants who came before us.

I can only tell you so much about David's show or about his story, and the other stories that follow. You must now suspend your disbelief and move on into the experience. I am certain you will find reading these tales as satisfying in its own way as watching David in person. And if I haven't made it clear, that is something I urge you to do the first time the opportunity presents itself.

—*Raymond E. Feist*
Rancho Santa Fe, California

Introduction

I AM TREMENDOUSLY GRATIFIED at the response to *Tales of the Impossible*, the first volume in this literary tribute to magic and illusion. Putting the book together was an amazing experience, which left me humbled, challenged, and in awe of the storytelling skills of the masters whom Janet and I invited into the book. I remain grateful to them for so readily accepting me into their fold.

Having played once in fields where angels fear to tread, I could not resist doing so a second time. Here, therefore, for your reading pleasure, is *Beyond Imagination*—more original stories by more masters. Each tale presented me with its own enjoyment, its own challenge.

—DAVID COPPERFIELD
April 1996

Eagle

DAVID COPPERFIELD

By the time I was the age of the boy in this story, I was beginning to experience magic. I also, by then, fancied myself a junior inventor. To a great extent, what happened to the Adam character in "Eagle" happened to me. I leave it to you to decide how much was magic, how much coincidence. . . .

—DC

Eagle

ADAM HAD ALWAYS BEEN A LONER. He was happiest when he was by himself, inventing things in his room, or walking along the beach near his house collecting shells and stones, or pieces of driftwood washed onto the sand by the tide and bleached by the sun.

Then, right before he turned eight, he was transferred to a new school, and a whole lot changed. He still liked doing what he had always done, but suddenly there were times when he wanted to share things. Of course he had his parents; they were always interested in what he did. But that wasn't the same as sharing his ideas with the kids at school.

Everyone else seemed to be running around the neighborhood in twos and threes and fours. In a way, he wanted to fit in with them, but he didn't want to be *like* everyone else. He wanted to be special, the way he was at home.

The trouble was, he didn't really enjoy most of the things they did. Some of it was okay, like flipping baseball cards and pitching pennies, but the kids at this school didn't seem to do much of that. It was already the end of the first week of second grade, and he hadn't made any friends.

"Hey, Adam, why don't you go and play kickball with everybody else?" the teacher on lunch duty asked, noticing him eating alone in a far corner of the school grounds.

Adam hesitated. "Nah," he said. "I'd rather play catch with my eagle at home."

Pretty soon, Adam had told the story about his eagle so many times, each time with new embellishments, that he had begun to believe it himself. He had started telling his parents stories about it, too. They smiled and nodded their heads, but he caught them winking at each other, which meant they were just being nice.

One Sunday afternoon, without any warning, four boys from school showed up at Adam's house and demanded to see the eagle. Put on the spot, he took them to the biggest tree in his backyard, the one next to the old boarded-up fishpond that his parents kept saying they were going to turn into a rock garden.

Standing on the planks, he glanced up into the branches, and said, "Look. Up there in the top leaves." He waited for a moment, until the wind rustled the leaves. "There he is. See him?"

They looked up into the tree. Some of them seemed to believe him and were doing a pretty good job of convincing the others, until one of them said, "There ain't no eagle up there."

"Sure there is," Adam insisted. "It's up in there, hiding inside the cluster of leaves."

The doubter was not convinced. "Yeah, right," he said. "Come on, guys, let's go."

The boys wandered off, laughing and kidding each other. Adam, feeling thoroughly miserable, went back into the house.

When Adam got to school that Monday, the boys were waiting for him.

"Hey, Adam, how's your eagle? Is he playing catch with your elephant?" the tallest one asked.

"I don't have an elephant," Adam said. "Just an eagle."

"Yeah, then why didn't we see him?"

"Well, because . . ." Adam thought fast. "Because he's an *invisible* eagle."

"Oh, an *invisible* eagle. Does that mean you have to have an invisible brain to see him?"

The boys taunted Adam all day. When school was over he went straight home and up to his room to think. The top of his desk was covered with strings and paper and random pieces of an old Erector set, hooked together to make puppets and gadgets.

He sat down on the chair in front of the desk, which was set against a window that overlooked the backyard, then got up and started to pace. There had to be some way to convince the boys.

He was pacing again, faster and faster. *I can rig something to make an invisible eagle believable.*

An hour later, he had come up with a plan. He figured out in his head the things he would need to put his idea into practice: for starters, he'd need a box with a flap that opened in front like a door, two strong magnets, lots of string, a piece of driftwood, and some wire. He'd also need someone to help him.

He went over to the window and looked down through the trees at the planks of wood that covered the old fishpond. It made a perfect stage for what he had in mind. And Sam, the old handyman and sometime gardener, who was down there working in the yard, was the perfect person to help him. He liked Sam, and often spent hours watching him do stuff with nails and wood, or helped him fix things around the house and garden.

"If you got nothing better to do, you can help me down here," Sam called out, noticing Adam at the window.

"I'm coming," Adam yelled back.

On his way outside, Adam went through everything in

his mind so that he could explain it to Sam. He'd use an inverted box, one without a bottom, sort of like one you'd use to trap a rabbit. There would have to be two strings which ran from the back of the box, under it, through the slits between the planks, and into the fishpond.

That was where Sam came in. He'd be hiding in the dried-up fishpond, under the planks, where the ends of the strings dangled down to him. He'd pull them, and the box would move. It would look as if the bird were inside, walking the box forward.

Sam would pull more strings; the door on the front of the box would be rigged to open, allowing the imaginary bird to exit. Next to the box, there would be a piece of hollowed-out driftwood that had a humongous magnet inside.

Sam would be holding a second magnet under the planks. He would use it to make the driftwood pivot down, so that it would look like his eagle had jumped onto it. A few seconds later, Sam would break the attraction between the two magnets. That would cause the driftwood to jump back up to its original position, as if his eagle had flown off.

The driftwood would be about ten feet away from the tree. There'd be wires running from the branches, going behind the tree, through a piece of garden hose, and down into the fishpond so that they couldn't be seen.

Adam would look up into the tree, to make it seem as if his eagle had flown off the driftwood into the branches. At the same time, Sam would be pulling the wires to shake the branches so that the leaves would rustle.

Finally, Adam would glance off toward the horizon as if he were following the eagle with his eyes as it flew away.

"Okay," Sam said, after Adam had explained the setup

to him. "Doesn't sound too hard so far, but you better go over it again for me from the beginning. I ain't so sure I've got it yet. I know you gotta prove to the guys that you . . . that you've got an invisible eagle, but the rest is still a little foggy."

Sam was real old. Sometimes it took him a while to catch on. He had come to Adam's house during the summer to fix and paint around the yard, mostly wooden stuff that had rotted from the sea air. They had become pals after Sam found out that Adam knew about magnets and liked using tools.

Adam had always had to explain his ideas to Sam more than once. "You'll be hiding under here," he said, walking onto the planks. Then he started from the beginning and talked it through.

"Now I see what you're getting at." Sam joined Adam on the planks. He took an old envelope and a stubby pencil out of his pocket and started drawing. "When did you say these kids are coming over?" he asked while he was sketching.

Adam thought for a moment. "Next Friday, before school."

"I dunno, that's awful soon. I still gotta job to do, you know."

"Please, Sam."

Sam smiled, and Adam knew he had him. He ran through the mechanics again, scene-by-scene. He could see it all clearly now. "It'll be like you're a puppeteer from under the ground."

"They'll all think they see the eagle. That it really exists." Sam's eyes were twinkling. "You're some kid, you know that?"

"Can you help me do it in time?"

"I can try," Sam said.

All week long, before school and after school, Adam and Sam worked together, setting everything up and rehearsing, so that Sam would know exactly what had to be pulled when. During class, Adam kept telling the kids about how he was going to prove to them on Friday that he did have an invisible eagle. By the time Wednesday came, he was getting really nervous. Nothing looked right to him, and they were having problems getting everything working properly. By Thursday, he and Sam decided they had better test the whole thing on Adam's parents, so, right before dinner, Adam called them outside. Everything worked on cue. His parents just loved it. Their eyes followed the invisible eagle up into the sky.

"My God, Adam," his dad said. "That's the most incredible thing I've ever seen."

He had his parents believing; he could see that from the way they looked at each other. "Did that really happen?" his mother kept asking.

"Yeah, it's the eagle. Pretty good, huh?" Adam knew they wouldn't ask him to reveal his secrets. Besides, they were used to his dreaming, his imagination. They would just kind of drop it after a while, the way they always did.

The next morning was Friday. Adam was up and dressed early, waiting near the window for the boys to show up. When he saw them, he hurried outside. He tried to look confident as he led them to the tree. After all, he and Sam had done fine with his parents, so there was nothing to worry about.

Then, again, what if this time something went wrong? He'd be humiliated—

He stopped a couple of feet from the box and gave the

boys a chance to line up next to him. It was too late to stop now.

"He's in there." Adam pointed to the box. The boys rolled their eyes.

"Eagle!" he called out, giving Sam the cue.

Nothing moved.

"Eagle!" Still nothing moved. Adam felt a small sense of panic. That was the cue he and Sam had used for his parents. Now the kids were here and he'd given the cue and nothing was happening. His panic grew. Sam must have fallen asleep in there, 'cause he wasn't used to starting work this early.

Wake up, Sam, Adam thought. "Eagle, c'mon," he pleaded.

And then it happened, exactly as they had planned. The box walked across the planks, and the front door opened up. He followed the invisible eagle with his eyes, directing the boys' attention to the next magical manifestation. They allowed their gaze to follow the driftwood, which dipped down on cue and rolled up again as the invisible bird jumped off.

Adam motioned his head upward, following the flight of the imaginary bird. He looked up at the leaves which were rustling in the trees, and followed the eagle with his eyes, off to the horizon, and into the early-morning sunlight.

The kids were silent for a moment. Then they all started to talk at once. They took off for school at a run, making sure that Adam kept up with them.

The day was incredible. About as perfect as it could be. When it was over, Adam could hardly wait to get home and tell his mother about it.

"It was great, Mom. Great. Unbelievable. You should have heard them. All morning. All afternoon. They hardly stopped talking about it. Hey, I gotta go tell Sam. Thank him—"

He charged outside, still talking.

"Adam, wait," his mom called out.

He stopped at the planks, waiting for his mom to catch up. She sat down next to him. "There's something I have to tell you," she said.

"Yes, but, I have to talk to Sam—"

"Adam." She held his shoulders and pulled him closer. "I didn't want to upset you this morning because you were going to show the boys the eagle, and I knew you were nervous about it. Yesterday, on his way home from work, Sam was in an accident."

"But Sam was all right this morning."

"No, Adam, he wasn't. Sam died last night."

16 Mins.

ERIC LUSTBADER

I was performing magic for many years before I even knew there was such a thing as public relations, let alone a public relations machine. It is important for anyone in the public eye to preserve the "person that was," the one who existed before "the fame that is."

Eric Lustbader ably tackles this theme. Author of such bestselling novels as The Ninja *and* Black Blade, *Eric spent fifteen years in the music industry. In his work for Elektra and CBS Records he helped introduce such stars as Elton John to the American music scene, so he certainly understands both the values and the dangers of a PR machine.*

In this story, he shows what can happen when a celebrity begins to believe in his own PR.

—DC

16 Mins.

THE TRUEST THING ANDY WARHOL ever said was that everyone gets his fifteen minutes of fame. Now that it's over, now that I've come down from the mountaintop and can breathe air that doesn't give me an adrenaline rush every time I inhale, I can talk about it. As you can see, I'm calmer now, and if it wasn't for those damn red lights in my eyes, I'd be dead cool. Those lights, splashing the night with color every second, make me think of when I was a kid. We had a clock at home, a black cat with eyes rocking back and forth with each swing of its tail, counting off the seconds. Tick-tock. Tick-tock. I can't get that clock out of my mind.

Here comes the body. They've had it in the house a long time, taking pictures, dusting for prints, whatever it is cops do in high-profile murders. And the news helicopters are there like vultures to record it all. The cops said I could make one call, and I called you. Not my lawyer, you. I've got to get this off my chest before it burns a hole in me; that's the way I feel, anyway.

So concentrate. Forget the clock, forget the red lights; forget the cops. I've already told *them* the story, or the parts of it they wanted to hear—over and over again until they understood. They've got to understand, for Randy's sake, not for mine. What newsmagazine did you say you work for? Forget it, don't interrupt. It doesn't matter anyway, we'll rehearse all this before we go on the air, won't we?

Okay, right. The story. The whole story.

I met Randy Gold five years ago. That was before all the hype, the media hoopla, the big bucks, and the public adulation. He was Ralph Neiman then, just slogging away, doing standard parlor tricks and illusions as an opening act for second-rate stand-up comics all across the country. You should have seen his act then—it was a zero. He'd go through the motions like he wasn't there at all, like he was eighty and already in Century Village, playing canasta, wearing his trousers up to his nipples.

We collided, so to speak, at a party in New York—a real wild thing with tons of booze and dope. Randy was so high his eyes were going in and out of focus. He looked so lonely, you know, inside, like that bright, brittle face he wore on stage had been smashed into a zillion pieces. I saw something, *felt* something, maybe, but don't ask me what it was. I'm not good with things like that, introspection and all. It's bad for life, setting up black vibes, you know?

Anyway, I took Randy home with me. He was awfully cute, even with that terrible haircut he had then. I tried to hump him, but, you know, he was so far gone I doubt he could feel anything. So I slept on his chest, curled up like a cat.

"Who the hell're you?" he said, peering into my face the next morning.

"Lorna," I said, and yawned a big one. I was hung over but good. "We met at the party last night, remember?"

"What party?" he said suspiciously, looking blearily around the apartment. "A party here?"

"No, silly." I giggled, out of nervousness, mostly because I had the disturbing idea that he was about to throw me off the bed, dress, and split. I didn't want that. "The party at Rick's place." I'd been waiting years for someone like him, a little lost boy, an empty vessel just waiting to be filled with magic—with life.

"Rick Sawgrass." Rick was a Wall Street gunslinger-wannabe who dealt commodities like coffee and frozen hog bellies. Also coke and horse.

"Right," I said, ruffling his chest hair with my Ultra Red nails. "Rick the prick."

He laughed then, and right away I could feel his muscles relax a little. That was good. He got up and went into the bathroom, not bothering to close the door. He had that loose-limbed gait of people who have nowhere in particular to go. *Yes*, I told myself. *He's just about perfect*.

"Rick can sure be a bastard given half a chance," he said. When he came back, he eyed me, naked and all, still curled up like a cat. You could tell he liked what he saw. "Hey, did we—?" He made a lewd gesture in the air.

"To tell you the truth," I lied, "I can't remember." I smiled at him, the kind of smile I use to cadge makeup from the girls at Saks. It gets to them every time. "But I *do* know I went to sleep satisfied."

He grinned, happy. Guys. They're all alike, you know? They respond on cue like well-trained dogs; you just have to know which cues to give them. As it happens, I know them all.

He sat down on the bed and put his hands on me, and I jumped up, not like I was scared or anything, but full of pep and energy. Now that I had him here, I wasn't going to give him what he wanted until I had established our working relationship. I'm not the kind of girl to fall into everybody's bed. Besides, guys like to work a little, just enough to make them think they're special.

"How 'bout some brunch?" I asked, slipping into the black sheath I'd worn the night before. It smelled of Nocturne and cigs. It also smelled of me, but I kind of liked that, like taking possession of an old friend.

I could see Randy staring at me in the sheath, which was a pretty sexy number. "I've got other ideas." He had that liquid look in his eyes that guys get when they're horny. "Let's stay here."

"I'm hungry." I put my fists on my hips and pouted. My pretty pout. "Feed me."

We went out for brunch.

In those days, I had a loft on Greene Street, downtown in SoHo. It fit my image at the time. Also, it belonged to a couple of gay guys I knew who were always out of town, so I could stay rent-free. Good thing, too, 'cause I had no money to pay rent. After you get enough hard knocks on the street, you learn what to do to get by.

"You know the truest thing Andy Warhol ever said?" I asked him as we sat at a booth and bit into bagels, smoked salmon, and cilantro cream cheese.

"No, what?"

"That everyone gets his fifteen minutes of fame."

Randy put down his bagel, looked around the dark interior of the SoHo restaurant. It was filled with people my age, you know, early twenties, all younger than he was by maybe ten years. Some R.E.M. song, "What's the Frequency, Kenneth?" was playing. I remember because I thought it was ironic, you know, because we were still trying to find each other's frequency and not, I will admit, having much luck. "Yeah, well, personally I think Warhol was full of shit," he said, his beautiful blue eyes locking on mine, " 'cause I've been working my ass off at this game for some time and I haven't even seen sixty seconds of it."

"That's 'cause you don't have an angle," I said, taking a big bite of my bagel.

Randy waited until I had swallowed. "An angle."

"Yeah, like what sets you apart, what makes you different from all the other jokers up there sawing a woman in half."

"I don't do that," he said sourly. "Sawing a woman in half is boring as hell."

"I know that. I saw your act last night. It was lousy."

"Thanks for your vote of confidence," he said, showing teeth like a monkey that's pissed off and about to throw his shit at you.

"You don't get it at all, do you? You've got potential, but you've got to exploit it."

"Who are you, Andy Warhol?" he sneered. "I do what I do."

I knew I was hitting him where it hurt most, his male ego. But as far as I could see he needed a wake-up call. He'd given me a glimpse of how he would end up without me: a broken-down nothing, not even a has-been 'cause he'd never get anywhere. I didn't like that; I liked him, responded to something inside him, like a pearl inside an oyster. I knew I could change him, and in the process he'd give me what I'd always wanted: my fifteen minutes of fame. As far as I could see, it was a fair bargain.

"You make things disappear, but lots of magicians do that," I said. "What do they use, mirrors or something?"

You know, it was strange, but right away his attitude changed. He got that look on his face that by now everyone all over the world's seen, if not in person, then on TV or on the covers of *People* or *Vanity Fair* or whatever. The Randy Gold Look. Aloof and icy and oh so mysterious. Anyway, he said, "I can't talk about that. It's sacred, you know, the tricks of the trade, something a magician never reveals."

I cocked my head and drew an imaginary X across my heart. "I swear I won't tell anyone."

"No dice."

"Okay." I wiped my mouth. "But back to the angle thing. Say I gave you a way for your act to be different than anyone else's."

"Different?" He made this face like I was a street vendor hawking bogus Chanel handbags. "What do you mean?"

I lowered my voice, even though the din inside the restaurant had risen about ten decibels since we had sat down. "You know, so different that people would *have* to take notice."

Now he rolled his eyes and guffawed. "Come on." He took a toothpick out of a small glass holder on the table, stuck it in his mouth. "What kinda crap is this? You're, what, twenty-six years old?"

"Twenty-three, actually."

"Oh, even better. What could you know?"

I put my feet on the vinyl of the booth bench, perching the way I used to see big black crows do at the tops of trees out on Long Island. "I know," I said, in that tone of voice that made people listen.

Only Randy didn't listen. "Right," he said, getting up. He gave me a weird look as he threw some money on the table. He started out of the restaurant.

"Wait!" I cried, running after him. I caught up with him in the street.

"Listen," I said. "I know what I'm talking about."

Randy kept right on walking. "Sure you do. And you have a bridge for me to buy, too, right?"

Something snapped inside me. This guy was my road

to fame, and he was too dense or proud or whatever the hell it is that makes guys add two and two and get three to see it. "You jerk!" I screamed. "I'm offering you the chance of a lifetime, and you won't give me the time of day!"

That's when I saw this squirmy thing, dark and ugly, swimming in his eyes like a shark near a reef. He reached out for me and, grabbing hold of my wrist, jerked me so hard I thought he'd dislocated my shoulder. I stumbled to my knees and he half dragged me into an alley smelling of grease, Thai spices, and garbage.

He towered over me, his face dark with blood and that squirmy thing. "Don't you ever raise your voice to me! Who d'you think you are, calling me a jerk?" He lashed out, struck the top of my head a glancing blow.

By his standards it was nothing, but, see, guys just don't get this threat of violence women live with all the time. Guys, basically *are* violent. That's why they go to war or find excuses to get into fistfights. I think it makes them feel good, strong and powerful. It's definitely a man thing that makes no sense to women. I mean, it made no sense to me, and my father had made me get used to it.

"D'you know how many times I've heard people tell me about the sure thing, the chance of a lifetime? Everybody claims to have an angle, but you know what they have in mind? A piece of my flesh. Well, I'm tired of it, damn sick and tired. I've been bounced around so many times my ass feels like a beach ball. Not again, I tell you. If this is my lot in life, so be it. At least it's mine!" He raised his hand to hit me again.

"Don't," I gasped. "Don't!" I tried to cover my head like I had when I was a kid, and my father had come at me after he'd done his work on my mom. But Randy grabbed both my wrists in one hand and shook me 'til my teeth rattled. You can see how small I am; I weigh just over a hundred pounds. There was nothing I could do. Nothing but show him how I could make his act different.

I squeezed my eyes shut real hard, and he disappeared.

It was only for a couple of seconds, not like the carving knife my father had taken up in a drunken rage the night I left home. I had made that disappear for good, right out of his fist. I could do that with inanimate objects and animals. Size was most important. The bigger the object, the shorter the time I could make it disappear. With a full-grown adult human it was only seconds.

But that was usually enough. It was with Randy. He reappeared in the alley, blinking, and gave a great shiver. His skin when he brushed against me was cool, and he was white-faced.

He stared at me, openmouthed. "What the hell happened?"

I just stood there, silent, cool as could be because I knew this would bug him the most. I was angry, real angry at the way he had scared me and brought back memories I had carefully tucked away.

He looked around him, apparently amazed to find himself still in the alley. All the rage was drained out of him, and that dark squirmy thing was gone from his eyes. He was cute again, and I could already imagine him in the new haircut I was going to give him. Not to mention the new outfits for his souped-up act I had already designed in my mind.

"What the hell happened?" he repeated in a voice thick with confusion.

I had regained my feet by this time. "For a minute, you were someplace else."

"No kidding." He rubbed his arms. "It was dark and very cold. Where was I?"

"I have no idea," I said truthfully.

He gave me this look that made me shiver inside with anticipation. It was the same shiver I'd get when I went fishing in the summer on Long Island, when the bluefish was just about to take the bait. It was a delicious sensation.

"You see what I'm trying to tell you," I said, "about the angle."

I could see he didn't disbelieve me, exactly, but I knew he needed something more, something he could see, hold in his hand.

"Take out your keys," I told him.

Almost as if he were in a trance, he did as I asked him. They glimmered in the palm of his hand, a dark pool of metal.

"Now keep your hand open. No, make sure your fingers are flat, away from the keys. Okay, now."

His eyes were on me with such heat, I could feel a kind of pressure. They seemed locked there. I knew he wanted to look at the keys, but at the same time he was frightened of what was going to happen next. But at last, his curiosity overcame his fear, and his gaze slipped away.

He stared at the keys with an almost obsessive intensity. I squeezed my eyes shut until I heard him shout. His palm was empty. He swallowed hard, flexed his fingers, turned his hand over as if he expected the keys to somehow fall to the filthy pavement. They didn't; nothing happened.

Slowly, so slowly I could see every vertebra in his neck move, he turned to look at me. "Where—" He licked his dry lips, started all over again. "Where are they?"

"Your keys?" I giggled, from delight now, not nervousness.

"Yeah." He swallowed again, poking at his empty palm. "My goddamned keys."

"Where would you like them to be?"

"Back in my hand, that's where!" he shouted.

I tilted my head at him. "Oh, you can do better than that."

He looked exasperated, as if he, the king of illusion or whatever, were in the process of being conned. "Okay, big shot, I want 'em in my left sock."

"You're the boss," I said, squeezing my eyes shut for an instant.

You know, I thought Randy was going to puke up his delicious brunch right there in the alley. He was staring at a bulge that had made the inside of his left sock bag out. Slowly, as if we were in some kind of slo-mo movie scene, he bent down and, with a shaking hand, rolled down the sock. Out dropped his keys, glittering on the pavement. He grabbed them up, hefted them, peered intently at each one, verifying what he already knew: they were his keys.

"I thought I knew all the cons backward and forward, but not this one." He flipped the keys into the air, caught them. "You didn't even come near me. How'd you do it?"

"It isn't a con; it isn't an illusion," I said. "It's real."

For a moment he said nothing. Then he grunted. "Sure. I get it. I wouldn't tell you mine, so why should you tell me yours. The tricks of the trade are sacred, right?" He nodded, seemingly satisfied, and he winked at me. "It takes a con man to recognize another con man, right?"

Wrong, but I said nothing. I had told him the truth, but people rarely believe the truth. They believe what they need to believe, and usually that's okay. It certainly was by me.

"I can see it all now," I said, trying to inject him with

my excitement. I could feel the clock ticking, bringing my fifteen minutes closer. "The costumes, the lights, the effects. You and me in the spotlight wowing audiences all over the world. News coverage, media attention, stories in *People* and *Vanity Fair*. We'll live in Hollywood and go to parties with Jack Nicholson and Sharon Stone. Charlie Sheen will invite us to be his houseguests. It will be so *cool!*"

"Yeah, this is big, all right," he said with a curious look in his eyes. "Really fucking monstrous."

We went back to my apartment. I could tell right away he didn't want to be there; something about the place suddenly made him nervous. Right then I wouldn't't've believed that it was me even if I'd heard it from God Himself.

He went over to the bar, an acid-stained, zinc-topped lab table the gay guys had scrounged up God knows where. He took some Cuervo Gold and sloshed it down. Then he took another triple-shot, convulsive like. He asked for a smoke, and I gave him one. He puffed on it like he couldn't wait to get to the filter. And all the while he walked around the room, not looking at me, not looking at anything. Every once in a while he'd stop back at the bar to guzzle more Cuervo. I'd had a coat once, black and so long it swished sexily against my ankles. I had lifted it from Saks in a particularly clever way, and so it was special to me. But the first time I put my hand in the left pocket, the stitching gave way and the two pieces of cloth parted. It was like that now with Randy: he looked like he was coming apart at the seams.

I shucked off my shift and he didn't even notice when I padded over to slip into one of the gay guy's silk dressing gowns from Victoria's Secret. "What's got into you?" I said. Maybe my voice was a bit too sharp and snappy. But, hell, I was as much confused as I was pissed off. Didn't this dude get it? Didn't he want to be saved from his lackluster life of trudging around the country, playing to indifferent audiences in one boozy dive after another? I asked him that, but he didn't say a word.

Nevertheless, I was going to get my answer all too soon. He was standing by the open window. Afternoon sunlight struck the windows of the converted warehouses across Greene Street, turning them into fiery mirrors. It looked almost biblical, like in that old movie when King Solomon used the polished shields of his army to reflect the sun into his enemies' eyes and blind them. Right then, it seemed to me that Randy had been struck down in his own private desert. Then he flicked what was left of the smoke out the window and went into the bathroom.

He was in there a long time. I remember having a queasy feeling in the pit of my stomach, but I put it down to the raw onions I'd piled on that bagel. I was dying to go into the bathroom and rinse my mouth out with Scope. I went over to the bathroom door and pounded on it.

"Ralph? Ralph, hey, I gotta get in there!"

Then I heard a high eerie sound, almost like a little girl having a nightmare. Something hard and metallic hit the floor. I pushed open the door, which he hadn't locked.

"Oh, God!" I said. "Oh, Jesus!"

There was blood running along the floor, not like that bright crimson stuff you see in the movies, but something dark and rich and sweet as raw sugar. Randy was sprawled up against the porcelain of the john. He was very pale, and he looked at me with blank eyes just as if I didn't exist. I saw the straight-edge razor I had learned to use to shave my legs, its blade dark with blood. The bastard was trying to kill himself by opening the veins in his wrists. I knelt down beside him. He'd done a pretty bad job on his left wrist and had apparently dropped the razor before he could get at the other one. He started that high eerie keening again.

I ran and got a scarf, tied it tight around his forearm, then I went to work on the wound. He hadn't the strength or the nerve to completely sever the veins; he might not even need stitches. I used peroxide, which almost made his hair stand on end. Then he passed out, which was best for both of us, I guess.

Dead man, I thought as I cleaned and dressed the ragged wound. *He's a dead man and he doesn't even know it.* I did a pretty neat job of it; being on the streets gives you lots of advantages over other folk. For instance, you learn real quick how to handle emergencies like a knife wound in the side or a razor slash to the wrist. Then I hauled his sorry ass back into the bedroom and loaded him into bed, swaddling him like an infant because he was already going into shock. He was going to need some antibiotics, which I had in the medicine cabinet, but that could wait until he woke up.

It took him six days before he would talk to me. I think he hated me for saving his life. It was just as well. I didn't want to tell him he had been a failure at suicide as well as everything else. He had lost weight, owing to the liquid diet I had him on and his lack of appetite, but that might have come from the antibiotics, which screw up your stomach something fierce. I got him yogurt specially—personally, I can't stand the stuff—but he wouldn't touch it.

He'd also grown a beard, a heavy black thing that made him look fierce and powerful and, amazingly, a bit evil. There was a place low on his right cheek where the beard was sparse. While he was asleep one day I took a closer look at it. It was a scar that I hadn't noticed before. It was long and looked as if it were part of some kind of plastic surgery. Really you couldn't even see it when he was clean-shaven, but now it made him look as if his face had been pieced together after some very nasty accident.

You know, thinking back on it, it was weird how different he looked, almost as if he had become an entirely different person. And maybe he had because, though he didn't know it yet, this empty vessel was beginning to take on the appearance of the image I had set for him in my mind's eye.

On the seventh day, he opened his eyes and said, "Fuck you, Lorna," in a voice made harsh by disuse. I'd had the radio on, Madonna singing one of her interchangeable pop songs, and the place smelled from toast and warm butter.

I stuck my tongue out at him and, scrambling onto the bed, straddled his thighs above the comforter. "You're welcome to try." I smiled at him, but he wasn't in any mood. The skin around his beautiful blue eyes looked bruised and puffy, as if he'd been in a bad fight. My mother'd had eyes like that. It was why she took to wearing dark glasses around the house, bumping into chairs while she was vacuuming.

I began to sing along with the Madonna song, and that seemed to loosen his mood.

"You've got a gift there," he said. "Your voice sounds so sweet."

"It's my mother's voice," I said, remembering.

"Then she must've been a professional singer."

"Nah, nothing like that. She just did it 'cause she

loved it." Which was why my father took it away from
her. I sang a little more because he liked it, and because it
brought my mother close again.

"Ralph," I said after a time, "why'd you do it? Don't
you want to live?" He turned his head away from me,
staring dully at the wall. "I don't get it; you'll have your
shot now, your chance at the big time. Isn't that what you
want?"

"Fuck you, Lorna," he intoned like a chant heard at
church.

Right then the weirdest thing happened. That damn
R.E.M. song came on again, the one we'd heard at
brunch the week before, "What's the Frequency,
Kenneth?" and right away I thought of frequencies and
how Randy and I were still on different ones.

I looked at him and thought hard. "It *isn't* what you
want," I said, getting it at last. "You've given up on ever
being famous."

For a long time he said nothing. The R.E.M. song
mingled with the homey smell of toast and warm butter.
Outside, a motorcycle swept by, making the hyper Jack
Russell terrier next door bark. The windows of the
houses across the street were opaque, as if they had been
painted over. It was getting dark and humid; I could smell
the rain coming, making the sooty sidewalks give off an
aroma as distinct as newly turned earth.

"What's the frequency, Ralph?" I asked him. "What's
your frequency?"

"Why would you care?" Guys, right? Didn't I tell you?
Now he was doing the sulky child thing. Didn't they
know they could get plenty of attention without pulling
that shit?

"Because," I said, leaning down and kissing him on the
temple, the tip of his ear, "I want to get on yours." Not

true, but what the hell, a lie is sometimes better than the truth in the service of necessity, I always say. It's always worked for me, anyway.

"I can't help you if you don't talk to me, Ralph."

"Why would you want to help me? I've been lying here trying to figure it out. I'm a fucking loser, a nothing."

My face was hanging just above his, my breasts pressed against his side, and at last he turned his head back, looked into my eyes. "Because when I look at you I see something more."

"There is nothing more."

"Why don't you let me be the judge of that," I whispered in his ear. "There will come a time when you'll see it yourself." I nipped his ear with my teeth. "Guaranteed."

He blinked. "I'm afraid," he said.

"Of what?"

"I dunno." He shrugged. "My life was placid, predictable. I knew how many gigs I was doing a year and where. I knew what dives I was staying in and how many days a year I'd be drunk. I even knew the towns where I could score coke and get laid without too much trouble. Until I met you. You turned everything on its head. My life—"

"Your life sucked, Ralph."

He hunched his shoulders as if my words were blows. "It was something I could count on. The *only* thing I could count on."

"But now you have me." I turned him over gently and could feel he wanted to come. "You can count on me. I'll always be here."

"With the loser. I've tried everything I can think of, but it doesn't seem to matter. Everything rolls against me."

"You're wrong. I see something you don't see. Trust

me." I took him in my arms and rocked him just as the first flash of thunder broke across the sky. It was like a neon light snapping on. A throaty rumble echoed down Greene Street, rattling the old panes of glass, replacing the homey odors of toast and warm butter with sizzling ozone.

"Do you know about the *I Ching*?" I asked.

He shook his head, mutely.

"It's called the Book of Changes. It's very old. The Chinese wrote it, and it's all about moving from one phase of life to another. See, it's about what's happening to you now. You tell me, I've done everything I can think of to change, but no change is happening. Here's where you're wrong. Meeting me was a change." I shifted around as another flash of lightning lit up the loft. "See, the *I Ching* says life is a bunch of opposing forces: success and failure, creativity and destruction, light and darkness. Think of these forces as wheels getting stronger or weaker as they roll around. The book says that when a force gets too strong, it turns into its opposite.

"So now in your life failure is dominant. You spend your time in useless resistance and now in abject defeat. What you need is optimism, patience, a sense of yourself. Consolidation and retreat."

"Retreat?" Had I hit a chord in him?

"Yes, retreat." Another flash and rumble. "Your act is a failure. Okay, recognize it and get rid of it. Retreat and consolidate, conserve your strength to create a new act. Otherwise you'll miss the moment—*this* moment— when the forces begin to change, when success begins to outweigh failure and is again on the rise.

"Think of what I'm offering you," I said as I held him close, as the lightning flashed and the thunder clashed. "Think of where we can go together."

For a long time he said nothing. I could almost hear him thinking. I thought of the *I Ching* and could feel the forces beginning to shift, like those underground plates that cause earthquakes when they move. I could hear the blood singing in my veins. I knew this was my moment, and very soon the clock would be ticking off my fifteen minutes.

"The idea of being famous, successful, frightens me," he whispered.

"Oh, but, darling, why?" I kissed him gently.

"I had a friend once who became famous, and do you know what happened? He was consumed by the fame. It was all he lived for, it defined him, and, then, finally, it *became* him, and he was lost inside it, and I could never get to him again."

"But that won't happen to you," I said, rocking him through the storm. "I'll see to it. I'll protect you from it." I sang him a song my mother used to sing to me before my father broke her jaw. It was a kind of lullaby, and it always had the power to calm me.

He turned his head, pressing his cheek against my breast. "It's why I tried to kill myself, Lorna."

"No," I said. "You tried to kill yourself because your life sucked." I said that because he needed to believe it in order to begin his transformation. I was put in mind of *My Fair Lady*, but with the genders switched. I was Rex Harrison, a professor of the human condition, and he was Audrey Hepburn, a nowhere slacker I was determined to transform into a media phenom. What a glorious undertaking, what a magnificent feeling it would be to succeed. I could already feel Rex Harrison's elation running through me like electricity. I could do it, I knew I could. All I had to do was convince Randy.

"Promise me you'll never let it happen to me."

"Of course I promise, but it's silly because it's never going to happen."

"No!" He grabbed my hand, placed it over my heart. He squeezed so hard it hurt. "Swear it."

"Okay, okay," I said. "I swear."

Another bolt of thunder crashed, and the loft was lit as if from a lamp that had been upended.

At last it seemed the right time to seal our bargain ,and as he reached up for me I melted against him. I could feel the heat rising from him, and I kicked frantically at the bedcovers, peeling them away from between us. Thick and clumsy, they clung to us like yesterday's dirt. But this was a new day, I thought as I tasted him in my mouth, a new dawn.

The thunder crashed and rolled down the street as we thrashed about. The rain clattered in through the open windows, and cars hissed by outside. Randy muttered something as he entered me, and then as I drew my thighs up and back, said it again. My own breath was coming in sweet gasps, and my heart was pounding so hard I couldn't make out what he was saying until it became one long string, like a chant or a prayer.

"Life," he was whispering over and over. "Give me life."

Much later, after we'd slept entwined only to be roused into another bout of feverish lovemaking, he said, "Even with this angle it's going to be difficult getting first-class gigs."

The storm was over, and in its place an eerie dusk had fallen; all the streetlights were haloed, and traffic seemed unaccountably muffled.

"I've been thinking about that this past week." I drew the covers around us. They were sweet with our mingled sweat and musk. "Maybe illusion is the wrong tack to take. There are a zillion illusionists around today, but there's nobody who's a first-rate escape artist."

"That's because they'd have Houdini to live up to, and no one has the abilities he once had. He was a fucking genius—not to mention some kind of mystic, teaching himself breath control, contortion, and all that." He waved a hand dismissively. "Forget Harry Houdini."

"I think you're wrong." I sat up, letting the covers pool around my waist. "Think of the tenor of the times. People are fed up with illusion—they get that all the time in films and TV and all the celebrity magazines. What people want is to escape. Don't you think they'd root hardest for an escape artist?"

I could see I had his attention. Somehow I could almost see our frequencies, once two parallel lines, now about to converge.

"Even if you're right," he said, "how's that gonna help me? I can't do what Houdini did."

That's when I pounced on him. "But that's the beauty part," I said. "You don't have to. You've got me. Remember what I did with your keys? Imagine this." And then I told him my idea. By the time I came to the part about the kiss he was sold.

So that's how it began with Randy and me.

I changed his name, his haircut, his clothes. I became his assistant. He used my talent to make objects held by audience members disappear before their very eyes, only to reappear at other places inside the theaters. Sometimes he'd ask a member of the audience to come up onstage and hold his or her hands open and—bam!—a wallet, pen, or photo from someone in the back of the theater would appear out of thin air. During this time I'd stand out of the spotlight, inconspicuous, quiet as a mouse, while all eyes were on Randy. It was a simple case of diversion, the basis of all classic cons. Everyone watched Randy do nothing at all while I performed the trick from the shadows at the side of the stage.

Then, at the very end of the act, as tension built to a crescendo, I would recruit members of the audience to bind him in chains, lock the chains, and test that the lock was real and could not be opened. I took the people over to the gleaming coffin I had rigged up with black bunting and fresh flowers and let them inspect it. I had had RANDY GOLD 1963–? painted in large gold letters on its side. Kind of hokey but, what the hell, that is what theater is all about. Then we got Randy into it. Just before the heavy lid was closed over him I bent down and gave him a kiss on the lips. The kiss became our trademark.

The stage lights went down to an eerie glow. A huge timer began to tick onstage. These were my ideas; really, Randy had none of his own. But I'll say this for him: he knew how to grab hold of an audience and not let go until he was finished with them. That was his true talent.

The audience was so quiet you could hear a pin drop in between the loud tick-tock of the timer. Tick-tock. Tick-tock. And then the coffin lid would rise up and out Randy would pop, like Dracula ready for a night full of fun. I hit the button on the timer to stop it, the stage lights came up, and the applause began to roll through the theater. Randy stepped out of the coffin to shake the hands of those audience members who had helped him and to invite them to inspect the coffin, chains, and lock again.

The applause built and built as Randy took his bows. Everyone was standing, including the crew. I looked out into the audience and saw all those sweaty faces. I could feel the applause like a tide raising him up, filling him with a warmth. Me, too, I guess, though I knew the applause was for him alone. Then he gave me my one bow, my single moment in the spotlight. Let me tell you, feeling all those eyes on me, Wow! What a rush! I couldn't get enough of it. It was sexual in a way, like the vibrations in a speeding car that are arousing and calming all at once. And then the spotlight would switch back to him, and he continued taking his bows. In the darkness at the edge of the stage I would shiver, and I always heard that clock ticking off my fifteen minutes.

Sometimes we'd vary the finale. I'd instruct the audience members to wrap him in rope and then the chains. We practiced the rope illusion together until he was sure of himself. He'd pump blood into his arms by flexing his fists. Later, inside the coffin, when he relaxed his arms, he'd gain the small space he needed to slip the knots. It was easy; it was foolproof. And, as I had predicted, the act hit a national nerve. He became a sensation virtually overnight, like it happened in a dream.

We played bigger and bigger houses, we got rave notices from amazed reviewers, and word of mouth spread like wildfire. The major newspapers sent people to do stories. They came to write a column, but after seeing the act they wrote double, triple the amount. Then came national coverage: TV, interviews on all the newsmags. The tabloids began dogging our every step. The thing was, though, it happened all at once. Randy would be doing four or five interviews a day. He acquired a manager, agent, accountant, a phalanx of others he now considered essential to his well-being: a bodyguard, hairdresser, masseuse, chef, astrologer, manicurist, physical trainer, two assistants. He bought a handgun and paid an ex–LAPD cop to teach him to shoot while they listened to John Lennon singing

"Instant Karma." And, of course, there were the dope dealers. He hired Rick the prick to supply him. In all these hangers-on he saw a kind of reflection of himself.

"Jesus, I can't believe this is happening," he'd confide to me time and again. "It's like a dream." Giving orders to all these people was like having an endless amount of cash in his pockets—it made his fame tangible. It made him believe.

But was it a dream or a nightmare? As, day by day, I saw Randy change, as I saw his celebrity take on a life and a hunger of its own, I was reminded of his fear of it, how he had seen his best friend consumed by fame. Was the same thing happening to Randy now? I didn't yet know, but I did suspect that somehow he had slipped the leash I had on him. The vessel, once empty, was now overflowing, turning into something I could no longer recognize.

Once, he had whispered "Life" into my ear while we made love; now I was no longer enough for him. He had become so much bigger than me—larger than that little lost boy who had whispered "Life. Give me life," at my breast. Now reality consisted of the stage, the spotlight, the rush of applause, the hanging out 'til 5 A.M. with the Mickey Rourkes and Sean Penns of the world, getting high and passing out. And, in between times, when the possibility existed of a crack of reality breaking into the crypt like a ray of sunlight, there were the professional friends he'd hired: people who knew their place and what obedience meant. Randy liked these people because they made him feel good. They were never in a down mood, never having PMS, never having a crisis at home, and were always at his beck and call. That was more than I could do for him—and a good deal less.

I used to think it bizarre when celebrities married

their bodyguards or their personal assistants; now it almost made sense.

And as I saw it happening, saw him drifting farther and farther away from me, I realized how unfair it was. And, you know, it's true that you never fully appreciate what you've got until you no longer have it. I began to realize that I loved him. He'd taken on a life of his own, and now even I could not imagine him as he had been.

I should have found a way to stop it then, but it had already gotten too big and, anyway, I was caught up in it, this creation of mine, this amazing *thing* which I had suckled to life: Fame.

We went on. I leaked to the press the deal with the kiss. It had been Houdini's habit to have passed to him through the kiss of his female assistant the keys to his chains. The press made the connection I wanted them to make between Randy and Houdini—the tabloids even started calling him Houdini's reincarnation.

Then, during the live TV special—the one that blew out all the ratings, beating even the Super Bowl—I arranged to have a uniformed New York City Police officer stop me at the last instant from kissing Randy as he was put in his coffin. I made a show of protesting, but the policeman, as we had arranged, was firm. The kiss didn't take place.

A hushed silence fell over the audience. As our ratings began to skyrocket, the lid was closed on Randy's coffin. If I was passing him the key to his locked chains by the kiss, everyone in America was asking, how was Randy Gold going to escape?

The clock began to tick. Tick-tock. Tick-tock. I looked around the Hollywood Bowl audience and knew by their rapt attention that we had them. This was the hardest ticket to come by since the last Barbra Streisand concert.

Everyone who was anyone in Hollywood, Washington, and Wall Street was crammed into the open-air amphitheater. And I could see that all of them—stars, managers, moguls, and cynics alike—had fallen hook, line, and sinker. They were ours to play with as we pleased. The feeling of power was so intense it was dizzying. After six agonizing minutes, the coffin lid opened, and Randy emerged. A collective gasp of astonishment rocked the theater—just as a similar reaction rocked the inside of every household tuned in. From that moment on, we were made.

And, of course, everything changed.

When I finally made my way backstage, the dressing room was already besieged. People from his publicity company guarded the door like Dobermans. They didn't even recognize me at first, and when I finally got in the place was bedlam. Celebrities were lined up to congratulate Randy. He was at the far end of the room, posing with a small army of people from the TV network. Next to them waited a couple of bearded money men who were producing his first film. Behind them were three twenty-something slacker-nerds who were programming something called "Randy Gold's Beyond Houdini" on interactive CD-ROM. I saw book publishers and editors and even some music-business people, who were anxious to get Randy into the studio to sing standards with Barry Manilow's band.

There was no way to get to Randy, and I could see that he was so busy, so flushed with triumph, that he was oblivious to almost everything. Still, you would have thought he'd want to share this moment with me, the person who had made it happen. But he wasn't even looking for me.

And, later, at the party the network had set up at the St. James Hotel, I saw him dancing with one of those supermodels with one name and a body you'd kill half of Santa Monica for.

"They sure look good together, don't they?" Mack said to me from the sidelines. As Randy's chief bodyguard he had the run of our house, our cars. Hell, he had the run of our lives. He knew the effect seeing Randy and the super-model was having on me, and I was enraged to see him enjoying my humiliation. Maybe he saw me as a threat. You could only be loyal to one person, and Randy was paying his hefty salary.

"He ought to be dancing with me." I couldn't help myself, though I knew it would only give Mack another measure of satisfaction.

"Nah. You know well as I do it's better for him to be seen with women like that. Pumps up the volume of his image."

When I said nothing, he edged closer to me, said out of the side of his mouth, "I've had all your clothes and things packed up." Just as if he'd been following some order I'd given him.

I whirled on him. "You did *what*?"

He was still looking at Randy and that damned girl with legs as long as I was tall. "Mr. G thinks maybe it would be better if you moved into the guesthouse."

We were living here in this huge house in Brentwood with the guest quarters. You know, we're right down the block from Meryl Streep's place. It's far too big for us, but who cares—size has nothing to do with need and every-thing to do with status. Besides, with the army of O.J. gawkers still flooding Rockingham Avenue, we got it for a steal. To be honest, I missed the grittiness of New York, but Randy loved L.A. He was like a kid who's had his nose pressed up against the window of a candy store for years and is now let in. He couldn't get enough of it.

"Says you, I'm moving," I told Mack hotly. "Well, forget it. I won't."

"It's already been done, Miss, per Mr. G's request."

I was so stunned all I could hear was my heart thumping over the big band music and the din of the glittering throng. "I don't understand." I said it like a tire losing air, and Mack knew it.

"Mr. G thinks people could get the wrong, you know, idea about the two of you." He flicked a thick finger in the direction of the golden couple whirling around the dance floor while cameras whirred and lightbulbs popped. "That he was tied down romantically, or something. That wouldn't be good for his image"—he leered at me—"or for his sex life, you know?"

I knew. "This is bullshit. I put him in that goddamned house and now he's throwing me out of it? I'll talk to him about this."

Now Mack pressed the full weight of his menacing look down onto me. "I wouldn't try that if I were you, Miss," he said. "I have orders."

"What kind of orders?" I asked suspiciously.

"Do you really want me to spell them out, Miss?"

"Yes," I said with a masochist's evil delight. "What exactly did Randy tell you to do?"

"I'm to keep you away from him during all but rehearsals and act time."

My stomach was doing fluttery things I didn't like, but I gritted my teeth and soldiered on. "What about business meetings? I'm always at business meetings; hell, I make up the agendas."

"No more business meetings," Mack said, with the sound of a prison door swinging closed.

For once I was at a loss for words, but Mack didn't take any notice. His voice filled up the silence. "Do yourself a favor. When you're done here you'll be driven to the guesthouse. Go to bed and forget tonight."

Forget tonight. That was rich. The clock was ticking out my precious fifteen minutes and I was being told by a mentally challenged steroid-stud to go to sleep. This bastard had no more business telling me what to do than my father, and yet what else could I do?

With a cold lump in my chest I watched the party unfolding without me. No one wanted to take my picture or interview me. No one asked me to make a record, though I was the one with the voice, not Randy; no one even asked me to dance. And when I went to find my table I discovered to my horror that I was sitting with the TV production people. The table was so far from Randy's, I might have been on Mars— or in New York. That cut it. Marooned at the lowly crew's quarters, my status was strictly nowheresville. It was now set in stone that no one of celebrity would give me the time of day.

I took Mack's smirking advice and left. I was no celebrity, and I certainly wasn't a hanger-on, so I had no business being there, right? Tick-tock. Tick-tock. My magic fifteen minutes were expiring without me.

I didn't go alone, however. How could I? That would have been too big a blow to my ego. And so even though I knew this was what Mack wanted, I got myself drunk enough to haul home some willowy young thing who needed to get his feet wet.

I'll say this, he got more than he bargained for. We did coke and Scotch, my favorite mind-wipe combo, and then I fucked his brains out until dawn. I was happy to see him having trouble walking on his way to the shower the next afternoon, but that was about all I had to be happy about. There was a sour taste in my stomach and the back of my nose that echoed the darkness of my mood, and when I looked in the mirror I wondered who the poor bitch was staring back at me.

The next evening I was unexpectedly invited up to the main house for dinner. For once, Randy was alone, but I passed the ubiquitous Mack, standing guard as always. He gave me an unaccountably exaggerated leer as he let me pass into the formal living room gaudily decorated in white and red.

"Sit down," Randy said. He was standing in front of his wide-screen TV, and he waved to a white-cushioned ottoman he seemed to have pulled up for the occasion. I sat and he touched a button on a remote. His VCR began to play, and I let out a little moan.

There I was in the nude, rolling around with the young man I had taken home from the party.

"Mack caught this," Randy said, "with the palmcorder I gave him for Christmas. Apparently you and your stud were too far gone last night to notice."

Now I knew what the great big leer had been all about. Mack had set me up, but it was no good telling Randy that. All he cared about was what had been caught on tape. And what a tape it was. I had seen pornography before, but it had always seemed so impersonal—actors going through the motions—that it had had no effect on me. This was different. It was so personal, so intimate an exposure, I cringed. It made me realize how private the sex act was—and what a violation its public display could be.

After all the sexual permutations had run their course, Randy threw the cassette at my feet and said, "Here, peddle it to *Penthouse,* why don't you. They took the Tonya Harding video; maybe they'll take this."

There was something about his face, it looked distorted by rage.

"You have no right," I said. "Not after your own behavior."

"Don't talk to me about behavior," he shouted. "You made me a promise."

"To what, be faithful to you?"

Now I could see it wasn't rage distorting his face, but something more. It was as if there were some inner beast distending the flesh, ballooning it outward, contorting it into an unrecognizable shape. I began to get frightened, because his beautiful blue eyes were dark with the squirmy, ugly thing, and he no longer looked like Randy. In fact, he didn't look human.

"You swore to me!" he thundered. His lips were pulled back from his bared teeth. "A sacred vow and now it's all gone. You've ruined everything and it can never be the same."

What was he talking about? I had no idea.

"Randy, I—"

And then I saw it: a small curling line of what I thought was snot crawling out of one nostril. But it wasn't snot. It was dark and long and moving, as if of its own volition. Then I jumped, gasping. Another curling line popped through the skin of one cheek where his scar was, and began to wave in the air.

I ran out of there as fast as I could. And I wiped that terrible image out of my mind as if it had never happened. An act of self-defense, I told myself.

I heard an evil laugh as I sped past the hulking presence of Mack, the hired hand. Mack, who had planned with studied objectivity my complete humiliation. And I knew in a flash that before the sun rose everyone in Randy's vast entourage would hear of this incident in minute detail. I'd be a laughingstock; I'd never again be able to look any of them in the eye.

It was clear that something was making Randy despise me. What? Did seeing me remind him of his old self? Of the fact that he was, essentially, a fraud?

Caught up in the web of celebrity, I didn't yet see the true nature of our dilemma. Maybe it was too terrible to face, so I shut it away with all my other awful memories of abuse. I got on with my obsession of making Randy Gold into the biggest superstar since Michael Jackson.

I know what you're going to ask: Why didn't I use my power to bring Randy back into line? After all, his "magic" was mine. I was the one who was getting him the implements he needed to make his astounding escapes. Without me, he was nothing. We both knew that, of course. It was a tacit agreement between us. And yet, we never spoke of it. The "magic" had taken on its own life. It existed because of the two of us, and in a weird kind of way neither of us was willing to mess with our arrangement, lest the magic go away and this fairy-tale life of celebrity and fabulous fortune disappear like a mirage in the desert.

In a real sense, we were both marooned in that desert, our feet set upon a path. In order to keep the celebrity alive we both had to keep going, not deviating an inch from the prescribed course. Because, you see, I might not have had Randy, but I had every other accoutrement I had ever imagined and enough money to blow on buying up my own little orbit of people, which is what I did, throwing all abandon to the wind. So Randy and I lived in the same compound, worked hard together, and never said a word off the set. I had my life and he had his, and deep in my soul I knew he was as unhappy with his as I was with mine. Still, neither of us could stop.

Sure. In retrospect, it seems sick. But that's now. In the

rarefied atmosphere up there during our fifteen minutes, it seemed natural, even right.

Then something happened, some cataclysmic moment when I saw the true nature of the precipice on which we both stood. Randy'd been off carousing with his paid buddies and had come home in such a debilitated state that Mack had had to support him through the door. Behind them I could see the white limo with the signature gold coffin painted on the doors. The headlights were on and the motor was still humming and I expected that the bimbo *du nuit* was sitting back comfortably somewhere behind the smoked-glass windows.

Anyway, Mack had brought Randy home like the good little retriever he was paid to be, and I said, "He looks like hell. You'd better put him to bed and have the limo driver take the girl home."

"He wants to sleep here," Mack said.

"Who says he's welcome?" I noticed that he didn't bother denying there was a girl in the limo.

Randy's head was bouncing around like one of those dogs with a spring-loaded neck. "Aw, shit, Lorna, don't be like that."

"Don't be like what?"

"You know. Cold." He turned his head, trying to find Mack's face. "Isn't she cold, Mack? Like a fucking meat freezer."

"Uh-huh," Mack said, sliding Randy around like a sackful of concrete. Randy stared at me. He looked lost and alone, just like the lovable dufus I'd met at Rick the prick's wild one. The fact was that despite everything that had happened, I still loved him.

"Ah, hell," I said. "Put him in my bed."

But as Mack began to maneuver Randy awkwardly

across the foyer Randy squirmed away. "Don't want bed," he said. "It's boring. In fact, sleep's boring."

"Listen, Randy," I began, "I think the best thing for you to do is—"

"Shut up!" he screamed. "Don't call me Ralph!"

"I said Randy." And turning to the bodyguard, "Didn't I say Randy, Mack?"

"You little New York slut, my name's Randy, got it?" Randy screeched. "Not Ralph! I forbid you to say that name in my house! There is no Ralph, see, he's dead, finished, kaput." He was weaving, that squirmy, ugly thing coming back into his eyes. "He never even fucking existed." Now he jerked his head as if it were on a string. "Am I right, Mack?"

"Right you are, Mr. G," Mack, the obedient servant said. "Right as ever."

"Damn straight, I am!"

I glared at Mack, but he contrived to ignore me. "Randy," I said, my voice as calm as I could make it under the circumstances, "all I meant was—"

Then he reached out and hit me. Not an open-hand slap, but a full-fledged punch with his balled-up fist. "Goddammit," he thundered, "I warned you not to call me Ralph. What's the matter with you, slut?"

I was on my knees and my head was spinning. My jaw hurt, and I could taste my own blood. He had hit me where my father had done his worst work on my mother. "I said Randy," I implored, coughing. "For God's sake, Mack, tell him I said Randy."

Rage and tension had drawn the booze- and drug-induced slackness out of Randy's face. "Yeah," he said, staring down at me. "Let's hear what Mack has to say. Mack, what do you think of Lorna here calling me Ralph?"

"She shouldn't ought to do that, Mr. G," the body-guard said. "Ralph's not your name, far as I know. Not anyone's name who lives in this compound."

Randy bent over me, his face in a twisted smirk that looked almost demented. "You hear that, baby? That comes from the source. Mack's not into bullshit. He tells it like it is."

No, Mack tells it like you want it, I thought. *Just like everyone else here but me.* I wanted to say that, anything to shake some reality back into the situation. But I knew that if I opened my mouth, Randy would hit me again. God knows, I've had enough experience with abuse to recognize the warning signs.

That's when the revelation washed over me, drenching me in cold sweat: It didn't matter what I did because this was Randy's reality now, and we were all a part of it— including me.

I bit my lip and looked up at him mutely. To my horror, I saw that the squirmy thing had changed again. It was now full-blown on his face like a parasite. It had a body and, I suppose, a head, and all these squirmy little tentacles, like on a squid. It had blossomed full force, devoured him whole. It owned him—it owned all of us. What was it? Right then I thought I knew. I was convinced that it was a physical manifestation of the celebrity I had created. This is what we all lived for, what we were marooned in our desert with. It had its own life now, and it was changing all of us to fit its needs.

I saw the precipice then. I couldn't walk away because there would be no escaping his stage coffin; he'd die in there. And now I saw I couldn't stay because the fame was killing both of us in slow, steady pieces.

I stared into Randy's altered face. A face crazed with rage and desperation.

I remembered holding him in bed that afternoon, infusing him with life—a new life—and thinking myself Rex Harrison to his Audrey Hepburn. "He's got it! By George, I think he's got it!" Imagine the exhilaration! A bright and oh so promising *My Fair Lady* come to life, and I was the creator!

But, as if someone had turned the kaleidoscope to show another pattern, I now remembered that moment differently. The Technicolor vision had turned to stark black and white, a world filled with menacing shadows. I recalled his newly lean face, the thick beard divided by the scar that ran down his cheek. I remembered the thunder and the lightning, and I saw that horrific moment for what it was and always had been: a scene played out between Dr. Frankenstein and his unholy creation.

I had constructed this persona, this star, from equal parts ambition and magic. He had been nothing when I had found him, and nothing he would have remained without my intervention. But that intervention had had unforeseeable consequences; it had gotten totally out of control.

"You ungrateful slut," he said, his rage coming to full flower. "You betrayed me!"

I looked at him as if he'd lost his mind, which, I suppose in a way he had. That dark, squidlike thing had a firm hold on him and wouldn't let go. It had taken shape and form like a squid spreading its mantle, waving its tentacles. It was crawling all over him. I wanted to shout out a warning to Mack, but his face was as placid as a stone god's. Didn't he, for Christ's sake, see the danger? Didn't he know what was happening?

"Don't give me that little-miss-innocent look; you know what I'm talking about, doesn't she, Mack?"

"She sure does," Mack soothed.

"Right," Randy said, reassured he was on the right

track. I could no longer see his face, only the dark, squid-like thing oozing its noxious ink all over him. His eyes were black pools, and he no longer looked human. Mack, calm as an iceberg, still saw nothing. "You promised me you'd keep Ralph dead. We buried him together, for Christ's sake. I could feel each spadeful of dirt covering him like a shroud, smothering him into the quiet of the grave. And you swore you'd keep him buried. You *swore*, goddammit!"

He was back on the same insane track as the one months back, when he'd shown me the video of my one sexual indiscretion. What was this obsession with a promise I'd made him? Something I'd sworn and now failed to do, betraying him.

And then something flew into my mind like a crow at midnight, delivering a message I'd deftly managed to miss:

You swore to me, he had said. *A sacred vow, and now it's all gone. You've ruined everything, and it can never be the same.* It was when he had spoken about his friend who had been consumed by his fame. Eaten alive, was the phrase Randy had used. That was what he had made me swear to do, what I hadn't done: to keep the same thing from happening to him. Randy was being consumed. I could see it happening right in front of my eyes, even if stupid Mack was blind. There was nothing of Randy left. The squid-like thing had taken root. It was dominant now, sinking its long, twisting tentacles through the pores of his skin, deep into the muscles, twining about the bones of his skull.

He had been calling out to me, and I had ignored his pleas. I had sworn to protect him from the very thing which had been eating at him for all these months. Randy! My Randy! What have I done to you?

Oh God, the rest is such a blur. I closed my eyes and tried to transport the squidlike thing off him, but I'd left it too late. It was too firmly entrenched. So I did the only thing I could think of. I leapt at him, got my hands on his face—on the squidlike thing. I ripped it and ripped it, and I could hear it howl, not with my ears but in my *mind*. It howled as I sunk my nails into it, and howled even harder when I closed my eyes, using my power again, straining.

Then, all at once, my body was torn away from Randy's, but I kept my hold on *it*, the horrid squidlike thing that was living off Randy, feeding and growing, turning him into its own plaything. I could feel a ripping, like a tooth being slowly pulled from its socket.

It was Mack, standing over me. He reached down and pried my hand off the squidlike thing. "No!" I screamed. "No!" I bit him in the back of his knee.

He swiped at me, releasing his hold on my hand. "You crazy bitch!"

I lunged back to Randy, digging into the squidlike thing with my long nails as it tried to reattach itself to Randy's facial muscles. Mack, one huge fist grabbing the material at the back of my neck, shook me so hard my teeth rattled, but I refused to let go. "I knew it would come to this one day," he said. "You've gone squirrelly." The other fist was curled to deliver a massive blow.

"No!" I cried. "Randy!" I could feel something in my hand, a thick viscous mass that dribbled and slid through my grasp. "Look!" I said, holding up my fist covered by the living mass. "Look! I have it!"

"You're nuts," Mack said. "There's nothing in your hand." He didn't see it, the dark, squidlike thing. Only I could see it. Only I could do something about it. I knew Mack was going to hurt me, but I didn't care. I had to protect Randy. I needed to take care of the dark, squid-like thing before it settled back into place on his face. I had undermined it enough so that it had let go its hold on him. Now, if only . . .

I closed my eyes and imagined it someplace else. Above me, I could feel the wind of Mack's first blow. I concentrated on the someplace else, on the dark squidlike thing, aligning the two until they merged. The gelatinous mass vanished.

Mack hit me at the same moment I heard the shot. Or at least that's how I remembered it. I cried out, tumbling head over heels, rocked with pain. And when I looked up I saw Mack sprawled on the carpet, a bullet hole in his huge chest. And there was Randy standing over him with the gun he had bought.

"Jesus," Randy whispered. Then he dropped the gun and just stood there, staring at me, his beautiful eyes blue again. They were as clear as a summer's sky, no trace of the dark, squidlike thing. It was gone to the same place I'd sent the carving knife my father'd tried to use on my mother.

"What happened?" he asked in a voice I hadn't heard in a very long time. "Are you okay?"

"I don't know," I said truthfully. I picked myself up off the floor. "Are you?"

Well, Randy's with the cops now, giving his statement, although what they'll get out of him is anyone's guess. I don't think he remembers all that much. The dark, squidlike thing remembers it all, I'll bet.

Randy's pal, the ex–LAPD cop, is doing his thing, and I suspect once all the media frenzy dies down they'll indict on a lesser charge, manslaughter or something, which, knowing the attorneys I've hired, will get reduced to aggravated assault, or maybe even self-defense. If Randy thought Mack was going to kill me, which Mack could've done easily enough with those fists, he'd be justified in trying to stop him. Or they could plead temporary insanity, which wouldn't be that far from the truth. In any event, the fame's gone, and things will never be the same. It's all for the best, really. Randy will get his life back again.

What's that? Why, yes, I could do it all again on camera. You like the way I photograph? The camera is kind to me, is that it? Nobody's ever told me before I'm a natural. But, yes, perhaps you're right. I shouldn't mention the dark, squidlike thing. Too hard to swallow, is it? But about my making things disappear, I can understand how you'd want a demonstration. I don't know about that. See, I've been thinking about it and I think that place I sent the carving knife and the squidlike thing to is where the squidlike thing was born. I let it come through the barrier every time I made the key appear inside Randy's coffin. I don't want to make things disappear again, 'cause I'm afraid the dark, squidlike thing will come back. You can understand that, can't you?

Let me see, what else? Yes, I'm free tomorrow after my police interview to have lunch with those publishers you mentioned. I tell the story, you write it, that's fair by me. But I don't want to give away film rights, that's understood right now. I want to be involved, okay? Good. This is going to work, I can feel it, you know? And maybe you're right, maybe I *can* do a demonstration for you guys, make something small disappear just once.

There it is again, hear it? The clock, I mean. It's ticking. Tick-tock. Tick-tock. My fifteen minutes may have expired, but my sixteenth is just about to begin.

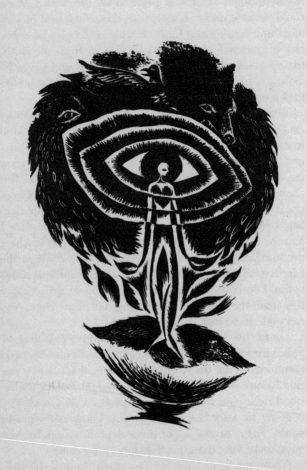

Disillusion

EDWARD BRYANT

We played with several subtitles before the first volume of Tales of the Impossible *went to print. One of them was* Illusions, *the other, like my current show, was* Beyond Imagination. *As the stories began to come in, the question arose as to which of these subthemes would best accommodate the most stories. Some of them seemed to fit the former, others the latter; in a few cases, it was a toss-up because the story dealt equally with both. That is certainly the case with this hauntingly strange love story.*

—DC

Disillusion

SHINING EYES.

The spotlit circle rippled across the audience in the orchestra section, reflected in astonished, delighted eyes. Amazed creatures, snared by the sudden glamour.

First they saw it. Then—a flash of dazzling white light. Now—

"That was absolutely amazing!" said Ingrid. Jack abruptly saw that her mouth was hanging slightly open. He couldn't help but notice the full redness of her lips. He suddenly wished they were back in the room, not here in this garish showroom approximately the size of the Astrodome. But if only she weren't— He crushed the thought, involuntarily squeezing the attaché case that sat on his lap. Ingrid turned toward him, eyes shining. The audience's wild applause crested around them. "What do you think, darling? Could it *really* be real? I mean real magic?"

"Misdirection," said Jack flatly. "There's no magic, and there are no *Star Trek* transporters. Leopards don't become giant condors—" He was rolling now. He ran out of breath and had to gulp some air. "And neither one of them turns into nubile young women."

"Well, you could fool me," said Ingrid, her wide smile shining almost as bright as the flashpots that had left dazzle floaters in each's eyes. "And I'm not a fool, Jack."

The words carried just the slightest edge. Jack looked at his new-but-maybe-not-much-longer lover sharply. Her smile softened.

"Watch the show," she said.

The Great Mandragore bounded back to center stage, wide grin dazzling the crowd. The wireless mike, limned in glowing crimson neon, spun slowly through the air from stage left. The eerie baton halted smoothly in front of the magician and parked itself in midair. The man reached out and plucked it from whatever invisible purchase.

"Not bad," breathed Ingrid.

Jack ignored her. "Look," he said. "See that gleam? The reflection?"

Ingrid shook her head impatiently. "I see nothing, Jack. Just another wonderful thing."

"It's a wire," he said. "Very thin. It caught the light." He thought he heard her sigh.

"No, Virginia," she said, almost too softly for him to hear. "There is no magic in this world. There's only wires, and mirrors, and trapdoors, and illusion."

"Deception," he said, recognizing the smug tone only too late, but still making no attempt to disguise it.

"Shut up, Jack." Ingrid said the words with no apparent malice. "Let him amaze me." It was like flipping a light switch. Her attention was . . . gone. It was up *there*. Onstage.

". . . and this is what I call my shell game," the Great Mandragore was saying. As he gestured, the serenely smiling young men and women of the stage crew smoothly pushed a series of what appeared to be clear Lucite pedestals into place. There were three, ranging from about six to ten feet in height. From the flies came what looked like huge hollowed and inverted shells of brown walnuts, each about four feet long. Lowered on wires, they hovered ten feet above the upper platforms of the pedestals.

The Great Mandragore clapped his hands. The leopard bounded smoothly from stage left and easily leapt to the nearest platform. It sat alert on its haunches, pink tongue protruding as it panted.

The magician clapped sharply twice. The rush of great wings buffeted the air from stage right as the condor flapped into sight. The huge bird alighted on the right-most platform and smoothly folded its twelve-foot wingspan. Its flat black eyes followed the Great Mandragore's every motion.

Then the magician clapped three times, the sounds as distinct as whip cracks. The beauty of the young woman who gracefully backflipped in a blur across to stage center was of a degree to take Jack's breath away. As tall as Mandragore, she vibrated to a stop upright, with arms and hands angled up in a victory pose. Her short, shining, russet hair shimmered in the spotlight. Emerald green eyes seemed to gaze into Jack's own.

"Ladies and gentlemen, Cybele."

The audience was already clapping wildly, and without prompting.

The young woman stepped into the air as two young male stagehands clasped hands below her foot. They snapped her upward; she tucked and flipped twice around—and landed with no wasted movement on the platform ten feet up. The crowd continued to roar.

"Now," said the Great Mandragore. Leopard, condor, and woman held their positions like stone as the magician snapped his fingers and two assistants carried a fourth large walnut-shell construction onstage and set it on the floor beside Mandragore.

The music cranked up.

"Wait!" said the magician. He gestured, and four stage-hands staggered out beneath the weight of what appeared to be a four-by-four square of sheet steel. They maneuvered it into place beside the shell, lowered it to a height of about six inches, and then jerked their hands and fingers back, dropping the square. It clanged to the stage with a sound like the tone of doom. Two of the stage-hands picked up the shell and set it in place on the steel square.

"*Now* we are ready!" He swept his arms around, and the shells on their wires lowered slowly to the three elevated platforms. The leopard lay down. The condor bowed its reddish head. The woman tucked to hands and knees. All three disappeared beneath their respective shells.

The drums rolled. The music took on a frenetic gypsy beat. While the stage lighting dimmed slightly, bright spots flashed strobelike on the four shells.

The Great Mandragore clapped his hands, this time amplified to a level that set Jack back in his seat. The lights came back up completely.

"So who's where?" called out the magician. He pointed at the shell on the upper right. When the covering rose, the audience gasped at the sight of the leopard. The sleek cat yawned, its tongue lolling.

The Great Mandragore pointed to the upper left. The shell rose. The great condor spread its wings, shaking out its feathers. The bird uttered a piercing, echoing *yawp*.

The magician motioned to the center shell. It rose, revealing no one and nothing on the platform atop the ten-foot transparent pedestal.

The drums thundered, the music and the audience both screamed with anticipation as the Great Mandragore turned his back to the audience and passed his hand over the shell on the metal sheet on the floor by his feet. The shell lifted into the air. A red-furred wolf rose to its haunches. The wild howl spiraled out from the grinning white jaws and filled the auditorium.

The leopard hissed and yowled. The condor shrieked.

A flash of intense light haloed the magician. When he turned to face the audience and take a bow, they realized it was no longer the Great Mandragore. He had, it seemed, become the young woman.

For the first time, she changed expression, grinning at the audience and waving.

The Great Mandragore descended from the flies, moving his arms gracefully, as if gently swimming toward the stage. He landed on his feet beside the young woman.

Taking her hand, he said simply, "Cybele and I thank you."

"No," said Jack under his breath, glancing to his side and seeing Ingrid staring raptly at the stage, "thank *you*." He squeezed the handle of his attaché case and felt, rather than heard, the *click*.

After the show, when the theater emptied, Jack and Ingrid walked back to their hotel and ordered a late snack in the all-night coffee shop. Jack had the feeling that Ingrid was still viewing the dazzle and mystery of the magic show. He also wondered whether she was seeing the Great Mandragore sitting in Jack's seat.

"It was wonderful," she kept saying.

The waitress brought them both more decaf.

"Good illusions," Jack said grudgingly.

"It was more than that," Ingrid said. "I'm sure of it."

For a quick disorienting moment, Jack thought he saw

the russet-haired assistant—Cybele, was it?—sitting in Ingrid's place. Then the blond hair was back, the eyes as blue as the sky at midmorning. Ingrid.

"What's wrong?" she said.

He shook his head. "Nothing."

She cocked her head like a tropical bird. "Are you having flashbacks to the performance tonight?"

"Maybe," he admitted.

"To the gorgeous assistant in the shell game finale?"

He stared at her, startled.

She nodded with some satisfaction, and half smiled. "We've been lovers for—what? A week? Now you're checking out the competition?" She shook her head. "Men." Her tone didn't sound amused.

Jack started to protest, then decided it probably wouldn't do any good. It was as though a voice inside him was telling him not to bother. He suspected everything was already written on his face. "That's not it at all."

Ingrid looked disgusted.

"You're the ace investigative reporter," he said, trying to sound neutral.

"Maybe I should have run a background check on you," she said sharply. "After the first two or three times guys burned me, I've been tempted. It just seems so cold . . ."

Jack suddenly had the feeling this was running downhill, all of a sudden out of control. He wanted to say the things that would make everything all right. "Ingrid—"

"Never mind." She turned away from him. "I'm on edge, doing this 'death of magic' article for the magazine. I've got to learn to keep my work out of my life, and my life out of my work."

He reached across and took her hand. It felt cold. "Listen," he said, "is this the professional on duty? I mean, you're the big enchilada writer, and I'm the lowly researcher with only a month's tenure at *RealWorld*."

Her expression softened. She cupped her hand like one of the Great Mandragore's giant walnut shells and set it down on the knuckles of his hand as he clasped hers. "Look, Jack, I don't mean to make things tense. Let's just go back to the room. Okay?" Her voice sounded genuinely hopeful.

But he realized he was looking at her now as a virtual stranger. What had he been thinking all this past week as they planned the Atlantic City junket? He tried to recall what he had felt for her only a few hours earlier. He didn't remember this disorienting sense of chaos before. His thoughts abruptly stalled in confusion. He *knew* he must have confronted situations like this: mutual attractions, kindled love affairs, relationships suddenly accelerating in feeling. Everyone dealt with this. Had Jack? *Hadn't he?*

"Are you going to prove to me that Mandragore's a fake?" she said. And then in exactly the same tone, "Are you going to break my heart?"

"Yes to the first," Jack said. He stared back at her. What was going *on*? With effort, he said, "As for the second—Let's go back to the room."

She looked away from his face again. "If he's a fake, how did he pull off that last trick, the shell game?"

"He's good," Jack said. "He's not a fake. It's just not real magic."

Ingrid's eyes momentarily lost focus. "Magic," she said. "I desperately crave some magic in my life. Not illusion."

Jack put down on the table twice the money he estimated was needed. "Let's go, okay?"

"No illusion," Ingrid repeated. "I don't need that. Jack, you told me last night you loved me. Do you?"

It was all going too fast to register. He couldn't remember last night. Jack shook his head, feeling suddenly that the hard bone of his skull was a sieve, and the rough-textured fabric of nightmare was filtering into his head. If he could just shake his head fast enough, the nightmare threads would fly out again. This was horrible. It was progressively and rapidly getting worse.

"What's the matter?" said Ingrid. "Have you got a headache?"

Jack massaged his temples. "Sorry. Just felt shaky for a moment. I'm okay." But he knew he wasn't. Okay, that is.

He waited until they were both back in the quiet of the room before he told her that, no, he didn't love her. Fortunately, when he said it, it was spoken only in his mind, and it was said after she'd dropped off to sleep and while he remained terribly awake, staring up in the dark at the invisible ceiling.

What was *happening* to him? For the smallest split of a second, he imagined he was being watched by hidden eyes.

The next day was Sunday and, after a leisurely room service breakfast, they took the train back to the city. They cabbed together from Penn Station. In front of Ingrid's building, with the meter ticking over, Jack argued her into seeing him after supper.

"It's important," he said. "It's something you'll need for the article."

Ingrid wasn't entirely sure she wanted to get together again so soon after the Atlantic City trip.

"I've got so much work this week," she protested. "I'm going to need the time at home."

"I've got something to show you," Jack answered. "I have something you really do need to see."

It took a little cajoling, but she finally agreed. "It's important?" she said doubtfully. "I mean, for real?"

"It is," he assured her.

Ingrid gave him a peck on the cheek and a quick hug, and told him she'd call before coming downtown. A shake of blond hair, a flash of blue eyes, and she was gone.

"Where now?" said the cabbie.

Jack told him.

Once back in his apartment off Sixth Avenue and Tenth, Jack set his overnight bag in the sleeping loft without unpacking it. He returned to the living room and carefully unsnapped the top of the attaché case. Gently he lifted the lightweight video camera out of its vibration-damping cradle and set it on the coffee table.

The tape cassette looked to be in good shape.

Mr. Constantine had quietly lent Jack the secretive camcorder. Mr. Constantine was Jack's boss. If the publisher had a first name, no one at *RealWorld* magazine seemed to know it. Perhaps "Mister" really was, as the office joke went, Constantine's given name.

Jack used the remote to turn on the Sony big-screen he used as a monitor. He registered that *CNN Headline News* was on the screen. It was close to the bottom of the hour. Feature stuff.

". . . magic or illusion?" the female reporter was saying.

Jack cranked the volume up.

"Tabloids across the country are asserting that the Great Mandragore is everything from a space alien with superhuman powers, to an ordinary sleight-of-hand artist who has posted a Faustian bargain with Satan. Mandragore has twice turned down requests by CNN for an interview opportunity to answer his accusers. A spokeswoman for his booking company offered regrets— but perhaps something more."

The shot cut to a close-up of the woman Cybele. Jack stared, the tape in his hand forgotten for the moment. "For the successful illusionist," she said, "the hand is indeed always quicker than the eye." She looked directly into the camera, green eyes afire. "The truth about the Great Mandragore is right there for all to see—if only you have the quickness of wit to look."

The picture cut back to the reporter, who then signed off.

Jack slipped the videotape cassette into the VCR's slot and punched the PLAY button on the remote. He watched for the better part of four hours, reversing the tape, hitting the PAUSE button, taking notes and timing numbers, running footage in superslow motion, taking more notes.

Finally he stopped when he realized his concentration was edging him close to exhaustion.

"You clever son of a gun," he said toward the Great Mandragore's jovial image frozen on the screen. "I've got you. Gotcha dead to rights. Even Ingrid will believe me now."

"You did *what*?" she said that night.

"I smuggled this into the performance," Jack said, gesturing at the minicam on the table. "Ultralight, completely quiet, autofocus, and perfect for low-light conditions. I taped the whole damned thing."

"I'm not sure this was a good idea," Ingrid said.

Jack stared at her in disbelief. "*Not a good idea*? We're journalists, my love. *Investigative* journalists. We're checking out a stage magician who's so good, half the country thinks he's the real McCoy. Sneaking a camera in may have broken a rule or two, but it's not a hanging offense. For crying out loud, Ingrid, I didn't pay off the leopard or the condor to give me the dirt."

She looked back at him, mute.

"Okay," he said. "I'm done. No more ranting. I just want you to watch some things. The show was about two hours, but I've culled a compilation of footage from all the really amazing stunts. You know, the shell game and all the rest."

Now Ingrid looked disgusted. "Okay," she said. "Show me."

"You'll love it," he said.

But she didn't.

He showed her all the ultraslow, frame-by-frame breakdowns of the vanishings and the transferences and the transpositions. He showed her how the camera could not be fooled by misdirection.

"No," she said.

"Oh, yes."

He pointed out the fractional moments when the lens caught the shine of a wire, the glimmer of a mirror, the suggestion of movement in a hidden compartment when the human eye of the perceiver wouldn't have noticed a thing.

Tears came to her eyes.

And then he showed her how the shell game had been performed.

"You son of a bitch," she said, starting to sob.

He couldn't stop. He showed her absolutely everything.

Then there was something else he could not stop.

He raised her chin with his hands and looked into her tear-glossed eyes. "By the way," he said, "I don't love you."

Her hand. His eye. The hand really *was* quicker. Her slap solidly smacked his cheek.

It echoed in his head for a long time; much longer than the time it took Ingrid to grab her coat and leave.

*   *   *

When Jack went to work at the midtown AusPub Tower the next day, Ingrid wasn't there. Lisa, the short, intense receptionist on the editorial floor of *RealWorld* magazine, told him that Ingrid had phoned in earlier and said that she'd be working at home the entire day.

Jack stared at the telephone in his cubicle before finally dialing her number.

She answered on the fourth ring. Her voice sounded logy, exhausted.

"It's me," he said.

"What do you want?"

"I'm sorry. I just needed to talk to you." That wasn't what he wanted to say at all, but it was a start. Jack tried to seize fast to the opening.

"Last night," said Ingrid. "Did you mean those things you said at the end?"

He was silent for a while. He wanted to deny what he had told her.

"Jack?"

He started at her prompt.

"Are you there?"

"Yes," he said. Horrified, he realized he had been presented with his agenda. "About last night, yes."

"Jack—" He heard infinite sadness in the single word. Saying nothing more, Ingrid hung up.

He dialed her back after hesitating. What was the use? But he still refused to set down the receiver and terminate the call. Jack got her answering machine and hung up without leaving a message. He stared at the phone long minutes more.

The moving feet of people traversing the wide expanse of offices, the keyboard clatter, the voices speaking urgently into phones, all faded into a soft white noise.

What was going on? The question haunted him. He had come to work at *RealWorld* barely more than a month before. He had met Ingrid, he had wooed her, won her, rejected her, all in that month. What kind of man was he? He didn't remember ever acting like this before.

His own character revelations bloomed in front of him like an endless series of silk handkerchiefs being pulled from a magician's sleeve.

Was it an illusionist's trick?

But this was not a stage in a theater supercharged with shattering sound and disorienting lighting. This was the real world. All the world's a stage. . . . The quotation reverberated in his brain, a basic musical echo that wouldn't go away, a language virus infecting his thoughts.

Which *was* quicker, thought Jack. The hand, or the eye?

Nothing made sense.

So he told the receptionist Lisa that he felt nauseated, he was probably coming down with Tehran A flu, he was going home for the day.

She should log his calls. Which didn't really matter, he thought. In his short tenure at the magazine, he had received few messages.

After leaving the office, he walked over to Forty-second Street, picked a martial arts film at random, and sat through the movie for three consecutive showings.

When he exited the dark theater in late afternoon, Jack realized he could recall nothing of the plot. Sonny Chiba? Some other fierce, lethal hero?

He couldn't remember.

That night, Jack extracted the last TV dinner from the freezer compartment of his refrigerator and cooked it in the oven. He wondered whether his life would be measurably different if he bought a compact microwave unit from the Korean electronics supermarket two blocks away.

He glanced around the apartment. There really were few amenities. The living room held a TV set on a metal folding chair. The windows had no curtains. He had pinned up some flowered sheets to keep the early light out. There were two more folding chairs over behind the nondescript coffee table. A cheap phone was centered on the coffee table.

The kitchen held a coffeemaker and a bag full of paper plates and plastic utensils. A mug with a Boston Red Sox logo rested by the sink. The refrigerator held a pound of ground coffee and a small container of Half & Half.

There were some clothes on hangers in the closet.

The bathroom contained an extra roll of toilet paper, but held too few towels.

It was, in short, an apartment that *looked* as though he had moved in yesterday and had been living out of a suitcase.

Jack spent much of the evening sitting and staring at the telephone. Should he call Ingrid? What good would it do if he reached her? What would he tell her? What was there at all to say? But he knew he wanted to talk with her.

When he dialed her number, Ingrid let the machine take the call—if indeed she was at home at all.

Jack left no message.

After he finally lay on his mattress in the sleeping loft, Jack quickly slept. He dreamed of his past. At first it was a lucid dream in which he knew he was journeying to his beginnings. Beyond a month, though, the details were frustratingly vague.

He recalled his parents, but they turned their faces inevitably away from him. So did his childhood friends, as well as his college schoolmates and the coworkers at his first job. He couldn't remember what that job was. Something . . . in a warehouse, he thought.

Now he *knew* he was being watched. He saw no watchers at first, but the sensation of being observed was unmistakable. He stood among lush trees and tall flowering plants, and felt certain the foliage hid eyes.

He would see those eyes if only he glanced in the right direction at precisely the right time. Branches moved without wind; bird sounds cooed and raucously cawed. Jack realized this was misdirection.

The next time he was tempted to redirect his vision, he deliberately gazed where he was obviously not supposed to.

That was when he made out the stone-still leopard gazing back at him from deep green eyes. But the more he stared at the great jungle cat, the more its furred outlines wavered and shifted into a huge bird whose shiny anthracite eyes fixed him dispassionately; and then the bird was a red wolf, a creature of long white teeth and hypnotic eyes.

Faces. The wolf's face deformed to a human face. The Great Mandragore grinned back at him. The face of Cybele took form superimposed over the illusionist's features. When she met Jack's eyes, she appeared wary.

Her expression softened, lips parting as though she were going to tell him something.

He awoke.

Jack wanted to return to the dream, but he also knew that was impossible. How he knew . . . he no longer understood.

*   *   *

When Jack walked into the glass-enclosed lobby of the AusPub Tower at nine in the morning none of his coworkers and acquaintances seemed to be meeting his eye.

Lisa, the receptionist on the editorial floor, appeared to gawk at him, startled.

"What's the matter?" he said.

She seemed to gather her wits. "Um, good morning, Jack."

"What's wrong?"

She said nothing, looked beyond his shoulder, and said, "Good morning, Mr. Constantine."

Jack glanced back at the publisher.

"Jack, would you mind coming back to my office for a minute, please?"

He nodded mutely, shooting an accusing glare at Lisa before turning on his heel.

This didn't look good. As they threaded through the maze of desks and cubicles toward Constantine's office, Jack thought that everyone else was studiously ignoring their passage. Or maybe he was just imagining that. But it was true that no one seemed to be looking up or offering a "hi" or "good morning."

They walked past Constantine's secretary, who looked up but didn't offer a greeting. Once in the corner office, Constantine shut the door behind them, gestured to the empty leather chair in front of his immaculately bare desk, and crossed to the west windows. He threw open the curtains with a dramatic rush of air—almost a gust of wind, Jack thought—and stood looking out at the tops of other midtown towers.

"Jack, Jack, Jack . . ." Constantine said. Still with his back turned, he shook his head.

"What?" said Jack tentatively.

"Ingrid turned in the rough of her 'death of magic' article early this morning."

"So how was it?" said Jack.

"Everything I could have hoped for." Constantine stared out over the city's suddenly Gothic-appearing towers.

"Everything?" Jack tried to smile.

"Indeed," said Constantine. "It will play as a wonderfully rationalist analysis of public gullibility and popular hysteria. The Great Mandragore is pictured as a consummate illusionist and nothing more."

"Which is what you wanted."

Constantine nodded. "There is a real tone of acute disappointment, of crushed romance in Ingrid's prose. I'm afraid her sense of joy in the infinite wonder of the universe may have been diminished a bit by this assignment."

"But that's what you wanted, too," said Jack.

The publisher nodded again, slowly. "You've been a good employee, Jack. You've done exactly what I requested of you, and more."

Jack wanted to smile, but couldn't quite manage it. "Is there a problem, sir? You said I'd get the nod for an editorial position if I brought this off."

"I'm afraid," said Constantine, "that I misrepresented matters a bit." He turned back from the window, and Jack saw the man's reflection waver like a desert heat shimmer.

The Great Mandragore faced him, hands palm-first at waist level.

Jack recoiled. A gentle hand touched his arm.

"It's all right, Jack," said Cybele from behind him.

Bewildered, shocked, Jack tried to jerk away from her. Her fingers tightened like spring steel.

"You're going to sleep for just a little while, Jack," said the Great Mandragore in Constantine's voice. "There won't even be a hangover." He nodded at the woman.

Cybele's fingers rose to the back of Jack's head. "Rest," she said.

Jack felt what he imagined a light switch might feel if it were conscious, as it was flipped off.

The light. First he saw it; then he—

Awoke.

Dim light, dust mote-laden light, the kind of light that made him think of late afternoons, light slanting down from high, narrow windows all around him. He stood in a spacious room cluttered on all sides with half-perceived heaps of things, piles of construction materials, vaguely apprehended equipment and tools.

Jack shook his head, trying to clear it. Meaning filtered back into his brain. Ahead and to his left, the thing that at first appeared to be the hummocks left by some sort of giant mole burrowing just under the concrete floor actually translated to a series of large, walnut-shell constructions.

He remembered. The props from the Great Mandragore's shell game.

Behind the shells, a row of Lucite pedestals shone in the window light. Off to the right, he saw shelves diminishing in perspective into the distance. The shelves held a variety of objects he couldn't even identify. What he *could* recognize included ropes, chains, handcuffs, manacles, leather masks. Was this some kind of S&M bondage and discipline emporium? No, he thought, these are props. For escapes.

Directly ahead, he could make out a steel tank on stilts, a container enigmatically labeled NAPHTHA.

Footsteps approached on the hard warehouse floor. Jack saw Cybele and Constantine materialize out of the dimness.

"Are you feeling all right?" said Cybele. It sounded like genuine concern in her voice.

Jack answered the question with his own question. "Where am I?"

"New Jersey," said Constantine. "We cabbed you out from the city."

"Cabbed?"

"I'm a publisher, Jack, not a magician."

"I'm not so sure about that." Jack gingerly touched his own face. "What the hell did you do to me?"

"We let you rest," said Cybele.

"What is this place?" Jack said.

Constantine spread his arms and turned to indicate the whole vast space. "It's a place to work; a place to rest; a place to find sanctuary." The publisher wore loose-fitting black clothes. As he raised his arms, for just a moment, the cloth of his voluminous shirt seemed to extend into wings.

Jack stared. He glanced to the side of the momentary condor-creature and thought he saw Cybele's skin take on the texture of fur as jungle cat rosettes began to pattern her body.

He blinked. Then the publisher and the magician's assistant were only a man and a woman again, and both smiled at him.

"How did you get me out of the building?" said Jack.

"AusPub?" the publisher said. "Why, you walked out under your own steam."

"I don't remember it."

"It seemed like a good idea," said Cybele, "not to debate the matter with you. We simply urged you to come with us."

"*Strongly* urged," said Constantine. "Now," he continued, "please accompany us further."

Jack had the feeling that this would be a bad time—or at least a useless time—to inquire about his promised editorial job. Things seemed to be accelerating quickly and out of all control, much as they had after the performance two nights ago. "Okay," he said. "Are you going to do anything bad to me?"

Constantine shook his head and smiled paternally. Cybele gently patted his cheek, a feather touch that still suggested all the force of a hurricane gale.

The publisher leading, the trio walked a narrow concrete path toward the distant wall.

"We owe you some explanation," said Cybele, her hand gently guiding his elbow to steer him around heaps and stacks of objects in the receding light.

"I guess I'd appreciate that," Jack said. They passed folded tarps and bolts of silk, an antique cannon and a series of nested glass boxes that looked like nineteenth-century aquariums. He frowned and slowed for a moment. "Is that a stuffed elephant?"

"A mammoth, actually."

Jack couldn't help but gawk.

Constantine smiled. "I picked it up as a curiosity awhile back. Mandragore caused it to disappear and then reappear nearly instantaneously in an aisle behind the entire audience."

They reached what had been the distant wall. All three of them stood in front of a heavy plank door. The door was evidently made to be secured with a thick brass padlock. Right now the locking hasp was open, the lock hanging by one post.

Constantine grasped the edge of the heavy door and swung it open with a creaking rasp of complaining hinges. Little light illuminated the inside. The three of them waited for their eyes to adjust.

Cybele said, "You will rest for a while. Then we'll have another job for you."

Jack stopped in some confusion. "Job? What about the editorial position?"

"Perhaps someday," said Constantine.

"Jesus!" said Jack. He realized he was staring at what looked for all the world like a human body dangling limply from a hook on the wall. "Who the hell is that?"

Cybele flicked a wall switch and a low-wattage bulb blinked on. Now Jack could read the sign beside the door. It read, PROPS. "Don't you recognize him?" she said.

Jack looked closer and realized he did, in fact, recognize the limp man hanging on the wall.

Eyes blank, every muscle at rest, the man on the hook was the Great Mandragore.

"Oh my God," said Jack. "The magician. What did you do to him?"

"Nothing," said Constantine. "We just keep him here until we need him."

"Until it's showtime," said Cybele.

"I'm missing something," Jack said. "None of this makes any sense at all."

The magician's assistant and the publisher exchanged glances.

"Conceive of strangers," said Constantine. "Imagine them dwelling in a strange land where they must survive the best way they can devise."

"Imagine strangers," said Cybele, "who perform what most inhabitants of their new home would perceive as wonders."

Jack looked at them, at the slack and suspended Great Mandragore, and then back at his companions again.

"You mean—" he started to say, then fumbled for the words. "You mean all the magic's real? Is that what you're saying?"

Cybele nodded. "But we can't let anyone else know that. We'd be imprisoned by the authorities, maybe dissected to see how our powers work."

"Or we would be torn apart by the population," said Constantine, "out of fear. We don't want to take over your reality. Our goals are more modest. We just would like sanctuary."

"So you want the public to be sure to think that the magic is only illusion," said Jack slowly. "That it's all a fake."

"And that is why we needed the cooperation of Ingrid," said Constantine. "And that is why we needed your help."

"You got my help," said Jack. "Ingrid did what you ultimately wanted her to do." He glanced sharply at the two of them. "Why did you make me do what I did to Ingrid?" Pain stabbed deep into him, sharp and edged as ice.

Neither said anything. Constantine looked away, but Cybele met his gaze. In her eyes, in the twist of her lips, Jack saw a flash of what he suspected must be jealousy. It was like the light glimmering off a sharpened tooth. "Now what about me?" He abruptly felt more bitter than fearful.

"We'll require you again," said Constantine. "Someday."

"Thank you," said Cybele. Her lips brushed his cheek as she stood on toe tips. Her hair was soft against his face for just a moment; but not as soft as Ingrid's had been. "I'll see you again, Jack," she said, in the doorway of the prop room.

Cybele reached with delicate transforming fingers to turn him off.

The last image he saw was not her eyes, but Ingrid's.

Jack wished futilely for that final wondrous shapechange. *Ingrid,* he thought, *love, if only you knew* . . . The miracle transformed solely in his mind.

He saw her magical eyes.

Disillusioned eyes.

The Stuff That Dreams Are Made Of

TAD WILLIAMS

Best-selling fantasy writer Tad Williams steps out of genre with this delightful parody of and tribute to both magic and the PI voices of such authors as Raymond Chandler, Mickey Spillane, and Dashiell Hammett. This is a very grown-up Tad, having fun. I cannot imagine the profile of the reader who would not enjoy this romp every bit as much as I did.

—*DC*

The Stuff That Dreams
Are Made Of

OKAY, I ADMIT IT. If a guy wants to get drunk in the middle of a weekday afternoon, he should have a lock on his office door. Usually Tilly runs interference for me, but this day of all days she'd left early to take her mother in to have her braces loosened. (Retired ladies who get a yen for late-life orthodontia give me a pain anyway. I told Tilly her mom's gums were too weak for such foolishness, but who listens to me?)

Anyway, Tilly is usually out there behind the reception desk to protect me. I don't pay her all that much, but somehow, despite the fairly small difference in our ages, I bring out some grumpy but stalwart mother-bear reflex in her. Actually, that describes her pretty well: any bill collector who's ever seen an angry Tilly come out from behind her desk, her bulky cable knit sweater and long, polished nails suggesting a she-grizzly charging out of a cave, will know exactly what I mean. If Tilly shacked up with Smokey the Bear, every forest arsonist in the country would move to Mexico.

Sadly, there was no lock, and for once no Tilly to play whatsisname at the bridge. The fairly attractive blond woman, finding the door to my inner office open, wandered in and discovered me in a more or less horizontal position on the carpet.

I stared at her ankles for a moment or two. They were

perfectly nice ankles, but because of all the blood that had run to one side of my head, I wasn't really in optimum viewing mood.

"Um," I said at last. " 'Scuse me. I'm just looking for a contact lens." I would have been more convincing if my face hadn't been pressed too closely against the carpet to locate anything on a larger scale than the subatomic.

"And I'm looking for Dalton Pinnard," she said. "Otherwise known as 'Pinardo the Magnificent.' See anybody by that name down there among the contact lenses?" She had a voice that, while not harsh, was perfectly designed to make ten-year-old boys goofing in the back of a classroom cringe. Or to make drunken magicians feel like brewery-vat scum. If she wasn't a teacher, she'd missed her calling.

"I have a note from a doctor that says I'm allergic to sarcasm," I growled. "If you don't want a whopping lawsuit on your hands, you'd better leave." Admittedly, I was still at a slight conversational disadvantage—this riposte would have been more telling if it hadn't been spoken through a mouthful of carpet fuzz—but how can you expect someone who's just finished off his tenth Rolling Rock to be both witty and vertical?

"I'm not going to go away, Mister Pinnard. I'm here about something very important, so you might as well just stop these shenanigans."

I winced. Only a woman who thinks that two pink gins at an educational conference buffet evening constitutes wild living would dismiss something of the profound masculine significance of a solo drunk as "shenanigans." However, she had already ruined my mood, so I began the somewhat complicated process of getting into my chair.

I made it without too much trouble—I'd be saying good-bye to the office soon anyway, so what difference did a few spilled ashtrays make? I was buoyed slightly by the knowledge that, however irritating this woman was right now, at least she wouldn't be around for the hangover. Not that she was unpleasant to look at. Except for a slightly sour look around the mouth, which turned out to be temporary, and a pair of glasses that belonged on one of those old women who wear garden gloves to play the slot machines, she looked pretty damn good. She had a slight tendency to go in and out of focus, but I suspected that might have something to do with what I'd had for lunch.

"Well," I said brightly once I had achieved an upright position. I paused to scrabble beside the chair rollers for one of the cigarette butts that still had a good amount of white left on it. "Well, well, well. What can I do for you, Miss . . . ?"

"It's Ms., first of all. Ms. Emily Heltenbocker. And I'm increasingly less sure that you can do anything for me at all. But my father sent me to you, and I'm taking him at his word. For about another forty-five seconds, anyway."

I hadn't managed to get my lighter going in three tries, so I set it down in a way that suggested I had merely been gauging the length of spark for some perfectly normal scientific purpose. "Heltenbocker . . . ? Wasn't that Charlie Helton's real name?"

"I'm his daughter."

"Oh." Something kicked a little inside me. In all the years I knew Charlie, I had never met his only child, who had been raised by her mother after she and Charlie divorced. It was too bad we were finally meeting when I was . . . well, like I was at the moment. "I heard about your dad last week. I'm really sorry. He was a great guy."

"He was. I miss him very much." She didn't unfreeze, but she did lower herself into the chair opposite me, showing a bit more leg than one expected from a schoolteacher type, which inspired me to assay the cigarette lighter again.

"Oh, for God's sake," she said a moment later, and pulled a lighter out of her purse and set it blazing under my nose. Half the admittedly foreshortened cigarette disappeared on my first draw. She dropped the lighter back in her bag. She struck me as the kind of woman who might tie your shoes for you if you fumbled at the laces too long.

"So . . . Charlie sent you to me?" I leaned back and managed finally to merge the two Ms. Heltenbockers into one, which made for more effective conversation. She had a rather nice face, actually, with a strong nose and good cheekbones. "Did you want to book me for the memorial service or something? I'd be honored. I'm sure I could put together a little tribute of some kind." Actually, I was trying desperately to decide which of the tricks I did at the children's parties which made up most of my business would be least embarrassing to perform in front of a gathering of my fellow professionals. I couldn't picture the leading lights of the magic world getting too worked up about balloon animals.

"No, it's not for the memorial service. We've already had that, just for the family. I want to talk to you about something else. Did you hear what happened to him?"

I couldn't think of any immediate response except to nod. In fact, it was despondency over Charlie's passing, and the awareness of mortality that comes with such things, that had been a large part of the reason for my little afternoon session. Well, not as large a part as the foreclosure notice on the office I had received that morning, but it had certainly fueled my melancholy.

What can you say about an old friend for whom The Basket and Sabers Trick went so dreadfully wrong? That, at a time when he was down on his luck financially, and on a day when he happened to be practicing without an assistant, it looks a little like your old friend may have been a suicide? Of course, a honed-steel saber sounds more like a murder weapon than a tool for self-slaughter, and most people don't choose to bow out inside a four-foot rattan hamper, but the door to his workroom was locked, and the only key had been found in Charlie's blood-soaked pocket. According to the respectable papers, he was working inside the basket and somehow must have turned the wrong way. The sharp blade sliced his carotid artery, just beneath the ear. "Accident" was the verdict most of them came up with, and the police (perhaps tactfully) agreed. Some of the lower-rent tabloids did hint at suicide, and ran lurid pictures of the crime scene under headlines like THE FINAL TRICK! and BASKET OF BLOOD!

(I would heap even more scorn on such journals except my most recent interview—only two years before—had been courtesy of *Astrology and Detective Gazette*, which shows they are not totally without discernment.)

"Yeah, I read about it," I said at last. "I was really shaken up. A horrible accident."

"It was murder." Phone-the-time ladies announce the hour with less certainty.

"I beg your pardon?"

"Murder." She reached into her bag, but this time she didn't produce a lighter. The envelope hit my desk with the loud smack of a card trick going wrong. "I went to see the lawyer yesterday. I expected Dad to be broke."

I was suddenly interested. She was here to hire me for *something*, even if I didn't know what. "And you were wrong?"

"No, I was exactly right. His net assets are a few hundred moth-eaten magic books, some tattered posters, a few old props, and an overdue bill for rental of his top hat. And that envelope. But I expected to receive something else, too, and I didn't get it."

I was already reaching for the envelope. She stilled me
with a glance. Yeah, just like they say in books. And if
any of you has ever received a note in class illustrated
with a dirty cartoon of your teacher and looked up to
find her standing over you, you'll know what I mean.
Real rabbit–in–the–headlights stuff. "Uh, you . . . you said
you didn't get something you expected?"

"Dad had been writing his memoirs for years. He
wouldn't let me read them, but I saw the manuscript lots
of times. When I didn't find it around the house
after . . . after . . ." For a brief moment her composure
slipped. I looked away, half out of sympathy, half to
escape the momentarily suspended gorgon stare. She
cleared her throat. "When I couldn't find it, I assumed
he'd given it to his lawyer for safekeeping. He'd fired his
agent years earlier, and he doesn't talk to Mom, so it
couldn't be with anyone else. But the lawyer didn't know
anything about it. It's just . . . *vanished*. And here's the suspicious part—there was a lot of interest in that
manuscript, especially from some of Dad's rivals in the
business. They were concerned that he might tell some
tales they'd rather weren't made public."

I straightened up. Repeated doses of her sit-up-
properly-class voice were beginning to take a toll on my
natural slouch; also, the effects of lunch were wearing off.
"Listen, Ms. Heltenbocker, I'm not a cop, but that doesn't
seem like grounds enough to suspect murder."

"I know you're not a cop. You're an out-of-work magician. Look in the envelope."

"Hey. I have a nice little thing going with birthdays and
Bar Mitzvahs, you know." That sort of defensive thrust
works best when followed by a quick retreat, so I picked
up the envelope. It had her name on it, written in an old
man's shaky hand. The only thing inside was an old

photograph: two rows of young men, all dressed in top hats and tailcoats, with a placard in front of them reading: SAVINI'S MAGIC ACADEMY, CLASS OF '48. Three of the faces had been circled in ink. None of the three was Charlie himself; I discovered him smiling in the front row, looking like a young farm boy fresh off the bus. Which in 1948, as I recalled, he pretty much would have been.

"This doesn't mean anything to me," I said. "How could it? I wasn't even born."

"Look on the back."

On the flip side of the photo, that same shaky hand had scrawled across the top: "If something happens to me or my book, investigate these three." At the bottom, also in ink but kind of faint, the same person had written: "Trust Pinardo."

"Yes, it's all my dad's handwriting. It took me awhile to find out who Pinardo was and to track you down. Apparently, you haven't been playing many of the big venues lately." She smiled, but I've seen more warmth from Chevrolet grillwork. "So far my dad's judgment looks pretty awful, but I'm willing to give you a chance for his sake. I still think it's murder, and I do need assistance."

I shook my head. "Okay, your father was a friend, but we hadn't seen each other for a long time. Even granting that it's a murder, only for the sake of argument, what do you—what did *he*—expect me to do, for Chrissakes?"

"Help me. My father suspected something about these three men who all went to the magic academy with him. His book has disappeared. I'm going to confront them, but I need somebody who understands this world." The facade slipped again, and I found myself watching her face move. The human woman underneath that do-it-yourself Sternness Kit was really quite appealing. "My mom and dad split up when I was little. I didn't grow up with him; I don't know anything about stage magic. I'm a teacher, for goodness sake!"

"Aha!" I said.

"What the hell does that mean?"

"Nothing, really." I pondered. "Okay. I don't buy any of this, but I'll do what I can. Charlie was a good guy, and he was there for me when I was starting out. I suppose that whatever I have, I owe to him."

"Hmmm," she said. "Maybe I trusted you too fast. You've certainly got a pretty good murder motive right there."

"Very funny. We'd better discuss my fee, because as it turns out, I can help you already. I've just recognized one of these guys." Quite pleased with myself, I pointed at a thin young man with a thin young mustache standing in the back row. "His name is Fabrizio Ivone, and he's working tonight at the Rabbit Club."

My none-too-sumptuous personal quarters are a suite of rooms—well, if a studio with a kitchenette and bathroom constitutes a suite—over my place of business. Thus, it was easy enough to grab a bite to eat, a couple hours' sleep, then shower and get back downstairs well before Ms. Heltenbocker returned to pick me up. If my head was starting to feel like someone was conducting folk-dancing classes inside it, I suppose that was nobody's fault but my own.

Tilly was again holding down the front desk, eating a takeout egg foo yong and going over the books. She was frowning, and no surprise: matching my income against my outgo was like trying to mend the *Titanic* with chewing gum and masking tape.

"Hey, you were supposed to have the day off." I

scrabbled in the filing cabinet for the aspirin. "How's your mom?"

Tilly gave me one of her looks. She'd probably noticed the pyramid of beer bottles I'd made on my desk. "If I stayed away from here a whole day, this place would just disappear under the dust, like Pompeii. Mom's fine. Her gums are still sore. I've been overheating the blender making her milk shakes all afternoon." She paused to contemplate a noodle that had fallen onto her sweater, where it lay like a python that had died climbing Everest. "By the way, who the hell is Emily Heltenbocker?"

"Client." I said it casually, although it was a word that had not been uttered within those walls for some time. "Also Charlie Helton's daughter. Why?"

"She left a message for you. Poor old Charlie—that was a real shame. Anyway, she says she'll be here at seven, and you should wear a clean shirt."

I did not dignify this with a reply.

"Oh, and two different reporters called—someone from the *Metropolitan*, and a guy from the *Defective Astronomer Gazette*."

"*Astrology and Detective*," I said absently, wondering what could have made me the center of such a media whirlwind. The *Metropolitan* was actually a rather high-toned organ: they only printed their car-accident pictures in black and white, and they ran tiny disclaimers underneath the alien abduction stories. I swallowed a few more aspirin and went to meet the press.

A couple of quick calls revealed that both had contacted me about the Charlie Helton Mystery, aka The Magical Murder Manuscript. Apparently the missing book angle had been leaked by Charlie's lawyer and was developing into a fair bit of tabloid froth. Some hack from the *Scrutinizer* called while I was still working my way through the first two. By the time I had finished my bout of semiofficial spokesmanship—not forgetting to remind them all that Pinnard was spelled with two n's, but Pinardo (as in the Magnificent) with only one—Tilly leaned in the door to tell me "my date" was waiting.

(There is a certain hideous inevitability to what happens when Tilly meets one of my female clients, at least if that client is under sixty years of age. It is useless to protest that I have no romantic interest in them—Tilly only takes this as evidence of my hopelessly self-deluding nature. As far as she's concerned, any roughly nubile woman who has even the most cursory business relationship with me falls into one of two categories: shallow gold diggers prospecting in my admittedly rather tapped-out soil, or blindingly out-of-my-league "classy ladies" over whom I am fated to make a dribbling fool of myself. Only the sheer lack of recent clients of any sort had caused me to forget this; otherwise, I would have been sure to meet Charlie's daughter downstairs in front of the laundromat, at whatever cost to dignity.)

All unknowing, Emily Heltenbocker had greatly increased the likelihood of such a reaction by wearing a rather touchingly out-of-date cocktail frock for our night-club sojourn. The black dress showed an interesting but not immodest amount of cleavage, so Tilly had immediately sized her up as a Number One.

"I'll just stick around for a while to keep out the repossession people," she informed me helpfully as I emerged. "Don't worry, boss. I won't let them take that urn with your mother's ashes like they did last time you went bust." She turned to Emily. "Call me sentimental, but I think however far in debt someone is, those loan sharks should stick to reclaiming furniture, not late relations."

I winced, not so much at the all-too-true reference to

my financial state as at the unfortunate subject of dead relatives, but Emily appeared to take no notice of my assistant's
faux pas. "What a loyal employee," she cooed. I thought I
detected a touch of acid beneath the sweetness. "She's
clearly been with the firm *forever.* Well, she should still get
back in time for Ovaltine and the evening news—even if
the repo men drop by tonight, it shouldn't take them long
to collect this lot."

Tilly raised an eyebrow in grudging approval—she liked
someone who could return serve. Before some thundering
new volley was delivered, I grabbed Emily's arm and pulled
her toward the stairs. Did I mention that there's been a
slight problem with the elevator lately?

"At least the shirt looks like it was ironed at some
point," she said. "Mid-seventies, maybe?"

She was driving. Her style refuted my ideas of what a
schoolteacher would be like behind the wheel, and in fact
rather enlarged the general concept of "driving."
Apparently, many of the other motorists felt the same: we
had traveled across town through an *1812 Overture* of
honking horns, squealing brakes, and occasional vivid
remarks loud enough to be heard even through our rolled-
up windows.

I chose to ignore her comment about my shirt and concentrated instead on clinging to my seat with one hand
while using the other to leaf through the autopsy report,
which Emily had somehow procured. (Privately, I suspected a coroner's clerk with guilty memories from high
school.)

Nothing in the report seemed to differ greatly from
what I had read in the papers. Karl Marius Heltenbocker,
aka Charlie Helton, had been in his early sixties but in
good physical health. Death was due to exsanguination,
the agent of same having been a large and very sharp steel

sword of the type known as a cavalry saber. A few rough drawings showed the position of the body as it had been found inside the basket, and a note confirmed that paramedics had declared the victim dead at the scene. The verdict was death by misadventure, and both autopsy and summary report were signed by George Bridgewater, the county's coroner-in-chief. If anyone in authority suspected it was a murder, it certainly wasn't reflected in the official paperwork.

"It sure *looks* like an accident," I said, wincing slightly as a pedestrian did a credible Baryshnikov impression in his haste to give Emily right of way through a crosswalk.

"Of course it does. If you were going to murder someone and steal his manuscript to protect yourself, Mister Pinnard, wouldn't *you* want it to look like an accident?" She said this with an air of such logical certainty that I was reminded of my firm conviction during my student years that all teachers were extraterrestrials.

"How fiendishly clever," I replied. I admit I said it quietly. I was saving my wittier ripostes until there was pavement under my feet again.

I hadn't been to the Rabbit Club in a while, and was faintly depressed at the changes. I suppose on the salary the school board forked out Emily didn't get out much, because she seemed quite taken with the place. Actually, set against the rather faded glories of the club—its heyday had roughly paralleled that of the Brooklyn Dodgers—she looked far more natural than me in my leather jacket and jeans. With her strapless cocktail dress and horn-rimmed glasses, she might have been sent over by Central Casting.

As I mused, she said something I didn't quite catch, and I realized I had stopped in the middle of the aisle to admire her shoulders (I have always been a sucker for a faint dusting of freckles). I hurried her toward a booth.

The show was not the sort to make anyone sit up in wonder, but the club was one of the few places left in town where young magic talent could get a start; looking around the darkened room, I felt a certain nostalgia for my own rookie days. Over the following hour we watched a succession of inexperienced prestidigitators fumble bouquets out of their sleeves and make coins jump across the backs of their hands while hardly ever dropping them. I nursed a soda water—rewarded for my choice with a restrained smile from my companion—but Emily drank two and a half glasses of champagne and applauded vigorously for one of the least sterling examples of the Floating Rings I'd ever seen. I decided sourly that the young (and rather irritatingly well-built) magician's no-shirt-under-the-tux outfit had influenced her appreciation.

After the break, during which the tiny house band wheezed through a couple of Glenn Miller numbers, Fabrizio Ivone was announced. The headliner had not changed much since the last time I'd seen him. He was a little older, of course, but aren't we all? His patter was delivered with a certain old-world formality, and his slicked-down hair and tiny mustache made him seem a remnant of the previous century. Watching him work his effortless way through a good group of standard illusions, it was easy to forget we were living in an era of jumbo jets and computers and special-effects movies. When he finished by producing a white dove from a flaming Chinese lacquer box, the smallish crowd gave him an enthusiastic ovation.

I took Emily backstage on my arm (at this point she was a wee bit unsteady on her pins) and quickly located the dressing room. Ivone was putting his brilliantined hair, or at least the part that wasn't real, back in its box.

"The world of illusion," said Emily, and giggled. I squeezed her wrist hard.

"That was a splendid show, Mister Ivone. I don't know if you remember me—we worked a bill together in Vegas about ten years ago, at the Dunes I think it was. Dalton Pinnard—Pinardo the Magnificent?"

"Ah, of course." He looked me up and down and went back to taking off his makeup. He didn't look like he cared much one way or the other.

"And this is my friend, Emily Heltenbocker." I took a breath and decided to go for the direct approach. "Her father was Charlie Helton."

A plucked eyebrow crept up that eggshell dome of a forehead. "Ah. I was sad to hear about him." He sounded about as sorry as he'd seemed glad to see me again.

"We were wondering if you might know anything about the book he was writing," said Emily. "Somebody stole it." She gifted Ivone with a dazzling smile. It was a good smile, but I couldn't match it since I was wincing at her sledgehammer approach.

The old magician gave her a look he probably used more often on sidewalk dog surprises. "I heard it was full of slanders. I am not unhappy to hear it has been stolen, if that were to be the end of it, but I have no doubt it will soon appear in the gutter press. If you are asking me if I know anything about this sordid affair, the answer is no. If you are insinuating I had anything to do with the theft, then you will be speaking to my lawyer."

I trod ever so gently on Emily's foot, preparing to steer the conversation in a friendlier direction. My new initiative was delayed somewhat by the wicked elbow she gave me back in the solar plexus. When I could breathe again, I said: "No, Mister Ivone, we don't think any such thing. We were just hoping that you might be able to tell us anything you know about Charlie's relationship with other magicians. You know, so we can decide once and for all if there's anything sinister in the disappearance. But you, sir, are of course above suspicion."

He stared at me for a moment, and I wondered if I'd overdone it. The cold cream was caked in his wizened features like a bad plastering job. "I would never harm anyone," he said at last, "but I must say that I did not like your father, young woman. Even in the Savini Academy—yes, we studied together—he was never serious. He and his friends, they were all the time laughing in the back row."

"And who were his friends in the academy?"

Ivone shrugged. "I do not remember. Pranksters, guttersnipes, not true artists. He was the only one of that sort who graduated."

I let out a breath. So if Charlie had known the other two men at school, they hadn't been close chums.

Ivone was still in full, indignant flow. "He did not show the respect for our great tradition, not then, not later. Always he was making jokes, even when he was on the stage, silly riddles and stories, little puzzles as though he were performing to entertain children." He placed his toupee in its box as carefully as if it were the relic of some dead saint, then solemnly shut the lid. "I have appeared before the crowned heads of Europe and Asia in my day, and never once on the stage have I made a joke."

I didn't doubt him for a moment.

"I wish you'd kept your mouth shut," I said. It didn't come across as forceful as it sounds, since Emily had already pulled away from the curb and I was frantically groping on the floor for the other half of my seat belt.

"Don't be rude—you're an employee, remember.

Besides, I didn't like him. He was a very small-souled man."

I rolled my eyes. "That's not the point. After you'd just gone and blurted that out about the book he wasn't going to give anything away. I couldn't very well ask him where he'd been when your dad died, for instance."

Emily made a face. "But I know that already. He was onstage at the Rabbit Club—he's been performing there for weeks. I checked."

"What?"

"I checked. I called the Performing Artists' Guild after you told me his name. He was working the night my father was killed."

I stared. The trained fingers I had once insured (okay, only for five thousand bucks on a twenty-six-dollar monthly premium—it was a publicity stunt) itched to throttle her, or at least to pull those stupid glasses off and see if she drove any better without them.

"He was *working*? Fabrizio Ivone, this supposed murderer, was on the other side of town pulling coins out of people's noses when your father died?"

"Yes, I just told you that I called the Guild. Don't get so defensive—I didn't expect you to do all the work, just the stuff that needed expert knowledge."

I threw myself back against my seat, but our sudden stop in the middle of an intersection catapulted me forward again microseconds later. "I can't believe I'm wasting my time on this nonsense," I growled. The light had turned green again, but Charlie's daughter seemed to be waiting for a shade she liked better. "The point I'm making, Emily, is that Fabrizio Ivone has an *alibi*. As in, 'Release this honest citizen, Sergeant, he's got an alibi.'"

She shook her head pityingly, as though I had just urged her to buy heavily into Flat Earth futures. "Haven't you ever heard of hired killers?" We lurched into motion just as the light turned red once more.

You just can't trust clients. It happens every time. They come through your door, wave money under your nose and make lots of promises—then boom! Next thing you know, that little party you were hired for turns out to be a smoker, and you're doing card tricks for a bunch of surly drunks because the stripper hasn't showed up.

Yeah, I'm a little bitter. When you've been around this business as long as I have, you get that way. You splurge on a Tibetan Mystery Box some guy swears is just like new and when you get it home it's riddled with woodworm. You order a shipment of doves from the mail order house, and they forget to punch airholes in the box. And women! Don't even talk to me about women. I can't count the number of times I've been standing around backstage somewhere, ten minutes before curtain for the Sunday matinee, arguing on the phone with my latest assistant, who isn't there because she's got water-bloat, or her boyfriend's in jail, or because I introduced her as "the lovely Zelda" the night before and her name's really Zena.

"Pull over," I snapped. "And try using the brakes instead of just glancing off streetlights until the car stops."

She followed my advice. In fact, she used the brakes so enthusiastically that I wore a very accurate impression of the dashboard grain on my forehead for hours afterward.

"Get the hell out, then," she said. "I knew you were a loser from the moment I first saw you crawling around on the floor."

"Well, I may be a loser . . . but *you* hired me." The effect of my clever comeback and sweeping exit was diminished slightly by the fact that I hadn't unbuckled the safety belt. The ensuing struggle also allowed me time to cool down a little. After I finally worked free and fell onto the sidewalk, I turned to look back, expecting to see the tears of a helpless woman, or perhaps a momentary glimpse of Charlie's features in hers, which would remind me of the old friend whose desperate daughter this was. Emily wasn't such a bad kid, really. I was half-ready to have my gruff masculine heart melted.

"Shut the damn door," she snarled. If there were any tears, I definitely missed them.

She did manage to run over my foot as she drove away.

I suppose I shouldn't have been too surprised, I reflected as I limped home. I had fallen out with Emily's father much the same way. Nobody in the whole damn family could admit they were wrong.

Charlie had been a wonderful guy, my mentor in the business. He'd helped me find my first agent, and had shared many of his hard-won secrets with me, giving me a boost that few young performers got. He'd been everywhere almost, had done things few other people had even read about, and could tell you stories that would make your eyes pop out. But he could be difficult and stubborn at times, and as Ivone had so vividly remembered, he had a rather strange idea of fun. After he and Emily's mother had broken up he had lived a solitary life—I hadn't even known he'd been married until several years into our friendship—and like a lot of bachelor types, his life revolved around what other people might consider pretty useless hobbies. In Charlie's case it was two: puzzles and practical jokes.

Unfortunately, not all of his jokes were funny, at least to the victims. One such, a particularly complicated operation, had involved my booking for a show at a naturist colony in the Catskills. I was very uncertain, since it required me to perform naked except for cape and top hat, but Charlie convinced me that a lot of big entertainment people were weekend nudists, and that I would be bound to make some great contacts.

When I arrived at the resort the night of the show I was met backstage by the club manager, who was definitely naked. He was a big fat guy of about fifty, and knowing that people like him could do it helped me wrestle down my inhibitions. See, when you perform, if the stage lights are bright enough, you hardly see the audience anyway; the manager assured me that it would be just like doing a show in my own bedroom. So, I stripped, squared my shoulders, calmed my quivering stomach, and marched out onto the stage.

And no, of course it wasn't a nudist colony. It was a regular Catskills resort, median audience age: almost dead and holding. The "club manager" was a confederate of Charlie's who'd taken off as soon as he'd finished his part of the scam.

The audience was not amused. Neither was I.

The sad thing was, Charlie and I fell out not because of the prank itself, nasty as it had been, but because I refused to admit there was anything humorous about it. I guess his pride was wounded—he thought he was the funniest guy in the world.

Things started to go downhill for me after that, but not because of my premature venture into performance art. I just caught some bad breaks. Well, a lot of bad breaks.

Maybe Charlie had been feeling guilty about our parting all these years, and about not being around to help me get back on my feet. Maybe that was why he'd told his daughter that if she ever needed someone to trust, to seek me out.

There was something else to consider, I suddenly realized. On the infinitesimal chance that Emily Heltenbocker was right and everyone else was wrong, maybe Charlie had been snuffed because one of his jokes had offended some-one. Maybe he'd made a bad enemy, and it didn't have any-thing to do with his manuscript at all.

I was pleased with this genuine detective-style thinking. Despite the misery of my long trudge home, I began to consider whether I should allow Emily—*if* she was suitably contrite—to rehire me. Charlie and I had been through a lot of good times before the bottom fell out. Maybe his daughter deserved a little patience.

Not to mention that she owed me for at least one night's work.

"Your girlfriend's on the phone," shouted Tilly.

I put down my self-help bankruptcy book and unhur-riedly picked up the receiver. I had known Emily would come crawling back, but I wasn't going to let her off too easily.

"You still have my father's graduation photograph," she said. "Send it back immediately, or I'll come over there and break your arm."

She was playing it a little more cagily than I'd expected. "Don't hurt me," I said. "My health insurance lists attack-by-schoolteacher as an act of God, and it'll be hell getting them to pay."

"Just send me the picture. Right now."

I was sure I detected an undercurrent of playfulness in her voice, albeit well camouflaged. "How about if I drop it by in person? Then we can discuss last night's little differ-ence of opinion."

"If you come within a mile of me, you're going to have to learn how to make balloon animals with your teeth."

She hung up loudly enough to loosen a few of my fill-ings, but I knew I basically had her.

*   *   *

Thus it was that after only a few dozen more phone calls (and a slight strategic modification on my part which might have been mistaken by some observers for a cringing apology) Emily Heltenbocker and I resumed our partnership.

"Tell me their names again." She revved the engine, although the light was still resolutely red.

I'd finally pinned down the other two mystery men, through laborious research in various trade booking guides. "Sandor Horja Nagy, the Hungarian Houdini— he's the one we're going to see right now. The other's Gerard O'Neill. And, just for your information, they were both doing shows on the night in question, just like Ivone. Two more airtight alibis."

"For goodness sake, Pinnard, you're so unimaginative. We're talking about magicians, people who disappear and reappear elsewhere for a living. Honestly, if this were a murder mystery in a book, you'd be the idiot cop they always have stumbling around to make the detective look good."

"Thank you for your many kindnesses." I reached into my pocket for my cigarettes. Emily had finally tendered my retainer, and I had splurged on a whole carton. "Whatever you may think, a stage magician nearing retirement age cannot disappear in the middle of a downtown performance, catch a cab to the suburbs, murder an old classmate, and be back before the audience notices. And he can't spin straw into gold or turn a pumpkin into a horse-drawn carriage either, just in case you still harbor some misconceptions about what real magicians do." I leaned back and withdrew my new, top-of-the-line disposable lighter.

"Don't you dare light that in my car. I don't want my upholstery smelling of smoke."

Obviously she had no similar problem with the scent of self-deceit and denial. I didn't say that, of course. Long years of working with the public have taught me that, although the customer may not always be right, only a fool behaves otherwise before he's been paid off. "Look," I said, "I'm just being sensible. You're a nice lady, Emily, but I think you're barking up the wrong tree. The police say it was an accident. The coroner said it was an accident. And all your suspects have alibis. When are you going to face up to what that really means?"

She started an angry reply, but bit it off. She stayed silent for a long while, and even when the light finally turned green, she accelerated with none of her usual gusto. I was pleased that I had finally made her see sense, but not exactly happy about it, if you know what I mean. Sometimes when something goes very wrong, we humans desperately want there to be a reason. It's not fun being the person who takes that possibility away.

"It's just not like my father," she said at last. "Suicide, never. Not in a million years. So that leaves accident. But you knew him too, Pinnard. You know how carefully he planned everything."

I had to admit that was true. Watching Charlie work up an illusion was like watching Admiral Nimitz setting out his bath toys—no detail too small for obsessive consideration. "But sometimes even careful people get careless," I pointed out. "Or sometimes they just don't give a damn anymore. You told me he was having real bad financial problems."

"You are, too, but I don't see you getting your throat slit."

"Not when I've got a whole carton of cigarettes," I said cheerfully. "I prefer my suicide slow."

"That's not very funny."

I immediately felt bad. "Yeah, you're right. I'm sorry. Look, let's go see this Nagy guy. Even if it turns out you're wrong about the murder angle, you'll feel better if you know for certain."

She nodded, but didn't seem very convinced. Or very cheerful. She was even still driving in an uncharacteristically moderate way. So, basically nice guy that I am, I sang a medley of Burt Bacharach songs for her as we made our way across town. I've always thought that if magic hadn't worked out, I could have made a tidy bundle warbling "Walk On By" in your better grade of dinner house.

It didn't jolly her up much. "I'll pay you the rest of tonight's fee right now if you shut up," was how she put it.

Sandor Nagy (I think you're supposed to say it "Nagy Sandor," but what I know for sure about Hungarian customs you could write on the back of a postage stamp and still have room for your favorite goulash recipe) had seen better days. As a performer, our pal Ivone was, by comparison, Elvis.

We warmed the plastic chairs in the hallway of the Rotary Club while we waited for Nagy to finish changing his clothes in the men's room. The show had been interesting—if watching a drunk perform for a bunch of guys offended because the entertainment was more blasted than they were is the kind of thing that interests you. Partly out of pity, we took him to the twenty-four-hour coffee shop across the street and bought him a Grand Slam Breakfast. (There is no time in places like that, so you might as well eat breakfast. Actually, there is time, but only the waitresses experience it, which is why they're all about a hundred and four years old. I've always thought someone should write a science-fiction book about this paradox.)

"I'm not quite sure what went wrong with that trunk

escape," Nagy said. Or slurred, to be more precise. "Usually it works like a charm."

After the grueling experience of his show, I had been planning to down a quick couple of beers—I wasn't going to drink club soda forever just because I was hanging around with Ms. Ruler-across-the-knuckles—but the old guy's breath and the bold yet intricate vein patterns on his nose persuaded me to order myself a Coke. Thus, I had my mouth wrapped around a straw and didn't have to comment.

"I'm sure you would have gotten out eventually," said Emily. "I didn't think they really needed to call the fire department."

Nagy eyed his soft-boiled eggs with great sadness. I think he would much rather have had a couple of belts himself, but we had declined to buy him anything with a proof content. He wasn't real coherent as it was, even after all the oxygen the fire crew had forced into him. "I'll let you in on a secret," he said. "I'm not as sharp as I used to be. A step slower these days, if you know what I mean."

"Well, you and my father were at the academy at the same time, weren't you? That was quite a way back."

I smiled. Emily was showing definite improvement. All the same, interrogating this guy made about as much sense as bringing down a pigeon with a surface-to-air missile. If he was a murderer, I was Merlin.

"Oh, that's right, you said you were Charlie Helton's kid. Shame about him. I heard he was writing a book. Wouldn't want to take time from my escape work, myself. There's a lot of practice involved." He pushed one of his eggs with the fork, as though unsure whether to commit to something so strenuous as eating. "He was a strange one, your dad. Drove a lot of people crazy."

"Did he? He made enemies?" Emily was leaning

forward, giving the old guy that penetrating would-you-like-to-share-that-with-the-class gaze that made me cringe even when it wasn't aimed at me. I refrained from pointing out that her elbow was in a puddle of catsup. Purely because I didn't want to distract her, of course.

"Not enemies, no. Not really." Sandor Nagy stopped to think, a process that clearly needed some ramping-up time. It was a good half minute before he came up with: "He was just . . . he bragged a lot. Told a lot of stories. Played tricks on people."

Now it was my turn to lean forward. My backfired-prank theory was sounding better. "Anyone in particular that he upset?"

Nagy shook his head. "Not that I could tell you—it's been a long time. He just pissed a lot of people off. Pardon my French, Miss."

I chewed on my straw, disgusted with myself for taking the idea of murder seriously for even a second. "Let me ask you another question," I said. "Are you really Hungarian? Because you don't have an accent."

Nagy frowned at me and squinted his bloodshot eyes. Starve Popeye the Sailor Man for a few weeks, then strap him into an extremely musty tux, and you basically had Nagy. "I sure as hell am! Both my parents were from the Old Country, even if I ain't been there. At least I got a family connection. One of those punks at the academy called himself 'Il Mysterioso Giorgio,' and he wasn't even Italian! Some chump kid from Weehawken!"

We left the Hungarian Houdini muttering angrily at his hash browns.

I had mixed feelings when I got downstairs to the office the next day. I was more convinced than ever that we were wasting our time, and that Emily—who was actually a pretty okay person—was going to get her feelings hurt. On the other hand, she'd paid me a nice little fee, and the story was playing big and bold in the tabloids.

It wasn't front page in the *Scrutinizer*, but it was near the front, and a full-page spread to boot. There was an artist's rendition of "The Death Basket" (which included far more swords than were actually involved in Charlie's demise), a photo of Charlie in his stage outfit, and one of the coroner and the police chief at a news conference, looking very serious. (In fact, the photo had been taken during some other and far more important case, but I must admit it gave the thing an air of drama.) The only item conspicuously missing was one of the publicity photos of yours truly I'd sent to them (there's no such thing as bad PR, especially when you've been stuck on the birthday party circuit for a few years), but I was mentioned prominently in all the articles, even if the *Metropolitan* managed to spell my name "Pinrod." So, all in all, it could have been worse.

Emily didn't seem to think so, though. When I called her she sounded tired and depressed. "I'm beginning to think you're right," she said. "Whatever was in the manuscript, it's gone. The tabloid reporters won't leave me alone. After I finish paying you, I'll be broke—my savings have gone on Dad's funeral. I think it's time to go fishing."

"Huh?" I had a sudden and disconcerting vision of Emily in hip-waders.

"It's just a family expression. When times are bad, when the bill collectors are after you, you say 'I think I'll go fishing.' And that's how I feel right now."

I was still thinking about the hip-waders. In a certain kind of way they can be a pretty sexy garment. I suppose it has something to do with my reading *Field & Stream* too much during my adolescence. In any case, distracted as I was, I did a wildly foolish and uncharacteristic thing.

"Listen, Emily," I said. "I don't want your money."

"What does that mean?" She sounded angry.

"I mean, I don't want any more of your money, and you can have back what I haven't spent yet. But we'll still go see O'Neill this afternoon. On the house, okay?"

She didn't say anything right away. I assumed she had been struck dumb by gratitude, but I wasn't sure. Charlie's daughter had proven herself a mite unpredictable. While I waited for the verdict, I rescrutinized the *Scrutinizer*. It was too bad they hadn't run a picture of Emily, I thought—she was a very good-looking woman.

I frowned. Something in the paper's coverage had been nagging at me since I'd read it, some little connection I couldn't make that was now bidding heavily for my attention, but between certain thoughts of an imaginary Emily in a fishing-gear pictorial and then the sudden reappearance of the actual Emily's voice, it didn't have much of a chance.

"That's . . . that's very kind of you, Dalton. You're a really nice person."

She'd never called me by my first name before. The nagging detail was abruptly heckled off the Amateur Night stage of my consciousness.

"And you're a nice person, too, Emily," I said. I hung up, feeling oddly as though I might be blushing.

Tilly was standing in my office doorway. She'd heard the whole conversation. Her expression of amused contempt was probably similar to what ancient Christians saw on the faces of lions.

"Your gills are showing, Pinrod," she said. "What an idiot—hook, line, and sinker."

I summoned up great reserves of inner strength and ignored her.

I spent all of O'Neill's performance trying to decide what Emily would do if I put my arm around her. I'd like to say we were paying close attention to the show, but we weren't. (I'm reasonably certain that murder investigators don't date each other, or that if they do, they keep the dates separate from the actual investigations. I hope so.)

Not that Gerry O'Neill's routine was the kind of thing that invited close attention. It was a mixture of old gags and fairly lame sleight of hand. Only the fact that it was a charity performance in front of a ward full of sick children made it something more than tiresome. And, to be fair, the kids seemed to like it.

O'Neill, it turned out, was the only one of the three who'd been on good terms with Charlie, and he'd kept in loose touch with him over the years. As we walked him out to his car, O'Neill wiped the perspiration from his round face and walrus mustache and told us with impressive sincerity how upset he'd been when he heard the news.

"He was a good guy, Charlie was. A little loco sometimes, but basically a heart of gold." He stuffed several feet of colored kerchief back into his pocket and patted Emily's arm. "You got my real best wishes, Missy. I was broken up to hear about it."

Emily's questions were perfunctory. She seemed a lot more cheerful than she'd been on the phone, but she seemed to be losing interest in the investigation. I wasn't really surprised—it was pretty difficult to feature any of our three suspects as the Fu Manchu criminal-mastermind type.

"When you say Charlie was a little loco sometimes," I asked, "what do you mean? His practical jokes?"

O'Neill grinned. "I heard about some of those. What a card. But I mostly meant his stories. He was full of stories, and some of 'em were pretty crazy."

"Like what?"

"Oh, you know, places he said he'd been, things he'd seen. He told me once he'd been in China, and some old guy there taught him how to talk to birds. Man, if you listened to him, he'd done everything! Snuck into a sultan's harem somewhere, hung out with voodoo priests in Haiti, tamed elephants in Thailand, you name it. Crazy stories."

Emily rose to her father's defense. "He did travel quite a bit, Mister O'Neill. He toured in a lot of places, took his show all over the world—Asia, South America, the Caribbean—especially when he was younger. He was a pretty big star."

O'Neill was a gallant man. "Then maybe all them stories were true, Missy. In any case, I'm sorry he's gone. He was a helluva guy."

We watched O'Neill drive off. As we strolled back across the parking lot, Emily took my hand.

"Maybe it *was* an accident," she said, and turned to look at me. The sunset brought out the deep gold colors in her hair. "Maybe that stuff he wrote on the photo was just another of his stories or silly tricks. But at least I did my best to find out." She sighed. "Talking to these people reminded me of all the parts of his life I missed out on. I didn't see a lot of him while I was growing up."

I didn't say anything. I was concentrating on the feeling of her warm skin beneath my fingers, and thinking about what I was about to do. I stopped, pulled her toward me, and carefully removed her glasses.

"Why, Miss Heltenbocker," I said, as if in surprise, "you're *beautiful*. Do you mind if I kiss you?"

She snatched them back and jammed them into place, brow furrowed in annoyance. "I hate it when everything's blurry. Kiss me with my goddamn glasses on."

What was it like? Do I have to tell you?

Magic.

*   *   *

I woke up in the middle of the night. The thing that had been bothering me had come back. Boy, had it ever come back.

I ran downstairs to my office, not bothering with a bathrobe. This should show you how excited I was—even though Tilly lived on the other side of town, wouldn't be in for hours, and the office was effectively part of my home, going there naked even at 4 A.M. made me feel queasily disrespectful.

A few minutes later I ran back upstairs and woke Emily.

(Look, just because she was a schoolteacher doesn't mean you should make old-fashioned assumptions.)

"Get up, get up!" I was literally jumping up and down.

"What the hell is going on, Pinnard?" She sat up, rubbing her eyes and looking utterly gorgeous. After the night we'd just spent, I wasn't at all worried about her use of my last name.

"I've solved it! And you're never going to believe it!" I grabbed her arm, almost dragging her toward the stairs. She very firmly pulled free, then went to get her glasses from the bedside table. Next—and clearly second in order of importance—she found my bathrobe and put it on. In a gesture of solidarity, I pulled my underwear off the ceiling light (don't ask), donned it, and led her to my office.

"Brace yourself," I said. "This is very weird." I took a breath, trying to think of the best way to explain. "First of all, you were right—it wasn't an accident."

Emily sat up straight. "Somebody *did* murder him?" A strange look came over her face. "Or are you going to tell me it was suicide?"

I was suddenly reluctant. Waking someone up in the middle of the night to give them the kind of news I was about to give Emily could have a number of shocking effects, and I felt very protective of her—and of what we suddenly seemed to have together. "Well, see for yourself." I spread the copy of the *Scrutinizer* on the desktop, then laid the graduation picture on top of it. "Something was bothering me about this article, but with everything else that happened today, well, I sort of forgot about it. Then, about fifteen minutes ago, I woke up and I knew." I pointed at the picture, at one of the faces that Charlie hadn't circled. "See this kid? You know who that is?"

Emily stared, then shook her head.

"That's Il Mysterioso Giorgio—the one Nagy mentioned. You know, the fake Italian from Weehawken."

"I still don't get it."

"You will. Remember Fabrizio Ivone talking about those delinquent friends of your dad's who didn't graduate the academy? Well, he was wrong—one of them did. It was young Giorgio here. Although he never made it as a working magician."

"How do you know that?"

I lifted the graduation picture and pointed to the *Scrutinizer*. "Because he would have had trouble being a stage magician *and* holding down the job of chief coroner." I put the graduation picture beside the news photo for comparison. "Meet Il Mysterioso Giorgio today—George Bridgewater."

She stared at the two photos, then looked up at me. "My God, I think you're right. But I still don't understand. What does it mean? Did he cover something up about my dad's death?"

This was the hard part. Suddenly, under the bright fluorescent lights, my certainty had dwindled. It would be unutterably cruel if I were wrong. I took her hand.

"Emily," I said, "I think your dad's alive."

She pulled away from me, stepping back as though I'd slapped her. The tears that suddenly formed in her eyes made me want to slap myself. "What are you saying? That's crazy!"

"Look, you said it yourself—Charlie'd never kill himself. And he wasn't the type to have an accident. But you said he'd traveled in the Caribbean, and he told O'Neill he'd studied with voodoo priests! They have chemicals they use in voodoo that make people look like they're dead. That's where the zombie legends come from. It's true—I read about it!"

She laughed—angry, frightened. "Where? In *Astrology and Detective Gazette*?"

"In a science magazine. Emily, they've done studies. Voodoo priests can use this stuff to put people in a kind of temporary coma. All the vital signs disappear. No paramedic struggling to keep your dad alive would know the difference, not if he'd made a real but shallow cut and spread a lot of blood around. It wouldn't even have to be human blood, since nobody would think of testing it when he was locked in a room by himself with the key in his pocket. But you'd have to have a confederate in place for later, 'cause nobody could live through a real autopsy. Chief coroners hardly ever do actual examinations, so it's a little bit of a coincidence he was writing the report at all. Even weirder that he wouldn't step aside when he found out it was an old school chum."

"So this guy Bridgewater helped my dad fake his own death? Why?"

"Who knows? A last prank for old times' sake, maybe? You said your dad was depressed and broke. Maybe it was a way for Giorgio the Mysterious to help a pal get out of a bad situation." I didn't want to mention it, but it was also possible that the deal had been a little less friendly—old

Charlie, collector of gossip and odd stories, might have had a wee bit of blackmail material on Bridgewater.

Emily stared at the pictures. When she turned back to me, she was calmer, but very grim. "I don't think you did this to be cruel," she said, "but this is so much more far-fetched than *anything* I suggested. It's just crazy."

I had a sick feeling in my stomach, kind of like something very cold was hibernating there. I knew I'd blown it. "But . . ."

She cut me off, her voice rising in anger. "I can almost believe my father would do something this wild, this outrageous—heaven knows, he loved a good trick, and he was having a lot of problems. But I can't for a moment believe that he would make me think he was dead, *not* let me know he'd survived, and then on top of it send me off to hook up with a bum like you and go on some insane hunt for a nonexistent murderer!" She waved the picture in front of my face. "Look at this! This is his handwriting! If he wanted to tip me off, why didn't he circle Bridgewater the coroner? Instead, he picks these three totally harmless . . ."

I was so far into my flinch that at first I didn't open my eyes. When she had remained silent for a good ten seconds, I peeked. Emily was still frowning, but it was a different kind of frown. "Oh, God," she said at last.

She flopped the photo over so the back was showing. I had written down the men's names as I identified them.

"Gerard O'Neill." Emily's voice was strained. "Fabrizio Ivone. Sandor Horja Nagy. Oh my God."

"What?"

"Look at the initials. G-O-N, F-I, S-H-N." The tears came for real now. " 'GONE FISHING.' "

★   ★   ★

There was a good deal more to the story, of course, but we didn't find out immediately. When we went to see Bridgewater, the coroner blustered at us about foolish accusations and the penalties for slander, but he didn't seem very fierce about it. (We later discovered that one of Charlie's academy-era jokes had yielded photographs of a naked Giorgio in bed with a sheep dressed in a garter belt. It had all been perfectly innocent, of course, but still not the kind of thing a local politician wants to see on the wire services.) Still, it was a few more months before we knew for sure.

Apparently Charlie Helton *did* have an agent Emily hadn't known about—a theatrical agent, but someone who had contacts in publishing. When, at the height of the tabloid fury about the Murdered Magician Mystery, the agent announced that he actually had the dead man's manuscript, it set off a bidding war, and the book sold for a very healthy advance. As Charlie's only heir, Emily received all but a small part of what was left after the agent took his cut. When the book quickly earned back its advance, she received all but that same small portion of the royalties that began flowing in. Even after the story lost its tabloid notoriety, *A Magical Life* continued to sell nicely. As it turned out, Charlie had written quite a good book, full of vivid stories about his life and travels, and lots of enjoyable but not-too-scurrilous backstage gossip about the world of stage magicians.

Even Fabrizio Ivone didn't come out too bad in Charlie's memoirs, although his inability to take a joke was mentioned several times.

That small portion of the income Emily didn't get? Well, every month the agent dispatches a check to a post office box in Florida—no, I won't tell you where exactly, just in Florida somewhere. Suffice it to say it's a small town with good fishing. The checks are made out to someone named Booker H. Charlton. Emily decided not to contest this diversion of royalties, and in fact we plan to go visit old Booker as soon as we can get out of town.

Why delay our visit to the mystery fisherman? Well, we've been real busy just lately setting up the Charlie Helton Museum of the Magical Arts. It's turned out to be a full-time job for all of us: Emily took early retirement from the school system to manage the operation, and Tilly answers the phone and handles the finances, which I'm happy to say are in the black. Tilly's mom works the ticket booth, flashing her expensive smile at the customers all day long. Me? Well, I've got the balloon animal concession pretty much wrapped up, and I'm working on a book of my own.

Oh, and in case anybody's disappointed that this has been a story about magicians without any real magic in it, I should mention one last thing. You remember how Charlie had scrawled on the back of his photo: "Trust Pinardo"? We found out a few months afterward that if Charlie's handwriting had been a little darker, we would have noticed a hyphen between the two words. See, we were going through some of his papers and found out that he'd stashed away a couple of hundred dollars so Emily wouldn't get stuck paying for his fake funeral. The deposit was in a trust fund at a small savings institution—Pinardo Thrift and Loan, no relation to yours truly.

In other words, the very beautiful woman who I am delighted to say now calls herself Ms. Emily Heltenbocker-Pinnard, the light of my life and (I hope) the warmth of my declining years, walked into my office that day on a completely mistaken assumption. We are an accident—a fluke of fate.

Love (as Bogart once said about a black bird, and

Shakespeare said about something I don't quite remember) is definitely the stuff that dreams are made of. It remains the greatest mystery and the only truly reliable magic.

Satisfied?

The Allies

KATHERINE DUNN

Our perception of reality is dependent on a combination of experience and individual needs. I may, for example, look at a stranger and find that person homely; someone to whom that person is a friend sees beneath the surface to an inner beauty hidden to strangers. Similarly, what I perceive to be fantasy may, in fact, be someone else's reality, and vice versa.

It is that dichotomy to which Katherine Dunn speaks in this story. She does so by taking a young, clumsy, and unattractive teenager from a dysfunctional family, and handing her a perception of reality which allows her to survive in a society which worships outer beauty.

—DC

The Allies

THE RADIO PURRED from the top of the refrigerator, and Mrs. Reddle paused, listening, with her smallest sable-hair brush an inch from the canvas.

"Another Unidentified Flying Object reported near the coast," said the radio. "And in Texas, an insurance salesman and a hitchhiker report that they were taken aboard a huge spherical vessel which stopped their car in the desert south of Burkburnett. More on these and other stories after this . . ."

Mrs. Reddle's brush moved forward delicately, laying a sliver of light on the face beneath her hand. The rough, two-by-four easel stood in the windowed bay of the kitchen, where anyone else would put a table and chairs. The Reddles' table was in the middle of the room with a discreetly rosy bowl in the center of its brown cloth. The bay was jammed with working rubble—boxes of magazine clippings and old photographs, a stained bench holding bottles, jars, cans stuffed with brushes, and rags smeared thick with pigments.

Mrs. Reddle sat with her left side to the daylight. The windows looked down the yellow grass knoll and across the highway to the service station. Her husband was leaning over a windshield; his massive arm swabbing at the glass, the grease on the belly of his overall threatening the finish of the car's hood. His laugh drifted in faintly, causing

Mrs. Reddle's mouth to press in on itself as she bent to the paint.

"Further sightings reported . . ." said the radio. "A squadron of white lights moving in patterns in the sky above this small coastal town . . ."

Mrs. Reddle lifted the last stroke of the paint until it melted smoothly into the surrounding shadow, and then fell back in her chair with a sly tilt at the corners of her mouth. She slid the brush into the turpentine can and squinted at the canvas through her eyelashes. The smells of turpentine and linseed oil and her own lean flesh drifted around her.

The bell on the pavement of the gas station rang. Her son stood on the bell cord in the shadow of the canopy. His child arms moved in wide circles, describing something to his father. A truck passed on the road, blocking the view, but her husband's laugh mingled with the engine noise and the rush of air. Further down the highway a familiar, squat figure toiled up the hill.

Edie Reddle heard her father's laugh rattling through the traffic and knew her mother was in a decent mood. On the days when her father laughed, or waved at her as she climbed the hill, Edie went straight in through the kitchen door to talk with her mother.

If her father moved heavily around the cars at the gas pumps or stared sullenly at her from the office window, she went around the house to the front door and directly up to her bedroom to listen until she could tell which direction the anger was moving.

Her mother was either happy or furious, with no mediocre moods for transition or warning. If Edie set off for the high school in the morning, leaving her mother whistling merrily, she could arrive home the same afternoon to grim, ripping accusations, screams of fury, breaking glass, flailing blows. It was a toxic mayhem that went on muttering and clanging into the night while Edie lay rigid, listening in the dark for the inexplicable escalation that could hurl a shrieking monster into her bedroom. Usually Edie's father or her younger brother was the target of the anger, but no one was safe until it passed, and the storm in the house froze them all.

It had to do, Edie figured, with what her mother thought about during the day. Whether she remembered something you'd done years ago or was imagining what you might be doing out of her sight. But it might also be triggered by something on the radio, or a phrase overheard in the supermarket, a chance comment by a clerk or passerby that twisted in her mother's mind and grew fangs.

But today she heard the laugh clearly and could see the swift flash of her father's heavy body working across the road, so Edie stepped up to the kitchen door and opened it.

Turpentine. A soothing oil seeping through the pungency. The brown kitchen with its cunning light was warm and neat. A faint hint of roasting meat softened the paint smells. As long as her mother was actually painting she was fine. Once she put her brushes down anything could happen. Edie took a full breath and put her books on the table.

"Further reports on the UFO sightings at Seaside on the news at 4:30. This is Radio AUZ, The Voice of Gold."

"Mama?" Edie fumbled with her coat buttons.

"Come here, dear."

The wilderness of the alcove ended precisely where it bordered the kitchen. No spot of paint or dropped rag, not even a leg of the chair she sat on was allowed to protrude into the clean kitchen. Only the smell went everywhere, gently.

Mrs. Reddle, with a fist full of brushes on her knee, sat

watching, waiting. Edie did not look at her. Looked only at the canvas. She waited a minute and then started the smile in her chest and let it flow up to her eyes first and then down to her mouth. She turned the smile on her mother. Mrs. Reddle smiled back hesitantly, her eyes anxious, her fist spreading the brushes into the denim of her dungarees at the knee. Edie used the line she had been practicing on the way home.

"Did religion make him look like that? I'm heading for the church right now. But no, I suspect it was you."

She watched her mother's eyes liven as though they were connected to her chuckle.

"Oh, he's a decent enough man," said Mrs. Reddle. "I'm just trying to cover up his stupidity by dressing it as enthusiasm."

"Is he dumb?" asked Edie. She bent to peer into the intense face on the canvas.

"I hope you can't tell from mine. But just look at these." Mrs. Reddle spread glossy photographs and snapshots on the base of the easel. Edie stared.

"You mean how close together his eyes are? And how small?"

Mrs. Reddle pointed with the tip of the brush.

"That's sometimes a clue, but it can go with a low kind of shrewdness, too. I've added some distance there and enlarged them a hair. But look how low his ears are set on his head. This is the dead giveaway. The top of each ear is a half inch below the level of his eye. And look at all that flab under his chin. That's not fat, that's just gaping room. He lets his jaw hang in private and has to think about jutting it out when he's in public."

Edie giggled and examined the painting. Mrs. Reddle watched the freckled skin pucker across her daughter's round face, the hunch of the plump shoulders, and the spread of the stubby white hands next to her own long, strong ones. The girl turned to her, brown eyes smiling.

"Is he taking this to Africa with him to impress the natives?"

"He's presenting it to his fan club, the ladies of the Overseas Mission Group. According to him all he's taking is his New Standard Bible and a million ccs of antibiotics. The ladies will send him care packages—homemade jam and silk undies."

They laughed as they set the table. Mrs. Reddle made the salad, and Edie stood at the sink peeling potatoes.

"And while the Highway Patrol and local police forces are continuing their investigations of the rash of sightings, this reporter asked Dr. A.R. Ziegler, professor of astrophysics at . . . 'What can I say? Anything is possible . . .'" said the radio.

The door slammed, and Edie's younger brother jostled her for room to wash his hands at the sink.

"Shove over, Fats."

Edie felt a sudden weight of hatred for his skinny, golden arms and the black grease that he sluiced and dripped over the coils of potato peel. Her mother's quick step behind her tightened the muscles of her neck but the punishing hand clipped the boy's head instead of hers.

"How many times, young man, have I told you to come home from school and change your clothes before you go over to that grease pit? Your father doesn't care. He doesn't have to wash your filthy clothes, nor his own either. There'll come a day . . ."

The voice soaring higher, losing control. The boy's face wrinkling in mute resentment near Edie's shoulder. He flipped water drops off his fingers at Edie and marched out of the room. Edie's ears strained to read the note of her mother's heels on the linoleum.

"Have you been listening to all the UFO reports, Mama? Everybody's talking about it at school." Edie's fingers turned the potato under her knife. She waited for the distraction to take effect.

"I have my own idea about them," said Mrs. Reddle. "I think they're looking for someone."

Edie turned to look at her. Mrs. Reddle shook back the stripe of stiff grey hair that sprang from her temples and nodded firmly at her daughter.

"Who?"

"Someone they can talk to."

Edie felt her mouth skewing in slow, embarrassed sarcasm, nearly giving her away before she turned back to the sink, her voice rattling ironically as she cut the potatoes into a pan.

"I got a talking-to today. Mr. Dolbeer stopped me in the hall."

"He's the algebra teacher?" Mrs. Reddle asked the cucumbers.

"He asked if it was my mother who'd painted the portrait of the president for the auditorium. When I said yes he kind of shook his head and said, 'How did she ever end up in this hole?' It made me mad. I said you hadn't ended up yet by a long way. And he apologized. He said he just meant that a talent like yours should be more widely recognized." Edie nonchalantly dumped peelings into the garbage can.

"What a nice man!" Mrs. Reddle's hands rested among the lettuce leaves and cucumber slices.

"He's not a nice man. He's critical of everything. The only people he likes in this world are Bach and Euclid. Everybody else is 'vulgar' or 'in poor taste.'"

Edie could feel the glow of her mother's pleasure filling the room. The soft laugh and the lighter touch of Mrs. Reddle's knife sliding on the cutting board.

"Well, you get good grades in his class. He must like you, too."

"He probably likes me better now that he knows who my mother is."

"Can you tell the listeners exactly what happened, Mr. Tindall?" said the radio. "I'm a salesman, see? I was coming back from San Antonio about 10 P.M. I'd got this hitchhiker, said he was going as far as Little Ross. He'll tell you this is true, what I'm saying."

The potatoes boiled wildly. Edie's plump hand lifted the lid slightly askew so the steam could escape. Mrs. Reddle stood in the open refrigerator door and stared at the small dark face of the radio.

"I'd think you were bats if you told me this . . . But there it was. Right in the middle of the road with a ramp leading up inside. Size of Wichita City Hall. What was I supposed to do?"

"Let's eat!" said Mr. Reddle coming through the door with a smile. Mrs. Reddle took the milk from the refrigerator and shut the door.

"Five minutes, I think. Have a wash."

"By God, Irma, I just sold four hundred dollars' worth of tires and got twenty recaps for nothing! What do you call that?"

"I'd probably call it fraud if I knew how you did it."

"Business, dear lady. Good business."

There was a hunk of yellow soap in a plastic dish near the sink. It was reserved for Mr. Reddle's use. His were the only hands it wouldn't scorch. A steady scent of unrefined petroleum followed him. Edie finished the table while Mrs. Reddle took the meat from the oven. Mr. Reddle grinned over his shoulder at the alcove as he scrubbed.

"You sure have been pecking away at the Reverend

Arn. You know that asshole drives all the way across town rather than buy his gas from me? I was figuring today there's not a person who goes to that church that *does* trade with me. Is that a coincidence? I don't know why in hell you're painting that for him. And what's he going to pay you? A hundred bucks! Shit. You've been fiddling with the thing for weeks."

Edie's fingers dug into the spoon handle.

"That's right, Mama," she hurried. "It's ridiculous to charge so little for your work. Any of your pictures would sell at five times the price."

Mrs. Reddle cocked a sarcastic eyebrow at her husband's splashing.

"I'm not a salesman like your father. Call your brother."

Dinner. The food passed. Talk of old farts in Ford Cortinas and the character with the four plumber's vans who'd been buying tires that day.

Edie's brother gave her a nudge under the table.

"Pass the spuds, Pudge."

"Don't call her that!" screamed Mrs. Reddle, slamming her fork onto the table and lunging up over her plate. The boy dropped down in his chair, arms guarding his head, squealing, "No, Ma! No, Ma! No, Ma!"

"Oh for Christ's sake, Irma," protested Mr. Reddle. "It was just a joke. That kid's teasing doesn't bother Edie. She's too smart to let a little ragging get to her."

Mrs. Reddle's arm still tensed, her body poised above the table, her eyes squinting rage at the boy. Her mouth folded tight 'til the full lips were completely invisible. She sank slowly into her chair. The boy sat up and turned a sullen face to his plate.

After dinner Mr. Reddle went back across to the station and took his son with him. The old man who helped him at mealtimes didn't know how to close up.

Dishes done, Mrs. Reddle wiped the kitchen counters while Edie arranged her homework on the table.

"Oh, I found this book in the school library. It's mostly landscapes, but it has some nice color plates of Velasquez portraits. The color reproduction is supposed to be a new thing, much more accurate."

Mrs. Reddle looked over Edie's shoulder at the vivid pages and then sat at the table, taking the book in her own hands. The radio sang and sold toothpaste softly.

The night came down tight. Only the red blink of the neon from the gas station appeared in the black windows. Mrs. Reddle bent over the picture book.

Edie's eyes flicked sideways from her work and took in the soft curve of her mother's cheek, the pale down that was becoming more pronounced as she grew older. The sculpted muscles of her mother's arms were graceful, beautiful to Edie. Her own thick arms grew heavier on the table.

"Is the Halloween dance fancy dress?" Mrs. Reddle's voice shook Edie to instant wariness.

"I think so."

The book lay open on dancers, their limbs thoughtful extensions of the lines of their bodies, skirts in clouds. Mrs. Reddle tapped the page.

"You'd look lovely in something like that. I'll get paid as soon as I deliver the portrait next week. I'll bet I can find real tulle even in this town."

Edie's face and neck oozed thin, cold sweat.

"I'm not going to that dance, Mama."

"Oh, you should! You don't go out enough at all. Hasn't that Jerry asked you?" Mrs. Reddle's face set in anxious lines, her brows tilting her whole forehead up in a little wrinkled tent beneath her hair.

"He asked me all right." Edie picked the corner of a

page, pinched it between her thumb and finger until the pain made her stop.

"But I said no. He's been skipping classes lately. And hanging out with some filthy people."

Edie's head sinking deeper into her shoulders, the hump of flesh on her shoulders riding up into the folds at the back of her neck.

"And I wouldn't want to go with anyone else. I'll just wait until he straightens out."

"Oh, my dear." Mrs. Reddle reached tenderly for her daughter's hand. "When you're older you'll know the best way to make that boy take a look at himself is to give him some competition."

Edie pulled her hand away and bit viciously on the flat of her thumbnail.

"I'm not going, Mama. I don't want to."

Mrs. Reddle looked down at the girls in their white dresses caught dancing before a mirror. She turned the page.

"The latest on the rash of UFO sightings across the nation on the news at 8:30. . . ." said the radio.

"This UFO business goes on practically every year around now, doesn't it? Halloween madness?" Edie grinned, her voice harsh with humor. Mrs. Reddle looked at her gently, lingering on the round flat face and the wispy hair lifting around it.

"I think it's real," said Mrs. Reddle. "Not all of it. Some of it is a joke, or people making themselves important for a minute or two."

Leaning toward her daughter, Mrs. Reddle poured urgency into her eyes, grave intensity into her voice. "But I think there are beings from . . . somewhere else . . . trying to contact us. Don't you see how careful they'd have to be? If they landed in a major city, they'd be attacked immediately. There would be total panic and nobody capable of communicating with them reasonably. The political leaders, if they didn't panic themselves, would be under enormous pressure from the populace to do something military. No, they couldn't do that. They have to take it this way, looking for a few individuals who can think without fear, who have minds open enough to accept what they see and yet are intelligent enough to understand whatever message it is that they have for us."

Mrs. Reddle's eyes fixed on Edie, her hands resting flat on the open pages of the book. Her voice was sure and eager as always when she was swept by an Idea.

Edie sternly prevented the left side of her face from quirking or lifting in irony.

"Well, nobody knows what's out there, I guess. And I can't think of one good reason there couldn't be a civilization more advanced than ours. . . ."

Edie shoveled the heavy words out slowly, and watched what she thought of as "The Idiot Glint" thrust the lids of her mother's eyes open, watched the protrusion of the eyes increase until a thin, precise line of white showed above and below her mother's irises. She nearly flinched when her mother's hand touched her own and closed over it.

"I have good reason to believe it. And I'll tell you now. You're old enough to understand. *You* are exactly what they're looking for."

The chill struck Edie's neck. A roar of air followed a truck past the house. She felt her own eyes spreading.

"Mama . . ."

"You must not be afraid, child." The sudden pity in her mother's voice spread a blankness over her thoughts, bundled her skeptic's logic up, and hid it away.

"There's nothing to be afraid of. I've always known.

Since you were born. I knew when I saw how your eyes would turn to watch things you shouldn't have been able to see. And I've watched it grow in you, this awareness, consciousness. You know it yourself. You sense your own uniqueness without being able to pinpoint it. But you must not doubt that it is for a purpose and that you will be called upon to use it." Mrs. Reddle's eyes filled with water, ran over, dripping, as they held Edie's eyes.

"To use it for the good of us all. The wide earth. So you must not be afraid if they come for you, if they need you. Do you understand, dear?"

Mrs. Reddle held Edie's hands in her own, and her tears fell on them. Edie's throat was closed tight. Her own eyes seeping, burning. She nodded convulsively.

"There, dear. It's all right. As long as you understand," said her mother. "Here come the men."

Feet hit the porch, and the women flicked quick hands at their tears and set their faces. The door opened. Edie bent over her book.

Her brother chirped, "Hey, there's a great movie on TV in about ten seconds."

"I've finished the bills if you want to mail them out tomorrow, Irma," said her father.

"I'm going to bed, folks. Good night," said Edie.

She paced the dark bedroom in flannel pajamas, rolling her bare feet carefully on the floor so no thump or shudder would be noticeable in the rooms below her.

"Uniquely ugly," she muttered.

A coward, a flatterer, a liar, she called herself, counting the night's crop of soft phrases spewed to control her mother's moods and fears. The imaginary conversation with Mr. Dolbeer. The shame of that long-standing invention,

"The Boy Friend," the mythical Jerry who had *almost* taken her to a dozen dances. That lie was the heaviest.

"Why won't she let me be ugly? Why does she blind herself and cripple me?" The streetlights threw bright grey across her as she passed the window. She saw herself in the mirror. "No. You're not a cute little girl," Edie mocked her wide reflection. "You're on your way to becoming a *beautiful* woman." She propped her hands on her waist and saw her own bulk shivering above and below them. "A very feminine figure, my dear," minced Edie. "A lovely little bosom," she hissed. "Mama," she whispered, "the boys moo at me in the halls. Mama," she muttered, "Mama, you're crazy, and I'm a sucker."

She sank down on the floor near the window and leaned her hot face against the cold glass. The white and red lights of the cars and the black night cooled her. "Space aliens," she whispered. "I should probably pack a bag and keep it by the window, just in case." She stifled a giggle. "Ah, Mama, you're slipping away from us."

But still, before morning she dreamed that the great ship came, whirring softly, shaped like a child's top. It hovered outside her window and the light of it filled her room. In the dream a silent door opened in the side and a ramp came out to her window. She stepped out onto it and walked lightly, gracefully, with her pajamas flowing around her, toward the opening where the silver beings reached toward her saying, "You must help us. We've looked for you so long."

The Magician
of Karakosk

PETER S. BEAGLE

*The voice in this story is uniquely, inimitably,
Peter S. Beagle's. While it is a fairy tale which
springs from Peter's imagination, it is also a
parable which says that if you do unto others,
but choose to do evil, you'd better watch out that
your victim not be wiser than you. If you don't,
there's always the outside chance that Beagle's
Boomerang Effect might turn you into the victim instead.*

—DC

The Magician
of Karakosk

WHAT, WHAT—IS IT MY TURN? No, I was not asleep—I would never be so unmannerly as to doze off when someone else was telling a story. I was thinking only, thinking about how long it has been since I sat like this with friends—oh, with anyone, really—listening to wonders and sillinesses and wonders again by firelight. I have lived an odd sort of life, and I am afraid that it has left me with little to tell that would not bore the young ones here and antagonize the old; and I would not do either tonight for worlds. You must indulge me—I promise to keep the tale short, and leave plenty of evening for Gri and Chashi and Mistress Kydra here. I am as eager as anyone else to be done with my rambling mumbles.

Well, then. Once, a very long time ago, in the land I come from, there was a magician who was too good at magic. Ah, you stare, you look at each other, you snicker, but it's so—it is quite possible to be too good at anything, and especially magic. Consider—if you only need a gentle shower to restore your thirsty fields, what good is a wizard who can bring nothing but storms that will wash them away? If you ask for a little kitchen charm to keep your man faithful, what's the use of a spell that will have him underfoot and at your heel every hour of every day, until you could scream for a single moment to yourself? No, no, when it comes to magic give me a humble mediocrity, always. Believe me, I know what I am saying.

Now the magician of whom I speak was a humble man in every way. He was of low birth, the son of a *rishu*-herder, and although he gave evidence of his abilities quite young, as most wizards do, there was never any possibility of his receiving the proper training in its use. Even if he could have had access to the teaching scrolls of Am-Nemil or Kirisinja, such as are preserved in the great thaumaturgic library at Cheth na'Bata, I much doubt that he could even have read them. He was a peasant with a gift, nothing more. His name was Lanak.

What did he look like? Well, if your notion of a magician is someone tall, lean, and commanding, swirling a black cape around his shoulders, you would have been greatly disappointed in Lanak. He was short and thickset, like all the men of his family, with their tendency to early baldness, I am afraid. But he had nice eyes, or so I have heard, and quite good manners, and large, friendly brown hands.

I repeat, because it is important: this Lanak was a humble man with no high dreams at all—most unusual in a wizard of any origin. He lived in Karakosk, a town notable only for its workhorses and its black beer, which suited our Lanak down to the ground, as you might say, for he understood both of those good creatures in his bones. In fact, the first spell he ever attempted successfully was one to strengthen his father's rather watery home brew, and the second was to calm a stallion maddened by the pain of a sand-spider bite. Left to himself, he'd likely never have asked to do anything grander than that with his magical gift. Spending his life as a town conjuror, no different from the town baker or cobbler—aye, that would have suited him right down to the ground.

But magic has a way of not leaving you to yourself, by its own nature. Magic has an ambition to be used, even if you don't. Our Lanak went along happily for many years, liked and respected by all who knew him—he even married a Karakosk woman, and I can count on the fingers of one hand those wizards who have ever wed. They simply do *not*; wizards live immensely alone, and there it is. But Lanak never really thought of himself as a wizard, you see. Lanak thought of himself as a Karakosk man, nothing more.

And if his talent had been as modest as he, likely enough he would have spent his life in perfect tranquillity, casting his backyard spells over fields, gardens, ovens, finding strayed children and livestock impartially, blessing marriage beds and melon beds alike—and yes, why not? bringing a bit of rain now and then. But it was not to be.

He was simply too good. Do you begin to understand me now? The colicky old horses he put his hands on and whispered to did not merely recover—they became twice the workers they had been in their prime, as the orchards he enchanted bore so much fruit that the small farmers of Karakosk found themselves exporting to cities like Bitava, Leishai, even Fors na'Shachim, for the first time in the town's history. There was a hard winter, I remember, when Lanak cast a spell meant only to ease the snowfall, just for the children, so their shoes would last longer—and what was the result? Spring came to Karakosk a good two months before a single green shoot stuck up its head anywhere else in the entire land. This is the sort of thing that gets itself noticed.

And noticed it was, first by the local warlord—I forget his name, it will come to me in a moment—who swept down on Karakosk one day with his scabby troop at his heels. You know the sort, you doubtless have a Night

Visitor or a Protector of your own, am I right in that? Aye, well, then you've an idea what it was like for Karakosk when their particular bravo and his gang came swaggering into the market square months before their yearly tribute was due. There were close on forty of them: all loud, stupid, and brutal, except for their commander, who was not stupid, but made up for it by being twice as brutal as the rest. His name was Bourjic, I remember now.

Well, this Bourjic demanded to see the great wizard folk had been telling him about; and when the townspeople appeared reluctant to fetch their Lanak on a bandit's whim, he promptly snatched the headman's little son up to his saddle and threatened to cut his throat on the spot if someone didn't produce a wizard in the next five minutes. There was nothing for it—Bourjic had made similar threats in the past, and carried them all through—so the headman himself ran to the very edge of town to find Lanak in his barn, where he was once more redesigning his fireworks display for the Thieves' Day festival. Lanak's fireworks were the pride of the region for twenty miles around, but he was forever certain that he could improve them with just a little effort.

When he understood the danger to the headman's son, he flushed red as a *taiya*-bush with outrage. Rather pink-faced as he was by nature, no one had ever seen him turn just that shade of redness before. He put his arm around the headman's shoulders, spoke three words—and there they were in the market square, face-to-face with a startled Bourjic trying to control his even more startled horse. Bourjic said, "Hey!" and the horse said, "Wheee!" and Lanak said the little boy's name and one other word. The boy vanished from Bourjic's saddle and reappeared in his father's arms, none the worse for the experience, and the spoiled envy of all his schoolmates for the next six months.

Lanak set his hands on his hips and waited for Bourjic's horse to calm down.

I've told you that Bourjic's men were all as stupid as gateposts? Yes, well, one of them cranked up his crossbow and let a quarrel fly straight for Lanak's left eye, as he was bending over the boy to make certain that he was unharmed. Lanak snatched the bolt out of the air without looking up, kissed it—of all things to do—and hurled it back at Bourjic's man, where it whipped around his neck like a noose and clung very tight indeed. Not tight enough to strangle, but enough so that he fell off his horse and lay there on the ground kicking and croaking. Bourjic looked down at him once, and not again.

"The very fellow I wanted to see," says he with a wide, white smile. Bourjic was a gentleman born, after all, and had a bit of manners when it suited him. He said now, "I've grand news for you, young Lanak. You're to come straightway to the castle and work for me."

Lanak answered him. "I'm not young, and your castle is a tumbledown hogpen, and I work for the folk of Karakosk and no one beside. Leave us now."

Bourjic reached for his sword hilt, but checked himself, keeping that smile strapped onto his face. "Let us talk," he said. "It seems to me that if I were offered a choice between life as a nobleman's personal wizard and seeing my town, my fields, my friends, all burned to blowing ashes— well, I must say I might be a bit more inclined toward see- ing reason. Of course, that's just me."

Lanak nodded toward the man writhing in the dirt. Bourjic laughed down at him. "Ah, but that has just made me want you more, you see. And I simply must have what I want, that's why I am what I am. So float up here behind me, or magic yourself up a horse, whichever you choose, and let's be on our way."

Lanak shook his head and turned away. Bourjic said nothing more, but there came a sound behind him that made Lanak wheel round instantly. It was the sound of forty men striking flint against steel at once and setting light to tallow-stiff torches they'd had ready at their saddles. The townsfolk looking on gasped and wailed; a few bravely, hopelessly, picked up clods to throw. But Lanak fixed his mild, washed-out-looking blue eyes on Bourjic and said only, "I told you to leave us."

"And so indeed I shall," the warlord answered him cheerfully. "With you or without you. The decision is yours for another ten seconds."

Lanak stood fast. Bourjic sighed ostentatiously and said, "So be it, then." He turned in the saddle to signal his men.

"Get back," Lanak said to the folk of Karakosk. They scrambled to obey him, as Bourjic's grinning soldiers raised their torches. Lanak folded his arms, bowed deeply—to the earth itself, it seemed—and began to sing what sounded like no more than a nonsensical nursery rhyme. Bourjic, suddenly alarmed, shouted to his men, "Burn! Now!"

But even as he uttered those two words, the ground before him began to heave and stretch itself and grumble, like an old man finally deciding to throw off his quilt and get out of bed. Where it stretched, it split, and some bits fell in and down and deep out of sight, and other bits swelled right up to the height of storm waves heading for shore. Bourjic's horse reared and danced back from the chasm that had just opened between him and Lanak, while all his men fought to control their own terrified beasts, and the folk of Karakosk clung to their children, to each other, to anything that seemed at all solid. The earth went on splitting, left and right, as though it were shedding its skin: raw red canyons were opening everywhere, and you could see fire crawling away and away in their depths. Shops and houses all around the square were toppling, bursting apart, and the angry, juddering, groaning sound kept getting louder, louder. Lanak himself covered his ears.

Bourjic and his lot crumbled like dry cheese. They yanked their horses' heads round and were gone, a good bit faster than they'd come, and it was hard to say who was doing the more screaming, man or mount. The ground began to quiet, by little and little, as soon as they were out of sight, and the townsfolk were amazed to see the fearful wounds in the earth silently closing before their eyes, the scars healing without a trace, the buildings somehow floating back together, and the Karakosk market square demurely returning to the dusty, homely patch of ground it had always been. And there stood Lanak in the middle of it, stamping out a few smoldering torches, wiping his forehead, blowing his nose.

"There," he said. "There. Nothing but an illusion, as you see, but one that should keep friend Bourjic well clear of us for some while. Glad to be of help, I'll be off home now." He started away; then glanced around at his dumbstruck neighbors and repeated, "An illusion, that's all. No more. The fireworks, now, those are real."

But the citizens of Karakosk had all seen one of Bourjic's soldiers—the one with the crossbow quarrel wrapped so snugly around his neck—plummet straight down into a bottomless crevasse that opened where he lay, and closed over him a moment later. And if that was an illusion, you could never have proved it by that man.

As I'm sure you can well imagine, the whole business made things even more difficult for poor Lanak. Bourjic was probably as interested as he in keeping the story from getting around; but get around it did, and it was heard in

towns and cities a long way from black-beer Karakosk.
Sirit Byar made a song out of it, I think. Lissi Jair did, I
know that much—a good song, too. There were others.

And the Queen, in her black castle in Fors na'Shachim,
heard them all.

None of you know much about the Queens in Fors, do
you? No, I thought not, and no reason why you should.
Well, there is always a Queen, which really means little
more than the hereditary ruler of Fors na'Shachim itself and
a scatter of surrounding provinces and towns—including
Karakosk—and even particular manors. Most of the
Queens have proved harmless enough over the years; one
or two have been surprisingly benign and visionary, and a
very few have turned out plain wicked. The one I speak of,
unfortunately, was one of those last.

Which does not mean that she was a stupid woman.
On the contrary, she was easily the cleverest Queen Fors
na'Shachim has ever had, and it is quite an old city. She
listened to new songs as intently as she did to the words of
her ministers and her spies; and it is told that she walked
often among her subjects in various guises, and so learned
many things that many would have kept from her. And
when she had heard enough ballads about the wizard
Lanak of little Karakosk, she said to her greatest captain,
the Lord Durgh, "That one. Get him for me."

Well now, this Durgh was no fool himself, and he had
heard the songs, too. He'd no mind at all to have as many
people laughing and singing about *his* humiliation by some
bumpkin trickster as were still laughing at Bourjic. So
when he went down to Karakosk, he went unarmed, with
only two of his most close-mouthed lieutenants for company. He asked politely to be directed to the home of a
gentleman named Lanak, and rode there slowly enough to
let the rumors of his arrival and destination reach the

house before he did. He'd been born in the country himself, Lord Durgh had.

And when he was at last face-to-face with Lanak in the wizard's front garden, he got off his horse and bowed formally to him, and made his men do so, too. He said, "Sir, I am come to you from the Queen on a mission of grave urgency for the realm. Will it please you to attend on her?"

Yes, of course it was a trick, and all of us here would doubtless have seen through it instantly. But no high personage had ever spoken to Lanak in such a humble manner before. He asked only, "May I be told Her Majesty's need?" to which Lord Durgh replied, "I am not privileged to know such things," which was certainly true. Then Lanak bowed in his turn and went into his house to tell Dwyla, his wife, that he had been summoned to the Queen's aid and would return in plenty of time for the Priests' Moon, which is when the folk around Karakosk do their spring sowing. Dwyla packed the few garments he requested and kissed him farewell, making him promise to bring their little daughter something pretty from Fors.

There's been a new road cut long since, but it is still three hard-riding days from the market square at Karakosk to the black castle. Durgh made a diffident half suggestion that the wizard might like to call up a wind to whisk them there instantly, but Lanak said it would frighten the horses. He rode pillion behind Lord Durgh, and enjoyed the journey immensely, however the others felt about it. You must remember, Lanak had never been five miles from Karakosk in his life.

Trotting over his first real cobblestones in the streets of Fors na'Shachim, he almost disjointed his neck turning it in every direction, this gawking peasant who could chase away winter and make the earth rend itself under bandits' feet. He was so busy memorizing everything he saw for

Dwyla's benefit—the marketplace as big as his entire town, the legendary Glass Orchard; divisions of the Queen's household guard in their silver livery wheeling right about and saluting as the Lord Durgh cantered by—that the black castle was looming over him before he realized that they had arrived. He did, however, notice Lord Durgh's poorly concealed sigh of relief as they dismounted and gave their horses over to the grooms.

Does anyone here know Fors at all, by any chance? Ah, your father did, Mistress Kydra? Well, I'm sure it hadn't changed much from Lanak's time when your father saw it, nor would it be greatly different today. Fors na'Shachim never really changes. For all its color, for all the bustle, the musicians and tumblers and dancers on every corner, the sharpers and the alley girls, the street barrows where you can buy anything from *namph* still wet from the fields to steaming lamprey pies—those *are* good—for all that, as I say, one never truly escapes the taste of iron underneath, of dutiful abandon working overtime to mask the cold face of power. And even if that power casts no shadow beyond the city gates, I can assure you that it is real enough in Fors na'Shachim. I have been there often enough to know.

But Lanak had never been to Fors, and he was thrilled enough for any dozen bumpkins to be marching up those obsidian stairs with Lord Durgh's hand closed gently enough just above his left elbow, and all those silver-clad men-at-arms falling in behind them. He was not taken directly to see the Queen—no one ever is. Indeed, that's rather the whole point of being Queen, as you might say. There have been those who forced their way into the presence, mind you; but these were a different sort of people from our modest Lanak. Most of them ended quite differently, too.

Lanak was perfectly content to be shown to his quarters

in what used to be called the Hill Tower because you can just make out the haze over the Ghost Range from the upper windows. They call it the Wizard's Tower now. There was food and drink and hot water waiting, and he used the time to wash, change from his grimy traveling clothes into something more suitable for meeting the Queen, and then to begin a long letter to Dwyla at home. He was still hard at it that evening when Lord Durgh came to fetch him.

What is the black castle really like? Well, it is as grand as you imagine, Hramath, but perhaps not exactly in the way you imagine it. It began as a fortress, you know, in the old times when Fors was nothing more than a military outpost; which is why it is black, being mostly built of dressed *almuri* stone from the quarries near Chun. Every Queen for the last five hundred years has tried in turn to make the castle a bit more luxurious for herself, if no less forbidding to her subjects: so there are a great many windows and rich carpets, and countless chandeliers even in places where you would never expect more than a rushlight. There is always music, and always sounding just at your shoulder, even if the players are a dozen galleries distant–that's a trick of *almuri*, no other stone does that. And, of course, the walls of every room and every corridor are hung with real paintings, not merely the usual rusty shields and pieces of armor—and the paintings are done on real cloth and canvas, not bark or raw wood, as we do here. The food and wine served to the Queen's guests are the best to be had south of the Durli Hills; the ladies of her court have Stimezst silk for their everyday wear; the beds are almost too comfortable for comfort, if you understand me. Oh, you would want for nothing you know how to dream of in the black castle at Fors, Hramath.

Even so, just like the city itself, it is always the stone fortress it always was, with the Silver Guard never more than a room away, and Lanak was not bumpkin enough to miss that for long. Not that he was especially on his guard when Lord Durgh bowed him into the Queen's presence—perhaps what I mean is that he was attempting from the first to see his marvelous adventure through his wife's eyes, and Dwyla was a shrewd countrywoman who missed very little. Wizard or no, he did well to marry her, Lanak did.

Yes, yes, yes, the Queen. She received Lanak in her most private chambers, with no one in attendance but Lord Durgh himself, and she packed *him* off on some errand or other before Lanak had finished bowing. I am told that she was quite a small woman, daintily made, with a great deal of dark hair, a sweetly curved mouth, skin as smooth as water, and eyes as shiny and cold as the gleaming black walls of her castle. She seemed no older than Lanak himself, but of course you never know with queens.

Well, then. She greeted Lanak most royally and courteously, even saying to him with an appealing air of shyness, "Sir, I have never received a great wizard in these rooms before. You must pardon me if I hardly know how to behave."

Those were her very words, as I was told them, and, of course, she could have said nothing more calculated to reach the heart of Lanak, who really was shy. He swallowed hard several times, finally managing to reply, "Majesty, I am no great wizard, but only a journeyman from a town of journeymen. As honored as I am, I cannot imagine why you have summoned me, who have your pick of masters."

And he meant it, and the Queen could see that he meant it, and she smiled the way a cat smiles in its sleep. She said, "Indeed, I must confess that I have made some small study of wizards. I know very well who the masters in this realm are, and who the journeymen—every one— and which lay claim to mastery who would be hard put to turn cream into butter. And nowhere have I heard tales to equal the word I have of you, good Lanak. Without ever stirring from your dear little town whose name I keep forgetting, you have become the envy of magicians whose names I am sure you cannot know. What have you to say of that, I wonder?"

Lanak did not know at all what to say. He looked at his hands, stared away at the pale rose canopy over the Queen's bed, and finally mumbled, "I think it is no good thing to be envied. If what you tell me is true, it distresses me greatly, but I cannot believe it is so. How could a Rhyssa, a K'shas, a Tombry Dar envy Lanak of Karakosk? You are mistaken, Majesty, surely."

"Queens are never mistaken," the Queen answered him, "as even great wizards must remember." But she went on smiling kindly and thoughtfully at Lanak. "Well, I will test your skill then, though for your reassurance, not my own. The water of my domain is not of the best, as you know."

Lanak did know. As you here cannot, even the oldest among us. In the time of which I tell you, the water of Fors na'Shachim and the country round about was renowned for its bitterness. It was not vile enough to be undrinkable, nor foul enough to cause sickness or plague, but it tasted like copper coins and harness polish, with a slight touch of candle wax. Clothes washed in any stream turned a pale, splotchy yellow, which came quickly to identify their owners to amused outsiders; indeed, citizens of Fors were often referred to as "pissbreeches" in those days. The term is still used now and then, even today, though no one in the city could tell you why.

The Queen said, "I have requested several wizards to improve the water of Fors na'Shachim. I will not embarrass such an unassuming man by revealing their names. Suffice it to say that not one succeeded, though all proved most wondrously gifted at vanishing when I showed my displeasure." She leaned forward and touched Lanak's rough brown hand. "I am confident that it will be quite otherwise with you."

Lanak answered helplessly, "I will do my best, Majesty. But I fear sorely that I will disappoint you, like my colleagues."

"Then I hope you are at least their equal at disappearing," the Queen replied. She laughed, to show him that this was meant humorously, and stood up to indicate that the interview was at an end. As Lanak was backing out of the room (Dwyla had read somewhere about the proper way to take leave of royalty), she added, "Sleep well, good friend. For myself, I will certainly be awake all night, imagining my subjects' surprise and pleasure when they brew their afternoon tea tomorrow."

But Lanak never even lay down in the grand, soft bed which had been prepared for him. He paced his room in the moonlight, trying as hard as he could to imagine which magicians had already tried their skills on Fors's water, and which charms they might have attempted. For there is a common language of magic, you know, just as there is in music: it is the one particular singer, the one particular *chayad*-player, the one particular wizard who makes the difference in the song or the spell. Lanak walked in circles, muttering to himself, that whole night, and at last he stood very still, staring blankly out of the window at the dark courtyard below. And when morning came, he ate the handsome breakfast that the Queen's own butler had brought to him, washed it down with the slop that still passes for ale in Fors, then belched comfortably, leaned back in his chair, and turned the water of the realm sweeter than any to be found without crossing an ocean. And so it remains to this day, though apparently he could do nothing with the ale.

The Queen was mightily pleased. She brought Lanak out on a high balcony and embarrassed him immensely by showing him to her folk as the wonder-worker who had done for them what the mightiest sorcerers in all the land had incessantly promised and failed to do. They cheered him deliriously, celebrated him all that day and the next, and were generally useless as subjects until the Silver Guard harried them back to work. Most of that last was done out of Lanak's sight, but not all.

"There," said the Queen. "Have you not satisfied yourself now that you are wizard enough to serve me?"

But Lanak said, "Majesty, it was merely my good fortune that I understand water. Water, in its nature, does not like to feel itself foul; it recoils from its own taste as much as you do. All I needed to do was to *become* the water of Fors na'Shachim, to feel my way down into the source of its old bitterness and become that, too. Your other wizards cannot have been country people, or they would have known this. In the country, spells and glamours are the very least of magic—understanding, becoming what you understand, that is all of it, truly. My Queen, you need a wizard who will understand the world of queens, ministers, captains, campaigns. Forgive me, I am not that man."

"Do not speak to me of my needs," the Queen answered him, and her tone was hard for the first time. "Speak of my desires, as I bid you." But she quickly hid her impatience and patted Lanak's hand again. She said, "Very well, then, very well, let me set you one last unnecessary test. It is known to me beyond any doubt that three high officers of my incorruptible Silver Guard are in the pay of a foreign lord whose name does not matter. I cannot prove this, but *that* would not matter"—and she showed just the tips of her teeth—" if I but knew who they were. Find these traitors out for me, simple country Lanak, and be assured forever of my favor."

Now even in Karakosk Lanak had resisted all efforts to make him, with his magical talents, a sheriff, a constable, a thieftaker. He wanted no part of the Queen's request, but even he could see that there was no courteous way to decline without offending her hospitality. So he said at last, "So be it, but give me the night once again to take counsel with my spirits." And this being just the sort of talk the Queen wanted to hear, and not any prattle of understanding and becoming, she smiled her warmest smile and left Lanak to himself. But she also left two trusted men-at-arms clanking back and forth outside his door that night, and another under his window, because you never know with wizards either.

So there went another night's sleep for our poor Lanak, who had been so peacefully accustomed to snuggling close to Dwyla, with his arm over her and her cold feet tucked in between his. As before, he brooded and pondered, proposing courses of action aloud to himself and each time breaking in to deride himself for an incompetent fool. But somewhere between deep midnight and dawn, as before, he grew very still, as only a wizard can be still; and by and by he began to draw odd lines and shapes in the dust on the windowsill, and then he began to say words. They made no more sense than the dust trails he was tracing, nor was there anything grandly ominous in the sound of them. By and by he stopped speaking and just leaned his head against the window like a child on a rainy day, gazing silently down at the courtyard. I think he even slept a little, with his eyes half-open, for he was quite weary.

And presently, what do you suppose?—here came the sound of quick hoofbeats on stone, and a horseman in the glinting livery of the Silver Guard clattered across the courtyard, past the inner gatehouse without so much as a glance for the drowsy sentry, and away for the portcullis at full gallop. Nothing stirred within the black castle, least of all the wizard Lanak.

An hour, maybe less, and by all the seagoing gods of the terrible Goro folk, here's another rider heading away from Fors as fast as he can go. Panting on his heels comes another, and what Lanak can see of his face in the icy moonlight is taut with fear, wooden with fear. No more after them, but Lanak leans at that window all the rest of that night, maybe sleeping, maybe not.

In the morning he went to the Queen in her throne room and told her to turn out the Silver Guard for review. Since she was used to doing this no more than once a week, she looked at Lanak in some surprise, but she did what he said. When she noticed that three of her highest-ranking officers were notable for not being there, nor anywhere she sent to find them, she turned on Lanak and raged in his face, "You warned them? You helped them escape me!"

"I did no such thing," Lanak answered calmly. Even a wide-eyed countryman can take the measure of royalty, give him time enough, and he had the Queen's by now. "Seeking to learn who your turncoats might be, I sent a spell of fear over your entire garrison, a spell of guilt and unreasoning terror of discovery. Those three panicked and fled in the night, and can do you no more harm."

"I wanted them," the Queen said. Her own face was very pale now, and her voice was gentle as gentle. "I wanted to see them with their bones broken and their skin stripped off, hanging from my balcony, still a little alive, blackening in the sun. I am very disappointed, Lanak."

"Well," Lanak murmured apologetically. "I did tell you I was not the right sort of wizard for a queen." He kept his face and his manner downcast, even somber, trying hard to keep his jubilation from spilling over. The Queen would be bound to dismiss him from her service on the spot, and, on his own, unburdened by mounted companions, he could be home in Karakosk for lunch, bouncing his daughter on his knee and telling Dwyla what it was like to dine in the black castle with musicians playing for you. But the Queen confounded him.

"No, you are not," she said, and there was no expression at all in her voice. "None of you are, not a preening, posturing one of you. But I realized that long ago, as I realized what I would have to do to attain my desire." She was staring at him from far behind her dark, shiny eyes; and Lanak, who—without ever thinking about it, feared very little— looked back at her and was afraid.

"You will teach me," the Queen said. "You will teach me your magic—all of it, all of it, every spell, every gesture, every rune, every rhyme of power. Do you understand me?"

Lanak tried to speak, but she waved him silent, showing him the tips of her teeth again. She said, "Do you understand? You will not leave this place until I know everything you know. Everything."

"It will take your lifetime," Lanak whispered. "It is not a business of learning one spell or learning a dozen. One is always becoming a wizard, always—"

"*Becoming* again," the Queen snapped contemptuously. "I did not order you to teach me the philosophy of magic—it is your magic itself I desire, and I will have it, be very sure of that." Now she softened her tone, speaking in soothing counterfeit of the way in which she had first greeted him. "It will not take nearly as long as all that, good Lanak. You will find me quite a good pupil—I learn swiftly when the matter is of interest to me. We will begin tomorrow, and I promise to surprise you by the end of the very first day. And Lanak"—and here her voice turned flat and hard once again— "please do not let even the shadow of a thought of taking wizard's leave of me cross your mind. Your wife and child in quaint little Karakosk would not thank you for it."

Lanak, who had been within two short phrases and one stamp of his foot of taking that very course, felt himself turning to stone where he stood. His voice sounded far away in his own ears, empty as her voice, saying, "If you have harmed them, I will have every stone of this castle down to make your funeral barrow. I can do this."

"I should hope you can," the Queen answered him. "Why would I want to study with a wizard who could do any less? And yes, you could have your dear family safe in your arms days before I could get any word to the men who have been keeping friendly watch over them since you left home. And you could destroy those same men with a wave of your hand if they and a thousand like them came against you, and another thousand after those—I know all that, believe me, I do." Her sleeping-cat smile was growing wider and warmer as she spoke.

"But for how long, Lanak? For how long could you keep them safe, do you think? Never mind the legions, I am not such a fool as to put my faith in lances and armor against such a man. I am speaking of the knife in the marketplace, the runaway coach in the crowded street, the twilight arrow in the kitchen garden. Is your magic—no, is your *attention* powerful enough to protect

those you love every minute of the rest of their lives?
Because it had better be, Lanak. I have my failings,
queen or no queen, but no one has ever said of me that I
was not patient. I will not grow weary of waiting for my
opportunity, and I will not forget. Think very well on
this, wizard, before you bid me farewell."

Lanak did not answer her for a long time. They stood
facing one another, alone in the great cold throne room,
hung with the ceremonial shields and banners of a hundred
queens before this Queen, and what passed between their
eyes I cannot tell you. But Lanak said at last, "So be it. I
will teach you what I know."

"I am grateful and most honored," replied the Queen,
and there was almost no mockery in her tone. "When you
have completed your task, you may go in peace, laden to
exasperation with a queen's gifts to your family. Until
tomorrow, then." And she inclined her head graciously for
Lanak to bow himself out of the room.

If no one would mind, I'll pass quickly over what Lanak
thought that night, and over what he felt and did in
solitude—even over whether he slept or not, which I certainly hope he did. I doubt very much that any of you
could have slept, or I myself, but magicians are very different people from you and me. It was the Queen's misfor-
tune that, clever as she was, she could not imagine just
how different magicians are.

In any case, she appeared in Lanak's quarters early the
next morning, just like any other eager student hoping to
make a good impression on her teacher. And the truth is
that she did exactly that. She had not been boasting when
she called herself a quick learner: by afternoon he had
already taken her through the First Principles of magic,
which are at once as simple as a nursery rhyme and as slip-
pery as buttered ice. Many's the wizard who will tell you

that nothing afterward in his training was ever as difficult as comprehending First Principles. Kirisinja herself took eight months—so the tale has it, anyway.

And the Queen did indeed surprise Lanak greatly that day when, illustrating the Sixth Principle, he made a winter-apple fade out of existence, and she promptly reversed his gesture and called the apple into being again. Elementary, certainly; but since the Sixth Principle involves bringing back, not the vanished object itself, but the last actual moment when the object existed, it is easy to understand why Lanak was a good deal more than surprised. A great many people have at least a small gift for magic, but most die without ever realizing this. The Queen knew.

Now I will tell you, the appalling thing for Lanak was that he found himself enjoying teaching her; even rather looking forward to their lessons. He had never taught his art before, nor had he ever had much opportunity to discuss it with other wizards. Dwyla was as knowledgeable as one could wish about the daily practicalities of living with magic, but as indifferent as the Queen to the larger reality behind the chalked circles and pentacles that she scrubbed off the floor many mornings. But the Queen, at least, was hungry to know every factor that might possibly affect the casting or the success of even the smallest spell. Lanak felt distinctly guilty at times to be enjoying his work with her as much as he was.

Because he had no illusions at all regarding what she proposed to do with the skills she was acquiring from him. She said it herself, more than once: "This whole realm south of the Durlis should be a true kingdom, an empire— and what is it? Nothing but a rusty clutter of overgrown family estates, with not even energy enough for a decent war. Well, when I am a wizard, we will see about *that*. Believe me, we will."

"Majesty, you will never be a wizard," Lanak would answer her plainly. "When we are done, you may have a wizard's abilities, yes. It is not at all the same thing."

The Queen would laugh then: a child's spluttering giggle that never quite concealed the iron delight beneath. "It will serve me just as well, my dear Lanak. Everything will serve me, soon enough."

And *soon enough* would arrive altogether too soon, Lanak realized, if the Queen kept up her astonishing pace of study. She was not so much learning as devouring, annexing the enchantments he taught her, as she planned to annex every one of the little city-states, provinces, and principalities she derided. He had no doubt that she could do it: any competent wizard could have done so straightforward a thing long before, if wizards were at all concerned with that sort of power, which they are not. Even the most evil wizard has no real interest in land or riches or great glory in the mortal world. That is a game for kings, and for queens—what those others covet is a tale I will not tell here.

This tale, now—it might have had a very different ending if Lanak had not been a married man. As I have said, magicians almost never take wives or husbands; when they lie sleepless, it is because they are brooding mightily over the ethics of conjuration, the logical basis of illusion, the influence of the stars on shape-shifting. But Lanak's nights were haunted by his constant worry about Dwyla and the little one, and about Dwyla's worry about him (he had not dared attempt to communicate with her for weeks, even by magical means, for fear of provoking her watchers), and the deep-growing anger of a mild man. And this last is very much to be wary of, whether your man is a wizard or no. But the Queen had never had to consider such things. No more had Lanak, when you come to think about it.

So. So the Queen came to know more spells than any-one but a wizard ever has known; and, also, she learned them far faster than a true apprentice wizard ever would have done. She walked through the walls of her castle, utterly terrifying her servants and soldiers, who took her for her own ghost; she caused the dishes being prepared for her in the great kitchens to rise and float solemnly through the halls to her dining table; at times she left a smiling, regal shadow to debate with ministers and counselors, and herself slipped away unnoticed to gaze from her highest tower far over the lands she intended to rule. There is a legend—no more than that—that as she grew even more accomplished, she took to prowling the midnight alleys of the city in the lean, man-faced form of a lourijakh, straight out of the Barrens. Further, it is told that she did not go hungry in that form, but that I do not believe. Lanak would never have allowed it, of that much I am sure.

Finally Lanak said to her, "I have kept our agreement, Majesty. You now know what I know—every spell, every gesture, every rune, every rhyme. Except, perhaps—" and he suddenly coughed and looked away, so plainly trying to swallow back the betraying word. But it was too late.

"*Except*," repeated the Queen. Her voice was light, her tone no more than respectfully curious, but her eyes were bright stone. "Except what, my master?" When Lanak did not answer, she spoke once again, and all she said was, "Lanak."

Lanak sighed, still not looking at her. "Sendings," he mumbled. "I did not teach you about sendings, because I do not use them myself. I would never employ a sending, for any reason. Never."

The Queen said, "But you know how it is done."

"Yes, yes," Lanak answered her. He rubbed his hands hard together and shivered, though it was a hot day for the time of year. He said, "A sending is death. That is its only purpose—whether it ever touches its victim or not, its presence kills. It may appear as an ordinary man or woman, as any animal from a snake to a *shukri* to a rock-*targ*—but it is in truth born of the very essence of the magician who controls it. And yet it is not the magician, not at all." His voice grew more urgent, and he did look straight at the Queen now. "Majesty, magic is neither good nor bad in itself, but a sending is evil in its nature, always. How you will use what I have taught you is your own affair—but ask me no more about sendings. I implore you, ask me no more."

"Oh, but I must," replied the Queen prettily. "I simply must ask, since you have so aroused my curiosity. And you must tell me, good Lanak." They stared at each other, and I think there was something in Lanak's eyes that made the Queen add, "Of course I have no intention of ever using such a thing. You are my master, after all, and I take your words most seriously. That is why I would hear all of them. All of them, Lanak."

So Lanak taught her about sendings.

It took him more than two weeks: still far less time than it should have, when you consider the memorizing alone, never mind the embarrassing rituals, the herbs that have to be gathered and cooked into stinking brews, the merciless disciplining of your mind—and all that for a single sending! But the Queen took it in as though it were no more than another lesson in predicting the sex of a child or the best month for planting. Truly, she was a remarkable woman, that one, and no mistake.

At the end, she said, "Well, Lanak, you have indeed kept your word, and I will keep mine. You may depart for home and hearth this very moment, if you desire, though I would be truly honored if you chose to dine with me this one last night. I do not imagine that we will meet again, and I would do you tribute if I may. Because I may have mocked you somewhat at times, but never when I call you *master.*" And she looked so young when she said this, and so earnest and so anxious, that Lanak could do nothing in the world but nod.

That night the Queen served Lanak a dinner such as he never had again in his life, and he lived to be very old and more celebrated than he liked. They drank a great deal of wine together—yes, you are quite right, Chashi, the vine-yards of this province have always supplied the black castle—and both of them laughed more than you might think; and Lanak even sang a few bars of an old song that the folk of Karakosk sing about their rulers in Fors na'Shachim, which made the Queen laugh until she spilled her drink. Nevertheless, when Lanak went off to his quar-ters, he was dreadfully, freezingly sober, and he knew that the Queen was, too. He turned in the doorway and said to her, "Above all, remember the very last word of the spell. It is a sure safeguard, should anything go ill."

"I have it perfectly," answered the Queen. "Not that I would ever need it."

"And remember this too," Lanak said. "Sendings call no one *master.* No one."

"Yes," said the Queen. "Yes. Good night, Lanak."

Lanak did not go to bed that night. By candlelight he carefully folded the clothes that Dwyla had packed for him—how long ago!—and put them back into his travel-ing bag, along with the gifts and little keepsakes that he had bought for her and their daughter, or been given for them by the Queen. When he had finished, the moon was low in the east, and he could hear a new shift of guards tramping to their posts on the castle walls. But he did not lie down.

If you had been there, you would have watched in wonder as he wrapped his arms around his own shoulders, just as precisely as he had packed his bag; and even if you missed the words he murmured, you would have seen him stand up on his toes—a little too high, you might have thought—and then begin to spin around in a curious way, faster and faster, until he rose into the air and floated up toward the arched ceiling, vanishing into a corner where the candlelight did not go. And how he remained there, and for how long, I cannot say.

By and by, when all the candles save one had burned out, and every other sound in the black castle had long been swallowed by other high, cold corners, there came the faint scratching of claws on stone in the corridor just outside his door. There was no rattling of the knob, no trying of the lock—which Lanak had left unturned—there was simply a thing in the room. The shadows by the door concealed it at first, but you would have known it was there, whether you could see it or not.

It took a step forward, halfway into the shivering light. It stood on two legs, but looked as though it might drop back down onto four at any moment. The legs were too long, and they bent in the wrong places, while the arms—or front legs, whichever they were—were thick and jointless, and the claws made them look too short. There were rust green scales glinting, and there was a heavy swag to belly and breast—like a *sheknath*, yes, Gri, but there was a sick softness to it as well, such as no one ever saw on a living *sheknath*. It was not dead, and not alive, and it smelled like wet, rotting leaves.

Then it took another step, and the candlelight twitched across its face. It was the face of the Queen.

Not altogether her face, no, for the delicate features had blurred, as though under layers of old cobwebs, and the rusty skin of it seemed to be running away from her eyes, like water crawling under a little wind. But there were tears on it, a few, golden where the light caught them.

In the darkness, Lanak spoke very quietly. "I have done a terrible thing." The Queen, or what remained of the Queen, turned ponderously toward his voice, her blank black eyes searching for him. Lanak said, "But I saw no other way."

The creature lifted its ruinous head toward the sound, so that Lanak could see for the first time just what had happened to the Queen's hair. The mouth was squirming dreadfully, showing splintery brown teeth, and the eyes had grown suddenly wide and deadly bright at the sound of his voice.

"A terrible thing," Lanak said again. "There was no need for me to mention sendings, knowing you as I do. I knew very well that you would command that I teach you to summon them, and that you would set about it as soon as I was out of your sight. For whom this first one was meant, I have no idea. Perhaps for the Council in Suk'kai, over the hills—perhaps for the Jiril of Derridow—perhaps even for me, why not? Sendings call no one *master*, after all, and you might easily feel that it might be safer to silence me. Was that the way of it, Majesty?"

The Queen-thing made a sound. It might have melted your bones and mine with terror, or broken our hearts, who can say? Lanak went on. "The last word of the summoning. I did not lie to you, not exactly. It is indeed a ward against the sending—but not for the sender. Rather, it balks and nullifies the entire enchantment by protecting the target itself against the malice of the enemy. Thus you set your arrow to the string, and let it fly, and struck it aside, all in the same spell. My doing." His voice was slow and weary, I should imagine.

"But sendings call no one *master*. I did warn you. Finding itself thwarted from its very birth, it turned back in fury toward its source and its one home—you. And when it could not unmake itself, could not reunite with the soul from which it was spun, then it chose to merge with your body, as best it might. And so. So."

Somewhere in the town a cock crowed, though there was no sign of morning in the sky. The Queen-thing lumbered this way and that, looking up at Lanak in raging supplication. He said heavily, "Oh, this is all bad, there is no good in it anywhere. I do not think I will ever be able to tell Dwyla about this. Majesty, I have no love for you, but I cannot hate you, seeing you so. I cannot undo what you and I have done together, but what I can I will do now." He spoke several harsh words, pronouncing them with great care. If there were gestures to accompany them, of course these could not be seen.

The Queen-thing began to glow. It blazed up brighter and brighter, first around its edges and then inward, until Lanak himself had to shut his eyes. Even then the image clung pitilessly to the insides of his lids, like the sticky burning the Dariki tribesmen make in their caves south of Grannach Harbor. He saw the outlines of the Queen and her sending, separate and together at once: her in her pride and beauty and cunning, and the other—*that other*—embracing her in fire. Then it was gone, but I think that Lanak never really stopped seeing it ever again. I could be wrong.

The room was indeed growing a bit light now, and the cock outside was joined by the wail of a Nounouri at his dawn prayers. There are a lot of Nounos in Fors, or there used to be. Into the silence that was not emptiness, Lanak said, "No one else will ever see you. I cannot end your suffering, but you need not endure it in the view of all men.

And if a greater one than I can do more, I will send him here. Forgive me, Majesty, and farewell."

Well, that is all of it, and longer than I meant, for which I ask pardon in my turn. Lanak went home to Karakosk, to Dwyla and his daughter, and to his fields, his black beer, and his fireworks; and he did the very best he could to vanish from all other tales and remembrances. He was not wholly successful—but there, that's what happens when you are too good at something for your own ambitions. But I will say nothing more about him, which would have made him happy to know.

As for the Queen. When I was last in Fors na'Shachim, not too long ago, there were still a few street vendors offering charms to anyone bound as a guest to the black castle. They are supposed to protect you from the sad and vengeful spirit that wanders those halls even now. Highly illegal they are, by the way—you can lose a hand for buying and a head for selling. I myself have spent nights at the castle without such protection, and no harm has ever come to me. Unless you count my dreams, of course.

The N Auntie

ANNE McCAFFREY

A new Anne McCaffrey short story is always an event for her millions of readers, so I know that they will be as pleased as I am that she chose to write a story for this anthology. Perhaps someday I shall have the pleasure of meeting and thanking her in person. Until then, it will have to suffice that we share the pages of this volume.

—DC

The N Auntie

I WAS A LITTLE SURPRISED to see Moira Flanaghan in the supermarket. Her son, Brendan, who was in the same class as my Kevin, was home sick with the whooping cough. I don't want to sound smug, but I'd made certain that all my children had been given the proper injections when they were babies: even the Salk vaccine though there hasn't been much of polio here in Ireland. Still, I'd had my brother, Dennis, as an awful example of what can happen. He'd died from the whooping cough. Maybe I was overly cautious, but if my mammy had given us those preventatives, my brother wouldn't have got so sick and would still be alive. After all the sorrow and grief over Denny's death, you may be sure I did the right thing by my children!

"Hi, Moira," I cried, waving at her down the aisle from me.

She looked up, and around, as someone interrupted from concentrating on something else. She nodded back, sort of peremptorily, and put the package she was studying into her shopping basket.

"Is Brendan better then?" I asked as soon as I got closer. She probably didn't want the entire population of the market to know her business. She was like that.

She made a grimace and gave a very tired sigh. She looked exhausted, and I knew by that alone that her answer would be negative.

"No, but my Aunt Nellie said she'd be glad to sit with him for a spell so I could get some shopping done. Paddy never follows my list."

Paddy was her husband, and I think he was even more distraught by Brendan's illness than Moira. The doctor was threatening to take him back into Crumlin's Sick Children's Hospital again. But Moira was the kind of mother who is sure her child is being neglected in a hospital situation.

"Your Aunt Nellie?" I asked. "I didn't know you had any relatives here in the east." The name "Nellie" is still enough to make me twitch.

"Yes, bless her," Moira said, again with a heavy sigh. "I don't know what I would have done without her these last few days. She's been a gem. Doing the cooking and amusing Brendan when he's whingeing. He never used to be a whinger." Another sigh. Then a smile. "I didn't even know I *had* an Aunt Nellie either. Great-aunt, I mean. She's quite old for all she's so spry and gay."

Moira's parents lived in Sligo, and she had scads of cousins and things, but, even with the best will in the world, you can't keep up with the cousins, much less the greats.

"She dropped by this afternoon just about the time I thought Brendan would drive me mad. I'd no warning she was coming, or even anywhere near Dublin, doncha know. But she took one look at me, heard Brendan whingeing, and before I knew it, she was in the door, making me a cup of tea, and so concerned . . . So when she said I should take some time out for myself, I . . ." Moira gave a helpless shrug. "I just did."

"Very good of her to give you a little time off," I said, and I shouldn't have felt so uncomfortable about such an opportune visit.

"What's she doing in Tallaght, so far from home?" I

knew that almost all of Moira's family lived in County Sligo. She missed them, and really, it was nice of a relative to put in an appearance just now.

"Oh," and Moira flicked her hand in the air, "she said something about being in Dublin for a spell. She likes to travel, and the tales she tells of the places she's been." Now a tired smile crossed Moira's face. "She's as good as a vacation herself. When I brought her up to Brendan, she took his hand and started telling him such fascinating stories that he stopped his whingeing altogether."

"Well, there's nothing like a little break to make you feel human, is there? I won't hold you up. I'll give you a jingle to find out how Brendan is."

"Oh, he'll be fine, I'm sure. Auntie Nellie says so."

So we parted, and I thought that really, people can be so helpful, given a chance. Like Moira's Great-aunt Nellie.

It was much later that night that I remembered why the phrase, "Great-aunt Nellie," had made me so uncomfortable. I had had a Great-aunt Nellie! At least, I once had thought I had.

It wasn't all that hard to pull the memory out of storage either, for all that I couldn't have been more than five or six at the time. But it was at that time that my brother Denny had had the whooping cough. And died of it. And my Great-aunt Nellie had let me in for a terrible scene with Mammy. I got whaled for one, telling such a fib and two, letting someone in the house at all.

My brother Denny had been two years younger, and what with whooping all night and Mammy not sleeping, Daddy had told her to go take a nap while he sat by Denny and read the paper. I remember that. It was why I had opened the door instead of waiting for my father to do so.

I had been told to keep very quiet so as not to wake Mammy, so it had seemed only logical for me to keep the person at the door from hitting the bell again. That house had had a loud one.

I remember the little woman standing there, with a bright red hat perched on her wavy silver hair, a hat that exactly matched the very nice red suit she was wearing that went with the cheerful smile on her face.

"My, but you're a pretty child, Ciara," she said. "Oh, my, of course you wouldn't remember your old Auntie Nellie. It isn't often that I stop by in Dublin on my travels." She also stepped into the house and closed the door behind her. "Give your great-auntie a hug now, won't you?" she added, holding her arms out to me.

Well, Mammy had taught me my manners, so I endured an embrace and a kiss on both cheeks. Indeed it was no hardship because she smelled of something floral and pleasant and she didn't have wet lips like Uncle Jamie nor thick lipstick like Auntie June. In fact, this great-auntie bid fair to be the nicest of all my relations. She was wearing silk, and it wasn't even Sunday.

She kept hold of my hand and sat down at the little table where the phone was kept.

"Now, tell me all about yourself, Ciara, before your mammy comes."

"Mammy's asleep," I said, putting a finger to my lips and keeping my own voice down. "Denny's sick."

"Yes, I'd heard," Great-aunt Nellie said, leaning in to me, her face sympathetic, but her eyes, and I remember them because they were much bluer than Mammy's and sparkled more than I'd ever seen anyone's eyes sparkle, were not really sympathetic. "That's the reason I came by. To see if I could help."

I shook my head. "Denny's got whooping cough."

"Oh, really?" she said, bending closer to me. "Very badly?"

"He never stops coughing, that's why Mammy's sleeping. Daddy's sitting with him now and reading his paper."

"Well, now, I'll just tiptoe upstairs and say a prayer for him and chat with your daddy, and we don't need to disturb your mammy, do we?" she said, and rose off the little stool. Then, putting me aside in a manner that told me I'd best stay where I was, she went slowly up the stairs, pulling herself along by the handrail.

I listened as sharp as I could and heard Daddy speaking to her. Then there was silence. I got bored with listening and went into the kitchen to find what I could to eat. I remember that because Daddy came down to the kitchen and put the kettle on.

"Is Auntie Nellie staying?" I asked.

"No," Daddy said in that heavy way he had then, "but she said a rosary for Denny, and even put his fingers on her beads . . . jade, they were, I think she said. Got them in Thailand or some such far-off place."

He made himself some tea and took it back up to Denny's room, and I was left, once again, to amuse myself.

It wasn't until that night, during tea, that Auntie Nellie was mentioned.

"Oh, by the way, Joan," Daddy said as he passed the veg back to Mammy, "your Great-auntie Nellie stopped by this afternoon to see Denny."

"My great-aunt who?" Mammy nearly dropped the dish. "I don't have an Aunt Nellie, great or otherwise."

"But . . . but . . ." and Daddy looked at me.

"That's who she said she was," I said. From the scowl on Mammy's face, I knew I'd better add something else. "She knew who I was and called me my name."

Well, the long and the short of it was that I got whaled

for letting in a stranger, since Mammy insisted she had no such relative, and, furthermore, one who would intrude on a household with a sick child.

My brother died that night, and I wasn't allowed to forget that I had let an absolute stranger into the house. And who knows what terrible infection she'd brought with her on that rosary that killed my brother.

I got in trouble at school, too, because I refused to say a rosary. I didn't want anyone to die because I'd said a rosary. Mammy had to come speak to Sister Assumpta about such blasphemy, but after that visit, I was always told to make my penances in Hail Marys and Our Fathers instead of saying a rosary.

Well, I told my adult self that night, such a coincidence would be vivid even thirty years later. And Moira's Greataunt Nellie couldn't possibly be my not-Great-aunt Nellie. At the time Denny died, we'd been living in the family home in Newbridge, County Kildare. And Moira's family were from Sligo—

I might have been able to push down that incident if Moira's Brendan hadn't also died the very next morning. One of the other mothers rang to tell me: he just stopped breathing sometime in the night.

I tried to remember if that's how my brother Denny had died, but I couldn't recall that detail. I felt awful, but even if, by any weird chance, that Great-auntie Nellie had also been the woman who called on our family, it had already been too late for Brendan.

I'll say this for that: a lot of women took their kids to get the pertussis injection that week.

Then, as those things sometimes work, I heard of another instance . . . a Great-auntie Nora, I'll admit . . . but it was just too much of a coincidence. Nellie/Nora . . . and both great-aunts, and in both cases another child died. A girl, and this time of scarlet fever. In an estate in south Dublin.

I heard the news at the Irish Countrywomen Association meeting. There was a good bit of chat, over tea, after the official agenda had been duly discussed and voted on. Meningitis was what most women were worried about: as much because it was so difficult to diagnose as because there was so much of it about.

"At least they get taken to hospital with it," I said, thinking that there'd be no great-aunts charming their way into an unsuspecting house. Though how just sitting with a sick child, or even saying a rosary with hands-on, could bring a child to its death, I certainly couldn't say. Or why?

"They can die in hospital just as easily," Rose O'Neill said bitterly.

"Oh no, not your Mary?" I cried.

"No, no, no," Rose said hastily. She's a nurse at Crumlin's Sick Children's Hospital. "But we had a meningitis death quite unexpectedly. The little girl was doing so well. We'd even allowed an aunt to visit with her because it's almost harder to keep the convalescents amused."

"Aunt?" Rose almost recoiled from the way I spit out the question.

"Yes, a great-aunt, in fact. A charming woman. Sister didn't think it would do little Onya any harm . . ."

"Great-aunt Nellie? Or Great-aunt Nora?" I asked so harshly that several other women stopped talking to listen to our exchange.

"Nancy. Yes, Nancy was her name."

"A small woman, with silver hair, and very well dressed?"

"Yes, and really, you don't think . . ."

"How did Onya die?"

"Quietly. In the night, before we could do anything to save her."

Rose's eyes didn't leave mine.

"Nellie, Nora, Nancy, oh it's much too close," I said, feeling sick in the pit of my stomach. "And the description fits, too. You don't happen to remember if she wore a floral scent, do you?"

Rose stared at me and said in a shocked whisper, "Yes, she did. But she was so nice and well-spoken."

"Yes, she is. And she's no one's relative!"

"Oh good Lord!"

Well, the Irish Countrywomen Association has a vast network and, when roused by an emergency, can cast a wide net. I won't say we had what the Gardai call an Incident Room or anything like that. To get grieving parents to talk about their dead child is painful, too, even if the cause is to prevent more such happenings. But, around the country, we located five more fatal cases in which a presumed great-aunt—Nellie, Nora, Nancy, Niamh, Nuala—had visited the child shortly before death occurred. We got three more descriptions of this auntie, which matched the others: except for details of dress. Dear great-auntie was always impeccable and very fashionably attired for a woman her age. Only what was her age?

One of our oldest members, and Mrs. Maitiand was in her nineties, remembered a pre-death visit of a Great-auntie Nellie when she was a child of six. (Granted Mrs. Maitiand's memory of what happened at the last meeting or even yesterday could be foggy, but details of her early childhood were as clear to her as when they had occurred.)

Sister Peg Kennedy, who was now in the Eastern Health Board District, remembered a series of unexpected infant deaths in the Cork District, where she had worked after finishing her training. Again measles had reached epidemic proportions one very wet winter: all the schools had been closed. She had been run off her feet, checking on the estates and the council houses. In several instances, a great-aunt had visited the premises shortly before the child had died. Peg was good enough to ask for the records and sure enough, Nellie, Nora, Niamh, Nuala, Nanny, Naomi had been doing the rounds.

"Why children?" Peg asked then, looking up from the pages, shock making her face awfully white.

"And children with the sort of ordinary illnesses from which children usually recover?" I added.

We did some more searching, through Peg's contacts with other district nurses. The Dread N auntie was found in five other counties, in the larger cities. Significantly, there were long periods when nothing about her could be found.

"You can't call her a Typhoid Mary," Rose said. "She carried the disease, but not everyone died of meeting her and getting it."

"What good does it do to know there's a lethal great-auntie doing the rounds?" Peg said in some despair.

We were all pretty upset by our findings now. But they weren't the sort of thing you could take to the Gardai. Or even a family doctor. There certainly wasn't any way to be discreet in a blanket warning.

Parents were already worried enough about the meningitis scare . . . to the point where phones at doctors' offices and hospitals were clogged with calls from the anxious.

"Well, we simply can't do *nothing*," I insisted.

"Well, what can we do?" Rose said in almost a wail. She was finding it hard to forgive herself letting the auntie in to see her little patient.

"Track her down to wherever she's staying," Peg said in a firm no-nonsense voice.

"How?" Rose demanded.

I began to see what Peg meant. Most of the latest fatalities had been right in the Dublin area. Great-auntie had always been very well turned out. Where did well-turned-out people stay? In good hotels.

"But there're hundreds of them in the Dublin area," Rose said, accepting failure.

"Yes, and there're a large membership of ICA, too," I said, beginning to see a plan. "We may not be great-aunties, but nothing keeps us from showing a picture to a receptionist to see if it matches a guest, is there?"

Rose's eyes popped out. "Could we?"

"I don't know why not. You know Grania Callaghan? Who did those quick sketches at our last fund-raiser? Well, there's me and Rose and Moira Flanaghan who've seen her . . ."

"Oh, you can't bother poor Moira so soon after Brendan's death . . ."

"I won't bother her . . . if I don't have to," I said, "but I will if Rose and I can't come up with a good likeness. You know, the way the Gardai and constables do on TV. A photo-fit sort of thing."

"I'll remember that woman's face until the day I die," Rose said, recovering her optimism and her resolve.

"She couldn't be a vampire, could she?" Rose asked, shocking herself.

"I don't remember fangs in her face," I said soothingly. "And vampires can only come out at night, can't they? Didn't you see *Interview with the Vampire*?"

"Yes, I did, and, besides, they were men."

"Until they also got that girl."

Rose moaned slightly, but before we had finished we had decided that a vampire Great-auntie N was not.

*　　　*　　　*

We didn't tell Grania Callaghan *why* we needed a photo-fit, but she was most cooperative. Rose and I gave her a good idea of the oval face, the placement of the cheek-bones, the eyes, the brows: I don't think we got the nose right, but full-face maybe that wouldn't matter. Rose also remembered the details of the fashionable outfit she'd been wearing during her hospital visit. Great-auntie certainly kept up with fashion trends. Where did she get her money? I wondered. But that was a minor detail. Possibly it was essential for her to look so pre-sentable to get into homes. You certainly wouldn't admit a tinker woman.

I got together a second committee to show copies of our result to reservation clerks in hotels and the better B&Bs. What I told them was that this lady had been at a meeting and dropped a valuable earring. We wanted to trace her to give it back, and all we knew was that she was staying in Dublin for a few weeks. She traveled a lot.

That gave us another area to work: the travel agencies in Dublin.

Two groups located her the same day.

"As if we were meant to find her," Rose said, exhaling a huge sigh of relief when I phoned her ward to tell her the news. "Only what do we do now? How can we possibly just approach her, and what do we say to her then?"

"Don't worry about that. Remember that psychiatric nurse you were telling me about?"

"Siobhan Hanley?"

"Isn't she married to a Gardai?"

"Yes, but she'll never believe this," Rose said.

"She will if we explain it to her. It's just weird enough to make her want to check out this sort of aberrant behavior."

"But . . . but . . . don't we have to catch the woman in the act, so to speak?"

"Yes, and that's dead easy now," I said with more confidence than I really felt. Because this was the very tricky part: confronting the woman and, God helping us, getting her committed. Preferably before she killed another child. Why children? And how?

An autopsy had been done on the meningitis child in Crumlin's. Rose had sneaked a glance at the report and the cause of death was heart failure due to the strain of the disease.

Great-auntieNellie/Nora/Naomi/Nuala/Niamh/Nana was staying at the Berkley Court, one of the most prestigious hotels. (We should have looked there first, but that's always the case, isn't it?) A few discreet questions about whether or not dear Auntie Nellie was in provided us with the last name.

"Oh, you mean Mrs. MacAvoy? Yes, she's in. She rarely leaves until midday," the bellboy said.

"Tips well, does she?" I asked.

He nodded his head several times and grinned.

"Well, I wouldn't like to disturb her this early," I said, looking at my watch.

So I waited out in my car. After I called Rose, Peg, and the others on my "committee."

It was after noon and I was getting pretty hungry, when Great-auntie Nellie emerged, looking not a day older than she had twenty-five years ago, the day before Denny died. She wore a lovely beige suit, with a white shirt and a frilly collar, a wisp of a hat, also beige and white, and beige high heels. She had very very good legs for a woman of her years. She *had* to be in her eighties. But she didn't walk or move like a stiffening geriatric.

She hailed a cab, and I followed. Excitement had adrenaline surging through me, and, by the time we started down the main road south, I was buzzing. Then I remembered that Peg had loaned me her mobile unit, so I gave her a call. Rose had one, too, so we could all stay in touch.

"She's heading south. Stillorgan maybe?"

"She hasn't been there. That we know of, has she?"

"No."

"Look, we'll head down the N-11, too. Rose has gone to get Moira," Peg said. "I've got the mother of the little girl she killed in Crumlin. And I'll get Siobhan. It's her day off, too. If we all catch up with Great-auntie, we should be able to manage."

I wasn't sure what we would have to manage. None of us were sick. Her victims were always children. But would we be able to force a confession out of the woman? And what good would that do anyway? She hadn't physically harmed them, had she? Even if somehow she had been instrumental in causing their deaths.

The taxi continued on its way south and then turned right at Leopardstown Avenue. How did Great-Auntie know where to go?

The taxi stopped at the little newsagent's, just before the biggest of Leopardstown estates. She got out. I was so nervous that I misdialed the phone first time, but when I got through to my confederates, I saw that they were right behind me.

"Look, we can drive right into the estate and just keep an eye on her until she stops," I said.

"But she'll notice us . . ." Rose replied, her nervousness obvious.

"Why should she? It's a big estate. There're lots and lots of cars coming and going. With women in them."

Great-auntie, walking as if she knew exactly where she

was going, turned right at the first junction. I went by her, still wondering why children? Why sick children? How were we going to stop her?

Because we *have* to, I told myself. She was now checking door numbers, and so I turned into a driveway. I must tell you that I nearly wet my knickers when she turned up the footpath to the same house.

A quick glance in my rearview mirror told me that Rose's blue Fiat was parking—well, scraping its tires on the curb—while Peg's white Nissan turned into the drive of the next house up. So I pretended to be getting things out of the back of the car while Great-auntie, smiling politely in my direction, rang the doorbell.

It took so long for someone to open it that I worried lest Great-auntie got suspicious. The door opened and she leaned slightly forward, making her request of the house-holder, smiling. She got in.

I got out and waved my confederates to hasten; Rose almost twisted her ankle; Moira was arguing with Peg; and Siobhan followed them, looking slightly amused and superior.

"It was *her*," Moira was saying. "I'd swear on it in court until the day I die. That was *her*!"

I was still leaning on the doorbell. It hadn't taken long, had it, for Great-auntie Nellie to talk me into going up to see my brother. And it hadn't taken Great-auntie long to convince Moira she was just the person to give her a break—while she made her arrangements to take Brendan's young life. Where was the mother of the house? Why was she taking . . .

The door opened so abruptly I nearly fell in. I must admit I very rudely pressed my way in.

"Great-auntie, she's here. We saw her come in. Where's the sick child?"

"Declan?" the woman replied, stumbling backwards as

the five of us pushed in. "He's upstairs. But who are you? I don't know you . . . any of you."

"Believe me, we're here to help Declan. Upstairs?"

How long did it take Great-auntie N to do her deed?

"But his great-auntie's with him," the woman called as we all made for the stairs. Rather dazed and uncertain, she followed. "I'd rather he not have too many visitors. Are you Health Board officials?"

"Yes, we are," Peg said authoritatively.

"Oh, well, I suppose you know what you're doing . . ."

Houses like these have four bedrooms on the upper floor. The front two would be the largest, the one on the left used by the parents. Two other doors were closed, but a murmuring voice told us which one was Declan's, and we burst in.

"How nice to see you, Great-auntie Nellie," I said, and, taking the one stride necessary to reach the lower bunk, I grabbed her upper arm and jerked her from her seat on the bedside. I don't think she had so much as touched the child yet, and he was sleeping peacefully, totally unaware that an angel of death had come to visit. The very blue eyes crackled up at me with such venom that had I been less involved in righteousness, I would not have dared handle her so.

Indeed she was a lot stronger than she ought to be and wrenched her arm free.

"It's her," said Moira, and reached past me to take Great-auntie's jacket lapels and started to shake her. "You killed my Brendan. You killed him. How did you do it?"

"You're insane, both of you," Great-aunt Nellie said, managing to release herself from Moira as well. "I've never seen you before in my life."

"That doesn't matter as much as that *we* have seen *you*,"

Rose said, and, when Siobhan stepped around, we had encircled Great-auntie Nellie.

"What is it you do to the children whose lives you take?" I demanded, clenching my fists at my sides to stop their trembling. I locked my knees so they wouldn't give me away. "You killed my brother Denny."

"My son, Brendan," and Moira gave way to tears though she didn't move from her stance.

"And the Sullivan child in Crumlin's," added Rose.

"And . . ." Peg began her litany.

"You're mad, all of you," Great-auntie said, looking from one to the other of us.

"What's going on here?" a male voice asked, and a disheveled father appeared in the doorway.

That's when Siobhan moved, getting a deft armlock on Great-auntie Nellie.

"It's like this, sir," she said in her best soothing voice. "This woman's a patient of mine and has escaped. We've been tracking her all over the city . . ."

"That is the most outrageous pack of lies . . ." Great-auntie Nellie said, and somehow she seemed to bulge beyond her former dainty self. I could see Siobhan struggling to keep her hold. "I ask you, do I *look* like a mad-woman?"

"Is she your Great-auntie Nellie, Tim?" asked the woman of the house behind him.

"No, I never saw her before in my life. Jaysus, Aisling, you know I was an orphan," Tim said with some indignation at his wife's stupidity. "Now then, what is all this?" he added in such a tone that I asked him was he Gardai.

"Yes, I am, but I'll just ask you ladies to move out of my son's room and let him rest. He had both of us up all night."

"I'm a ward sister at Crumlin's," Rose said. "What's wrong with him?"

"We don't know if it's meningitis or not, Sister," said Tim, his eyes shadowed with anxiety. "Here, you, all of you, clear out of here downstairs. If you wouldn't mind, Sister?"

"I'm Eastern Health Board," Peg said then when she noticed Siobhan giving her a high sign.

Siobhan then pushed Great-auntie toward the door, and I followed as closely as I could, leaving the distraught parents and the other women with the sick child.

"We'll just have a few words, Auntie, while I call an ambulance. Easy now, you wouldn't want to fall down these steep stairs, would you?"

The stairs were steep and narrow, so I had to follow behind Siobhan, who kept giving little twists to the hold she had on the woman as they descended. The front door stood open, and I wondered how I could get past the two women and close it against any possible run by our captive.

"How do you do what you do, that kills the children?" Siobhan asked. "Do you steal their breath?"

"I need it more than they do," Great-auntie said, to my surprise. I hadn't hoped for any information out of her. Certainly not a tacit admission of culpability. "There are far too many children in this country. I only visit families who have more than their fair share. I really only take what I have to have."

"Their lives?" I demanded.

"Their youth," she answered. "They have youth. I need that youth to *live!*"

She had just reached the bottom step when she kicked backwards, catching Siobhan on the shins with her spiky heels. It was the surprise of pain that caught Siobhan so unawares. Somehow she got out of the armlock, though that arm hung down as she made it out the front door and slammed it behind her.

"Damn her," cried Siobhan, limping to the door even as I got to it. We both fumbled with the stiff lock for precious seconds before we got it open and rushed down the foot-path.

"I'll go right," said Siobhan, so I turned left.

"She didn't come this way," I cried.

"I don't see her either."

In fact the only thing that was moving on the footpath was a little black Siamese which was favoring one front paw as it made its way across the street. And there was a motorbike coming down, I remember thinking, far too fast for this narrow road.

"Around the side?" Siobhan suggested, but we had only turned to see that there would have been no escape to the side of the house when we heard brakes squeal and an ago-nized scream.

The biker had run over the little black cat.

"Oh, Jaysus, seven years bad luck," the boy was saying as he jammed down the bike rest and trotted back to the mangled body of the cat.

"I don't think so, lad," Siobhan said, as we joined him where he knelt by the mangled body. His wheels had crushed its torso, probably breaking the backbone instantly, but somehow missing a few of the rosary beads on the chain around its neck. "Don't take it so hard. It wasn't looking where it was going, you know. Cats panic so eas-ily."

"You're sure about the luck?" he asked, his face twisted.

"You'll never know how lucky we just got," she said, and, giving him a clout on the arm, gestured for him to go on his way.

"But shouldn't I find out who the owner was?"

"You're a good lad, but it was only some ancient stray that had used up all its nine lives."

As we heard the bike start up, Siobhan and I exchanged glances. I didn't know whether to laugh or cry from relief.

"Well, that's true enough, isn't it?" she asked.

And, of course, it was.

The Fall of the House of Escher

GREG BEAR

*Imagine a world where technology allows everyone to per-
form seemingly impossible feats with great ease. Imagine
this same world to be a place where you eat what you
want by thinking it, even create people by thinking them.
Then hypothesize that boredom has set in and the search
is on for some new and unique diversionary entertainment. Add to that another complication: death is impossible. Along comes a magician, trained and experienced
in stage illusion and legerdemain, one who is too
"young" a member of this society to control anything but
his own abilities. Who, in such a world, would be king?*

—DC

The Fall of the House of Escher

"HOC EST CORPUS," said the licorice voice. *"Lich, arise."*

The void behind my eyes filled. Subtle colors pin-wheeled against velvet. Oiled thoughts raced, unable to grab.

The voice slid like black syrup into my ears.

"Once dead, now quick. Arise."

I opened my eyes. My fingers curled across palm, thumb touched pinkie, tack of prints on skin, twist and pull of muscles in wrist, the first things necessary. No pain in my joints. Hands agile and strong. Tremors gone.

I shivered.

"I'm back," I said.

"Quick and quick," the voice said.

I turned to see who spoke in such lovely black tones. My eyes focused on a brown oval like rich fine wood, ivory eyes with ruby pupils, face square and stern but unmarred by age.

"How does it feel to be inside again, and whole? I am a doctor. You can tell."

I opened my mouth. "No pain," I said. "I feel . . . oily, inside. Smooth and slick."

"Young," the face said. I saw the face in profile and decided, from the timbre of the voice and general features, that this was a woman. The smoothness of her skin reminded me of the unlined surface of a painting. She wore long black robes from neck to below where I lay on an elevated bed or table. "Do you have memories?"

I swallowed. My throat felt cool. I thought of eating and remembered one last painful meal, when swallowing had been difficult. "Yes. Eating. Hurting."

"Your name?"

"Something. Cardino."

"Cardino, that's all?"

"My stage name. My real name. Is. Robert . . . Falucci."

"That is right. When you are ready, you may stand and join them for dinner. Roderick invites you."

"Them?"

"Roderick suggested you, and the five voted to bring you back. You may thank them, if you wish, at dinner."

The face smiled.

"Your name?" I asked.

"Ont. O-N-T."

The face departed, robes swishing like waves. Lights came up. I rolled and propped myself on one elbow, expecting pain, feeling only an easeful smoothness. I suspected that I had died. I surmised I had been frozen, as I had paid them to do, the Nitrogen Fixers, and that . . .

Lich, she had called me. Body, corpse. In one of my flashier shows I had reanimated a headless woman. Spark coils and strobes and a big van de Graaf generator had made the hair on her free head stand on end.

I slipped my naked legs down from the table, found the coolness of a tessellated tile floor. My fumbling fingers found the robe on the table as I stared at the floor: men and women, each a separate tile perfectly joined, in a flow of completion advanced to the far wall: courtship, embracing, copulating, birth.

I felt a sudden floating happiness.

I've made it.

*   *   *

On a heavy black oak table, I found clothes set out that might have come from a studio costume department—black stiffly formal suit out of a 1930s society movie, something for Fred Astaire. To my chagrin, I tended to corpulence even in this resurrected state. I put the robe aside and stuffed myself into the outfit and poured a glass of water from a nearby pitcher. A watercress sandwich appeared, and I nibbled it while exploring the room.

I should be terrified. I'm not. Roderick . . .

The table on which I had been reborn occupied the center of the room, spare and black and shiny, like a stone altar. It felt cold to my touch. A yard to the right, the heavy oak table supported my sandwich plate, the pitcher and glass of water, the discarded robe, and a pair of shoes.

Lich, she had called me.

I stood in bright if diffuse illumination. No lights were visible. The room's corners lay in shadow. Armless chairs lined the wall behind me. A door opened in the next wall. Paintings covered the wall before me. The room seemed square and complete, but I could not find a fourth wall. No matter which direction, as I made a complete turn, I counted only three walls. The decor seemed rich and fashionable, William Morris and the restrained lines of classic Japanese furniture.

Obviously, not the next decade, I thought. *Maybe centuries in the future.*

I walked forward, and the illumination followed. Expertly painted portraits covered the wall, precise cold renderings of five people, three pale males and two dark females, all in extravagant dress. None of them were Roderick—if Roderick was who I thought he might be— and Ont did not appear, either. The men wore tights and seemed ridiculously well endowed, with feathers puffed on their shoulders and immense fan-shaped hats rising from the crowns of their close-cropped heads; the women in tight-fitting black gowns, reddish hair spread like sunbursts, skin the color and sheen of rubbed maple.

I wondered if I would ever find employment in this future world. "Do you like illusions?" I asked the portraits rhetorically.

"They are life's blood," answered the male on the left, smiling at me.

The portrait resumed its old, painted appearance.

Assume nothing, I told myself.

Startling patterns decorated the wall behind the portraits. Flowers surrounded and gave form to skull-shapes, eyes like holograms of black olives floating within petaled sockets.

"Where is dinner?" I asked.

The portraits did not answer.

The room's only door opened onto a straight corridor that extended for a few yards, then sent me back to the room where I had been reborn. I scowled at the unresponsive portraits, then looked for intercoms, doorbells, hidden telephones. Odd that I should still feel happy and at ease, for I might be stuck like a mouse in a cage.

"I would like to go to dinner," I said in my stage voice, precise and commanding. The door swung shut and opened again. When I stepped through, I faced another corridor, and this one led to a larger double door, half-ajar.

I opened the door and stepped outside. I faced an immense ruined garden and orchard, ranks of great squat thick trees barren of any leaves and overgrown with brown creepers and tall sere thistles spotted with black crusty patches. Hundreds of acres spread over low desolate hills, and on the highest hill stood an edifice that would have seemed unlikely in a dream.

It rose above the ruined gardens, white and yellow-gray like ancient chalk, what must have once been a splendid mansion, its lowest level simple and elegant. An architectural cancer had set in, however, and tumorous wings and floors and towers and bridges thrust from the first level with malign genius, twisting and joining in ways I could not make sense of. These extrusions reflected the condition of the garden: the house was overgrown, thick with its own weeds.

Above the house and land rose a sky at once gray and dull and threatening. Coils of cloud dropped from a scudding ash-colored ceiling like incipient tornadoes, and the air smelled of stale ocean and electricity.

A slender spike of alarm rose in me, then faded back into a general euphoria at simply being alive, and free of pain. It did not matter that everything in this place seemed nightmarish and out of balance. All would be explained, I told myself.

Roderick would explain.

If anyone besides me could have survived into this puzzling and perhaps far future, it was the resourceful and clever friend of my youth, the only Roderick of my acquaintance: Roderick Escher. I could imagine no other.

I let go of the door and stepped out on a stone pathway, then turned to look back at the building where I had been reborn. It was small and square, simply and solidly constructed of smooth pieces of yellow-gray stone, without ornament, like a dignified tomb. Frost covered the stones, and ice rime caked the soil around the building, yet the interior had not been noticeably cooler.

I squared my shoulders, examined my hands one

more time, flexed the fingers, and spread them at arm's length. I wiped both of my hands quickly before my face, as if to pass an imaginary coin between them, and smiled at the ease of movement. I then set out along the path through the trees of the ruined garden, toward the encrusted and cancerous-looking house.

The trees and thistles seemed to consent to my passage, listening to my footfalls in silent reservation. I did not so much feel watched as measured, as if all the numbers of my life, my new body, were being recorded and analyzed. I noticed as I approached the barren trunks or the dry, lifeless wall of some past hedge, that all the branches and remaining dry leaves were gripped and held immobile by tiny strands of white fiber. *Spiders, mites,* I hypothesized, but saw no evidence of anything moving. When I stumbled and kicked aside a clod of dry dirt, I saw the soil was laden with thicker white fibers, some of which released sparkles like buried stars where tiny rocks had cut or scratched them. As I walked, I dug with my toe into more patches, and wherever I investigated, strands underlay the topsoil like fine human hairs, a few inches beneath the dusty gray surface. I bent down to feel them. They broke under my fingers, the severed ends sparkling, but then reassembled.

The house on the hill appeared even more diseased and outlandish, the closer I came. Among its many peculiarities, one struck me forcibly: with the exception of the ground floor, there were no windows in the building. All the walls and towers rose in blind disregard of each other and of the desolation beyond. Moreover, as I approached the broad verandah and the stone steps leading to a large bronze door, I noticed that the house itself was also layered with tiny white threads, some of which had been cut and sparkled faintly. What might have seemed cheerful—a house pricked along its intricate surfaces and lines by a myriad of stars, as if portrayed on a Christmas card—became instead flatly dreadful, dreadful in my inner estimation, yet flatly so because of my artificial and inappropriate *calm*.

Another wave of concern swept outward from my core, and was just as swiftly damped. *Part of me wants to feel fear, but I don't. Something in me desires to turn around and find peace again . . .*

A *lich* would feel this way . . . Still half-dead.

From the porch, the house did not appear solid. Fine cracks spread through the stones, and to one side—the northern side, to judge from the angle of the sun—a long crack reached from the foundation to the top of the first floor, where it climbed the side of a short, stubby tower. I could easily imagine the stones crumbling. Perhaps all that held the house together were the white threads covering it like the fine webs of a silkworm or tent caterpillar.

I walked up the steps, my feet kicking aside dust and windblown fragments of desiccated leaves and twigs. The bronze door rose over my head, splotched with black and green. In its center panel, a bas-relief of two hands had been cast. These hands reached out to clasp each other, desire apparent in the tension and arc of the phalanges and strain of tendons, yet the beseeching fingers could not touch.

I could not equate any of this with the Roderick I had known for so many years, beginning in university. I remembered a thin but energetic man, tall and handsome in an ascetic way, his hair flyaway fine and combed back from a high forehead, double-lobed with a crease between, above his nose, that gave him an air of intense concern and concentration. Roderick's most remarkable feature had always been his eyes, set low and deep beneath straight brows, eyes great and absorbing, sympathetic and sad and yet enlivened by a twist and glitter of sensuous humor.

The Roderick I remembered had always been excessively neat, and concerned about money and possessions, and would have never allowed such an estate to go to ruin . . . Or lived in such a twisted and forbidding house.

Perhaps, then, I was going to meet another of the same name, not my friend. Perhaps my frozen body had become an item of curiosity among strangers, and resurrection could be accomplished by whimsical dilettantes. Why would the doctor suddenly abandon me if I had any importance?

The bronze door swung open silently. Along its edges and hinges, the fine white threads parted and sparkled. The door seemed surrounded by tiny embers, which faded to orange and died, silent and unexplained.

Within, a rich darkness gradually filled with a dour luminosity, and I stepped into a long hallway. The hallway twisted along its length, corkscrewing until wall became floor, and then wall again, and finally ceiling. Smells of food and sounds of tableware and clinking glasses came through doors at the end of the twisted hall.

I followed the smells and the sounds. I had expected to have to scramble up the sloping floor, to crawl down the twisted hall, but up and down redefined themselves, and I simply walked along what remained, to my senses, the floor, making a dizzy rotation, to a dining room at the very end. Doors swung open at my approach. I expected at any moment to meet my friend Roderick—expected and hoped, but was disappointed.

The five people pictured in the portraits sat in formal suits and gowns around a long table set with many empty plates and bottles of wine. Their raiment was of the same period and fashion as my own, the twenties or thirties of my century. They were in the middle of a toast, as I entered. The woman who had presided at my rebirth was not present, nor was anyone I recognized as Roderick.

"To our revivified *lich*, Robert Falucci," the five said, lifting their empty glasses and smiling. They were really quite handsome people, the two women young and brown and supple, with graceful limbs and long fingers, the three men strong and well muscled, if a little too pale. Veins and arteries showed through the translucent skin on the men's faces.

"Thank you," I replied. "Pardon me, but I'm a little confused."

"Welcome to Confusion," the taller of the two women said, pushing her chair back to walk to my side. She took my arm and led me to an empty seat at the end of the table. Her skin radiated a gentle warmth and smelled sweetly musky. "Tonight, Musnt is presiding. I am Cant, and this is Shant, Wont, and Dont."

I smiled. Were they joking with me? "Robert," I said.

"We know," Cant said. "Roderick warned us you would arrive."

Musnt, at the head of the table, raised his glass again and, with a gesture, bade me to sit. Cant pushed my chair in for me and returned to her seat.

"I've been dead, I think," I said in a low voice, as if ashamed.

"Gone but not forgotten," Dont, the shorter woman, said, and she hid a brief giggle behind a fist clutching a lace handkerchief.

"You brought me back?"

"The doctor brought you back," Cant said with a helpful and eager expression.

"Against the wishes of Roderick's poor sister," Musnt

said. "Some of us believe that with her, and perhaps with you, he has gone too far."

I turned away from his accusing gaze. "Is this Roderick's house?" I asked.

"Yes and no," Musnt said. "We oversee his work and time. We are, so to speak, the bonds placed on the last remnants of the family Escher."

"Roles we greatly enjoy," Cant said. She was youthfully, tropically beautiful, and I suspected I attracted her as much as she did me.

"I think I've been gone a long time. How much has changed?" I asked.

The four around the table, all but Cant, looked at each other with expressions I might have found on children in a schoolyard: disdain for a new boy.

"A lot, really," Musnt said, lifting knife and fork. Food appeared on Musnt's plate, a green salad and two whole raw zucchinis. Food appeared on my plate, the uneaten remains of my watercress sandwich. I looked up, dismayed. Then a zucchini appeared, and they all laughed. I smiled, but there was a salt edge to my happiness now.

I felt inferior. I certainly felt out of touch.

I did not remember Roderick having a sister.

After dinner, they retired to the drawing room, which was darkly paneled and decorated in queer rococo fashion, with many reptilian cherubs and even full-sized dog-headed angels, as well as double pillars in spiral embrace and thick gold-threaded canopies. The materials appeared to be lapis and black marble and ebony, and everywhere, the sourceless lights followed, and everywhere, the busy and ubiquitous fibers overlay all surfaces.

I heard the distant murmur of a brook, rushes of air,

sounds from some invisible ghostly landscape, and the voices of the five, discussing the spices used in the vegetable soup. Wont then added, "*She* persists in calling our work a blanding of the stew."

"Ah, but *she* is only half an Escher—" Wont said.

"Or a fading reflection of the truly penultimate Escher," Shant added.

"She would do anything for her brother," Cant said sympathetically.

"You've always favored Roderick," Dont said with a sniff. "You sound like Dr. Ont."

Cant turned and smiled at me. "We are judges, but not muses. I *am* the least critical."

Musnt opened a heavy brocaded curtain figured with seashells, and they looked out upon the overgrown garden. Orange and yellow clouds moved swiftly in a twilight azure sky. Musnt flung open the glass-paneled doors, and we all strode onto a marble patio.

Cant put her arm through mine and hugged my elbow against her ribs. "How nice for you to arrive on a good day, with such a fine setting," she said. "I trust the doctor remade you well?"

"She must have," I said. "I feel young and well. A little . . . anxious, I think."

Cant smiled sweetly. "Poor man. They have brought back so many, and all have felt anxious. We're quite used to your anxiety. You will not disturb us."

"We're Roderick's antitheticals," Wont said, as if that might explain something, but it still told me nothing useful. Mired in a dense awkwardness and buried unease, I looked back at the house. It reached to the sky, a cathedral, Xanadu and the Tower of Babel all in one. Towers met with buttresses in impossible ways, drawing my eye from multiple perspectives into hopeless directions.

"What did you do, in your life?" Musnt asked.

"I was a magician," I said. "Cardino the Unbelievable." The name seemed ridiculous, from this distance, in the middle of these marvels.

"We are all magicians," Musnt said disdainfully. "How boring. Perhaps Roderick chose poorly."

"I do not think so," Cant said, and gave me another smile, this one eerily reassuring, an anxiolytic bowing curve of her smooth and plump lips. To my shock, nipples suddenly grew on her cheeks, surrounded by fine brown areolae. "If Robert wants, he can add another layer of critique to our efforts."

"What could he possibly know, and besides, aren't we critical enough?" Shant asked.

"Hush," Cant said. "He's our guest, and we're already showing him our dark side."

"As antitheticals should," Musnt said.

"I don't understand . . . What am I, here?" I asked, the salt taste in my mouth turning bitter. "*Why* am I here?"

"You're a *lich*," Musnt said, staring away from me at nothing in particular. "As such, you have no rights. You can be an added amusement. A spice against our blanding, if you wish, but nothing more."

"Please don't ask if you're in hell. Not so soon," Shant said with a twist of disgust. "It is *so* common."

"Who is this Roderick?"

"He is our master and our slave," Shant said. "We observe all he does, bring him his audience, and bind him like chains."

"He is a seeker of sensation without consequence," Cant said. "We, like his audience, are perfect for him, for we are of no consequence whatsoever." Cant sighed. "I suppose he should come down and say hello."

"Or you can find *him,* which is more likely," Shant suggested.

I opened my mouth to speak, then closed it again, turning to look at the five on the patio. Finally, I said, "Are you real?"

Cant said, "If you mean embodied, no."

"You're dreams," I said.

"You asked if we like illusions," Cant said shyly, touching my shoulder with her slender hand. "We can't help but like them. We are all of us tricks of mind and light, and cheap ones at that. Roderick, for the time being, is real, as is this house."

"Where is Roderick?"

"Upstairs," Shant said.

Wont chuckled at that. "That's very general, but we really don't know. You may find him, or he will find you. Take care you do not meet his sister first. She may not approve of you."

At a noise from within the patio doors, I turned. I heard footsteps cross the stone floor, and looked back at Cant and the others to see their reactions. All, however, had vanished. I took a tentative step toward the doors, and was about to make another, when a tall and spectrally thin figure strode onto the patio, turned his head, and fixed me with a puzzled and even irritated glare.

"So soon? The doctor said it would take days more."

I studied the figure's visage with halting recognition. There were similarities: the high forehead, divided into two prominences of waxen pallor, the short sharp falcon nose, the sunken cheeks hollowed even more now as if by some wasting disease . . . And the eyes. The figure's eyes burned like a flame on the taper of his thin, elongated body. The voice sounded like an echo from caverns at the center of a cold ferrous planet, metallic and sad, yet keeping some of the remembered strength of the original, and that I could not mistake.

"Roderick!"

The figure wore a tight-fitting pair of red pants and a black shirt with billowing sleeves buttoned to preposterously thick gloves like leathern mittens, while around his neck hung a heavy black collar or yoke as might be worn by an ox. At the ends of this yoke depended two brilliant silver chains threaded with thick white fiber. Around his legs twined more fibers, which seemed to grow from the floor, breaking and joining anew with his every step. He seemed to walk on faint embers. Threads grew also beneath his clothes and to his neck, forming fine webs around his mouth and eyes. Looking more closely, I saw that the threads intruded *into* his mouth and eyes.

Still his most arresting feature, the large and discerning eyes had assumed a blue and watery glaze, as if exposed to many brilliant suns, or visions too intense for healthy witness.

"You appear alert and well," Roderick said, turning his gaze with a long blink, as if ashamed. His hair swept back from his forehead, still thin and fine, but white as snow, and tufted as if he had just awakened from damp and restless sleep. "The doctor has done her usual excellent work."

"I feel well ... But so many irritating ... evasions! I have been treated like a ... I have been called an amusement—"

Roderick raised his right hand, then stared at it with some surprise and, slowly, pulling back florid lips from prominent white teeth as at the appearance of some vermin, peeled off the glove by tugging at one finger, then the next, until the hand rose naked and revealed. He slowly curled and straightened the slender, bony fingers and thumb. A spot of blood bedewed the tip of each. One drop fell to the floor and made a ruby puddle on the stone.

"Pardon me," Roderick said, closing the naked hand tightly and pushing it into a pocket in his clinging pants. "I am still emerging. You have come from a farther land than I—how ironic that you seem the more healthy for your journey!"

"I am renewed," I said. Upon seeing Roderick, I began to feel my emotions returning, fear mixing now with a leap of hope that some essential questions might be answered. "Have I truly died and been reborn?"

"You died a very young man—at the age of sixty," Roderick said. "I took charge of your frozen remains from that ridiculous corporation twenty years later and secured you in the vaults of my own family. I had made the beginnings of my huge fortune by then and arranged such preparations very early, and so you were protected by many forces, legal and political. None interfered with our vaults. If not for me, you would have been decanted and rotted long ago."

"How long has it been?"

"Two hundred and fifty years."

"And the others—Wont, Cant, Musnt, Shant, Dont . . ."

Roderick's face grew stern, as if I had unexpectedly uttered a string of rude words. Then he shook his head and put his still-gloved hand on my shoulder.

"All the world's people lie in cool vaults now, or wear no form at all. People are born and die at will, ever and again. Death is conquered, disease a helpmeet and plaything. The necessities of life are not food but sensation. All is servant to the quest for stimulus. The expectant and all-devouring Nerve is King."

I was suddenly dizzied by a vertigo of deep time, the precipitous awareness of having emerged from a long well or tunnel of insensate nullity, leaving almost everyone and everything I had known behind. And perhaps Roderick, the friend I had once known, was no longer with me, either. I felt as if the stones beneath me swayed.

"You alone, of all our friends, our family . . . are alive?"

"I alone keep my present shape, though not without some gaps," Roderick said with some pride. "I am the last of the embodied and walkabout Eschers . . . I, and my sister, but she is not well." His face creased into a mask of sorrow, a well-worn expression I could not entirely credit. "I have mourned her a thousand times already, and a thousand times she has returned to something like life. She feigns death, I think, to taunt me, and abhors my quest, but . . . I could ask for no one more obedient."

"I don't remember your having a sister," I said.

Roderick closed his eyes. "Come, this place is filled with unpleasant associations. I no longer eat. The thought of clamping my jaw and grinding organic matter . . . ugh!"

Roderick led me from the dining room, back to the foyer and a staircase which rose opposite the main door. The stairs branched midpoint to either side, leading to an upper floor. Roderick ascended the stairs with an eerie grace, halting and surveying his surroundings unpredictably, as if motivated not by human desires, but by the volition of a hunting insect or spider. His eyes studied the fiber-crusted walls, lids half-closed, head shaking at some association or memory conjured by stimuli invisible to me.

"You must find a place here," Roderick said. "You are the last in the vault. All the others have long since been freed and either vapored or joined with some neural clan or another. I have kept you in reserve, dear Robert, because I value you most highly. You have a keen mind and quick fingers. I need you."

"How may I be useful?"

"All this, the house and the lands around us, survive by whim of King Nerve," Roderick said. "We are entertainers, and our tenure wears thin. Audiences demand so much of us, and of everything around us. You are new and unexplored."

"What kind of entertainment?"

"Our lives and creations—the lives of my sister and I— are one illusion following on the tail of another," Roderick said. "All that we do and think is marked and absorbed by billions. It is our prison, and our glory. Our family has always had conjurers—do you remember? It is how we met and became friends."

"I remember. Your father—"

"I have not thought of him in a century," Roderick said, and his eyes glowed. He smiled. "Fine work, Robert! My mind tingles with associations already. My father . . . and my mother . . ."

"But Roderick, you did not get along with your father. You abhorred magic and illusions. You called them 'tricks,' and said they 'deceived the simple and the unobservant.' "

"I remained a faithful friend, did I not?"

"Yes," I said. "You must have. You brought me back from the dead."

"Sufficient time shows even me how wrong I am," he murmured.

We reached the top of the stairs. A familiar figure, the doctor named Ont, passed down the endless hallway, black robes swirling like ink in water. She stopped before us, paying no attention to me, but staring at Roderick with pained solicitousness, as if she might cry if he grew any more pale, or thinner.

"Thank you, Dr. Ont," Roderick said, bowing slightly. She nodded acknowledgment.

"He is what you wanted, what you need?"

"So soon, and unexpected, but already valuable."

"He can help you?"

"I do not know," Roderick said. Ont looked now at me.

"You must be very *cautious* with Roderick Escher," she warned. "He is a national cleverness, a treasure. It is my duty to sustain him, or to do his bidding, whichever he desires."

"How is *she?*" Roderick asked, hands clasped before him, naked fingers preposterously thin and white against the thick leathern glove.

Ont replied, "Even this vortex soon spins itself out, and this time I fear the end will be permanent."

"Fear . . . more than you hope?" Roderick asked.

Ont shook her head sternly. "I do not understand this conceit between you."

With another tip of her head, Ont walked on, and the hall curled into a corkscrew ahead of her. Remaining upright, she trod along the spiraling floor and vanished around the curve. The hall straightened, but she was no longer visible.

"A century ago, I chose to come back into this world refreshed," Roderick said to me, "and took from myself a kind of rib or vault of my mind, to make a sister. She became my twin. Now, let me show you how the house works . . ."

Roderick gripped me by the elbow and guided me to a steep, winding stair that must have coiled within the largest tower surmounting the house. He gave what he meant to be an encouraging smile, but instead revealed his teeth in a conspiratorial rictus, and climbed the steps before me. I hesitated, palms and upper lip moist with growing dread of this odd time and incomprehensible circumstance. Soon, however, as my friend's form vanished around the first curve in the stair, I felt even more dread at being left alone, and hoped knowledge of whatever sort might ease my apprehensiveness. I raced to catch up with him.

"As a race, in the plenitude of time—a very short time—we have found our success," Roderick said. "Lacking threat from without, and at peace within, our people enjoy the fruits of the endeavors of all civilizations. All that has been suffered is repaid here." His voice sounded hollow in the tower, like the mocking laughter of a far-off crowd.

"How?" I asked, following on Roderick's heels up the stairs. That which might have once winded me now seemed almost effortless. Whatever shortness of breath I felt was due to nerves, not frailness of body.

"All work is stationary," Roderick said, again favoring me with that peculiar grimace that had replaced a once fine and encouraging smile. We had made two turns around the tower.

"Then why do we walk?" I asked.

"We are chosen. Privileged, in a way. We—my sister and I, Dr. Ont, and now you—maintain the last links with physical bodies. We give a foundation to all the world's dreams. The entire Earth is like the seed in a peach, all but disposed of. What matters is the sweet pulp of the fruit—communication and expansion along the fiber-optic lines, endless interaction, endless exchange of sensations. Some have abandoned all links with the physical, the seed, having bodies no more. They flit like ghosts through the interwoven threads that make the highways and rivers and oceans of our civilization. Most, more conservative, maintain their corporeal forms like shrines, and visit them now and then, though the bodies are cold and unfeeling, suspended and vestigial. You were reborn in one such vault, made to hold such as you, and eventually to receive my sister and me—though I have decided not to go there, never to go there. I think *death* would be more interesting."

"I've been there," I said.

"Yes, and I always ask my *liches* . . . What do you recall?"

"Nothing," I said.

"Look closely at that excised segment in your world-line. You were dead two and a half centuries, and you remember nothing?"

"No," I said.

He smiled. "No one has. The demands . . . The voices . . . Gone." He stopped and looked back at me. We stood more than halfway up the tower. "A blankness, a darkness. A surcease from endless art."

"In my life, you were more concerned with business than the arts."

"The world changed after you died. Everyone turned their eyes inward, and riches could be achieved by any who linked. Riches of the inner life, available to all. We made our world self-sustaining and returned to a kind of cradle. I grew bored with predicting the weather of money when it hardly mattered and so few cared. I worked with artists, and found more and more a sympathy, until I became one myself."

He stood before a large pale wooden door set in the concrete and plaster of the tower. "Robert, when we were boys, we dreamed of untrammeled sensual delights. Soon enough, I saw that experiences that seemed real, but carried no onerous burdens of pain, would consume all of humanity. Before my rebirth, I directed banks and shaped industries . . . Then I slept for twenty years, waiting for fruition. After my rebirth, my sister and I invested the riches I had earned in certain industries and new businesses. We *directed* the flow and shape of the river of light, on which everyone floated like little boats. For a time, I controlled—but I never retired to the vaults myself."

He touched the door with a long finger, smearing a

spot of blood on the unpainted and bleached surface. "Physical desire," he whispered, "drove the growth. Sex and lust without rejection or loss, without competition, was the beginning. Primal drives directed the river, until everyone had all they wanted . . . In a land of ghosts and shades."

The door swung open at another touch of his finger, leaving two red prints on the wood. Within, more river sounds, and a series of breathless sighs.

"Now, hardly anyone cares about sex, or any other basic drives. We have accessed deeper pleasures. We restring our souls and play new tunes."

A fog of gossamer filled the dark space beyond the door. Lights flitted along layer after layer of crossed fibers, and in the middle, a machine like a frightened sea urchin squatted on a wheeled carriage. Its gray spines rose with rapid and sinuous grace to touch points on conjunctions between threads, and light seeped forth.

"This is the thymolecter. What I create, as well as what I think and experience, the thymolecter dispenses to waiting billions. And my thoughts are at work throughout this house, in room after room. Look!"

He turned and lifted his hand, and I saw a group of thin children form within the gossamer. They played listlessly around a bubbling green lump, poking it with a stick and laughing like fiends. It made little sense to me. "This amuses half the souls who occupy what was once the subcontinent of India."

I curled my lip instinctively, but said nothing.

"It *speaks* to them," Roderick whispered. "There is torment in every gesture, and triumph in the antagonism. This has played continuously for fifteen years, and always it changes. The *audience* responds, becomes part of the piece, takes it over . . . and I adjust a figure here, a sensibility there. Some say it is my masterpiece. And I had to fight for years to overcome the objections of the five!" His cheeks took on some color at memory of the triumph. He must have sensed my underwhelming, for he added, "You realize we experience only the tip of the sword here, the cover of a deep book. You see it out of context, and without the intervening years to acculturate you."

"I am sure," I muttered, and was thankful when Roderick extinguished the entertainment.

"You've had experience with live audiences, of course, but never with a hundred billion respondents. My works spread in waves against a huge shore. At one time they beat up against other waves, the works of other artists. But there are far fewer artists than when you were first alive. As we have streamlined our arts for maximum impact, competition has narrowed and variety has waned, and now, the waves slide in tandem; we serve niches which do not overlap. Mine is the largest niche of all. I am the master."

"It's all vague to me," I said. "Isn't there anything besides entertainment?"

"There is discussion of entertainment," Roderick said.

"Nothing else? No courtships, relationships, raising children?"

"Artists imagine children to be raised, far better than any real children. Remember how horrid *we* were?"

"I had no children . . . I had hoped, here—"

"A splendid idea! Eventually, perhaps, we will reenact the family. But for now . . ."

I sensed it coming. Roderick's friendship, however grand, had always hung delicately upon certain favors, never difficult to grant individually, but, when woven together, amounting to a subtle fabric of obligations.

"I need a favor," Roderick said.

"I suppose I owe you my life."

"Yes," Roderick said, with an uninflected bluntness that chilled me. Roderick drew me from the gossamer chamber, and, as he was about to close the door, I glimpsed another play of lights, arranged into curved blades slicing geometric objects. A few of the objects—angular polyhedra, flushed red—seemed to try to escape the blades.

"Half of Central America," Roderick confided, seeing my puzzlement.

"What sort of favor?" I asked with a sigh, as the door swung silently shut.

"I need you to perform magic," Roderick said.

I brightened. "That's all?"

"It will be enough," Roderick said. "Nobody has performed magic of your sort for a hundred years. Few remember. It will be novel. It will be concrete. It will play on different strings. King Nerve has gotten demanding lately, and I feel . . ."

He did not complete this expression. "Pardon my enthusiasm, you must be exhausted," he said, with a tone of sudden humility that again endeared him to me. "There is a kind of night here. Sleep as best you can, in a special room, and we will talk . . . tomorrow."

Roderick led me through another of those helical halls, whose presence I keenly felt in every part of the house, and soon came to hate. I wondered if there were no doors or halls at all, only illusions of connections between great stacks and heaps of cubicles, which Roderick could activate to carry us through the walls like Houdini or Joselyne. In a few minutes, we came to a small narrow door, and beyond I found a pleasant though small room, with a canopy bed and a white marble lavatory, supplying a need I was beginning to feel acutely.

Roderick waited for me to return and chided my physical limitations. "You still need to eat, and suffer the consequences."

"Can I change that?" I asked, half-fearfully.

"Not now. It is part of the novelty. You are a *lich*. You subscribe to no services, move nothing by will alone."

"As do the five?"

Again he shook his head and frowned. "They are projections. To you, they feel solid enough, real enough, but there is no amusement in them. They can *seem* to do anything. Including make my life a torment."

"How?"

"They express the combined will of King Nerve," he said, and answered no further questions. He then showed me the main highlights of the room. It was much larger than it seemed, and wherever I turned I beheld new walls, which met previous walls at square angles, each wall supporting shelves covered with apparatus of such rareness and beauty that I lost all of my dread in a bath of primal delight.

"These can be your tools," Roderick said with a flourish. I turned and walked from wall to apparent wall, shelf to shelf, picking up Brema brasses, numerous fine boxes nested and false-bottomed and with hidden pockets and drawers, large and small tables covered with black and white squares in which velvet-drop bags might be concealed, stacks of silver and gold and steel and bronze coins hollow and hinged and double-faced and rough on one side and smooth on the other, silk handkerchiefs and scarves and stacks of cloths of many colors; collapsing birdcages of such beautiful craftsmanship I felt my eyes moisten; glasses filled with apparent ink and wine and milk, metal tubes of many sizes, puppet doves and mice and white rats and even monkeys, mummified heads of many expressions, some in boxes; slates spirit and otherwise, some quite small; pens and pencils and paintbrushes with hidden talents; cords and retracting reels and loops; stacked boxes à la Welles in which a young woman might be rearranged at will; several Johnson Wedlocks in crystal goblets; tables and platforms and cages with seemingly impassable Jarrett pedestals; collapsible or compressible chess pieces, checkers, poker chips, potato chips, marbles, golf balls, baseballs, basketballs, soccer balls; ingenious items of clothing and collars and cuff links manufactured by the Magnificent Traumata; handcuffs and straitjackets . . .

As I turned from wall to wall with delight growing to delirium, Roderick merely stood behind me, arms folded, receiving my awestruck glances with a patient smile. Finally I came to a wall on which hung one small black cabinet with glass doors. Within this cabinet there lay . . .

Ten sealed decks of playing cards.

I opened this cabinet eagerly, aching to try my new hands, wrists, fingers, on them. I unwrapped cellophane from a deck and tamped the stack into one hand, immediately fanning the cards into a double spiral. With a youthful and pliant fold of skin near my thumb I pushed a single ace of spades to prominence, remembering with hallucinatory vividness the cards most likely to be chosen by audience members in any given geography, as recorded by Maskull in his immortal *Force and Suit*. I turned and presented the deck to Roderick.

"Pick a card," I said, "any card."

He stared at me intensely, almost resentfully, and his left eye opened wider than the right, presenting an expression composed at once of equal mix delight and apprehension. "Save it. There is altogether too much time."

But like a child suddenly brought home to familiar toys, I could not restrain myself. I propelled the deck in

an arc from one hand to the other, and back. I shuffled
them and cut them expertly behind my back, knowing
the arrangement had not even now been disturbed. With
my fingers I counted from the top of the precisely split
deck, and brought up a queen of hearts. "Appropriate
for your world," I said.

"Impressive legerdemain," Roderick said with a slight
shudder. He had never been able to judge my lights of
hand, or follow my instant sleights and slides and crosses.
With almost carnivorous glee I wanted to dazzle this man
who controlled so much illusion, to challenge him to a
duel.

"It's magic," I said breathlessly. "*Real* magic."

"Its charm," he said in a subdued and musing voice,
"lies in its simplicity and its antiquity." He seemed doubt-
ful, and rested his chin on the tip of an index finger. "Still,
I insist you need to rest, to prepare. Tomorrow . . . We will
begin, and all will be judged."

I realized he was correct. Now was not the time. I
needed to know more. It was possible, in this unreal futu-
rity, anything I might be able to accomplish with such simple props would be laughed at. Sooner expect a bird to fly
to the moon . . .

With a brief farewell, he departed, and left me alone in
the marvelous room. My heart hammered like a pecking
dove in my chest.

Nowhere in this room, unique I supposed in all the
rooms of the house of Roderick Escher, did there creep or
coat or insinuate any of the pale light-guiding threads or
fibers. I was alone and unwatched, unconnected to any
hungry external beings, be they kings or slaves . . .

I fancied I was Roderick's secret.

I undressed and showered. The bathroom filled with
steam, and I inhaled its warm moistness, returning again to

the euphoria I had experienced upon my arrival. I toweled and picked up a thick terry cloth robe, examining the sleeves and pockets. In a table drawer I found needle and many colors of thread, and marveled at Roderick's thoroughness.

Far too restless and exalted for sleep, I began to sew hooks and loops and pockets into the robe, for practice, and then into my suit of clothes. My fingers worked furiously, as agile as they had ever been in my prime.

I turned to the laden walls and spun through a dozen displays before finding clamps, tack, glue, brads, wire, springs, card indexes, and other necessities. I altered the suit for fit as well as fittings. I had long centuries ago learned to be a tailor and seamstress, as well as a forger and engineer.

There were no windows, no clocks, no way to learn the time of evening, if evening it actually was. I might have spent days of objective time in my obsessive labors. It did not matter here; I was not disturbed and did not rest until I became so tired I could hardly stand or clasp a needle or bend a wire.

I removed the robe, climbed into the small, comfortable bed, and immediately fell into deep slumber.

I know not how many minutes or hours, or perhaps years later, I felt a touch on my face and jerked abruptly to consciousness. My eyes burned, but my nerves pulsed as if I had just drunk a dozen cups of black coffee. In the darkened room (had I turned off any lights? there were no lights to control!) I saw a whitish shape, tall and blurred. Now came to me a supreme supernatural dread, and I was immediately drenched with sweat. I rubbed my eyes to clear them.

"Who's there?" I cried.

"It is I, Maja," the form said in a thrilling contralto.

"Who?" I asked, my voice breaking, for I only half

remembered my circumstances. I did not know what might face me in this unknown place and time.

"I am Roderick's sister," she said, and came closer, her face entering a sourceless, nacreous spot of glow. I beheld a woman of extraordinary character, her countenance as thin as the faces of the women in Klimt's darker paintings, her eyes as large as Roderick's, and of like cast and color. I could have sworn her high twin-lobed forehead would have blemished her femininity, had it been described so to me, yet it did not.

"What do you want?" I asked, my heart slowing its staccato beat. I felt no danger from her, only a ruinous sadness.

"Do not do this thing," she warned, eyes intent on mine. I could not break that gaze, so frightened and yet so strong. "It is a change too drastic for the Eschers, a breach, a leap to disaster. Roderick wishes our doom, but he does not know what he does."

"Why would he wish to die?"

This she did not answer, but instead leaned forward and whispered to me, "He believes we *can* die. That is his madness. He has told me to go before, to prove certain theories."

"And you have agreed—to die?"

She nodded, eyes fixed on mine, drawing me in as if to the doors of her soul. In her there was more of the cadaver already than a living woman, yet she seemed sadly, infinitely beautiful. Her beauty was that of a guttering candle flame. The fire of her eyes was a fraction of that of Roderick's, and her body, as a taper, might supply only a few minutes more of the fuel of life. Unlike the brown women, Cant and Dont, who were unreal yet seemed solid and healthy, she was all too real, and I could have blown her away with a weak breath. "I am his twin. He took me from his mind, shaped me to equal him, in all but will. I have no will of my own. I obey him."

"He made his own sister a slave?"

"It is done that way here. We may create versions of our self that do not possess a legal existence."

"How bitter!" I exclaimed.

"Oh, I may protest, may try to show him my love by directing his will with persuasion. But he is stronger, and I do whatever he tells me. Now, it is his wish I try again to die. I only hope this time I might succeed."

Behind her I saw the approach of the solicitous Dr. Ont. The doctor took Roderick's sister by one skeletal hand, pushed her lips close to Maja's almost translucent ear, and murmured words in a tongue I could not understand. Maja's head fell to one side, and it seemed she might collapse. Dr. Ont supported her, and they withdrew from the room.

I felt at once a heavy swell of resentment, and a commensurate surge of bluster. "How dare she come here, smelling of death. I've left *death* behind." But in my declining terror, I was exaggerating. Roderick's sister, Maja, had had no smell at all.

She had smelled no more intensely than a matching volume of empty air.

I felt I slept only a few minutes, yet when Roderick's voice boomed into my room, waking me, I was completely refreshed, confident, ready for any challenge. *I* was no slave of Roderick Escher. "Dear friend—have you made the necessary preparations?" he asked. I looked around for his presence, but he was not there, only his voice.

"I'm ready," I said.

"Do you understand your challenge?"

"Better than ever," I said. I had the confidence of an innocent child, thinking tigers are simply large cats; even the appearance during the night of Maja Escher held no awe for me.

"Good. Then eat hearty and build up your strength."

Roderick did not enter my room, but breakfast appeared on a table within the room. The apparatus I had chosen the night before lay beside the plates of warm vegetables, broth, breads. I put on my robe, manifested an ace of spades in my right hand, and threw it at the stack of toast, piercing the top slice. The card stuck out of the toast upright. I lifted the card, retrieving the toast with it, and took a bite, chewing with a broad smile. All my fears of the day before (if indeed a day had passed) had faded. I had never in my first life felt so confident before going onstage, or beginning a performance.

As I ate, I wondered at the lack of all meat. Had the world's inhabitants suddenly and humanely ended the slaughter of innocent animals? Or did they simply distance themselves from the carnal, in sympathy, as most of them had assumed the character of frozen meat in chilly refrigerators?

Were there any animals left to eat?

In truth, what did I know about Roderick's brave civilization? Nothing. He had not prepared me or informed me any further. Yet my confidence did not fade. I felt instinctively the challenge that Roderick was about to offer—to compare the overwhelming and undeniable magic of this time, against my own simple legerdemain, as Roderick had called it.

Roderick visited me in person as I finished my breakfast.

"Did you enjoy yourself?" he asked as he entered through the door. His arm rose slowly to indicate the changeable wall of cases, now frozen to the apparatus associated with cards. He walked over to the glass case, opened it, and removed a reel manufactured by my inspiration,

Cardini, who had died just after my first birth, but whose effects I had learned by heart. "Did you know," Roderick said, holding the tiny reel in his palm, "that a century ago, children played with dollhouses indistinguishable from the real? Little automata going about their lives, using tools perfect for their scale, living dolls sitting on furniture accurate in every way . . . And these houses were so cheap they were made available to the poorest of the poor?"

"I didn't know that," I said.

Roderick smiled at me, and for the first time on this, my second day in my new life, I felt a narrow chilliness behind my eyes, a suspicion of the unforeseen.

"Yet we have advanced beyond that time as gods march beyond ants," he said. "All pleasures available at will. Every nerve and region within the brain—and without!—charted, and their affects explored in endless variations. Whole societies devoted to pain from injuries impossible in all past experience, to the ghostlike exertion of an infinite combination of muscles in creatures the size of planets, to the social and sexual dalliances of phantoms conjured from histories and times and places that never were."

"Remarkable," I said stiffly.

"An audience of such intense discernment and sophistication that nothing surprises them, nothing arouses their childlike amazement, for they have never *been* children!"

"Extraordinary," I said with some pique. Did he wish for my defeat, my failure, to enjoy some petty triumph over an inferior? I steeled myself against his words, as I might have armored against the complaints of an older and better magician, criticizing my fledgling efforts.

"There are audiences of such size that they dwarf all of the Earth's past populations," he added.

I saw my bed fold into itself until it vanished into a corner. The wall of cases shrank into a narrow box the size of a book, leaving me with only the table and the apparatus I had chosen the night before.

"Prepare, Robert," he said. "The curtain rises soon."

Then his voice took on a shadowed depth, betraying a mix of emotions I could not comprehend, relief mixed with heavy grief and even guilt, and something else beyond my poor, unembellished range. "Dr. Ont came to me last night. Maja has succumbed. My sister is no more. Ont certifies that she has truly died. She has even begun to decay."

"I'm sorry," I said.

"It's a triumph," he said quietly. "She goes before . . ."

I put on the suit I had tailored and adjusted, and inwardly smiled at its close fit and how it flattered my pudgy form. I had never been handsome, had always lacked the charms of magicians who combined grace and artistry with physical beauty. I compensated by simply being better, faster, and more ingenious.

Roderick looked around the room. Fibers grew from the floor, climbing the walls like mold, until they shrouded everything but me and my table and cards. I seemed surrounded by a forest of fungal tendrils, glowing like swarms of fireflies.

"Billions of receptors, hooked into webs and matrices and nets reaching around the Earth," Roderick said. "Tiny little eyes like stars that have replaced any desire to leave and venture out to real stars, to other worlds. We have our own interior infinities to explore."

I made my final arrangements, and stood in the center of the lights, the tendrils. "Tell me when I'm to begin."

"We've already begun, except for the time you've spent in this room," Roderick said. "Even Maja's protests to me, and her death, have been watched and absorbed. I've used the drama of my own war to stay at the top of the ratings, my preparations and agonizing. Even the five, the antitheticals—I have made them part of this!"

The same nacreous light that had bathed Maja's face now surrounded me, and the fibers arranged themselves with a sound like the motion of a horde of chitinous sea creatures rubbing their claws.

Roderick backed away until he stood in shadow, then lifted his hand, giving me my cue.

I had never had such a draw in my life—nor felt so alone. But was this really so different from appearing on television? I had done that often enough.

"Once upon a time," I said, focusing ahead of me at no space in particular, and smiling confidently, "a young man on a luxury cruise was caught in a horrible shipwreck, stranded on a desert island with nobody and nothing but a crate of food and water, and a crate of unopened packs of playing cards."

I brought out a deck of cards and peeled away the plastic. "I was that young man. I knew nothing of the magical arts, but in three solitary years I taught myself thousands of manipulations and passes and motions, until I felt I could fool even myself at times. And how was this done? How does a magician, knowing all the methods behind his effects, come to believe in magic?"

I swallowed a lump in my throat and leaped into the abyss.

"In those three years, I learned to make cards *confess*." I riffled the deck of cards and formed a rippling mouth, and with one finger strummed the edges.

"We spoke to each other," the cards said in a breathless stringy voice. "And Cardino taught us all we know."

I produced another deck, opened it with one hand, removed the cards and arranged them on my palm, and made them speak as well, in a *female* voice: "And we taught him all that we know."

I squeezed both decks up in a double arc and caught them in opposite hands. From the top of each deck I produced a queen of hearts, and clamped the two cards together in my teeth. "I learned the secrets of royalty," I said through clenched teeth. Holding the decks in one hand, separated by my pointing finger, I plucked the cards from between my teeth and revealed them as two jacks. "The knaves whispered to me of court intrigues, and the kings and queens taught me the secrets of their royal numbers."

In my hands, the two cards quickly became a pair of threes, then fives, then sevens, then nines, and then queens again. "Finally, I was rescued." I riffled the decks together, blowing through them to make the sound of a ship's horn. "And returned to civilization. And there, I practiced my new art, my new life. And now, having returned from that island called *death*, where all magic must begin—"

I looked around me, unsure what effect my next request would have. "I call for volunteers, who wish to learn what I have learned."

The overgrown chamber whispered and lights passed among the fibrous growths like lanterns on far shores. Five figures appeared in the chambers then: Wont, Cant, Shant, Musnt, and Dont. Cant approached first, smiling her most wistful and attractive smile. "I volunteer," she said.

Roderick, standing in the background, his feet almost rooted to the floor by thick cables of fiber, lifted his hands in overt approval. Why encourage those he loathed—those who shackled him with so many strictures?

Was he flaunting the strength of his chains, like Houdini?

"Am I a physical person?" I asked Cant, dismissing all questions from my thoughts.

"Yes," she said. "Very."

"Am I the last untouched human on this world?"

"In this house, to be sure."

"Do I have a connection with any of the external powers that can make things appear and disappear, make illusions by wish alone?"

"You do not subscribe to any services," Cant said. "This we guarantee, as antitheticals."

I hesitated just a moment, and then took her hand. She felt solid enough—like real flesh. "Are *you* real?" I asked.

"Who can say?" she replied.

"Is your form solid enough to forgo false illusions, illusions of will isolated from body?"

"I can do that, and guarantee it," Cant said. Her companions took attitudes of rapt attention.

"It is guaranteed," they said as one.

I began to get some sense of what their function was then, and how they constrained Roderick. What would they do to constrain me?

"If I told you there were cards rolled up in your ears, what would you say?"

"All things are possible," Cant said musically, "but for you, that is not possible."

I held my hand up to her ear and drew out a rolled-up card, making sure to tap the auricle and the opening to the canal. She reacted with some puzzlement, then delight.

"You have doubtless been told that in the past, illusion was possible only through tricks. Tell me, then—how do I do such tricks?"

"Concealment," Cant said, prettily nonplussed.

I showed her my hands, which were empty, then removed my coat, dropping it to the floor, and rolled up my sleeves. I pulled another card from her other ear, unrolled it, showing it to be ruined as a playing card, then converted it to a cigarette by pushing it through my fist.

"Everyone can do that," Cant said, her smile fading. "But you—"

"*I can't do such things,*" I said with a note of triumph. "I am an atavism, an innocent, an anachronic . . . A *lich.*" I held out the cigarette. "Does anybody smoke anymore?" I asked. The five did not speak. Roderick shook his head in the shadows. "I didn't think so. King Nerve needs no chemical stimulants. All drugs are electronic. There is no one else on this planet—or in this house, at least—who can make the world dance, the *real* world. Except me—and I was taught by the cards."

The remaining antitheticals came forward. Musnt, as it happened, unknowingly carried a deck of cards in the pocket of his solid but unreal dinner jacket. Producing a fountain pen, I had him mark his name on the edge of the deck, grateful that these phantoms could still write, and blew upon the ink to help it dry. "These cards have friends all over the world, and they tell tales. Have you ever heard cards whisper?" I patted the deck firmly into his hands. "Hold these. Don't let them go anywhere." I borrowed his jacket and put it on Dont, helping her into the sleeves with courtesy centuries out of date. They hung over her hands.

"Hold up your deck of cards, please," I said to Musnt. He lifted the cards, his face betraying anticipation. I was grateful for small favors.

"I believe you have a set of pockets on the outside of your jacket," I told Dont. "Investigate them, please."

She reached into the pockets and removed two cellophane-wrapped decks of cards.

"Sneaky devils, these cards. They go anywhere and everywhere, and listen to our most intimate words. You have to be discreet around playing cards. Open the decks, please."

She pulled the cellophane from one deck. On the edge of the deck was the awkward scrawl of Musnt, written in fountain pen. Musnt immediately looked at his deck. The edges were blank.

Fibers formed curious worms and squirmed closer, lights pulsing.

"The other deck, now," I told Dont. She unwrapped the second deck, and there, in fountain pen, was written, *Wont.*

"Hand the deck to the person whose name is written on the side," I said. She passed the deck to Wont.

"Write on the other side your name and any number," I told Wont, giving him the pen. "And then, on a card within the deck, write the name of anybody in this room—in big, sloppy, wet letters. Show the card to everybody *except* me, and put it within the deck and press the deck together firmly."

He did this.

"Now give the deck to Cant."

He passed the deck to her. "How many decks do you carry now?" I asked. She reached into her pockets and found two more decks, which she handed to me, keeping Wont's deck with his name written on it.

"Now find the card Wont has written on, and the card immediately next to it, smeared with the wet ink from that card. Write your name on the face of that card, and another number. Show them to everybody but me."

She did so.

"How many decks do we all have now?" I asked.

I went among them, counting the decks presently in circulation—five. I redistributed the decks one to each of the five Negatives.

"The cards have told each other all about you, and you

have no secrets. But I am the master of the cards—and from *me* not even the cards have secrets!"

I reached behind their ears, one by one, and pulled the cards that had been written on, with the names Cant, Musnt, Dont, and Wont. "The gossip of the cards goes full circle," I said. "Show us your decks!"

On the top of each deck, the cards bearing the suit and number of the written-on cards—for all had been number cards—appeared, bearing a newly written number, and a new name—*Cardino*.

The Negatives seemed befuddled. They showed the cards to each other and to the questing fibers.

They had forgotten the art of applause, and the fibers were silent, but no applause was necessary.

"How is this done?" Musnt asked. "You must tell . . ."

I pitied them, just as a caveman might pity a city slicker who has lost the art of flint knapping. From the beginning of their lives to the present moment, they had truly fooled nobody. They had lived lives of illusion without wonder, for always they could explain how things were done—all their magic was performed by silent, subservient, electronic demiurges.

"Turn to the last card in your decks," I said. "Show me who is king."

On every one of their decks, the king of hearts was inscribed with two names. They held the cards out simultaneously. Each Negative carried a card bearing his or her name, and in larger letters, RODERICK ESCHER.

The fibers seemed to give a mighty heave. Roderick came forward, and I saw the fibers fleeing from his legs, his suit, his face and skin.

The Negatives turned to each other in confusion. Cant giggled. They compared their decks, searched them. "They're made of matter," Wont said. "They aren't false—"

"Tricks," Shant said.

"Can *you* do them?" Wont asked.

"In an instant," Shant said. Cards fluttered down around him, twisted, formed a tall mannequin, and danced around us all. The fibers withdrew from around him as if singed by flames.

"Not the point," Roderick said, free of fibers now. "You can do anything you want, but you *subscribe*. Cardino does these things by himself, alone."

The fibers bunched around my feet. Shant made his cards and the mannequin vanish. "How?" he asked, shrugging.

"Skill," Roderick said.

"Skill of the body," Shant said haughtily. "Who needs that?"

"Self-discipline, training, years of concentrated effort," Roderick said. "Isn't that right, Cardino?"

"Yes," I said, the confidence of my performance fading. I was caught in a game whose rules I could not understand. Roderick was using me, and I did not know why.

"Nothing any of us can experience compares to what this man does all by himself," Roderick continued.

The five froze in place for a moment. I could see some change in their structure, a momentary fluctuation in their illusory solid shapes.

Roderick lifted his arms and stared at his body. "I'm free!" he said to me in an undertone, as if confiding to a priest.

"What's all this about?" I asked.

"It's about skill and friendship and death," Roderick said.

The five began to move again. The fibers touched my shoes, the hem of my pants. Instinctively, I kicked at them, sending glowing bits scattering like sparks. They recoiled, toughened, pushed in more insistently.

"My time is ending," Roderick said. "I've done all I can, experienced all I can."

The five smiled and circled around me. "*They* favor you," Cant said, and she bent to push a wave of growing fibers toward my legs. I backed off, kicked again without effect, shouted to Roderick, "What do they want?"

"You," Roderick said. "My time is done. Maja is dead; I go to follow her."

I turned and ran from the room, sliding on the clumps of fibers, falling. The fibers lightly touched my face, felt at my cheeks, prodded my lips as if to push into my mouth, but I jumped to my feet and ran through the door. Roderick followed, and, behind him, a surge of fibers clogged the door.

Wherever I ran in the house, eager fibers grew from the walls, the floor, fell from the ceiling, like webs trying to ensnare me. Cant appeared in a twisted hallway ahead. I fell to my hands and knees, staring as the floor twisted into a corkscrew, afraid I would pitch forward into the architectural madness.

Dr. Ont appeared, shoulders dipped in failure, hands beseeching to explain. "Roderick, do not—"

"It is done!" Roderick cried.

A cold wind flowed down the hall, conveying a low moan of endless agony. Roderick helped me to my feet, his thin fingers cold even through the fabric of my suit.

"Can you feel it?" he whispered to me. "King Nerve has released me. I'm dying, Robert!" He turned to Dr. Ont. "I'm dying, and there's nothing you can do! I know all the permutations! I've experienced it all, and *I am bored. Let me die!*"

Dr. Ont stared at Roderick with an expression of infinite pity. "Your sister—"

Roderick gripped my shoulders. "We are walled in like

prisoners by the laziness of gods, all desires sated, all refinements exhausted. Let them crown the new master!"

The moaning grew louder. Behind Dr. Ont, Roderick's sister appeared, even more haggard and pale, the feeblest energy of purpose animating a husk, her dry and shrunken mouth trying to speak.

Dr. Ont stood aside as Roderick saw her. "Maja!" Roderick cried, holding up his hands to block out sight of her.

"Still alive," Dr. Ont said. "I was wrong. She cannot die. We have all forgotten how."

The five brushed past Roderick, smiling only at me.

"The House of Escher loses all support," Cant said, touching my arm lightly. "The flow is with you. The world wants you. You will teach them your experience. You will show them what it feels to be *skilled* and to have fleshly talents, to *work* and *touch* in a primal way. Roderick was absolutely correct—you are a marvel!"

I looked at Roderick, frozen in terror, and then at Maja, her eyes like pits sucking in nothing, as isolated as any corpse but still alive.

The walls shuddered around me. The fibers withdrew from the stones, and where they no longer held, cracks appeared, running in crazed patterns over the white and yellow surfaces. The tiles of the floor heaved up, the tessellations disrupted, all order scattered.

Cant took my hand and led me through the disintegrating corridors, down the shivering and swaying stairs. Behind me, the stairs buckled and crumbled, and the beams of the ceiling split and jabbed down to the floor like broken elbows. Ahead, a tide of fibers withdrew from the house like sea sucked from a cave, and above the ripping snap of tearing timbers, the rumble and slam of stone blocks falling and shattering, I heard Roderick's high, chicken-cluck shriek, the cry of an avatar driven past desperation into madness:

"No death! *No Death!* King Nerve forever!"

And his bray of laughter at the final jest revealed, all his plans cocked asunder.

The antitheticals blew me through the front door like a wind, and down the walk into the ruined garden, among the twisted and fiber-covered trees, until I was away from the house of Roderick Escher. All of his spreading distractions and entertainments, all of his chambers filled with the world's diversions, the pandering to the commonest denominators of a frozen or disembodied horde . . . the impossible and convoluted towers leaned, shuddered, and collapsed, blowing dust and splinters through the door and the windows of the first floor.

The fibers pushed from the ground, binding my feet, rising up my legs toward my trunk, feeling through my suit, probing for secrets, for solutions. I felt voices and demands in my head, petulant, childish, *Show us. Do for us. Give us.* The fibers burrowed into my flesh, with the pricks of thousands of tiny cold needles.

Cant took my arm. "You are favored," she said.

The voices picked at my thoughts, rudely invaded my memories, making crude and cruel jokes. They seemed to know nothing but expletives, arranged in no sensible order, and they applied them accompanied by demands that went beyond the obscene, demands that echoed again and again; and I saw that this new world was composed not of gods, but of mannerless children who had never faced responsibility or consequences, and whose lives were all secrecy, all privilege, conducted behind thick and impersonal walls.

Tingles shot up my hands and feet and along my spine, and I felt sparks at the very basement of my reason.

Do for us, do everything, live for us, let us feel, all new and all unique, all superlatives and all gladness and joy, and no death, no end.

My hands jerked out, holding a pack of cards, and I felt a will other than mine—a collective will—move my fingers, attempt to spread the cards into a fan. The fingers jerked and spilled the cards into the dirt, across the creeping fibers. "Get them away from me!" I cried in furious panic.

The blocks and timbers and reduced towers of the House of Escher settled with a final groaning sigh, but I pictured Roderick and Maja buried beneath its timbers, still alive.

The fibers lanced into my tongue. The voices filling my head hissed and slid and insinuated like snakes, like *worms in my living brain,* demanding *tapeworms,* asking numbing questions, prodding, prickling, insatiable.

Cant said, "You must assert yourself. They demand much, but you have so much to give—"

The fibers shoved down my throat, piercing and threading through my tissues as if to connect with every cell of my being. I clawed at my mouth, my throat, my body, trying to tug free, but the fibers were strong as steel wires, though thinner than the strands of a spider's web.

"Newness is a treasure," Musnt said, standing beside Cant. Wont and Shant and Dont joined her.

My legs buckled, but the fibers stiffened and held me like a puppet. I could not speak, could only gag, could hardly hear above the dissonant voices. *Amuse. Give all. Share all. Live all.*

"Hail to the new and masterful," Cant said worshipfully, smiling broadly, simply, innocently. Even in my terror and pain that smile seemed angelic, entrancing.

"A hundred billion people cannot be wrong," Shant

said, and touched the crown of my head with his outspread hand.

"We anoint the new Master of King Nerve," the five said as one, and I could breathe, and speak, for myself, no more.

Chin Oil

GEORGE GUTHRIDGE

Like me, Guthridge has traveled to Thailand many times, and has fallen in love with the people and the culture. This is his first story drawn from those travels.

In describing chin oil, Guthridge writes, "Carefully administered, a drop of chin oil—colorless and odorless, and so viscous it feels gelatinous—can turn someone into a love slave. An overdose causes insanity." He goes on to say that a corpse's chin oil is, ". . . literally worth its weight in gold. If injury or insanity results from someone's toying with chin oil, the offender is reborn five hundred times as a mad dog."

Read on if you dare.

–DC

Chin Oil

How aware she was of the day! Oranges like lanterns above the path that wended amid Ayutthaya's lawns. Odor of mimosa, orchid, tapioca. She even could hear the beating wings of the butterflies that followed her up from the river. Never before in this life or any other, she decided, had her senses been so acute. A day to remember.

Stonemasons and women mixing mortar stopped work on the gate and moved aside, wordless, eyes downcast, as she shuffled past, awkward in her pregnancy. How confident of her love was Lord Samut, she told herself, letting her walk to her new home alone!

Her life was just as her brother, now a soldier in the king's army, had predicted when they were children. Whenever he divided up an orange, she invariably received the last piece. He would laugh and tease her, for that told her future: *lucky in love*.

This was not as she had imagined—releasing a *Phii Tai Thang Klom* ghost and being part of a nobleman's house forever. She always felt she would marry a farmer. But in many ways the turn of events transcended her childhood dreams.

Compared to the balance of the world, what Samut asked in return for all he had given her was no more than a falling leaf. She was but a northern hill woman, a Shaw Karen, and poor even by tribal standards. Unworthy even to touch his shadow. He had given her parents a fine farm. Her brother, a place of leadership in the army. And her, more than muscular lovemaking beside the river, while moths danced in moonlight. She smiled inwardly, regardless of her fear, a hand on her belly.

She had touched more than his shadow; for had he not often told her he loved her? Samutsakorn Charhala was a man of his word, a man of god, a warrior who had helped lead the armies that again freed Siam from the Burmese. She owed him everything, and he asked so little, she assured herself. Release the ghost and live, she and the child, in his house forever.

She wished she could hurry—her knees were trembling—but castle protocol, the pregnancy, and the confines of her sarong dictated small steps. She was relieved to reach the shade beneath the lamyai trees that lined the final path. It seemed to curtain off the curious.

Then she saw Samut, his attendant holding the ever-present tasseled umbrella, and her heart thudded harder. From love, not fear, she decided.

He stopped walking toward her and, sadly smiling, looked at her as he so often did, as though she were delicate as an orchid. She lowered her eyes and head, pressed her palms together, and dipped expertly at the knee despite her belly. He returned the greeting and, taking hold of her fingertips, lifted her to her full height. The setting sun gleamed against the gems of his helmet and vest, and his sarong hugged a muscular waist. God, but she loved him! When he ran his hand down her waist-length hair, she shivered. A shocked whisper went through the crowd, only to end when Samut cast a hard eye their way.

"The day draws to a close," he said softly.

Yes, my lord, she tried to reply, but only nodded, afraid her voice would reveal her fear.

A hand on her elbow, he walked her toward the sharpened posts and teak lintels meant for his—*their*—new home. When they stopped, he seemed loath to let her go, suddenly looking awkward as an adolescent.

Daring to glance up into his downcast eyes, she saw in their sorrow the love she and her pregnancy gave him, and her courage and conviction were renewed. As she turned away, she allowed her fingertips to touch his side, the fine flesh. She descended the ladder into her new home.

At the bottom of the pit was a bed of flowers. She lay down, brought an orchid to her nose, and inhaled, trying to slow her heart. The scent reminded her of oranges.

Somewhere a toucan cawed, as if announcing sunset.

She kissed the orchid, closed her eyes, and pulled open the special seam in her sarong, exposing her distended navel. She felt as she had that first time Samut took her, she shifting her weight beneath him so he would enjoy her virginity without it impeding him. He was watching her now, she was sure, probably flanked by attendants with torches, but she feared looking up lest she see tears in his eyes. Might he later wish she had not witnessed his weakness? She could not abide hurting him.

Only when she heard the post against the pit did she look up. Five Burmese slaves were wrestling with it, aiming its point toward her belly, ready to free the ghost from deep within her womb, as custom commanded for a castle gate or noble house.

She raised and slightly parted her knees despite the sarong, as if better to assist the release. Petals fluttered down, and she saw Samut's hand above her, his wrist adorned with tattoos—*yantra* that protected him from human swords and evil spirits.

"I am yours," she whispered. "Forever."

"My love." His voice, tremulous, echoed off the walls, despite the pit's being rich and odorous earth rather than rock. "Dearest, deepest love."

As the last petal reached her, she tightened her lips and fists, trying to hold back, but when the slaves let go of the log and it pierced her belly, her scream was so shrill that the crowd drew back in terror. She never saw the young soldier who fought his way to the front and collapsed to his knees, crying, a section of orange cupped in his outstretched hands.

"I lied," he kept saying. *"Lied!"*

-1995-

On the roof of the world, amid a world of roofs, I awaken from Malee again calling me to Ayutthaya.

Instead of being among the graves where she and my son lie, I am once more on red tile beneath a smog-browned sun, a sea of smog around me. Smog chokes the city, suffocates sanity. Engines roar, horns blare. Cancer and cacophony. Each day, Bangkok traffic grows—and eats its own.

As it did, thanks to Laud, with my Malee and our beautiful boy.

The two-way radio crackles from the tiny platformed tent where I keep my things. I relegate my hatred to its sacred place within my heart and reach inside the tent for the mike.

"Soi Two off Sukhumvit," Sak says.

He has seen her ghost again.

"Roger that." Sak loves when I talk B-grade movie. "On my way."

I slip on my flip-flops, slide down the tile, grab hold of a vent pipe, spin toward the backstairs. I wish I were not camped on a sloped roof, but I was too late in the beat-the-smog game and too *farang*—foreigner—to score a flat one. I could have stayed in Malee's grocery, but after the traffic took her and Bat, and the monks threw me out of Phra Khu, I put the place up for lease. Every Lipovitan-D or UFC's Rambuton in Syrup I sold was a bitter memory, every *baht* I took in a silver teardrop.

Nor could I return to the States, where Malee's nightmares began.

"*Samut,*" *she sometimes shrieked when she awakened.* "*Why—!*"

She would lie speechless for several minutes, staring at the ceiling of our chalet but seeming to see nothing, her face and tank top wet with sweat—even though when she worked out on the Nordic Track or Soloflex she rarely perspired. I would hold her, feeling foolish at being so helpless.

So I sold my salon and we came back to Thailand, hoping her agony would end. Now she and our son are gone, the solace of chanting at Phra Khu is gone, and there is no going back—or forward. There is only death. And smog.

I trundle out my 350 from amid the others and roar from my soi—side street—and onto Sukhumvit. When Malee was alive I could not steer a cycle down a deserted straightaway, much less thread through the world's worst traffic. True expertise on a motorcycle in Bangkok depends on not caring if you survive.

I see smoke before I reach the wreck. A truck laden with chicken crates, its driver probably strung out on amphetamines and overwork, has plowed into a Toyota Corolla. Several fallen crates have burst open, and burning chickens flop around. A charred body hangs headfirst from the car, arms out like black wings. Three Ruam Katanyu corpse collectors in orange jumpsuits are using fire extinguishers, the car frothy with foam, the Katanyu van's red light blipping through the smoke. A policeman keeps a crowd in check while directing traffic, arms snapping precisely, whistle shrilling.

I have arrived too late.

Sak strolls, hands in pockets, from behind the truck. He is tall for a Thai, his height accented by the composure he emanates—his years as a monk. Above one pocket of his white shirt is embroidered THAI TOURS; over the other, POR TECK TUENG FOUNDATION. He alternates between taxiing tourists and collecting corpses, though for three thousand *baht* he will combine the occupations and send *farang* home with a *real* vacation tale.

The Ruam Katanyu collectors work smoothly, two now loading the smoldering body into the van. Like those of us in the Por Teck Tueng Foundation, with whom they compete for bodies, neither worker wears gloves, despite the possibility of burns or of being exposed to contaminated blood. A matter of pride and public scrutiny. Gloves might denote irreverence toward the dead.

"Money-grubbers," I say, watching them.

"The living must make a living," Sak replies.

He is right, of course. Mine is merely a competitor's carping; there is only one Ruam Katanyu worker I hate. I did not mean to step on the toes of Thai tradition. The two foundations, operating since the sixties, combine Buddhist and business principles, but most corpse collectors work more for spiritual merit than for money. In a city whose few ambulances often get stalled in traffic, the collectors cruise the streets, listening to police calls—ready to help the injured but to serve the dead. Assuring that the violently dead receive proper care lessens the chance they will return as vengeful ghosts, and earns collectors indulgences to improve their next life or ease the afterlife of a deceased loved one.

My wife and son did not receive that care. After three days of red tape I found them slabbed among other mangled bodies in the morgue.

My fault.

I summon my courage. "She cause the wreck?"

"Spectators say so." Sak's voice is devoid of emotion.

"Don't tell me any more."

It is so often the same. Malee is at almost every accident along this section of Sukhumvit. Drivers are distracted by a ghost woman wrapped in blue flames, bearing a crying child. I cannot stop trembling.

I close my eyes. *I am in a cocoon with Malee, legs entwined, arms around Bat. The three of us naked—safe from a world of ghosts and guilt. But then she whispers in my ear about the woman in the dreams, the one who wants to know why Samut chose her to impregnate. And kill.*

The cocoon shatters like thin glass.

"Late again, Mister John?" a too-familiar voice sarcastically addresses me.

I open my eyes to see Laud offer Sak a cigarette. Sak drags deeply and returns it, nodding his thanks. Tires and siren screeching, the van shrieks away—as if the dead don't have enough screaming!—and the driver manages fifty meters before being blocked in the snarl. The vehicle sits like a tortoise at a wall, pawing desperately, going nowhere.

"You should unpack your hair dryer and find woman's work," Laud says. "Leave the dead to us."

"Don't start it."

"Or you'll what . . . Mister *John*." A former professional kick-boxer, he eyes me insolently, his body looking muscular even in the baggy Ruam Katanyu jumpsuit.

Most of my Thai friends cannot pronounce *George*, so they use what to them is the closest English. Laud, fluent in half a dozen languages, uses my nickname for its derogatory value—as though I were just another john on a sex tour, come to spread indignity and AIDS in the Land of Smiles.

Yet it was he who proposed to Malee and took her virginity before informing her he was married—in a culture where few men of status are willing to marry a nonvirgin, regardless of her upbringing and morals.

Bat was Laud's child.

But I was Bat's father.

The monks threw me out for wanting to learn *saiyasat*—black magic.

They should have expelled me because I never learned not to hate.

"You could kill me." I make sure his eyes follow mine, and I look toward the policeman. "And he would do nothing. Nor would anyone else. Just another stupid *farang* who picked a fight with the wrong Thai."

Laud smirks, acknowledging the truth of my words, and I have to constrain myself from putting a hand on his head—the ultimate insult to a Theravada Buddhist. Do that, and he *will* hit me, and I am still too cowardly for suicide. Nor would it make me an avenging ghost; I would not be among the violently dead. Suicide involves contemplation, no matter how brief, which mitigates the violence.

Except Laud would not think of his hitting me as being my suicide. For him it would be murder. Sweet. Simple.

"Would you really want me walking Sukhumvit forever?" I ask.

The smirk fades. His eyes register neither insolence nor anger. They register nothing—he seeking to be a stone wall; and I, a tortoise.

Walking beside Malee as she burns, he knows I mean.

"We had a deal," I remind him.

"You don't pay enough." He has switched from English to Thai. "I'm upping the ante."

This part of Sukhumvit is the only place where I help collect corpses. I work not for money or merit, but to be near Malee. Laud and the other Ruam Katanyu workers had agreed to stay away—for a price. The Chinese businessmen who sponsor the foundations, and thus achieve merit without doing any collecting, approved the arrangement without knowing its real reason. In the past there were fistfights for bodies. Loss of teeth over loss of life meant loss of face. Territoriality between the two foundations, even resulting from extortion, made good business sense.

I clench my fists at my sides. Regardless of how futile—and feudal—trying to hit Laud would be.

Sak, always the mediator, steps between us, takes the cigarette from Laud, takes a drag. Laud's arrogance visibly shrinks. He is aware of Sak's background. No one touches, much less harms, a monk. *No one.*

"How much?" Sak asks.

"More than your foundation can afford."

"You didn't care about her when she was alive," I tell him. "Why *now*?"

Laud narrows his eyes toward me. "Because I care that you care."

The admission is more frightening than his physical prowess. Despite seeming carefree and priding themselves on being the world's most humble hosts, Thai men are extremely macho. For him to reveal emotions, especially to a foreigner, shows how deeply I offended him.

"Fucking *farang*. She'd have been my second wife if you hadn't showed up. "

He is wrong. Thai culture officially no longer recognizes multiple marriage. And Malee—*never*.

"No amount of money will keep me out of Sukhumvit," he adds. "Bat . . . is mine."

After quietly appraising him, Sak says, "We'll give you chin oil to stay away."

"Big deal. I can get it by the mason jar, if I want."

"This isn't some over-the-counter crap," I tell him in a hard voice.

"You think I don't have connections . . . *farang?*"

We eye one another, each waiting for the other to make a move.

"We can get chin oil from a golden child," Sak says.

"Sure you can. And in the next life I'll be king."

"You come with us when we extract it," Sak says. "Come—we'll give it to you—and then you leave this section of Sukhumvit alone. Forever."

Laud is suddenly silent. Even the traffic noise seems to still.

Though its properties vary with the age and condition of the corpse from which it is extracted, chin oil is colorless and odorless, so viscous it feels gelatinous, so slow to dilute in another liquid it would never work for spiking drinks quickly. Carefully administered, a drop can turn someone into a love slave. An overdose causes insanity.

I used to think Malee was a love slave. Or just plain crazy.

"Samut!" she'd shriek, and I would hold her until her semi-catatonia broke. *She would tell me nothing, nothing.*

"You wouldn't understand," she'd sob.

Only once, the morning after we received word that Laud was suing for custody of Bat, did she talk about the nightmares—and then in broken sentences imbued with bitterness.

"Royalty used to create Phii Tai Thang Klom—*the most*

ferocious ghosts of the violently dead. That happens when . . . when a woman's spirit combines with her child's. The nobles would impale pregnant women under tower and palace posts . . . protect the place forever. . . .

"*The Burmese sacked Ayutthaya, but Samut drove them out. The capital had to be rebuilt. . . . Many pregnant women were sacrificed . . .*

"*. . . I was among them.*"

I didn't know whether to laugh or cry—I was still too Western to understand—but when she spoke again I had my first real taste of terror.

"*I'm still impaled!*" she cried. "*After all these lifetimes!*" She shook the papers at me. "*Samut's back, too—but meaner, uglier.*"

Perhaps she was crazy. Perhaps I am. Or perhaps what is crazy is a Western world that believes earthly existence ceases with death.

Is it crazy that Thais see ghosts as natural phenomena? Or that an American wracked with grief would spend every waking moment trying to be near his dead wife and son?

No less crazy than my attempting to figure out how to destroy Laudiwisi Charhala without killing him and risk having his ghost join Malee's among the violently dead. He who, upon our return to Thailand, secretly sent her word to visit him. They would *negotiate* about the child.

The night of the fiery wreck.

He had never seen the boy he fathered, nor did he care to.

Cared only that he lost a woman to a *farang*. A hair-dresser, no less.

Each spade of sacred soil Sak and I unearth in the cemetery is heavy with hate. Buddhists believe in 136 hells. I wish I could send Laud to all of them.

It is a moonless night; Sak and I wear headlamps. Laud

scoffs when we offer one. As if his soul is such tempered steel that he sees in the dark.

"Arrogance and ingots," Sak mutters.

Laud is not listening, intent as he is on watching us dig. The graves are shallow, for the burials are temporary. Buddhist cemeteries are filled with the violently dead who might arise and kill others the same way they themselves died. The bodies are interred only until the evil spirit dissipates and relatives are safe to have the body cremated.

Sometimes the dead can be persuaded to release small amounts of essential oil through their chin.

We have come to conjure the spirit of the rarest of corpses: a dead child whose spirit is still trapped in the body and whose desiccated flesh has turned golden. The corpse's chin oil is literally worth its weight in gold.

We work carefully but quickly, knowing that if injury or insanity results from someone's toying with chin oil, the offender is reborn five hundred times as a mad dog. And being caught tampering with Ayutthaya grounds means punishment in *this* life.

We begin uncovering the golden boy—dead three months. As Laud stoops, my headlamp reflects his greedy eyes. Quivering with rage, I grip the shovel to keep from ramming it into his throat.

Earthly evil first coalesces in the lower extremities, so we leave the golden boy's bottom half buried. We sit him up and, after deeply bowing in a *wai* several times, palms pressed together and touching the forehead, we use sacred string to tie him to the aged post that marks his grave.

As we peel off the wax death mask, Laud gasps. The infant's features are crimped, the skin so golden that he looks like an idol onto which penitents press squares of gold leaf, traditional in Buddhist temples.

"He's . . . beautiful," Laud says, fumbling an amulet from

his shirt and clutching it so tightly he seems about to break its chain.

"He should be," I say. "He's my son."

Laud's face is momentarily blank. Then he moves closer, eyes filling with anger. "You bastard. You dug up my boy!"

He hits me, his hand a blur, and the next thing I know I am on my back on the ground, my T-shirt and the corpse spattered with blood. Sak is holding Laud away from me and saying, "Surely it is Buddha's will that the body never decomposed. Maybe the boy is to have great value for you in death because he was taken so early from you in life."

"Only some faggot *farang* would dig up my boy." But Laud has shifted his weight backward, his desire for golden-boy chin oil too strong for him to kill me.

"Let's continue," Sak says. "Before the police find us, and we all end up in jail."

Laud adjusts his shirt and points toward me. "Later. *After* you rebury him."

It is not the first time Sak and I have unearthed Bat, and this time we do not intend to return him to the ground. But Laud doesn't know that.

"Get on with it," Laud says. "Let's get the hell out of here."

I wipe my nose, sniff back the blood, and use a toucan's feather to brush dirt from the boy's face, careful not to let my fingers touch the skin. Sak and I circumscribe a holy circle with a second string. He motions for Laud to join us. Laud hesitantly steps inside the circle and stands looking around as if in a cloistered room. Sak and I arrange our things: Candle of Victory, eight drawings depicting holy Pali text—each set equidistant around the string—and the wide-brimmed collecting vial.

We sit cross-legged. Sak and I shine our headlamps through the darkness to make sure we are alone, and then

Sak begins to chant softly. The words rise into the night like willow wisps. The dead child seems to watch through his wrinkled, golden lids.

Halfway through the recitation, Sak's features cloud with frustration. Without opening his eyes he holds out a hand toward Laud.

"Give me the amulet," he says. "It interferes with communication."

Reluctantly Laud hands him the triangular stone and chain.

Sak kisses the stone and throws it over his shoulder into the night. Laud lurches up, scanning the darkness to see where it lands. I laugh inwardly—my rage a bomb no one will defuse.

I glance from the boy, to Malee's grave beyond, then to Sak. *Do it!*

Bat's body slumps forward, the forehead touching Sak's. Sak's hand trembles as he lights the Candle of Victory. Laud moves forward to help, but I gesture him away.

Bat's hands levitate from his sides, and he grips Sak's elbows.

Now *I* struggle to keep from helping when I shouldn't. Sak and I never anticipated really conjuring the child.

Sak accepts the spirit's presence. His trembling lessens, and he maneuvers the vial and lit candle beneath Bat's chin.

As Sak chants, clear liquid drools from the chin into the test tube. I look at Laud; his eyes betray his greed. Sak shifts position, as if to block Laud from disturbing the process. The drool becomes a small but steady stream.

The oil dies to a dribble, then stops, and Sak hands me the vial, which I cork. Laud grabs it.

Sak moves his head away from Bat's, places the candle beneath the boy's hands to release the grip, and the arms fall. Only the strength of the string holds up the body.

"We'll finish here," I tell Laud. "Go."

He eyes me suspiciously. "You see he gets taken care of. Properly."

"Of course."

"I wouldn't want someone . . ."

"Cutting into your monopoly?"

"Especially not you," he says, "Not anyone."

"Wouldn't think of it. But there'll be no second time for you, either."

"Makes it all the more valuable." He lifts the vial into the glow of my headlamp, lips pursed in satisfaction. "I fucked the living shit out of her, you know," he says in English. "The night she died."

"The hell you did. She was on her way *to* your place."

Countering his ugliness makes me feel ugly, fills me with revulsion and greater guilt. There was a time, Malee once told me, when Laud was quick with *pak wan*—sweet mouth . . . flattery. But his interest in her was lust, not love. Now, jealousy has displaced the lust.

"Well, I would have fucked her, had she arrived." His face and voice have not changed expression. "We both know that . . . *farang*."

"She had Bat with her. With him there she wouldn't have touched you no matter what you offered. She would have given him up first."

But why, I ask myself, had I not realized where she was going? I had seen Bat's papers too many times not to know.

Laud snorts. "So you've got it all figured. You take me for a fool." He holds the vial tauntingly in front of me. "I know why you're giving me this. It's not a bribe. You wanted me here. You wanted *this* to possess me once I left the circle."

He steps outside the string and uncorks the vial.

I envision a vapor swirling up and choking his neck

like a python, but I know the oil is a low-power variety
Sak purchased from the Tiger Monk shop in Thonburi—
the extraction from Bat merely parlor magic.

"I could drink it," Laud threatens, "and it wouldn't
affect me. I'm protected!"

He recorks the vial and pulls up his sleeve. The intricate
geometry of his newest protective *yantra* tattoos is crusted
with scab.

"Took out a little insurance, asshole. Just in case you
really were digging up a golden boy."

Ever since my training at Phra Khu, I am calm, logical,
articulate when I am angriest. I smile a lot.

"And we knew you'd get new *yantras*," I say in a measured voice, "and that you always use that artist on Soi Si
Bamphen. They say his tattoos can stop a knife. I've seen
him test it."

"This is one of his finest designs." Laud is admiring his
wrist. "Shows my power, affording someone like him."

"He can be bribed, I'm told."

"Everyone has a price. How do you think I get him to
give me his best?"

"I paid him to use the needles I gave him, Laud—
infected needles."

For a moment we stare silently at each other. Then he
blanches.

"I knew that something as power-charged as a golden
child would assure your visiting the tattoo artist." I smile.
"Killing you would put you with Malee in the afterlife.
But not if you died by suicide—or sickness."

His kick snaps beneath my head and I feel my shoulders
wrench as I hit the ground. He leans over, hawks deeply,
drools spit into my eyes.

"You think you've infected me? I'll return the favor.
Some guys I know go both ways, my friend—and they're

not nice people. What you *farang* call 'rough trade.' They may not be infected—but they'll make sure you end up that way. We'll die together, Mister *John*."

"I'm not . . . gay," I gasp.

"You will be when they're through with you."

Backing away, he looks around tensely, as wary of the golden boy as of the possibility of my having a gun. He is at the edge of the circle of light and Sak has turned his back to him, busy replacing the wax mask onto Bat's face, when he slowly lifts the vial again and studies it.

Glowering even deeper than before, he strides toward the post, shoves Sak aside, and grabs the mask.

Bat's features are now streaked with discolor rather than being evenly golden-sheened. One of my finer efforts: gold-highlighted evening foundation followed by Shiseido bronzing gel, topped with bronze shimmer facial powder.

Laud wipes his fingers across Bat's cheeks, revealing charred skin, and slaps the mask back down. He crosses to me and kneels, eyes on fire. "I sell this shit"—he sticks the tube against my nose—"and people find out it's not what I claim it is, I lose face. Not to mention my bankroll."

Stooping, Sak gently puts a hand on Laud's shoulder.

Laud jabs with an elbow. As Sak drops, clutching his guts, groaning, Laud grips my T-shirt collar and pulls my head up. "Just what did you hope to prove!"

"That I can get to you . . . somehow . . . no matter what . . . you do."

"Not if you're nuts, you won't. Not if you're a goddamn basket case."

He jams the test tube into my mouth. I sputter and slam my fists against the sides of his head. Then I choke, and oil oozes down my throat.

They say chin oil clogs veins and clings to organs so steadfastly an exorcist may die trying to remove it. It courses through me in seconds. My mouth and esophagus flame, and hot pressure pulses behind my eyes. My hips begin involuntarily heaving, my penis is a thermometer about to burst. My testicles are red coals.

"Malee!" I call out.

"My friends will love having you," I hear Laud say, but I no longer see him. Malee is in my arms. We make love with a passion beyond even that of our honeymoon, she crying out not from nightmares but in abandon. Her hips are against mine, lips against mine—the taste and smell of oranges.

Somewhere I hear Laud scream.

I open my eyes briefly—through delirium I see him slumped against the post that marks Bat's and Malee's graves. He is staring at his crotch—his pants stained with blood.

I do not live on the roof any longer. Sak hooked up one of those air filters the Japanese build here but claim as their own, and has taken over the grocery. It disgusts me when he feeds me, but I like to watch him work with customers—always the mediator.

The store is open-air front, and I sit all day on the bench at the small marble table, my back against the wall. Customers and passersby wave and say "Hello, George" as best they can, and on days when the chin oil does not swathe me in dreams, I sometimes manage to smile. No one calls me "John" anymore. Sak must have said something.

I often wonder what became of Laud. Sak says he was carted off to the hospital and then to jail after the police found him by Bat's body. Supposedly he sits staring at his crotch night and day, whimpering about his missing genitals. It can't be pleasant for the other prisoners, given the overcrowded conditions.

Sometimes I hear him howling through five hundred futures.

It is not how I wanted things. I lied about the tattoo needles. I only wanted to make Laud realize there were ways we could get to him if we wished. There are always ways.

I don't know what seized him that night. Sak trundled me away before the police arrived. Was there power or memory in the post that marked the graves? Did Bat and Malee combine into a *Phii Tai Thang Klom?* Had they somehow called up a ghost from the past?

Malee asked me once: *Can a ghost be reincarnated?*

She wanted to be buried at Ayutthaya should anything happen to her. I think she sensed her time was coming— the Thais and their awarenesses—and she wished to meet former selves . . . but worried about former spirits.

When the sun clears the building tops and shines through the smog, I bask in the light and think about Malee. What future lives will she have? To the outside world I appear mindless, looking as if through unseeing eyes, but behind the invalid's wall the chin oil created, my days are dreams.

We drive toward Ko Chang, the languid island to the southeast, where I plan to ask her to marry me. I peel an orange. We share the sections, me feeding her; she dares not take her hands from the wheel.

"They say love binds souls for eternity," she tells me. "Only personalities and relationships change."

She laughs when I offer her the last section, for she knows I often cheat so she gets what she wants.

for Noi

I love you

Crossing into the Empire

ROBERT SILVERBERG

I am writing this while on tour. As a matter of fact, right now I'm in Nashville, Tennessee. Tomorrow I'll be in Memphis. Yesterday I was in LA. With a schedule like that, you can understand how cities seem to overlay themselves in my mind.

In the universe that Robert Silverberg created for this anthology, that sense is taken a step further, as a city from the distant past visits modern Chicago, for a little while.

—DC

Crossing into the Empire

MULREANY IS STILL ASLEEP when the Empire makes its midyear reappearance, a bit ahead of schedule. It was due to show up in Chicago on the afternoon of June 24, somewhere between five and six o'clock, and here it is only eight goddamned o'clock in the morning on the twenty-third and the phone is squalling and it's Anderson on the line to say, "Well, I can't exactly tell you why, boss, but it's back here already, over on the Near West Side. The eastern border runs along Blue Island Avenue, and up as far north as the Eisenhower Expressway, practically. Duplessis says that this time it's going to be a fifty-two-hour visitation, plus or minus ninety minutes."

Dazzling summer sunlight floods Mulreany's bedroom, high up above the lake. He hates being awake at this hour. Blinking, grimacing, he says, "If Duplessis missed the time of arrival by a day and a half, how the hell can he be so sure about the visitation length? Sometimes I think Duplessis is full of shit. —Which Empire is it, anyway? What are the towers in the Forum like?"

"The big square pointy-topped pink one is there, with two slender ones flanking it, dark stone, golden domes," Anderson says.

"Basil III, most likely."

"You're the man who'd know, boss. How soon do we go across?"

"It's eight in the morning, Stu."

"Jesus, we've only got the fifty-two hours, and then there won't be another chance until Christmas. Fifty-one and a half, by now. Everything's packed and ready to go whenever you are."

"Come get me at half past nine."

"What about nine sharp?" Anderson asks hopefully.

"I need some time to shower and get my costume on, if that's all right with you," Mulreany says. "Half past nine."

It's the Empire of Basil III this time, no question about that. What has arrived is the capital city from the water-front all the way back to the Walls of Artabanus and even a little strip of the Byzantine Quarter beyond—the entire magnificent metropolis, that great antique city of a hundred palaces and five hundred temples and mosques, green parks and leafy promenades, shining stone obelisks and eye-dazzling colonnades. The Caspian Sea side of the city lines up precisely along South Blue Island Avenue, with the wharves and piers of the city harbor high and dry, jutting from the eastern side of the street. The longest piers reach a couple of blocks beyond Blue Island where it crosses Polk, stretching almost to the southbound lanes of the Dan Ryan Expressway, which seems to be the absolute boundary of the materialization zone. A bunch of fishing boats and what looks like an imperial barge have been taken along for the ride this time, and sit forlornly beached right at the zone's flickering edge, cut neatly in half, their sterns visible here in Chicago but their bows still back in the twelfth century. The whole interface line is bright with the customary shimmering glow. You could walk around the outside edge of the interface and find yourself in the Near West Side, which has been intruded upon but not harmed. Or you could go straight ahead into that glowing field of light and step across the boundary into the capital of the Empire.

One glance and Mulreany has no doubt that the version of the capital that has arrived on this trip is the twelfth-century one. The two golden-domed towers of black basalt that Basil III erected to mark the twentieth anniversary of his accession are visible high above the Forum on either side of the pink marble Tower of Nicholas IX, but there's no sign of the gigantic hexagonal Cathedral of All the Gods that Basil's nephew and successor, Simeon II, will eventually build on what is presently the site of the camel market. So Mulreany can date the manifestation of the Empire that he is looking at now very precisely to the period between 1150 and 1185. Which is good news, not only because that was one of the richest periods of the Empire's long history, making today's trading possibilities especially promising, but also because the Empire of the time of Basil III turns up here more often than that of any other era, and Mulreany knows his way around Basil's capital almost like a native. Considering the risks involved, he prefers to be in familiar territory when he's doing business over there.

The usual enormous crowd is lined up along the interface, gawking goggle-eyed at the medieval city across the way. "You'd think the dopey bastards had never seen the Empire get here before," Mulreany mutters, as he and Anderson clamber out of the limo and head for the police barricade. The usual murmuring goes up from the onlookers at the sight of them in their working clothes. Mulreany, as the front man in this enterprise, has outfitted himself elegantly in a tight-sleeved, close-fitting knee-length tunic of green silk piped with scarlet brocade, turquoise hose, and soft leather boots in the Persian style.

On his head he wears a stiff and lofty pyramid-shaped hat of Turkish design, on his left hip a long curving dagger in an elaborately chased silver sheath. Anderson, as befits his lesser status, is more simply garbed in an old-fashioned flowing tunic of pale muslin, baggy blue trousers, and sandals; his headgear is a white bonnet tied by a red ribbon. These are the clothes of a merchant of late imperial times and his amanuensis, nothing unusual over there, but pretty gaudy stuff to see on a Chicago street, and they draw plenty of attention.

Duplessis, Schmidt, and Kulikowski wait by the barricade, gabbing with a couple of the cops. Schmidt has a short woolen tunic on, like the porter he is supposed to be; he is toting the trading merchandise, two bulging burlap bags. Neither Duplessis nor Kulikowski is in costume. They won't be going across. They're antiquities dealers; what they do is peddle the goodies that Mulreany and his two assistants bring back from their ventures into the Empire. They don't ever put their own necks on the line over there.

Duplessis is fidgeting around, the way he always does, looking at his watch every ten seconds or so. "About time you got here, Mike," he tells Mulreany. "The clock is ticking-ticking-ticking."

"Ticking so fast the Empire showed up a day and a half early, didn't it?" Mulreany says sourly. "You screwed up the calculation a little, eh?"

"Christ, man! It's never all that precise, and you know it. We've got a lot of complicated factors to take into account. The equinoctial precession—the whole sidereal element—the problem of topological displacement—listen, Mike, I do my best. It gets here every six months, give or take a couple of days, that's all we can figure. There's no way I can tell you to the split second when it's going to—"

"What about the calculation of when it leaves again? Suppose you miss that one by a factor of a couple of days, too?"

"No," Duplessis says. "No chance. The math's perfectly clear: This is a two-day visitation. Look, stop worrying, Mike. You sneak across, you do your business, you come back late tomorrow afternoon. You're just grouchy because you don't like getting up this early."

"And you ought to start moving," Kulikowski tells him. "Waxman and Gross went across an hour ago. There's Davidson about to cross over down by Roosevelt, and here comes McNeill."

Mulreany nods. Competitors, yes, moving in on all sides. The Empire's already been in for a couple of hours; most of the licensed crossers are probably there by now. But what the hell: there's plenty for everybody. "You got the coins?" he asks.

Kulikowski hands Mulreany a jingling velvet purse: some walking-around money. He shakes a few of the coins out into his palm. The Emperor Basil's broad big-nosed face looks up at him from the shiny obverse of a gold nomisma. There are a couple of little silver argentei from the time of Casimir and a few thick, impressive copper sesterces showing the hooded profile of Empress Juliana.

Impatiently Kulikowski says, "What do you think, Mike, I'd give you the wrong ones? Nothing there's later than Basil III. Nothing earlier than the Peloponnesian Dynasty." Passing false money, or obsolete money that has been withdrawn from circulation by imperial decree, is a serious mercantile crime over there, punishable by mutilation for the first offense, by death for the second. There are no decrees about passing money of emperors yet to be born, naturally. But that would be stupid as well as dangerous.

"Come on, Mike," Duplessis says. "Time's wasting. Go on in."

"How long did you say I can stay?"

"Like I told you. Almost until sundown tomorrow."

"That long? You sure?"

"You think it does me any good if you get stranded over there?" Duplessis says. "Trust me. I tell you you've got until sundown, you've got until sundown. Go on, now. Will you get going, for Christ's sake?"

There's no need for Mulreany to show his transit license. The police know all the licensed border-crossers. Only about two dozen people have the right combination of skills—the knowledge of the Empire's language and customs, the knack of doing business in a medieval country, the willingness to take the risks involved in making the crossing. The risks are big, and crossers don't always come back. The Empire's official attitude toward the merchants who come over from Chicago is that they are sorcerers of some kind, and the penalty for sorcery is public beheading, so you have to keep a low profile as you do your business. Then, too, there's the chance of catching some archaic disease that's unknown and incurable in the modern era, or simply screwing up your timing and getting stuck over there in the Empire when it pops back to its own period of history. There are other odd little one-in-a-thousand glitch possibilities also. You have to have the intellectual equipment of a college professor plus the gall of a bank robber to make a successful living as a crosser.

The easiest place to enter today, according to Kulikowski, is the corner of Blue Island and Taylor. The imperial city is only about four feet above Chicago street level there, and Kulikowski has brought along a plank that he sets up as a little bridge to carry them up the slight grade. Mulreany leads the way; Anderson follows, and Schmidt brings up the rear, toting the two bags of trade goods. As they pass through the eerie yellow glow of the interface Mulreany glances back at Duplessis and Kulikowski, who are beginning to fade from view. He grins, winks, gives them the upturned thumb. Another couple of steps and Chicago disappears altogether, nothing visible now to the rear except the golden flicker, opaque when seen from this side, that marks the border of the materialization zone. They are in the Empire, now. Halfway across the planet and nine centuries ago in time, waltzing once more into the glittering capital city of the powerful realm that was the great rival of the Byzantines and the Turks for the domination of the medieval world.

Can of corn, he tells himself.

In today, out tomorrow, another ten or twenty million bucks' worth of highly desirable and readily salable treasures in the bag.

The imperial barge—its back half, anyway—is just on their left as they come up the ramp. Its hull bears the royal crest and part of an inscription testifying to the greatness of the Emperor. Lounging alongside it with their backs to the interface glow are half a dozen rough-looking members of the Bulgarian Guard, the Emperor's crack private militia. Bad news right at the outset. They give Mulreany and his companions black menacing glances.

"Nasty bastards," Anderson murmurs. "They going to be difficult, you think?"

"Nah. Just practicing looking tough," says Mulreany. "We stay cool, and we'll be okay." Staying cool means telling yourself that you are simply an innocent merchant from a distant land who happens to be here at this unusual time purely by coincidence, and never showing a smidgeon of uneasiness. "But keep close to your gun, all the same."

"Right." Anderson slips his hand under his tunic. Both he and Schmidt are armed. Mulreany isn't. He never is.

He figures they'll get past the guardsmen okay. The Bulgars are a wild and unpredictable bunch, but Mulreany knows that nobody over here wants to go out of his way to find trouble at a time when the weird golden light in the sky is shining, not even the Bulgars, because when the light appears and everything surrounding the capital disappears from the view of its inhabitants it means that the powers of sorcery are at work again. Events like this have been going on for eight hundred years in this city, and everyone understands by now that during one of the sorcery-times there's a fair possibility that some stranger you try to hassle may come right back at you and hit you with very mighty mojo indeed. It's been known to happen.

This is something like Mulreany's twenty-fifth crossing—he doesn't keep count, but he doesn't miss an Empire appearance, and he's been a licensed crosser for about a dozen years—and he knows his way around town as well as anybody in the trade. The big boulevard that runs along the shore parallel to the wharves is the Street of the Eastern Sun, which leads to the Plaza of the Customs-Brokers, from which five long streets radiate into different parts of the city: the Street of Persians, the Street of Turks, the Street of Romans, the Street of Jews, and the Street of Thieves. There are no Jews to be found on the Street of Jews or anywhere else in the capital, not since the Edict of Thyarodes VII, but most of the best metalworkers and jewelers and ivory-carvers have shops in the quadrant between the Street of Jews and the Street of Thieves, so it's in that section that Mulreany will make his headquarters while he's here.

Plenty of citizens are milling around in the Plaza of the Customs-Brokers, which is one of the city's big gathering places. Mulreany hears them chattering in a whole bouill- abaisse of languages. Greek is the Empire's official tongue, but Mulreany can also make out Latin, Persian, Turkish, Arabic, a Slavic dialect, and something that sounds a little like Swedish. Nobody is very upset by what has happened to the city. They've all had experience with this sort of thing before, and all of them are aware that it's just a tem- porary thing: when the sky turns golden and the capital goes flying off into the land of sorcery, the thing to do is sit tight and wait for everything to get back to normal again, which it eventually will do.

He and Anderson and Schmidt slide smoothly into the crowd, trying to seem inconspicuous without conspicu- ously seeming to be trying to seem inconspicuous, and leave the plaza on the far side by way of the Street of Jews. There was a decent hotel seven or eight blocks up that way the last time he was here in the reign of Basil III, and though he doesn't know whether the date of that visit, in Empire time, was five years ago or five years yet to come, he figures there's a good chance the hotel will be there today. Things don't change really fast in the medieval world, except when some invading horde comes in and rearranges the real estate, and that isn't due to happen in this city for another couple of centuries.

The hotel is exactly where he remembers it. It's not quite in a class with the Drake or the Ritz-Carlton: more like a big barn, in fact, since the ground floor is entirely given over to straw-strewn stables for the horses and camels and donkeys of the guests, and the actual guest rooms are upstairs, a series of small square chambers with stiff clammy mattresses placed right on the stone floors, and tiny windows that have actual glass in them, almost clear enough to see through. Nothing lavish, not even really very comfortable, but the place is reasonably clean, at least, with respectable lavatory facilities on every floor and a relatively insignificant population of bugs and ticks. A pleasant smell of spices from the bazaar next door, ginger and aniseed and nutmeg and cinnamon, maybe a little opium and hashish, too, drifts in and conceals other less savory aromas that might be wandering through the building. The place is okay. It'll do for one night, anyway.

The innkeeper is a different one from last time, a gaptoothed, red-haired Greek with only one eye, who gives Mulreany a leering smirk and says, "In town for the sorcery-trading, are you?"

"The what?" Mulreany asks, all innocence.

"Don't pretend you don't know, brother. What do you think that ring of witch-fire is, all around the city? Where do you think the Eastern Sea has gone, and the Genoese Quarter, and Persian Town, and everything else that lies just outside the city walls? It's sorcery-time here again, my friend!"

"Is it, now?" Mulreany says, making no great show of interest. "I wouldn't know. My cousins and I are here to deal in pots and pans, and perhaps do a little business in daggers and swords." He colors his Greek with a broad, braying yokel accent, by way of emphasizing that he's much too dumb to be a sorcerer.

But the innkeeper is annoyingly persistent. "Merely let me have one of those metal tubes that bring near what is far off," he says, with a little wheedling movement of his big shoulders, "and my best rooms are yours for three weeks, and all your meals besides."

He must mean a spyglass. Binoculars aren't likely to do

him much good. Even more broadly Mulreany says, "Pots, yes, my good brother. Pans, yes. But miraculous metal tubes, I must say ye nay. Such things are not our commodities, brother."

The lone eye, ice-blue and bloodshot, bores nastily in on him. "Would a knife of many blades be among your commodities, then? A metal box of fire? A flask of the devil's brandy?"

"I tell you, we be not sorcerers," says Mulreany stolidly, letting just a bit of annoyance show. He shifts his weight slowly from leg to leg, a ponderous hayseed gesture. "We are but decent simple merchants in search of lodging in return for good coin, and if we cannot find it here, brother, we fain must seek it elsewhere."

He starts to swing about to leave. The innkeeper hastily backs off from his wheedling, and Mulreany is able to strike a straightforward deal for a night's lodging, three rooms for a couple of heavy copper sesterces, with tomorrow's breakfast of rough bread, preserved lamb, and beer thrown in.

Wistfully the innkeeper says, "I was sure at last I had some sorcerers before me, who would favor me with some of the wondrous things that the high dukes possess."

"You have sorcerers on the brain," Mulreany tells him, as they start upstairs. "We are but simple folk, with none of the devil's goods in our bags."

Does the innkeeper believe him? Who knows? They all covet the illicit stuff the sorcerers bring, but only the very richest can afford it. Skepticism and greed still glitter in that single eye.

Well, Mulreany has told nothing but God's truth: he is no sorcerer, just a merchant from a far land. But real sorcerers must have been at work here at some time in the past. What else could it have been but black magic,

Mulreany figures, that set the city floating in time in the first place? The capital, he knows, has been adrift for most of its lengthy history. He himself, on various crossings, has entered versions of the city as early as that of the reign of Miklos, who was fourth century A.D., and as late as the somber time of Kartouf the Hapless, right at the end, just before the Mongol conquest in 1412. For Chicagoans, the periodic comings and goings of the city are just an interesting novelty, but for these people it must be a real nuisance to find themselves constantly floating around in time and space. Mulreany imagines that one of the imperial wizards must have accidentally put the hex on the place, long ago, some kind of wizardy experiment that misfired and set up a time-travel effect that won't stop.

"Half past ten," Mulreany announces. It's more like noon, actually—the sun's practically straight overhead, glinting behind the spooky light of the interface effects— but he'll stay on Chicago time throughout the crossing. It's simpler that way. If Duplessis is right, the city is due to disappear back into its own era about eleven o'clock Thursday morning. Mulreany likes a twelve-to-fourteen-hour safety margin, which means heading back into Chicago by seven o'clock or so Wednesday night. "Let's get to work," he says.

The first stop is a jeweler's shop, three blocks east of the Street of Jews, that belongs to a Turkish family named Suleimanyi. Mulreany has been doing satisfactory business with the Suleimanyis, on and off, for something like a century Empire time, beginning with Mehmet Suleimanyi early in Basil III's reign and continuing with his grandfather Ahmet, who ran the shop fifty years earlier in the time of the Emperor Polifemas, and then with Mehmet's son Ali, and with Ali's grandson, also named Mehmet, during the reign of Simeon II. He does his best to conceal from the various Suleimanyis that he's been coming to them out of chronological order, but he doubts that they would care anyway. What they care about is the profit they can turn on the highly desirable foreign goods he brings them. It's a real meeting of common interests, every time.

Mulreany gets a blank look of nonrecognition from the man who opens the slitted door of the familiar shop for him. The Suleimanyis all look more or less alike—slender, swarthy, hawk-nosed men with impressive curling mustachios—and Mulreany isn't sure, as he enters, which one he's encountering today. This one has the standard Suleimanyi features and appears to be about thirty. Mulreany assumes, pending further information, that it's Mehmet the First or his son Ali, the main Suleimanyis of Basil's reign, but perhaps he has shown up on this trip some point in time at which neither of them has met him before. So for all intents and purposes he is facing an absolute stranger. You get a lot of mismatches of this sort when you move back and forth across the time interface.

A tricky business. He has to decide whether to identify himself for what he really is or to fold his cards and try someplace else that seems safer. It calls for an act of faith: there's always the chance that the man he approaches may figure that there's more profit to be had in selling him out to the police as a sorcerer than in doing business with him. But the Suleimanyis have always been on the up-and-up, and Mulreany has no reason to mistrust this one. So he takes a deep breath and offers a sweeping salaam and says, in classier Greek than he had used with the innkeeper, "I am Mulreany of Chicago, who once more returns bringing treasure from afar to offer my friend the inestimable master Suleimanyi."

This is the moment of maximum danger. He searches Suleimanyi's face for hints of incipient treachery.

But what he sees is a quick warm smile with nothing more sinister than balance-sheet calculations behind it: a flash of genuine mercantile pleasure. The jeweler eagerly beckons him into the shop, which is dark and musty, lit only by two immense wax tapers. Anderson and Schmidt come in behind him, Schmidt taking care to bolt the door. Suleimanyi snaps his fingers, and a small solemn boy of about ten appears out of the shadows, bearing an ornate flask and four shallow crystal bowls. The jeweler pours some sort of yellowish green brandy for them. "My late father often spoke of you, O Mulreany, and his father before him. It gives me great joy that you have returned to us. I am Selim, son of Ali."

If Ali is dead, this must be very late in the long reign of Basil III. The little boy is probably Mehmet the Second, whom Mulreany will meet twenty or thirty years down the line in the time of Emperor Simeon. It makes him a little edgy to discover that he has landed here in the great Emperor Basil's final years, because the Emperor apparently went a little crazy when he was very old, turning into something of a despot, and a lot of peculiar things were known to have occurred. But what the hell: they don't plan to be dropping in for tea at the imperial palace.

Before any transactions can take place an elaborate ritual of sipping the fiery brandy and exchanging bland snippets of conversation must occur. Selim Suleimanyi politely inquires after the health of the monarch of Mulreany's country and asks if it has been the case that unruly barbarians have been causing problems for them lately along their borders. Mulreany assures him that all is well in and around Chicago and that the Mayor is fine. He expresses the hope that the Empire's far-flung armies are meeting with success in the distant lands where they currently campaign. This goes on and on, an interminable spinning of trivial talk. Mulreany has learned to be patient. There is no hurrying these bazaar guys. But finally Suleimanyi says, "Perhaps now you will show me the things you have brought with you."

Mulreany has his own ritual for this. Schmidt opens one of the big burlap bags and holds it stolidly out; Mulreany gives instructions in English to Anderson; Anderson pulls items out of the bag and lays them out for Suleimanyi's inspection.

Five Swiss Army knives come forth first. Then two nice pairs of Bausch & Lomb binoculars, and three cans of Coca-Cola.

"All right," Mulreany orders. "Hold it there."

He waits. Suleimanyi opens a chest beneath the table and draws out a beautiful ivory hunting horn encircled by three intricately engraved silver bands showing dogs, stags, and hunters. He rests it expectantly on his open palm and smiles.

"A couple of more Cokes," Mulreany says. "And three bottles of Giorgio." Suleimanyi's smile grows broader. But still he doesn't hand over the hunting horn.

"Plus two of the cigarette lighters," says Mulreany.

Even that doesn't seem to be enough. There is a long tense pause. "Take away one of the Swiss Army knives and pull out six ballpoint pens."

The subtraction of the knife is intended as a signal to Suleimanyi that Mulreany is starting to reach the limits of his price. Suleimanyi understands. He picks up one of the binoculars, twiddles with its focus, peers through it. Binoculars have long been one of the most popular trading items for Mulreany, the magical tubes that bring far things close. "Another of these?" Suleimanyi says.

"In place of two knives, yes."

"Done," says Suleimanyi.

Now it's the Turk's turn. He produces an exquisite pendant of gold filigree inlaid with cloisonné enamel and hands it to Mulreany to be admired. Mulreany tells Anderson to bring out the Chanel No. 5, a bottle of Chivas, two more pairs of binoculars, and a packet of sewing needles. Suleimanyi appears pleased, but not pleased enough. "Give him a compass," Mulreany orders.

Obviously Suleimanyi has never seen a compass before. He fingers the shiny steel case and says, "What is this?"

Mulreany indicates the needle. "This points north. Now turn toward the door. Do you see? The needle still points north."

The jeweler grasps the principle, and its commercial value in a maritime nation, instantly. His eyes light up and he says, "One more of these and we have a deal."

"Alas," says Mulreany, "compasses are great rarities. I can spare only one." He signals Anderson to begin putting things away.

But Suleimanyi, grinning, pulls back his hand when Mulreany reaches for the compass. "It is sufficient, then, the one," he says. "The pendant is yours." He leans close. "This is witchcraft, this north-pointing device?"

"Not at all. A simple natural law at work."

"Ah. Of course. You will bring me more of these?"

"On my very next visit," Mulreany promises.

They move along, after Suleimanyi has treated them to the spicy tea that concludes every business transaction in the Empire. Mulreany doesn't like to do all his trading at a single shop. He goes looking now for a place he remembers near the intersection of Baghdad Way and the Street of Thieves, a dealer in precious stones, but it isn't there; what he finds instead, though, is even better, a Persian goldsmith's place where—after more brandy, more chitchat—he warily lets it be known that he has unusual merchandise from far-off lands for sale, meets with a reassuring response, and exchanges some Swiss Army knives, binoculars, various sorts of perfume, a bottle of Jack Daniel's, and a pair of roller skates for a fantastic necklace of interwoven gold chains studded with pearls, amethysts, and emeralds. Even at that the Persian evidently feels guilty about the one-sidedness of the deal, and while they are sipping the inevitable wrapping-up tea he presses a pair of exquisite earrings set with gaudy rubies on Mulreany as an unsolicited sweetener. "You will come back to me the next time," he declares intensely. "I will have even finer things for you—you will see!"

"And we'll have some gorgeous pruning shears for you," Mulreany tells him. "Maybe even a sewing machine or two."

"I await them with extraordinary zeal," declares the Persian ebulliently, just as though he understands what Mulreany is talking about. "Such miraculous things have long been desired by me!"

The sincerity of his greed is obvious and comforting. Mulreany always counts on the cheerful self-interest of the bazaar dealers—and the covetousness of the local aristocrats to whom the bazaaris sell the merchandise that they buy from the sorcerers from Chicago—to preserve his neck. Sorcery is a capital offense here, sure, but the allure of big profits for the bazaaris and the insatiable hunger among the wealthy for exotic toys like Swiss Army knives and cigarette lighters causes everybody to wink at the laws. Almost everybody, anyway.

As they emerge from the Persian's shop Schmidt says, "Hey, isn't that our innkeeper down the block?"

"That son of a bitch," Mulreany mutters. "Let's hope not." He follows Schmidt's pointing finger and sees a burly red-haired man heading off in the opposite direction. The last thing he needs is for the innkeeper to spot the purported dealers in pots and pans doing business in the jewelry bazaar. But red hair isn't all that uncommon in this city, and in all likelihood the innkeeper is busy banging one of the chambermaids at this very moment. He's glad Schmidt is on his toes, anyway.

They go onward now down the Street of Thieves and back past the Baths of Amozyas and the Obelisk of Suplicides into a district thick with astrologers and fortune-tellers, where they pause at a kebab stand for a late lunch of sausages and beer, and then, as the afternoon winds down, they go back into the bazaar quarter. Mulreany succeeds in locating, after following a couple of false trails, the shop of a bookseller he remembers, where a staff of shaven-headed Byzantine scribes produces illuminated manuscripts for sale to the nobility. The place doesn't normally do off-the-shelf business, but Mulreany has been able on previous trips to persuade them to sell books that were awaiting pickup by the duke or prince who had commissioned them, and he turns the trick again this time, too. He comes away with a gloriously illustrated vellum codex of the *Iliad*, with an astonishing binding of tooled ebony inlaid with gold and three rows of rubies, in exchange for some of their remaining knives, Coca-Cola, cigarette lighters, sunglasses, and whiskey, and another of the little pocket compasses. This is shaping up into one of the best buying trips in years.

"We ought to have brought a lot more compasses," Anderson says, when they're outside and looking around for their last deal of the day before heading back to the inn. "They don't take up much space in the bag, and they really turn everybody on."

"Next trip," says Mulreany. "I agree: they're a natural."

"I still can't get over this entire business," Schmidt says wonderingly. This is only his third time across. "That they're willing to swap fabulous museum masterpieces like these for pocketknives and cans of Coke. And they'd go out of their minds over potato chips, too, I bet."

"But those things aren't fabulous museum masterpieces to them," Mulreany says. "They're just routine luxury goods that it's their everyday business to make and sell. Look at it from their point of view. We come in here with a sackful of miracles that they couldn't duplicate in a hundred years. Five hundred. They can always take some more gold and some more emeralds and whack out another dozen necklaces. But where the hell are they going to get a pair of binoculars except from us? And Coke probably tastes like ambrosia to them. So it's just as sweet a deal for them as it is for us, and— Hello, look who's here!"

A stocky bearded man with coarse froggy features is waving at them from the other side of the street. He's wearing a brocaded crimson robe worthy of an archbishop and a spectacular green tiara of stunning princely style, but the flat gap-toothed face looking out at them is pure Milwaukee. A taller man dressed in a porter's simple costume stands behind him with a bag of merchandise slung over his shoulder. "Hey, Leo!" Mulreany calls. "How's it going?" To Schmidt he explains, "That's Leo Waxman. Used to carry the merchandise bags for me, five, six years ago. Now he's a trader on his own account." And, loudly, again, "Come on over, say hello, Leo! Meet the boys!"

Waxman, as he crosses the street, puts one finger to his lips. "Ixnay on the English, Mike," he says, keeping his voice low. "Let's stick to the Grik, okay, man? And not so much yelling." He casts a shifty look down toward the end of the block, where a couple of the ubiquitous Bulgarian Guardsmen are lolling against the wall of a mosque.

"Something wrong?" Mulreany asks.

"Plenty. Don't you know? The word is out that the Emperor has ordered a crackdown. He's just told the imperial gendarmerie to pull in anybody caught dealing in sorcery-goods."

"You sure about that? Why would he want to rock the boat?"

"Well, the old man's crazy, isn't he? Maybe he woke up this morning and decided it was time finally to enforce his own goddamned laws. All I know is that I've done a very nice day's business, and I'm going to call it a trip right here and now."

"Sure," Mulreany says. "If that's what you want. But not me. The Emperor can issue any cockeyed order he likes, but that doesn't mean anyone will pay attention. Too many people in this town get big benefits out of the trade we bring."

"You're going to stay?"

"Right. Till sundown tomorrow. There's business to do here."

"You're welcome to it," Waxman says. "I wish you a lot of joy of it. Me, I'm for dinner at Charlie Trotter's tonight, and to hell with turning any more tricks here just now, thank you. Not if there's a chance I'll miss the last bus back to the Loop." Waxman blows Mulreany a kiss, beckons to his porter, and starts off up the street.

"We really going to stay?" Schmidt asks, when Waxman has moved along.

Mulreany gives him a scornful look. "We've still got almost a bag and a half of goods to trade, don't we?"

"But if this Waxman thinks that—"

"He was always a chicken-shit wimp," Mulreany says.

"Look, if they were really serious about their sorcery laws here, they'd have ways of reaching out and picking us up just like that. Go into the bazaar, ask the dealers who they got their Swiss Army knives from, and give them the old bamboo on the soles of the feet until they cough up our full descriptions. But that doesn't happen. Nobody in his right mind would want to cut off the supply of magical nifties that we bring to town."

"This Emperor isn't in his right mind," Anderson points out. "But everybody else is. Let Waxman panic if he wants to. We finish our business and we clear out tomorrow afternoon as scheduled. You want to go home now, either of you, then go home, but if you do, this'll be the last trip across you ever make." It's a point of pride for Mulreany to max out his trading opportunities, even if it means running along the edge occasionally. He has long since become a rich man just on the twelve and a half percent he gets from Duplessis and Kulikowski's placements of the artifacts he supplies them with, but nevertheless he isn't going to abort the trip simply because Leo Waxman has picked up some goofy rumor. He detests Waxman's cowardice. The risks haven't changed at all, so far as he can see. This job was always dangerous. But the merchants will protect him. It's in their own best interest not to sell the golden geese to the imperial cops.

When they get back to the hotel, the innkeeper grins smarmily at them out of his cubicle next to the stable. "You sell a lot of pots and pans today?"

"Pretty good business, yes," Mulreany allows.

An avid gleam shines in the lone eye. "Look, you sell me something, hear? I give you a dozen girls, I give you a barrel of fine wine, I give you any damn thing you want, but you let me have one of the magic things, you know what I mean?"

"Gods be my witness, we are but ordinary merchants and let there be an end on this foolishness!" Mulreany says testily, thickening his yokel accent almost to the point of incoherence. "Why do you plague us this way? Would you raise a false charge of sorcery down on innocent men?" The innkeeper raises his hands placatingly, but Mulreany sails right on: "By the gods, I will bring action against you for defaming us, do you not stop this! I will take you to the courts for these slanders! I will say that you knowingly give lodging to men you think are sorcerers, hoping to gain evil goods from them! I will— I will—"

He halts, huffing and puffing. The innkeeper, retreating fast, begs Mulreany's forgiveness and vows never to suggest again that they are anything but what they claim to be. Would the good merchants care for some pleasant entertainment in their room tonight, very reasonable price? Yes, the good merchants would, as a matter of fact. For a single silver argenteus the size of a dime Mulreany is able to arrange a feast of apples and figs and melons, grilled fish, roasted lamb stuffed with minced doves and artichokes, and tangy resinated wine from Crete, along with a trio of Circassian dancing girls to serve them during the meal and service them afterward. It's very late by the time he finally gets to sleep, and very early when half a dozen huge shaggy Bulgarian Guardsmen come bashing into his room and pounce on him.

The bastard has sold him to the Emperor, it seems. That must have been him in the bazaar at lunchtime, then, watching them go in and out of the fancy shops. Thwarted in his dreams of wangling a nice Swiss Army knife for himself, or at least a fifth of Courvoisier, he has whistled up the constables by way of getting even.

There's no sign of Anderson and Schmidt. They must

have wriggled through their windows at the first sound of intruders and scrambled down the drainpipe and at this moment are hightailing it for the interface, Chicago-bound. But for Mulreany there's a cell waiting in the dungeon of the imperial palace.

He doesn't get a very good look at the palace, just one awesome glimpse in the moment of his arrival: white marble walls inlaid with medallions of onyx and porphyry, delicate many-windowed towers of dizzying height, two vast courtyards lined by strips of immaculately tended shrubbery stretching off to left and right, with crystalline reflecting pools, narrow as daggers, running down their middles.

Then a thick smelly hood is pulled down over his head and for a long while he sees nothing further. They pick him up and haul him away down some long corridor. Eventually he hears the sound of a great door being swung back; and then he feels the bruising impact of being dropped like a sack of potatoes onto a stone floor. Mulreany remains weirdly calm. He's furious, of course, but what good is getting into a lather? He's too upset to let himself get upset. He's a gone goose, and he knows it, and it pisses him off immensely, but there isn't a damned thing he can do to save himself. Maybe they'll burn him or maybe, if he's lucky, he'll be beheaded, but either way they can only do it to him once. And there's no lawyer in town who can get him off and no court of appeals to complain to. His only salvation now is a miracle. But he doesn't believe in miracles. The main thing he regrets is that a schmuck like Waxman is home free in Chicago right now, and he's not.

He lies there for what feels like hours. They took his watch away when they tied his wrists together, and in any case he wouldn't be able to see it with this hood on, but he knows that the day is moving along and in a matter of hours the interface between the Empire and Chicago is going to close. So even if they don't behead him, he's going to be stranded here, the dumbest fate a crosser can experience. The ropes that encircle his wrists start to chafe his skin, and he feels nauseated by the increasingly stale, moist air within the hood covering his face.

Eventually he dozes: sleeps, even. Then he wakes suddenly, muddleheaded, not knowing where he is at first, feeling a little feverish, and starving, besides; he's been cooped up in here, he figures, twelve or eighteen hours, or even longer than that. The interface certainly has closed by now. Stranded. Stranded. *You goddamned idiot*, he thinks.

Footsteps, finally. People coming. A lot of them.

They pull him to his feet, yank the hood off, untie his wrists. He sees that he's in a big square stone room with a high ceiling and no windows. On all sides of him stand guardsmen in terrific Arabian Nights uniforms: golden turbans, baggy scarlet pantaloons, purple silk sashes, blousy green tunics with great flaring shoulder pads. Each of them carries a scimitar big enough to cut an ox in half at a single stroke. Right before him is a trio of cold-eyed older men in the crimson robes of court officials.

They've brought him a hard crust of bread and some peppery gruel. He gobbles it as if it's five-star-quality stuff. Then the chilliest-looking of the officials pokes him in the belly with an ornate wooden staff and says, "Where are you from?"

"Ireland," Mulreany says, improvising quickly. Ireland's a long way away. They probably don't know much more about it here than they do about Mars.

The interrogator is unfazed. "Speak to me in the language of your country, then," he says calmly.

Mulreany is utterly innocent of Gaelic. But he suspects that they are, too. "Erin go bragh!" he says. "Sean Connery! Eamon de Valera! Up the rebels, macushlah!"

There are frowns, and then a lengthy whispered conference among the three officials. Mulreany is unable to catch a single word of it. Then the hood is roughly pulled down over his head and everybody leaves, and once more he is left alone for a long hungry time that feels like about a day and a half. Finally he hears footsteps again, and the same bunch returns, but this time they have with them a huge wild-eyed man with long, flowing yellow hair who is wearing rawhide leggings and a bulky woolen cloak fastened across the breast by a big metal brooch made of interlocked flaring loops. He looks very foreign indeed.

"Here is a countryman of yours," the chilly-faced court official informs Mulreany. "Speak with him. Tell him where in Ireland you are from, and name your lineage."

Mulreany, frowning, ponders what to do. After a time the newcomer unleashes a string of crackling gibberish, utterly incomprehensible to Mulreany, and folds his arms and waits for a reply.

"Shannon yer shillelagh, me leprechaun," Mulreany offers earnestly, appealing to the Irishman with his eyes for mercy and understanding. "God bless St. Paddy! Faith and begorrah, is it known t'ye where they'd be selling the Guinness in this town?"

Looking not at all amused, the other says in thick-tongued Greek, "This man is no Irishman," and goes stalking out.

They threaten him with torture if he won't tell them where he really comes from. He's cooked either way, it seems. Tell the truth and go to the block, or keep his mouth shut and have it opened for him by methods he'd rather not think about. But he knows his imperial law. The

Emperor in person is the final court of appeal for all high crimes. Mulreany demands then and there to be taken before His Majesty for judgment.

"We will do that," says the frosty-faced one. "As soon as you admit that you're from Chicago."

"What if I don't?"

He makes disagreeable racking gestures.

"But you'll take me to him if I do?"

"Most certainly we will. But only if you swear you are from Chicago. If you are not from Chicago, you die."

If you are not from Chicago, you die? It doesn't make any sense. But what does he have to lose? One way they'll rack him for sure, the other there's at least a chance. It's worth the gamble.

"I am from Chicago, yes," Mulreany says.

They let him wash himself up and give him some more bread and gruel, and then they take him to the throne room, which is about nine miles long and six miles high, with dozens of the ferocious Arabian Nights guardsmen everywhere and cloth-of-gold on the walls and thick red carpeting on the floor. Two of the guardsmen shove him forward to the middle of the great room, and there, studying him with an intent frown as though he is looking at the Ambassador from Mars, is the Emperor Basil III.

Mulreany has never seen an emperor before. Or wanted to. He comes over twice a year, does his business, goes back where he came from. It's merchants and craftsmen he comes here to see, not emperors. But there's no doubt in his mind that this is His Nibs. The Emperor is a trim, compact little man who looks to be about ninety-nine years old; his skin has the texture of fine vellum, and his expression is mild and benign, except for his eyes, which are dark and glossy and burn with the sort of fire that it takes to maintain yourself as absolute tyrant of a great empire for forty or fifty years. He is dressed surprisingly simply, in a white silk tunic and flaring green trousers, but there is a golden circlet on his brow and he wears on his chest a many-sided gold pendant, suspended from a heavy chain of the same metal, that bears the unmistakable crossed-thunderbolt symbol of the imperial dynasty inlaid upon it in lapis lazuli. Standing just to his right is a burly florid-looking man of about forty, imposing and almost regal of presence, garbed in an absurdly splendid black robe trimmed with ermine. Dangling from his hand, as casually as if it were a tennis racquet, is the great scepter of the realm, a thick rod of jade bound in gold, which, as Mulreany is aware, marks this man as the High Thekanotis of the Empire, that is to say, the prime minister, the grand vizier, the second-in-command.

There is a long, long, long silence. Then finally the Emperor says, in a thin, faint voice that seems to come from ten thousand miles away, "Well, are you a sorcerer or aren't you?"

Mulreany draws a deep breath. "Not at all, Your Majesty. A merchant is what I am, nothing but a merchant."

"Would you put your right hand on the holy altar and say that?"

"Absolutely, Your Majesty."

"He denies that he is a sorcerer," the Emperor says pleasantly to the High Thekanotis. "Make note of that." There is another great silence. Then the Emperor gives Mulreany a quick lopsided smile and says, "Why does the sorcery-fire come so often and take the city away?"

"I don't know," Mulreany says. "It just does."

"And when it does, people like you step through the

sorcery-fires and move among us, bringing the magical things to sell."

"Yes, Your Majesty. That's so." Why pretend otherwise?

"Where do you come from?"

"Chicago," Mulreany says. "Chicago, Illinois."

"Chicago," the Emperor repeats. "What do you know of this place?" he asks the High Thekanotis. The High Thekanotis scowls. Shrugs. It's obvious that he finds this whole event irritating and is already eager to ship Mulreany off to the executioner. But the Emperor's curiosity must be satisfied. "Tell me about your Chicago. Is it a great city?"

"Yes, Your Majesty."

"In what part of the world is it to be found?"

"America," says Mulreany. "In northern Illinois." What the hell, he has nothing to lose. "On the shore of Lake Michigan. We have Wisconsin to the north of us and Indiana to the east."

"Ah," the Emperor says, smiling as if that makes everything much clearer. "And what is this Chicago like? Describe it for me."

"Well," Mulreany says, "it has, oh, two or three million people. Maybe even more." The Emperor blinks in surprise, and the High Thekanotis glares with such ferocity that Mulreany wonders whether he has made a slip of the tongue and used the word for billion instead. But three million would be amazing enough, he decides. The imperial capital is one of the biggest cities of this era, and its population is probably around half a million, tops. "We have some of the tallest buildings in the world, like the Sears Tower, which I think is 110 stories high, and the Marina Towers, which are pretty big, too, and some others. We have great restaurants, any kind of food you might want. The Art Institute is a really fine museum and the Museum of Science and Industry is pretty special, too."

He pauses, wondering what else to say. As long as he keeps talking they aren't going to cut his head off. Does the Emperor want to hear about the dinosaurs at the Field Museum? The Aquarium? The Planetarium? He might be impressed by some statistics about O'Hare Airport, but Mulreany isn't sure he has the vocabulary for that. Then he notices that the Emperor is starting to look a little strange—turning pale, rocking weirdly back and forth on the balls of his feet. His eyes have taken on a really odd look, a mixture of profound cunning and utter wackiness.

"You must take me there," the Emperor says, whispering fiercely. "When you return to your city, take me with you and show me everything. Everything."

The High Thekanotis makes a choking sound, and his florid face turns an even brighter red. Mulreany is aghast, too. No imperial citizen has ever come across into Chicago, not even one. They are all terrified of the sorcery-fire, and they have no way of seeing beyond the interface anyway to know that there's another city out there.

But is the old man serious? The old man is crazy, Mulreany reminds himself.

"It would be an honor and a privilege, Your Majesty," he says grandly, "to show you Chicago someday. I would greatly enjoy the opportunity."

"Not someday," says the Emperor Basil III. "Now."

"Now," Mulreany echoes. An unexpected twist. The Emperor doesn't want to chop off the heads of the sorcerers he has sent his police to round up; the Emperor just wants one to give him a guided tour of Chicago. This afternoon, say. Mulreany smiles and bows. "Certainly, Your Majesty. Whatever Your Majesty wishes." He wonders how the old Emperor would react to his first glimpse of the downtown skyscrapers. He wonders what sort of greeting Chicago would give the Emperor. The whole thing is nutty, of course. But for him it's a plausible way out. He continues to smile. "We can leave immediately, if you desire, Your Majesty."

The High Thekanotis seems about to have a stroke. His chest heaves, his face puffs up furiously, he brandishes the jade scepter like a battle-axe.

But it's the Emperor who keels over instead. The excitement of the prospect of his trip across the line has done him in. He turns very pale and puts his hands to his chest and utters a little dry rasping sound, and his eyes roll up in his head, and he pitches forward headfirst so rapidly that two of the guardsmen are just barely able to catch him before he hits the stone floor.

The room goes berserk. The guardsmen start moaning and chanting; court officials come running in from all directions; the Emperor, who seems to be in the grip of some sort of seizure, arches his back, slaps his hands against the floor, stamps his feet, babbles wild nonsensical syllables.

Mulreany, watching in astonishment, feels the High Thekanotis's powerful hand encircling his forearm.

"Go," the grand vizier tells him. "Get yourself out of here, and never come back. Out now, before the Emperor returns to consciousness and sees you again. Now." The vizier shakes his head. "Chicago! He would visit Chicago! Madness! Madness!"

Mulreany doesn't need a second invitation. A couple of guardsmen grab him under the arms and hustle him from the room and down the hall and through the palace's endless hallways and, at long last, out through an immense arch into the broad plaza in front of the building.

It's the middle of the day. The fifty-two-hour visitation is long over; the gateway between the eras is shut.

Go, the High Thekanotis said. But where? Afghanistan?

And then, to his amazement, Mulreany sees the interface still glowing in the sky down at the eastern end of town. So there must have been another match-up with Chicago while he was in the imperial hoosegow. He can get across after all, back to good old Chi. The Loop, the Bears, the Water Tower, Charlie Trotter's, everything. Sprinting as if six demons are on his tail, he rushes toward the waterfront, jostling people out of his way. He'll be coming back empty-handed this trip, but at least he'll be coming back.

He reaches the Street of the Eastern Sun. Rushes out onto one of the wharves, plunges joyously into the golden light of the interface.

And comes out in a lovely green forest, the biggest trees he's ever seen this side of California. Everything is wonderfully silent. He hears the chirping of birds, the twittering of insects.

Oh, shit, he thinks. *Where the hell is Chicago?*

He looks back, bewildered. The interface line is gone, and so is the imperial capital. There's nothing here but trees. Nothing. Nothing. He walks for half an hour, heading east into the sun, and still he sees only this tremendous virgin forest, until at last he stumbles forward out of the woods and discovers himself to be at the shore of a gigantic lake, and then the awful truth strikes him with the impact of a tidal wave.

Of course. It's an era mismatch.

The interface must have closed right on schedule, and opened again a little while afterward, but this time the Empire had lined itself up against some other sector of the time stream very distant from his own. Just as the Empire that arrives in his Chicago is the one of Basil III sometimes and sometimes the one of Miklos and sometimes the one of Kartouf the Hapless, so too does the Empire of Basil's time line itself up sometimes with Chicago-1990, and sometimes Chicago-l996, and sometimes Chicago-2013—

And sometimes, probably, the one of 1400 A.D. Or of l400 B.C., not that it makes much difference. Before 1833, there wasn't any city at all here beside Lake Michigan.

A mismatch, then. He has heard rumors of such things occurring. One of those little thousand-to-one glitches that hardly ever actually happen, and that you assume never will happen to you. But this one has. He's known a few crossers who didn't come back. Schmucks, he always figured. Now it's his turn to be the schmuck. Mulreany wonders what it's going to be like living on nuts and berries, and trying to kill a deer if he feels like having a little protein. It's goddamned embarrassing, is what it is.

But he's an optimist at heart. There's cause for hope, right? Right? Sooner or later, he tells himself, the golden light will glow in the sky again behind him, and the Empire will return, and he'll go through the interface to the glorious city beyond, and eventually, after skulking around in it for a while, waiting for the right Chicago to come along, he'll go back across and find his way home.

Sooner or later, yes.

Or maybe not.

Natasha's Bedroom

ROBYN CARR

In my show I perform an illusion where I predict graf-fiti. Robyn Carr tells a story about an artist who's painting leads to a different sort of surprise.

—DC

Natasha's Bedroom

IT WAS A REFLEX that caused Natasha to pick up a paint-brush. Not an act of survival. Not a creative vent.

Natasha felt as though she were disappearing. Fading away. Her very cells, she believed, were becoming weaker and more transparent with every month that followed John's death. She had expected losing him would cause great pain, but had never envisioned this kind of diminishing.

But why not? she asked herself. *Since I feel less alive every day.*

She had met John in 1980 and married him three years later. She had loved him immediately. He'd been studying a painting at the Scottsdale Center for the Arts for so long that she, an artist herself, felt compelled to ask him what he saw. "A lot of anger," he'd answered. "I was just wondering if it's the anger that drives the painting or the painting, and its inherent difficulty and poverty, that drives the anger."

"Not many people would feel that," she replied. "You must be a painter."

But no, his art was in design. He dabbled in painting, sculpting, and building for his own personal pleasure. He was an architect. He'd been with a firm then, already aching at the age of twenty-four to be out on his own. An award and layout in *Architectural Monthly* just a few years later did the trick.

Since they both worked hard, long hours and had tremendous talent, they hadn't thought of their lives as charmed, but in retrospect they were. It had taken John only a few years to have his own design firm and only a few months to have many clients. Natasha had her first one-woman show just a couple of years out of college. As a team—John creating impressive spec houses decorated with Natasha's paintings, wall hangings, and sculptures— they became well-known and moderately rich in Scottsdale, Arizona. John built their desert foothills home of tile, adobe, and glass so that the sunlight was maximized and the heat minimized. From there they worked, enter- tained artists, builders, and patrons, and dreamed large airy dreams. Desert wildlife wandered near their patio, and the lights of the city twinkled below them. Natasha's work hung in galleries all over town, and John's houses speckled the valley.

They'd been devoted and selfish, not even letting chil- dren and pets into their perfectly balanced life together. Used to having what they wanted when they wanted it, they never made any contingency plans for a time when things wouldn't go according to their desires. Then John began to have pains in his chest and shallowness in his breath. It was a rare and fatal virus that only a heart trans- plant would cure. There wasn't time. Just when the fall drizzle began to gray the Arizona skies, after only three months of illness, John died in his sleep.

The first month of Tasha's widowhood was filled with tears and insomnia. The second month she took on a hol- low feeling, as if there were nothing left inside of her. In the third month she became morose and lethargic and learned how to order groceries to be delivered, but other things that needed to be done to maintain her home and life were neglected. She stopped cleaning, and the trash stood by the kitchen door, rarely going all the way to the cans and almost never getting carted out to the street to be picked up. By the fourth month her friends, frustrated and helpless, began to call less often and Tasha stopped leaving the desert foothills house John had built. She wandered aimlessly from room to room, and if she was hungry, which was rare, she ate something out of a can, over the sink. She didn't do any of the things she'd done as John's wife; didn't brew coffee, read the newspaper, budget her money, cook meals. She rarely dressed; she showered irregularly. Her electricity was cut off once and she didn't care. She drank diet sodas, warm, out of the can, and let the swimming pool turn green. It took her two weeks to summon the energy to call the power company to make amends, but when they asked her to bring a cashier's check to their office, she told them she was an invalid and would have to complete the process by mail.

"Tasha, there's a whole world out here," a friend would entreat. "You've got to get out, meet people, socialize again!" But she couldn't imagine. She eschewed all offers of help—of support groups, counseling, antidepressants, and even outings with friends. She had been with John, his best friend and lover, for fifteen years. There was nothing else she could imagine that would make her life worth living. She found the notion that life went on to be absurd. There was nothing in life that mattered to her in any way. To say that she was suicidal would be to misunderstand; she was not committed enough to anything or anyone to end her own life. She'd just go on—alone and without any plans of any kind for herself—until she faded completely away. The regular sale of her artwork, scattered among dealers in the valley, allowed this lifestyle, or the lack thereof, to continue.

Then she began to paint again, after six months of grief.

It was one of the few things she knew how to do alone.
And it required no explanation. She painted flowers, cacti,
fruit, birds, and mountains. She didn't really care how the
paintings turned out; she was only interested in the process. The smells, the colors, the angles, the strokes, the
light.

The paintings were not what she would consider good;
a lot was still missing from even this single, autonomous
portion of her existence without John's input: "I like the
hopefulness of these lines." "There's such joy in this face."
By far the most exhilarating comment from John was his
silent approval—when he viewed one of her works that he
particularly liked, he would lay a daisy on the easel tray
underneath that painting. She would often find herself
standing on daisy petals as she worked.

What was still there, even without John's presence, was
Tasha's fundamental ability to put brush to canvas. She had
studied painting for years, yes, and John's encouragement
and pride had fleshed it out, true, but whatever spark of
chimera she had begun with had been a gift. It had been
free. It had been hers. And what her life had been about
before John.

Small changes occurred in Tasha's life, a transition so
slow that she barely noticed herself. Her trash made it to
the curb. She ran the dishwasher. She put on her tennis
shoes and shorts and walked the familiar desert trails near
her house. She drove into Scottsdale for paint and stopped
at the grocery store. She heated food in the microwave and
balanced her checkbook and called to ask that newspaper
delivery be resumed. She flipped through the channels and
found something to watch on TV. She never for a second
considered that she was making herself a life.

Spring came to the desert in a flood of color, more
resplendent than any spring Tasha had ever seen, and she

began painting a mural on the bedroom wall. The bedroom because, if she ever did have guests in her house again, they wouldn't see it and think her mad. And because she could look at it late at night as she was snuggling into bed or early in the morning as she was rising with the sun. It would look just as if John were standing in the yard, his back against the desert and mountains. Blankets of lupines, poppies, daisies, and wildflowers seemed to wave at towering saguaros and yuccas.

She painted him in jeans, boots, and a work shirt, rolled up at the sleeves. The sky blue and cloudless, air still, desert in bloom, mountains cast in red-brown and peppered with sprigs of plant life. It was his face she first had trouble with; which of her favorite expressions would be right? Should his hair be longish, as it sometimes became when he ignored it? Or clipped and styled, which gave him such a polished look? Bearded or bare?

It didn't look like him, and this caused grief to roil up in her anew. She pulled out all the photos and other paintings she'd done of him, but to no avail. She painted and repainted, wiped away and tried again, but invariably the jaw was too square, the cheekbones too broad, the mouth too slim and wide, the hair too wavy, the eyes too deepset, the brows too thick, and the nose too sculptured. Just when she'd get the eyes right, the mouth would go wrong. She'd fix the mouth and the nose wasn't right. Fix the nose and the eyes, after all, were not his. Then she noticed the physique was flawed—John's legs were not proportionally that long; his neck was not that thick. John's body was more lithe and boyish than the man in the mural. The man on her wall kept changing shape and dimension and even color as she worked.

Then, suddenly, a new phenomenon occurred. Tasha would work all day, John would look as close to himself as she could manage, and when she left the room or fell asleep, he would change into a man she didn't know. She might have been frightened by this if she weren't so frustrated. All she wanted was to be able to look at the image of her dead husband once in a while. Why was this so impossible?

In the late night, with the moon lighting the desert around her house and the flash of heat lightning and thunder over the valley in the distance, Tasha sat in her bed and looked at the mural in the dim light of a single bedside lamp. The spring breeze through the screens cooled the sheets and made her linen nightgown seem inadequate, and she hugged her knees while she studied the man on the wall. His hair was sandy brown, while John's had been honey blond. His eyes were heavily shrouded, while John's had been bright and open. His face was square, and John's had been angular. She had made him John's height; it seemed she had that much control, yet the man on the wall looked much taller, much larger. It mystified her that he could be so thoroughly different from what she intended. Leaning back into her pillows, drowsily considering her failure, she wondered if she'd be forced to start from scratch. Again.

"Who *are* you?" she said to the wall.

The wall blurred as if she had begun to drift into sleep. The flowers appeared to be swaying in the wind, and the man seemed to move and stretch. As if the wall were a window to her desert, the man walked through the yard. Toward her. As he moved, she could see the muscles beneath his jeans and shirt. The reddish hue of his hair sharpened and moved in the wind, and his face came into focus, his jaw strong, eyes hooded, nose long and straight. With every step he resembled John less and less. She slowly rose up, sitting taller and straighter and more alert as he approached. Within seconds he stood at the foot of her bed, looking down at her.

"You're beautiful," he said, smiling. He walked around to the side of the bed where she sat. "You're so beautiful," he whispered.

Tasha was struck dumb by the vision, which she assumed must be a dream. Vivid, colorful dreams were not unusual for her, but she was such a practiced dreamer that she often knew the dream lacked sense or logic even while she was in it. This time, however, there was such incredible logic—the wall was blank where the man had been painted, and now he stood before her.

He knelt beside the bed and reached for her hands. He pulled them to his lips and kissed her fingers. She could feel the pressure of his hands as though he were real; she felt calluses on his fingers and the moist softness of his lips. When he looked into her eyes she could see that he was handsome and that his eyes were dark and sleepy. His mouth had a gentle turn, and his touch was strong but tender. "Who *are* you?" she asked.

"Shhhh," he responded, whispering. "Don't talk. Don't make this stop. Just let me look at you."

"A dream," she said, but she squeezed his hands, and he was solid. She wondered if he had broken into her house and was there to assault her. A shiver of fear ran through her, and she pulled away from him, scooting across the bed.

"I'm sorry," he said. "Did I hurt you? Did I do something wrong?"

His voice was very deep, almost hoarse, as though he should clear his throat. He didn't grab at her when she withdrew, but relaxed his arms and gave her a moment to collect herself. She studied his suntanned face, a face that had been struggling to emerge on her mural. He would be in his thirties—perhaps forty. The shirt was as she had painted it; the jeans were the ones she created; the boots were tan, laced work boots. Then she looked at the wall. There was still no man in her mural. This was not someone who had broken into her house. This was the man she had painted. Come into her bedroom.

"Are you all right?" he asked softly. "Did I scare you? Hurt you?"

"No. Yes. You didn't hurt me, but you scared me," she said.

"Give me your hand. Here."

She reached out her hand, and he took it in his. He turned it over and looked at her palm, then pressed his lips into it. With her other hand she reached gingerly toward him and cautiously touched his shoulder. His chambray shirt was soft under her fingertips. She pressed harder, half-wondering if her hand would pass through him, but he was as flesh and bone as she.

"Come closer," he whispered, pulling her toward him. He put both his hands on her shoulders and touched her bare skin, massaging her neck with his roughly textured fingers. He let his fingers creep up her scalp and then, like combs, pulled them through her shoulder-length hair. He touched her face as if he also had to be sure she was real, and so her fingers seemed automatically to reach his. She felt his cheeks—bristly. She combed her fingers through his hair—thick and wiry. She traced his heavy brows, and his eyes fell closed. She touched his mouth, and it opened, pulling in her fingers.

"Why are you here?" she asked him.

"Why are *you*?" he replied.

"This is my bedroom," she answered, but her voice was growing softer, more sleepy, liquid.

"Then there can be only one thing," he said, putting his

arms around her and pulling her to the edge of her bed. "I must be here for you. You must be here for me." His mouth covered over hers in a warm, wet, and searing movement that was at once tender and passionate. As she began to smell him—a combination of outdoors, soap, sweat, and skin—and taste him—coffee, bread, and the smallest bit of Irish whiskey—she knew that, whether apparition or painting or dream or invader, he was real and solid and considerate and pleasant.

Tasha thought, very briefly, about the many options she had. She could ask him to leave and see what happened. She could force him into a conversation and see what she could learn. She could begin to scream—though she didn't feel like screaming—and see if he withdrew or ran or disappeared. She could excuse herself, go to the phone, call the police, and judge his reaction. Or, she could be wholly selfish and foolish and enjoy what she was feeling without being practical or curious. She hadn't been feeling much lately, and this was a storm of emotion.

"Take this off," she said, tugging at the blue chambray shirt.

He discarded it immediately. He had to sit on the edge of the bed to pull off his boots and socks. Then he stood, loosened his pants, and dropped them, presenting her with a lovely view of a solid, white, smooth rump. No underwear under those jeans. When he turned toward her, naked, she silently mused, mmmm, looks like there is only one reason. And a handsome one at that. She pulled back the comforter.

As he knelt before her to help her out of her nightgown, she ran her hands down his chest, hips, and thighs. He was powerfully built, a man whose labors were physical. The hair on his chest, groin, and legs was reddish brown, and he was tanned, except where his swimsuit would have been. While she studied his body with her hands, he did likewise. "You are so beautiful," he kept saying.

"I haven't been told that in a very, very long time," she confessed. In fact, she realized, she had completely forgotten that, indeed, she had physical assets. At thirty-six she was petite and firm. Her skin was pale and her eyes large and dark. Her hair was thick brown, and her lips light peach. She was covered, head to toe, with a light layer of freckles that as a child she had hated, but as a woman she had found sensual. Her teeth were small, straight, and white, and her breasts were at least adequate. She had a wholesome look with a naughty edge.

"If you tell me what you like, you'll have everything you want," he told her. Then he covered her body with his and waited.

This had never, ever happened to Tasha before, not even in dreams or in her imagination. He was wonderful, but what she liked best was that he smiled and laughed. When she gave him some order, and he fulfilled it to her groaning pleasure, he chuckled deep in his throat as though it were all a fun game. "You taste of apples," he said once. "Your skin is like satin." And, "I could do this forever, it feels so wonderful."

In the aftermath, lying in the damp sheets and studying his face as she wound a finger into his curling hair, she thought of the months of devastating pain she had endured.

"I don't understand why you're here," she said. "Or how."

"I usually don't question it," he answered.

"This has happened to you before?"

Again he chuckled, low in his throat. "Not as often as when I was young. But, I have to admit, it's getting better."

"You think you're in a dream, don't you?"

"What do you think I'm in?"

"My bedroom." She tapped his chest. "And you're real."

He ran his hands down her body, smiling into her eyes as if he greatly appreciated her curves. The softness of her skin. "It always feels so real. But then I wake up, alone, and realize that it was just my hard-to-shed adolescence, kicking up again. One thing is different this time, though. I never talked about my dream in my dream."

Tasha tried to remember if she had. But this was no dream, she reminded herself. He had left her mural and come into her bed.

"Why are you alone?" he asked her.

"My husband's been dead about seven months," Tasha said.

"Dear Lord. Was he old?"

"No, he was young. Maybe younger than you."

"God, you poor thing. I wish there were some way I could fill that space he left behind."

"I don't think I'd want that," she said. "I don't think I could bear to take that kind of chance again. To become that enmeshed with someone again. It's too much when . . . You know. The bad part is, it doesn't kill you."

"Wouldn't he have wanted you to go on? Have a good, full life?"

"What he would have wanted and what I'm capable of are two different things."

His brow furrowed as he considered that. "You shouldn't live your life alone," he finally said. "Not you."

"If there's any alternative to that, I don't know what it is," she said, and she meant this most sincerely. In her state of mind it had been impossible to comprehend the idea of fitting herself back into the world.

"Come here," he said, pulling her close. "We'll see."

Again, he made love to her. This time there was no talking afterward. She fell asleep in his arms. She slept deeply. For the first time in months.

While she was standing under the pounding stream of the shower, she came awake. The night before was vivid in her mind. Real. She jumped out of the shower, wrapped her towel around her without drying herself first, and bolted into the bedroom. She expected to see him in her bed, but her bed was made. The pillows were fluffed, her comforter was pulled straight, and her nightgown lay draped at the foot of the bed.

Tasha tore the comforter and sheet back, looking for telltale wrinkles or reddish brown hairs. None. She plunged her face into the pillow on which his head had lain and breathed in deeply, but inhaled only laundry detergent and fabric softener. She looked at her mural, and there he stood.

"I'm a candidate for madness," she said aloud. She looked down at her own hand and saw that she appeared to be more solid flesh than she had been the day before. Her skin no longer seemed translucent; her body felt more real. Her cheek felt pink and sensitive where his whiskers had rubbed her.

The meaning of her experience was a complete mystery to her. Perhaps a dream so spectacular was meant to be savored, nothing more. She left her desert house, careful to lock the doors and set the alarm. It was too early in the morning for her to buy paint or stop by any of the Old Scottsdale galleries that carried her works, so she went to a favorite bagel shop on Camelback Road. She bought a newspaper and tried to read, but in her mind she kept wondering what miracle had allowed her to paint a man— a sweet and handsome man—who could come to life long enough to make love to her. And, in some incredible flash of hopefulness, cause her to drive into town for a morning cup of coffee and bagel, as she'd done in bygone days. For the first time since John's death, she realized with a start, she was acting as though she were among the living.

That thought caused her to lower her newspaper, and she saw him. He sat at a table on the patio. Yes, it was he. He was dressed in jeans and a plaid shirt, rolled up at the sleeves. His hair was still damp from his morning shower, and his newspaper was spread out on the table before him. His cellular phone was propped up on the table; a workingman; a foreman or contractor or builder. This was too real to be coincidence. But did she want him in her life? Did she want *anyone* in her life? Fading away had its merits.

"Excuse me," she said to him. "Can you tell me what time it is?"

He looked up at her, and there was instant recognition in his eyes. He was stunned. Taken aback.

"Is something wrong?" she asked.

"I'm . . . Sorry," he said, glancing at his watch. "Seven-forty-five. It's just that I know you. I bought one of your paintings. Tasha Scott, isn't it? Your picture was on the brochure."

So, he wasn't remembering her from last night. Still . . .

"Oh, which one?" she asked.

"*Dew and Grass*," he said. Remarkably, a slight flush touched his cheeks.

The painting was an old one, but special. She had nearly kept it for John. It was a self-portrait. When she was twenty-six, ten years ago. She was sitting up in a four-poster bed that sat in a field of waving grass. Her hair was long and dark then, her eyes downcast and her arms stretching out as though she were just coming awake in the morning.

"I'm surprised you can even recognize me," she said. "That was such a long time ago. When I was young."

"You don't seem to have changed at all," he said. "This is a real pleasure. Can I . . . um . . . buy you a cup of coffee?"

"I have coffee, thanks."

"Will you sit down? Are you rushing off?"

Yes, she would sit for just a few minutes. No, she wasn't rushing—just waiting for the stores to open.

His name was Elliot Lowell, a builder. He knew nothing about art, he said, but that particular painting was a favorite of his. It looked like something that should hang in the bedroom of a teenage girl, he said, and his older sister had been trying to talk him out of it for years, but however odd it seemed for a middle-aged man to hang on to such a work, he happened to be partial to it. Was it the only one she'd done of herself? he wanted to know.

There had been several, but that was the only one she'd done of herself in a bed. It had been the only self-portrait she'd really liked, and she'd stopped doing them years ago. Her last series *had* been young girls, she told him. In faddish dress-styles. Every one had gone quickly. Great, expensive decor for well-off Scottsdale bedrooms, she supposed.

They had chatted for twenty minutes when he asked her if she'd go on a date sometime. "Dinner or a movie or something?"

"Actually, I'm a recent widow. . . ."

"Oh. I'm sorry to hear that. It's pretty presumptuous of me. But what are the odds I'll run into you at the bagel shop again? I thought I'd better take a chance."

"I'm not ready," she said.

"I can understand. I come here for coffee a lot," he said, by way of letting her know where she might be able to find him.

"Maybe we should exchange phone numbers for now,"

she suggested. "I might be more inclined in, say . . ." but she didn't finish. Two weeks? Two months? Two years?

He produced a card immediately and wrote an additional phone number on the back. A private number?

"You're not married, are you?" she asked, just to be sure.

"Never been," he said. "Very set in my ways. Very single. Very eligible?" And then he laughed. She recognized the laugh, and it sent a shiver through her like an aftershock.

Have you ever dreamed of me? she wanted to ask him. But she couldn't. She took his card and stood. "It was very nice to meet you," she said. "I'm glad you like the painting."

"I love the painting. It's my favorite thing."

"Maybe I'll call you sometime," she said. "If you're sure you're not seeing anybody."

He smiled handsomely. Tenderly. "I'm not seeing anybody," he said. "Only you." He took her hand, and she instantly recalled those calluses. "Thank you for asking the time. I'll hope for your call."

She didn't go to the store or any of the local galleries. Instead she went directly home. She dropped her purse on the kitchen counter and went to her bedroom to inspect the mural. There he stood. She thought perhaps he looked a bit more confident than when she'd left him.

On the carpet beneath the mural, as though they had dropped from the flowers she had painted, were a dozen or so daisy petals.

TechnoMagic

KEVIN J. ANDERSON

In the story Kevin wrote for the first volume of Tales of the Impossible, *he juxtaposed two people who live in a freak show, with the so-called normal "outside" world. In this story, he juxtaposes an alien's view of earth magic, with the view of a technologically advanced society. Though his approach in this story is far more lighthearted, the results of his explorations are not entirely dissimilar, for both lead to similar conclusions: reality and illusion can only be defined by the eye of the beholder.*

—DC

TechnoMagic

"Any sufficiently advanced technology is
indistinguishable from magic."
—ARTHUR C. CLARKE

"Twenty-seven years for a rescue ship? You've got
to be kidding! What am I supposed to do on this
planet in the meantime? How am I—"
—TAURINDO ALPHA PRIME, LAST TRANSMISSION
FROM SCOUT VESSEL BEFORE CRASHING IN THE NEVADA
DESERT (LOOSELY TRANSLATED)

THE FIRST GARISH POSTERS had said *The Great
Taurindo!*—some overenthusiastic publicist's idea, not
mine—but my fame grew so rapidly that within a few
years the marquees in the Las Vegas amphitheaters shouted
my name in letters even taller than I was. (And I am
slightly greater in height than the average Earthling,
though I look just like one of them.)

The evening's crowd was sprawled out at various tables,
more than could comfortably fit in the room, thanks to the
outrageous ticket prices people were willing to pay to see
me perform. The rich ones sat in the best seats, drinking
expensive cocktails, while busloads of budget tour groups
crammed together at the long tables, jabbering their
schemes for how to win at the nickel slots.

Everyone fell silent as the show began. I cracked my knuckles in the shadows at the edge of the stage, waiting, making sure my smile looked right. Many species in the Galaxy believe the flashing of one's teeth to be a threatening gesture, but on Earth it's considered friendly. Just another of the odd details about Earthlings.

The master of ceremonies announced me as the "World's! Greatest! Magician!" Sometimes I'm called a magician, other times an "illusionist"—neither of which is truly accurate, since what I do is not magic or illusion, but the real thing . . . courtesy of my planet's highly advanced technology. None of the spectators knew that, though.

The broad stage reminded me of when I had taken my oral exam before the xenosociology degree committee back on the homeworld. I strode out and took my bow as I introduced the evening's first spectacle.

"Remember the old saw about the woman being cut in half in a box?" I said. The audience chuckled. No one from my planet would have understood the reference, but this was a hoary old trick performed ad nauseam by Earth magicians. Simple enough to master, but I had added a new twist. "Tonight I'll show you a new saw, a very large saw in fact." I smiled again.

The lights flashed. Hot white beams reflected from the highly polished, stainless-steel teeth of the giant chain saw blade that would slice me in two before their very eyes.

The audience loved the show so far—my lovely assistants were wearing even skimpier outfits than usual.

"I won't hide in a box, I won't use mirrors or distractions. I will lie on this table in plain sight, and this chain saw will cut me in half—as you watch! You'll see it all, every second of it."

The music built. The lights dimmed.

I stepped back into the artificially deep shadows at the

back of the stage, and then I sent my perfect clone forward out into the brilliant light. He was an identical match for my body, cell for cell, although his brain was completely blank. It was all the vapid simulacrum could do to stagger across the stage and lie down on the table under the motionless chain saw.

The beautiful assistants strapped him down, and he didn't resist, instinctively smiling out at the audience like an idiot. All clones smile. It's a secret they seem to share in their brainlessness.

The eyes of all the men in the audience were trying to catch a glimpse of just a bit more through my assistants' scanty uniforms and paid little attention to the mechanics of the actual trick. Others were trying to figure out what the gimmick was—while some few, the blessed ones, remained happy enough just to be entertained.

The music swelled loud and dramatic. The chain saw blade spun up with a loud roar that built to a threatening whine, like a dentist's drill for King Kong.

The lighting technicians slipped a thick red gel over the spotlights, bathing the stage in an ominous crimson glow, as the deadly blade began to descend, rattling as the chain teeth whipped around and around in a circle. The clone lay twitching on the table, bound by the restraints and staring with uncomprehending eyes up at the sharp spinning blade about to rip him to shreds.

That's showbiz, as they say.

Timing was everything now, and I had to depend on my crew. They knew what they were supposed to do.

The chain saw slammed down, ripping through the clone's rib cage and sparking on the steel tabletop. Blood flew in a bright arc—one of the more picturesque ones, I thought. The clone let out a shriek of instinctive pain that was abruptly cut off . . . then all the lights went out for an instant to be replaced by only a single faint spotlight on the retracting chain saw blade still slowly spinning, dripping blood.

The audience swelled with thin screams. I wondered how many of them would faint this time, though I had done this trick many times, and they must have known there would be no accident. Not this time. Not any time.

I could have kept the lights up, of course, since this was all real. I could have shown the audience the gory, anatomically correct mess on the table. But that would have gone beyond the bounds of good clean entertainment. Instead, the glimpse of the bloodied saw and the clone's genuine scream was all they needed to know.

As the lights dropped to black, the automatic nanocritters—microscopic destructive robots—began the busywork of taking my clone apart cell by cell, dissolving him into a simple protein mass in the space of less than a minute. And when the entire body was denatured, the liquid obediently seeped into drains in the table (placed there ostensibly for spilled blood). I would use the protein mass to grow a clone for another performance.

The lights came up again with enough flash and dazzle to blind the audience temporarily, and there I stood in the middle of the stage, intact and smiling, taking my bow to thunderous applause—as always.

Outside the bright lights of the casino, I melted into the crowd, where I could study the way humans interact. I've never gotten tired of it, even after so many years.

On the sidewalk at a street corner, where impatient pedestrians waited for DON'T WALK to change to WALK, I saw an aspiring magician walking among the people, pestering them, showing off to the best of his ability. Doing card tricks, pulling colored scarves from his sleeves—amateurish stuff, but I stopped in midstride with a warm glow of nostalgia. Perhaps he hoped for some sort of special attention as he stood overshadowed by the huge marquee for *The Great Taurindo*!

I watched him for a while. This struggling magician with stars in his eyes and the reckless hope for fame reminded me of one of the first Earthlings I had ever met. . . .

Just before my burned-out scout ship crashed out on this planet's desert wastelands, I was able to salvage only a few things from the hulk. After transmitting my distress call and pinpointing my position for the eventual rescue ship, I hurried away from the ship as the self-destruct nanocritters began to turn the hull and engines to indefinable dust.

Swallowing hard, I hiked across the rocky scrub in the general direction of the large city I had spotted just before impact.

Because of my profession studying alien cultures, I had been through the "first contact" routine numerous times before, and this one went off without a hitch. But as I ambled through the streets of Las Vegas, trying to fit in while staring wide-eyed around me, I came upon a street magician. He had a battered cardboard box open on the sidewalk, in which had been scattered bits of paper and round metal (obviously the monetary currency in use).

The magician extended a deck of playing cards to passersby, asking them to select a card, whose identity he would then guess. In another trick he hid a bright red ball under one of three bowls, rapidly shuffled them around, then asked someone to find it—and invariably they guessed wrong.

At first, I suspected these humans had telepathic powers, but as I watched I soon realized this was not the case. The magician was merely fooling his audience with sleight of hand. And people were tossing him money for it.

I watched him for some time, but since I had no local currency to give for the performance, I wandered away.

I began to think that I could do such stunts, only better—given my superior technology. Among the few items I had snagged from the ship before its quiet self-destruct was the wonderful Central Autonomic Molecular Device—a complex whirlwind computer, synthesizer, and nanotechnology processor. I called it the "gizmo," ignoring the pretentious technical terminology that I didn't understand anyway. The machine was far beyond my level of education and training—I was a xenosociologist and observer, not an engineer. The palm-sized gizmo *worked*, and that was all I needed to know during my exile here.

I was stuck on Earth for twenty-seven years, and I would have to make something of myself in the meantime. And magic fascinated these people.

As I assimilated into this culture I came upon an interesting observation called Clarke's Law. It said that "Any sufficiently advanced technology is indistinguishable from magic." The postulate had been derived by a visionary who also developed the concept for this planet's geosynchronous communication satellites, had popularized the idea for the space elevator as an alternative to expendable launch vehicles, and had also written the story for an amusing film called *2001: A Space Odyssey*, which I enjoyed very much. (I wonder if Mr. Clarke's awe of alien intelligences might have been so great if he'd had the pleasure of meeting the bovine slugs of Merricus or endured the screeching carrion ballets of Vulpine Five, however.)

Clarke's postulate about technology and magic gave me an idea. With the gizmo to serve me, I simply had to learn what sort of magic the Earthlings wanted to see and how to make a good show out of it.

Showmanship proved to be the hardest part. Simply displaying an endless string of miracles would not be enough. (Besides, Central Authority back home would have been very annoyed if I accidentally started a new religion on Earth.)

I watched Earth's best performers, astonishing magicians and illusionists, trying to learn the secret to a good show. At times I was confounded, wondering if these showmen somehow had access to contraband extraterrestrial technology themselves. It didn't matter—I knew my gizmo was superior to anything they might have. I could do better.

It took me a long time to understand their attitude toward entertainment—but once I did, it became a key to grasping the human psyche. While Earthlings are endlessly curious and easily perplexed, these people honestly didn't want to know *how* a magic trick was performed. They might claim so, and half mean it, but they would rather be intrigued and amazed. They'd be outraged if every magician went on their endless talk shows and explained all the secrets.

That would squash the thrill for them, the *magic*.

One of my simplest tricks (and therefore one of my favorites) was transporting myself instantaneously from one part of the arena to another. It was a trivial teleportation gimmick—but with the appropriate buildup, the music, the lights, the smoke and mirrors, the gorgeous assistants, and pounding drums, it became an amazing feat. Other Earth magicians had done similar acts, some with people, some with animals—but no one did it with my method (so far as I know).

After selecting a volunteer from the audience—a fidgety

young man with too-short pants and a sweat-stained polyester shirt—I climbed into a vertical metal box at the back of my stage, holding the lid open. An identical box stood at the far end of the seats, a good distance away, containing my unwitting volunteer. The young man stood inside the box as if it were a coffin, looking out and wanting to shrink away from the sudden attention.

The assistants sealed the door of his box. The young man's eyes were bugging out and his Adam's apple bobbed as he gulped.

Waving from the stage, I closed the door on my box, activating the instantaneous teleportation circuit in the gizmo strapped to my waist.

Less than a second later, I emerged intact in the opposite booth, while assistants opened the box on the stage, allowing the wide-eyed volunteer to stumble out, gawking in amazement and completely at a loss as to how he had traveled a hundred meters in an instant. He rubbed his still-tingling skin and blinked into the bright lights and the applause. He grinned like a clone.

My promoters and agents (*these* people are true aliens, even among Earthlings) kept insisting that I do bigger and more daring stunts—and I obliged, attempting to surpass even the greatest illusions ever performed by master magicians. Though some of the spectacles required more power, my precious gizmo had a century-and-a-half useful life span, according to its warranty. I trusted the engineers from my planet. They knew what they were doing.

Most outrageous trick: I made the Empire State Building vanish at midnight, right under floodlights and helicopters and in front of the slack-jawed faces of the gathered crowd.

In the blind instant when the spotlights shut off, I touched the gizmo at my waist to *disintegrate* the entire skyscraper, all 102 stories (plus television tower). When the lights came back up again, only shaven foundations remained of one of the tallest buildings on this planet. A few disconcerting sparks flickered up from severed electrical cables, nothing more.

I sincerely hoped the publicists had evacuated the building as they'd promised.

Once the cheers and applause began to subside, we dropped the lights again and I reintegrated the building, according to its molecular pattern stored in the gizmo's computer. Simple enough, when you think about it, given a little bit of engineering know-how . . . or at least a machine that can do it all for you.

Then I made my big mistake.

It was a trick I had done dozens of times, and it had never proved difficult before. Overconfident, I let my guard down, forgetting how truly alien these Earthlings are, how they panic when there isn't the least bit of danger. I "screwed up," to use their own quaint phrase.

For the finale of my act I had taken to levitating while juggling—my trademark performance, as it were. I strapped an auxiliary antigravity pack to my chest just below the gizmo itself, using it to levitate and flit about the stage as I taught and caught dangerous objects.

If the truth be told, I wasn't all that talented a juggler, but it was an Earth skill I had learned, and I was ridiculously proud of doing it without technological assistance. With the gizmo at hand, levitating is easy—juggling is *hard*!

While drifting high above the stage, and sometimes out

over the audience, I tossed a blur of swords and spiked balls. I was probably more impressed by my own trick than the audience was. They loved the levitation part, but juggling isn't as exciting to Earthlings as is disintegrating buildings, for some reason.

Because I had a tough audience this evening, I tried to show off, incorporating an extra spiked sphere into the mix with my twirling swords. The audience applauded, and I grinned proudly.

I let my concentration falter for only an instant . . . just enough to let one of the spiked balls slip above my chest as I reclined in thin air. It fell against me, and I reflexively twitched in midair, trying to avoid a sharp poke. Instead, the spiked ball struck the hidden gizmo, dislodging it.

As I yelped in surprise more than hurt, the whole mess—spiked balls, throwing knives, and the miraculous gizmo—tumbled to the stage with a discordant tinkle and thud.

The audience laughed, delighted to see the great performer fumble, and I covered my despair and my botched trick with a joke. "Ladies and gentlemen, you are very fortunate this evening. Never before has an audience seen *all* juggling items tumble thirty feet to the stage at once! Consider yourselves lucky I wasn't juggling with a volunteer from the audience!" (Showmanship, showmanship!)

This brought a chuckle as I lowered us to the far end of the stage, using the last trickle of reserve power in the anti-grav belt. I felt sick inside, but "the show must go on," so I took my bows and said my good-nights.

When the lights went down, I dashed across the stage to retrieve the debris and hurried back to my dressing room, where I refused all visitors for the rest of the night. . . .

I stared down in dismay at the broken innards of the gizmo, the convoluted circuits, the delicately imprinted control paths and microchips far beyond any technology Earth has ever created. The warranty wouldn't do me any good now.

As I said before, I am a xenosociologist, not an engineer. I stared down at my ruined miracle-working machine and thought again of Clarke's Law. The electronic paths and schematics meant absolutely nothing to me. The high-tech gizmo might as well have been magic.

I knew this would be my last night of performing. Without the gizmo the Great Taurindo was nothing, unless I learned how to do magic the hard way. . . .

So the years passed. I had amassed a considerable fortune during my years as a star, and I was able to continue living comfortably, though I never set foot on the stage again. I became something of a legend, the reclusive master illusionist who had suddenly quit performing and would tell no one why. I gave no interviews. Numerous books were written about me and my reasons, offering wild speculations, though none so preposterous as the truth.

In the privacy of my home, I continued to practice a few tricks for my own entertainment. I became quite proficient, actually, but nothing good enough to meet the expectations of those who had seen me perform before.

When at last the twenty-seven years had passed, and I received the signal from the rescue ship, I felt an overwhelming joy . . . as well as a not-inconsiderable sadness at leaving this interesting backwater planet.

I rushed into the desert to the pickup point, abandoning my home and all my possessions at the darkest hour of night—my sudden disappearance would only increase the mystique about me—and ran to meet the ship.

The pilot and crew were in a great hurry. A Cultural

Inspector from Central Authority hustled me off to my seat in the passenger compartment, and we roared back out through Earth's atmosphere. Finally, when we had reached our hypercruise speed, the Cultural Inspector came to debrief me—and I had been waiting for her.

"So, Taurindo Alpha Prime," she said, "you have spent many years on this planet. Tell me what you have learned of their culture."

I smiled. "I can do better than that—I can show you."

From a pocket in my jumpsuit I withdrew a standard deck, shuffled with a dazzling flourish and a snapping blur of sound, then fanned and extended them toward her.

"Pick a card," I said, "any card."

The Queen of Hearts and Swords

KAREN JOY FOWLER

Any Karen Joy Fowler story is a special experience. Her voice is unmistakable, her take on life uniquely her own. Here, she draws from Mammy Pleasant, *a biography by Helen Holdgredge, to tell a story about a woman whose major talent is the reinvention of herself. The setting is San Francisco in the middle of the nineteenth century. Through the protagonist, an extraordinary woman with one blue eye and one brown, Fowler shows us that people treat you according to who they think you are, not who you really are.*

—DC

The Queen of
Hearts and Swords

THE QUEEN OF HEARTS AND DIAMONDS:

IN 1852, WHILE ON HIS WAY from Valparaiso to San Francisco aboard the steamship *Bolivia*, Thomas Bell met a woman named Madame Christophe. Mr. Bell was a clerk for Barron, Forbes and Company, a firm specializing in cotton, mining, and double deals. Madame Christophe was the most beautiful woman he had ever seen, very tall, with clouds of dark hair and rosy, satiny skin. Her most remarkable feature was her eyes, for they didn't match. One was blue and one was brown, and yet the difference was subtle and likely to be noticed only on a close and careful inspection, and only when she was looking right at you. She did this often.

One night they stood together at the rail. The stars were as thick and yellow as grapes. There was a silver road of moonlight on the black surface of the ocean. Thomas Bell was asking questions. Where had she come from? Madame Christophe told him she was a widow from New Orleans. Where was she going? Who was she? Whom did she know in San Francisco?

She turned her eyes on him, which made him catch his breath. "Why do you look at me like that?" he asked.

"Why do you ask so many questions?" Her voice was full of slow vowels, soft stops. "Words were invented so that lies could be told. If you want to know someone, don't listen to what they say. Look at them. Look at me," she said. "Look closely." Her voice dropped to a whisper. "What does that tell you?"

Mr. Bell couldn't look closely. His vision was clouded by his ardor. But he saw her shiver. He rushed to his cabin for a wrap to lend her, a green-and-black tartan shawl.

They debarked in San Francisco in a crush of people. She got into a carriage, and he lost sight of her.

She should have been easy to find. There were so few women in San Francisco. Fewer still were beautiful. He sent inquiries to all the hotels. No one had a Madame Christophe registered. He asked everyone he knew, including his good friends Nora and Alexander Radford, he spoke of her everywhere, but could only say that she was a widow from New Orleans, that her eyes didn't match, and that she had his shawl. He was forced to return to Mexico, where he was in the middle of negotiations concerning the New Almadén Mine, without seeing her again.

Most of the people who made up San Francisco's society in the 1850s had once been or still were distinctly disreputable. In 1856, when the Vigilance Committee ran San Francisco and Belle Cora, a popular madam, had inadvertently caused the murder of a United States marshal simply by going to the theater and sitting with the wives, it was not always easy to explain why one person was top-drawer and another was not.

But Mrs. Nora Radford's case was simple. Her husband had died owing everyone money. Her conversation, she overheard Mrs. Hill say, was interesting enough, only there was too much of it. This observation was as hurtful as it was inaccurate. She had always been considered rather witty. Mrs. Hill and everyone else knew that she was more surprised by her husband's debts than anyone.

Only she refused to blame her husband for this. In fact, she was impressed. How clever he must have been to have fooled them all.

And she was touched. How hard he must have worked to give her such a sense of security. Much harder to accomplish than if he'd actually had money. She moved into rooms and missed her husband hourly.

Her new home was in the country, overlooking a graveyard. This was not as dismal as it might sound. Her room had a curtained bed and a carved dressing table. The cemetery was filled with flowers. On a warm day, the scent of them came into the room on the sunshine.

Her landlady was a tireless Southern woman named Mrs. Ellen Smith. Mrs. Smith took in laundry and worked as a housekeeper for Selim Woodworth, a prominent San Francisco businessman. It was young Mr. Woodworth who had suggested the arrangement to Mrs. Radford. Mr. Woodworth was a prominent philanthropist, a kind man, whose marked attentions to her after her husband's death, in contrast to the disregard of others, vouched for his quality. "My Mrs. Smith," he said warmly. "She works hard and makes canny investments. I don't know why she continues on as my housekeeper. Perhaps her fortunes have been so vagarious, she can never be secure. But she is a wonderful woman, as devoted to helping the unfortunate as she is to making a living in the world. That's where her money goes." He tipped his hat, continued his way down the little muddy track that was Market Street. Mrs. Radford hoisted her heavy skirts, their hems weighted with bird shot as a precaution against the wind, and picked her way through the mud. She took his advice immediately.

Mrs. Radford's initial impression of her landlady was that she was about thirty years old. And she was beautiful. The first time Mrs. Radford saw her, she was sitting in a sunlit pool on the faded brocade of the parlor sofa. In Mrs. Radford's mind she always retained that first golden glow.

"You'll find me here when the sun is shining," Mrs. Smith told her. "I'll never get used to the cold."

"It gets colder and colder," Mrs. Radford agreed. The words came out too serious, too sad. There was an embarrassing element of self-pity she hadn't intended.

Mrs. Smith smiled. "I hope we can make you feel at home here." She looked straight at Mrs. Radford. Her eyes didn't match. There was a shawl on the sofa, of green-and-black plaid.

Mrs. Radford couldn't remember the name Mr. Bell had given her, but she was sure it wasn't Ellen Smith. Something foreign, she'd thought. Something Latin. Mrs. Smith's beauty was darkly Mediterranean. She stood and was surprisingly tall, a whole head above Mrs. Radford. "Would you like a cup of tea?" she asked.

The kitchen was an elegant place of astral lamps and oil chandeliers. There were golden cupids in the wallpaper. There was a young black man who swept the floor and washed the dishes while they talked. Mrs. Smith filled her cup half with cream, heaped it with sugar. She stirred it and stirred it.

"I can't quite place your accent," Mrs. Radford said.

"I don't wonder. I've lived so many places." Mrs. Smith stared down into her clouded tea. She lifted the cup and blew on it. She set it down.

"I lived on the hill," Mrs. Radford said, coaxing her into confidences by offering her own. "Until my husband died. I am quite come down in the world."

"You'll rise again. I started out with nothing."

Mrs. Radford had often been embarrassed at how much beauty meant to her. At the age when Mrs. Radford might have been beautiful herself, she suffered badly from acne. It pitted her skin and her lovely hair was little compensation. At the time she'd thought her life was over. But then it had hardly seemed to matter. She'd made such a happy marriage. God had granted her a great love. And yet she had never stopped wishing she were beautiful, had apparently learned nothing from her own life. She would have been the first to admit this. It would have hurt her to have had ugly children, and this was a painful thing to know. As it turned out she had no children at all. "You had beauty," said Mrs. Radford.

Mrs. Smith raised her extraordinary eyes. "I suppose I did." The day was clouding. The sun went off and on again, like a blink. Mrs. Smith turned her head. "I've learned not to count on it. My mother was beautiful. It did her no particular good. I lost her very early. She was so worried about me—what would happen to me, who would take care of me. She told me to go out to the road and stand so that people could see me. It was the last thing she said to me."

It had been just a little back lane, without much traffic. The fence was falling into ruins; she stepped over it easily. She could see the end of the road, shimmering in the distance like a dream. There was an apple tree over her head, blossoming into pink and filled with the sound of bees. She stood and waited all morning, crying a little from time to time, about her mother, until she was sleepy from the sun and the buzzing, and no one came by.

Finally, in the early afternoon, when the sun had just started to slant past her, she heard a horse in the distance. The sound grew louder. She raised her hand to shade her eyes. The horse was black. The man was as old as her grandfather, who was also her father, truth be told.

He almost went by her. He was nodding himself on the slow-moving horse, but when he saw her he stopped so suddenly that saliva pooled around the silver bit and dripped slowly, like honey, onto the road. The man looked her over and removed his hat. "What's your name?" he asked. She said nothing. He reached out a hand. "Well, I'm not fussy," he told her. "How would you like to go to New Orleans?" And that's how she moved up in the world, by putting her foot in the stirrup.

"I was ten years old."

"Oh, my dear." Mrs. Radford was shocked and distressed.

Mrs. Smith put her hand on Mrs. Radford's arm. Mrs. Radford had rarely been touched by anyone since her husband died. Sometimes her skin ached for it, all over her body. Where did an old woman with no children go to be touched? Mrs. Smith's hand was warm. "It wasn't that, after all. He turned out very kind," she said.

Mrs. Radford adjusted to country living as well as could be expected. The laundry was a busy place. The cemetery was not. She especially enjoyed her evenings. She would join Mrs. Smith. The parlor would be brightened by a busy fire. They would drink a soothing concoction Mrs. Smith called "balm tea," with just a drop of rum. It went straight to Mrs. Radford's head. In these convivial surroundings, she told Mrs. Smith how she had planned once to teach. "I had a train ticket to Minneapolis. I had a job. I had only known Alexander for a week. But he came to the station and asked me to marry him instead. 'I want to see the world before I get married,' I told him. 'See it after,' he said. 'See it with me.'"

"And did you?"

In fact, his language had been much more passionate—things Mrs. Radford could hardly repeat, but would never forget. His voice remained with her more vividly than his face. She grew warm remembering. It calmed her to speak of him; she was grateful to Mrs. Smith for listening. "I saw my corner of it. It was a very happy corner."

In her turn, Mrs. Radford learned that Mrs. Smith's original benefactor, a man named Mr. Price, had taken her to a convent school in New Orleans. She spent a year there, learning to read and write. Then he sent her to Cincinnati. She lived with some friends of his named Williams. "I was to go to school for four more years and also to help Mrs. Williams with the children. She made quite a pet of me, at first.

"But then Mr. Price died. I know he had already paid the Williamses for my schooling, but the Williamses pretended he hadn't. They sent me to Nantucket as a bonded servant."

The weathered wood and sand of Nantucket was a new landscape for her. Her mistress had been the Quaker woman who owned the island's general store. She came from a line of whalers—very wealthy. She had taken Ellen, now twelve, to the Friends' meeting house, where they sat in the darkness on hard wooden benches and waited for the Spirit. "It didn't take with me, I'm afraid," said Mrs. Smith, fingering the locket she wore at her throat. "I'm too fond of nice things. But she was also very kind. I called her Grandma. I worked for her until she died, quite suddenly, and then again there were no provisions made for me. This time I was quite alone. Sixteen. I sold off some of her stock, and I went to Boston. Her real granddaughter lived there, and I thought she might take me in, but she didn't." It was there that Ellen met James Smith, a wealthy and prominent businessman. They were married. He died.

"It's been a sort of pattern," Mrs. Smith conceded. "Life is full of loss."

Mrs. Radford could see that she had not loved her husband. It was nothing she said; it appeared on her face whenever she spoke of him.

Mrs. Radford had not decided what to do. Thomas Bell had returned from Mexico almost a year ago. He was an old friend, so she owed him some loyalty, although he hadn't, in fact, been to see her since his return. Served him right, really, if he'd come to call, to express his condolences, he might have seen the woman. Virtue was its own reward.

And what of her loyalty to her new friend? Mr. Bell was not the sort of man who married. There were rumors that he had been seen going into a house of assignation on Washington Street.

Before her husband's death, Mrs. Radford would have only had to write the invitations and San Francisco's most eligible men would have gathered at her dinner table. Sometimes at night, alone in her curtained bed, she allowed herself to imagine the dinner. Alexander pouring wine. The gold-rimmed china. The sensation of the beautiful Mrs. Smith.

But Mr. Bell had been so overheated, so single-minded, so desperate. Mrs. Radford was a great believer in love. She longed to do her little bit to help it along. Marriage was the happy ending to Mrs. Smith's hard and blameless life. The right man had only to see her; and it still might be Thomas Bell, who already had.

The most enjoyable parts of a social occasion are often the solitary pleasures of anticipation and recollection. But it is sadly true that one cannot relish these without having had an invitation to the party itself.

The MacElroys, who were special friends of Thomas Bell's, had announced the engagement of their middle daughter. There was to be a fabulous ball. Although Mrs. Radford had, with her husband, been a guest at the party celebrating the engagement of their first daughter and also at the marriage of their youngest daughter, there was no certainty that she would be included now.

It was only a party. Only a fabulous ball. She did not mind for herself, not so much, really, although she had always enjoyed a party. But it would be just the setting for Mrs. Smith. With this in mind, Mrs. Radford finally called on Thomas Bell. He was living in the bachelor club on Grove. He apologized for the cigar smoke, which did not bother her, but not for the fact that he had never come to see her, which did. His blond hair had receded some in the last four years, giving him a high, wide forehead. He had always been a handsome man, but he'd attained a dignity he had lacked before. He looked marriageable. "Did you ever find your lovely shipmate?" she asked him, quite directly, with no cunning preamble.

"Madame Christophe?" he said immediately. "No. I looked everywhere."

"In the servants' quarters?"

He responded with some heat. "She was a queen."

"And if she were not?" Mrs. Radford watched his face closely. She was looking for true love. She thought she saw it.

And also rising comprehension. "You know where she is." Mr. Bell reached excitedly for her arm. "Take me to her at once."

"No. But if she were invited to the MacElroys' ball, I would deliver the invitation. Then you could take your turn with every other eligible young man in San Francisco." She meant this quite literally, but she allowed a familiar, teasing tone to come into her voice to hide it.

"Dear Mrs. Radford," he said.

"She is a working woman," Mrs. Radford warned him. "With quite a different name."

"She is a queen," Mr. Bell repeated. "Whatever she does, whatever she calls herself. Blood will tell."

Mrs. Radford was in black. Mrs. Smith wore a gown of pink silk. It was fitted at the bodice, but blossomed at the hips with puffings and petals. The hem was larger still and laced with ribbons. She came into the MacElroys' drawing room, cleared for dancing, like a rose floating on water. The redowa had just finished. The lancers had not yet begun. Every head was turned. Mr. Bell made a spectacle of himself in his effort to get to her first. He was just slightly shorter than she was.

"Mrs. Radford," he said politely. "How lovely to see you here. And Madame Christophe. I mustn't imagine that you remember me, simply because I remember you."

"But I do," she said. She glanced at Mrs. Radford and then back to Mr. Bell. "And I'm afraid my name is not Madame Christophe. Doubtless I owe you an explanation. What a lovely room this is." There was a pause. Mr. Bell rushed to fill it.

"All you owe me is a dance," he assured her. He was eager, nervous. He drew her away from Mrs. Radford, who went to sit with the older women. The music began. She watched Mr. Bell bend in to Mrs. Smith to speak and bend away again. She watched the pink skirt swinging over the polished floor, the occasional glimpse of Mrs. Smith's bronze-toed boots. She attended to the music and the lovely, familiar sense of being involved in things. She watched two men watch Mrs. Smith. Mr. Ralston, the banking executive, engaged her for one waltz. Mr. Edward Barron took the next. And Mr. Bell danced with no one else, spent the time while she danced with others pacing and watching for the moment she came free.

In her own small way, Mrs. Radford also triumphed. People spoke to her who hadn't done so since her husband's death. Small, innocuous pleasantries, but she could no longer take such attentions for granted. Eventually every conversation arrived at Mrs. Smith.

"That lovely woman you came with," said Mrs. Hill. "I've not seen her before."

"She's an old friend," said Mrs. Radford contentedly. "A widow from New Orleans." She said nothing else, although it was clearly insufficient. Let Mrs. Hill remember how she had accused Mrs. Radford of talking too much!

At the end of the evening, Mr. Bell went to find their cloaks. "I had a wonderful time," Mrs. Smith told Mrs. Radford. "I'm grateful to you for arranging it."

"I'm so pleased I could. You'll have many nights like this now. Many invitations. You were such a success."

Mrs. Smith had a gray velvet cloak. Mr. Bell returned with it, settled it slowly over her shoulders. He was reluctant to release her. "About my name," she said. They were walking outside, the women's skirts crushed one against the next, like a bouquet. On the steps, they joined a crowd waiting for carriages. Next to them were the Hills and the Ralstons. "I was forced to change my name to get out of New Orleans. I was born into slavery in Georgia," Mrs. Smith said. Everyone could hear her. "I became a white woman in order to escape it. Ellen Smith isn't my real name either."

Mrs. Smith and Mrs. Radford were alone in their carriage. The ride to the country was a long one. Mrs. Radford's feelings were too tender to bear examination. It seemed as though Mrs. Smith had deliberately humiliated her. "Is it true?" she asked first.

"Everything I've told you is true."

"Why pick that moment to say it?"

"It was time. I've been a white woman for so many years. It wasn't aimed at you," Mrs. Smith said. "Or your ideas about love and beauty." The horses' hooves clapped. The carriage wheel hit a stone. It threw Mrs. Radford against Mrs. Smith. Mrs. Smith caught her by the arm. She was wearing gloves, so they didn't actually touch.

THE QUEEN OF WANDS AND SWORDS:

Mrs. Radford went to live with her sister in Cincinnati, and Ellen Smith began calling herself Mary Ellen Pleasant. By 1858 she was a familiar figure in San Francisco. In that year, a slaveholder from Mississippi came to California with a slave named Archy. Archy escaped, but was found and taken into custody in Sacramento. He was quickly released by the Sacramento judge, who said there was no law in California that could force him back to Mississippi against his will.

The slaveholder had Archy rearrested in San Francisco. Once more he was released by the state, but before he could leave the courthouse, the federal marshal, invoking the Fugitive Slave Law, had him placed in jail. Archy's imprisonment was strenuously protested by the black population, and the cause was also enthusiastically taken up by many prominent whites. But it was Mary Ellen Pleasant who told the slaveholder right to his face, right on the courthouse steps, that he had been foolish to bring to California a slave who wasn't faithful by attachment.

"He belongs to me," the slaveholder told her with chivalrous ice. "I paid for him."

"With money some other slave made for you," she answered. "He's not yours now, because he never was yours." The exchange delighted San Francisco society, which recounted it over drinks and cigars until it had assumed many different shapes and shadings. Sometimes Mrs. Pleasant towered over the tiny slaver. Sometimes he was even taller than she, and she stood on the step above him to look him spiritedly in the eye. Always she was our Mammy Pleasant. Once again, Archy was released.

That night when the slaveholder had Archy seized and put aboard the *Orizaba*, it was to Mrs. Pleasant that the ship's cook sent a midnight message. It was at her instruction that a police officer rowed out to the ship and took Archy from the slaveholder with a writ of habeas corpus. It was Mary Ellen Pleasant who stood on the dock in the dark, with blankets and whiskey, to welcome Archy home. Mrs. Pleasant was widely and warmly congratulated. She gave a party to celebrate Archy's final release and invited all of white society.

Mrs. Pleasant was admired for many things. Everything about her was exceptional—her beauty, her industry, her intelligence. Through hard work and a genius for investment, she became a wealthy woman. She built herself a mansion on the hill, but she spent as much in charity. She knew the indigent and unfortunate. They depended on her. She also knew the most prominent families in the city. Best of all she knew her place. She could be invited to any social gathering and be counted on to send her polite regrets.

But now it was clear that too much of a fuss had been made over her. By giving a party herself, she created the kind of awkward occasion San Francisco society expected her to avoid.

It was not her color, or at least it was not only her color.

There were suspicions, whispers too faint to be called rumors. She had lovers, they said, some black, some white. Thomas Bell, perhaps, and more. She had a second husband, hidden somewhere. She dined with prostitutes and Chinamen. She had too much power over the blacks in San Francisco, who adored her—and yet, weren't they also afraid of her?

But all the invitations were accepted.

In the days before the party Mrs. Pleasant gave up her aprons, her collars, and her black bonnet. She began to wear bonnets that were gayer, dresses that were daintier. She favored earrings that dangled and bracelets that clinked.

The night of the party she dazzled. Her gown was a twilight blue, designed in New York, and embroidered with sequins made of actual fish scales. She wore a necklace of diamonds. George Willard, her butler, told the people in his church that she was having gardenias grown in hothouses in San Jose. There was a bouquet for the window and a single flower, the largest flower, for her hair. Mr. Willard answered the door and brought the guests, one by one, to the ballroom, where the floor had been polished by hand as if it were glass.

The guests were all men. One by one, they offered the excuses and regrets of their wives. They found it very hard to endure her eyes.

Mrs. Pleasant had told Mr. Willard that her mother was sold by the overseer, because of the way she looked at him. No one wanted a slave he was afraid of. Two months later the overseer sickened and died. "It was your mother," the other slaves had said. "Your mother had the power. It's a matter of blood."

At midnight Mrs. Pleasant excused herself and went to her room, leaving Mr. Bell to say good-night to her guests. In the morning when she came back downstairs, the servants saw that she was wearing her housekeeping apron again. "Take the flowers away," she said to Mr. Willard. "Go and put them on someone's grave."

Mr. Bell was not Mrs. Pleasant's lover. He wasn't sure why. She fascinated and frustrated him. He called on her constantly. He didn't care at all what color she was, although black was better—she wouldn't expect him to marry her if she were black. She was interested in his finances, in his investments, in his company. She urged him not to settle for being a clerk, no matter how trusted, but to demand to be made a partner. She seemed happy to see him, but she always managed to turn the conversation to business. If he sat next to her on the sofa, she moved to a nearby chair. If he followed her into the kitchen, she circled the table and left for the pantry.

He invited her to go with him to visit the New Almadén Mine. Once it had been a frequent getaway for its owners and their mistresses. But the ownership was currently in dispute. The mine was deserted.

They took the stagecoach to San Jose and spent the night in a hotel called the Hacienda because it was made of adobe and tile. They ate dinner together and then went to their separate rooms. Mr. Bell did not fall asleep until almost dawn. The sheets on his bed were twisted and damp with his sweat.

The following day they rode out together, up the hillside, through the manzanita and dust to the entrance. Then they left the horses and walked along the tracks into the mouth of the mine. Soon there was no light at all. Mr. Bell lit a candle and put it in his hat. The walls of the tunnel were wet so that they shone like obsidian. There was the smell of water and money.

"You're the most beautiful woman I've ever seen," Mr.

Bell said suddenly. She was behind him. He couldn't see her at all. He turned and the candlelight swept across her face. He reached into his pocket. "I have something for you."

It was a necklace of gold, set with engraved medallions. She had to step very close to him to see it. "It's lovely," she said. She let him clasp it about her neck. He had to lift her hair to do so.

"I'm not the sort of man who marries," he told her, standing with her neck in his hands. He was shaking from the touch of her skin.

"I don't want to marry you." Her tone was agreeable. She turned to him, half her face in shadow. "You're only a clerk," she said.

Mrs. Pleasant refurbished the now empty laundry and boardinghouse in the country, renaming it Geneva Cottage. She decorated it with dark polished woods, gold-leaf mirrors, marble basins, fountains with erotic statues. She paid special attention to the landscaping. It had a large, lush yard with many hidden groves and private grottoes, cool shaded places where ferns and violets could grow. There were small bits of sunny grass perfumed by hidden flowers. It took a year to finish. When she was done she sent out invitations to a second party.

This time she invited only men, ten of the most power-ful men in San Francisco. The invitations were delivered secretly by black messengers. She had picked her guests carefully. She had their pictures in a room upstairs, the room once occupied by Mrs. Radford, with a candle beneath each one. Two of the men were bankers; there was a railroad millionaire, a mine owner, and a newspaper baron. There was a senator, and a judge from the state supreme court. The guest list has never been made public.

She promised them a special evening in the country without their wives. The paper the invitations were written on was red; the ink was silver. They all came.

When Ellen Smith left New Orleans, disguised as Madame Christophe, she was only a step ahead of the hangman. She had been stealing slaves, connecting them with the Underground Railroad, when the planters closed in. She escaped through the help and intervention of her patroness, Marie Leveau, the voodoo queen of New Orleans. Marie Leveau had taught her many things. One of them was how to give a party.

There was little to eat and much to drink. They called the drink champagne, but it was really something far more lethal. Mrs. Pleasant had put it down herself. "The entertainment tonight will be voodoo," she told the men. There were ten beautiful young women, dressed like princesses, but with the skin of slaves, to sit with the men while they smoked and dance the calinda with them after. There were drums. There were ritual incantations. The ballroom grew hot from the dancing and the liquor. There were drums.

One of the women was a sixteen-year-old named Malina. She wore yellow roses on her wrist and yellow silk on her shoulders. She caught the attention of one of the men, perhaps a banker, perhaps the mine owner. What appealed to him most was her shyness. She couldn't answer his questions, couldn't smile at his jokes. Her movements during the dance were slight, but this, he thought, made them even more suggestive. He drank, and she didn't. When he put his hand into the space between her skirt and her leg, she froze suddenly, awkwardly, and asked another of the women to change places with her. There was a silence in the room. When the dancing began again, the man had a different partner.

Mrs. Pleasant could see that he was angry and very drunk. She took Malina aside and told her she was a fool to be rude to a man who could do her so much good. Mrs. Pleasant wanted the men entangled, wanted the women installed as mistresses, draining whatever time and money they could from the men's wives. Malina refused to be reasonable.

"I hate him," she said, and it was loud enough to be heard. She was sobbing, salty tears that would ruin the yellow silk, which belonged to Mrs. Pleasant and not to her.

Malina ran from the room and the man went after her. She ran through the pink-and-white parlor and out into the courtyard. She ran into the trees. The man followed. There was a time of silence, and then there was a scream. Just one. It might have been the peacocks Mrs. Pleasant had purchased to patrol the grounds.

By the time Mrs. Pleasant and the other men and women reached the outside, Malina was returning. Her hair was falling about her face. She came between the two fountains with their statues of naked women—two stone figures, stroking their own breasts. She was not wearing her roses or her shoes.

The moon was an insufficient rim of light. Malina was stumbling, her head at a strange angle. She dripped. She fell in the courtyard. Her throat had been cut.

When Mrs. Pleasant next looked up, she saw that all the other women had fled. "I'll take care of it," she told the men. "You must rely on my discretion." She removed her house-keeping apron and covered Malina's face with it. She would never put it on again. "No one will ever know that you were here tonight. Your wives will never know," she said.

*   *   *

Mrs. Pleasant meant, of course, that no one white would ever know about the party. By morning the circumstances of Malina's death had been told throughout the black community. Although she had had few friends, her funeral was so large it had to be moved outdoors. The casket was open. Malina's neck had been wrapped in discreet chiffon.

Mrs. Pleasant dressed in a fresh yellow. Some of the mourners felt it was an inappropriate color. They fell silent when she arrived, and there was something hostile in the silence. Most of them owed Mrs. Pleasant their jobs. Some owed her their lives. They owed Malina nothing so tangible. So their hostility angered Mrs. Pleasant.

"I am the equal of anyone," she told them. "Even you."

She knelt beside Malina and put a painted egg in the dead girl's hand. It mollified the mourners somewhat. The egg would give Malina power from the grave over the man who killed her. He would not escape without payment.

The murderer had never returned from the lawn to Geneva Cottage. Thomas Bell, who had carefully stayed away from the party himself, went to see him the next morning. When Mr. Bell entered the house, the man he was visiting turned pale. Clearly he had not slept. The two men walked together out to the street, away from the ears of the servants, away from the eyes of his family. It was a foggy San Francisco day. You couldn't see from the porch to the curb. Droplets collected on Mr. Bell's muffler and gloves. The other man was in his dressing gown.

Mr. Bell let the silence go on for a while.

"You weren't there," the man said finally. "But there was magic. I wasn't myself. You know I couldn't do such a thing. You know me. I was her instrument."

A shroud of fog wrapped the house behind him. Mr. Bell could barely see the lights of the upstairs windows, hanging like vague, golden moons. "Why would Mrs.

Pleasant want you to kill Malina? Mrs. Pleasant told Malina to be nice to you." The man hadn't known Malina's name. He didn't want to hear it now. He raised his hand to stop Mr. Bell from saying it.

"Mrs. Pleasant is doing her best to protect you," said Mr. Bell. "She does want you to know that she couldn't go so far as to perjure herself in a court of law."

"The colored cannot give evidence against a white person," the man said. Perhaps he was the judge.

Mr. Bell wiped the moisture off his upper lip. "Are you certain that Mrs. Pleasant is a colored person?"

"Of course I'm certain." There was a pause. The next time the man spoke his voice betrayed his shock. "I have her own word."

"Words were invented so that lies could be told. When you look at her, do you see a colored woman?"

"Of course I do. No one would pretend to be colored if they were white." The man had begun to shiver. "This is nonsense. Everyone in San Francisco knows she was a slave."

"You may be right," Mr. Bell said. "I confess I'm curious myself. I'd like to see what she would say under oath. But it might be satisfying my curiosity rather at your expense. In any case, I'm sure it won't come to that."

A month later Mary Ellen Pleasant gave a third party. It was at her home on the hill. She invited the ten gentlemen from the second party, their friends and business associates, and all the wives. They all came. The conversation was nothing to remember; there wasn't very much of it. The men were awkward and strained. The wives were angry and confused. But the mansion was strung with lights and the food was extraordinary. There were seven courses. There were smoked and fresh meats, out-of-season vegetables, pâtés and wines from France, jewelry boxes which contained teas from China, fruits glazed with liqueurs. There was the novelty of Cajun stews. Mrs. Pleasant was publishing a cookbook.

After dinner she announced that she was going east to help John Brown arm the slaves. She was taking many thousand dollars of her own fortune to give to him. "I always knew there would be blood," she said. "I always knew in the end there would be no other way."

Some of the most prominent white businessmen said that they, too, had always thought the slaves would have to be armed. They insisted on making large donations of their own to John Brown. Mr. Bell made helpful suggestions as to the amounts.

Mary Ellen Pleasant lived in San Francisco until her death in 1903. As she aged, the colors of her eyes faded until they matched, even when she looked at you directly. She had done many things in her last forty-three years, but she had never given another party. She always remembered her final one vividly, although the time came when she could no longer remember the names of all the men who had been her lovers, nor the names of all the men who had been at Geneva Cottage that evening, nor the name of the murdered woman. "It was Christmastime. The trees were iced and the house was lit from cellar to roof," she said. "You never saw such dresses. I chose the menu myself. Everyone who was any-one was there."

with acknowledgments to Helen Holdgredge's biography, *Mammy Pleasant,* published by GP Putnam's Sons, 1953.

The Invisibles

CHARLES DE LINT

*Now you see it, now you don't. That's the old illusion-
ist's directive. When I'm onstage, I direct your attention
to objects and events, and you see them only when I tell
you to. In life, there are also those objects and people we
don't see until our attention is suddenly directed to
them. Then, it's as if there were no way we couldn't
have seen them in the first place. Another question is, do
these people know they are, in effect, invisible? Did they
make themselves disappear? And if so, why?*

—DC

The Invisibles

"What is unseen is not necessarily unknown."
—WENDELESSEN

1

WHEN I WAS TWELVE YEARS OLD, it was a different world.

I suppose most people think that, turning their gazes inward to old times, the long trail of their memories leading them back into territory made unfamiliar with the dust of years. The dust lies so thick in places it changes the shape of what it covers, half-remembered people, places, and events, all mixed together so that you get confused trying to sort them out, don't even recognize some, probably glad you can't make out others. But then there are places, the wind blows harder across their shapes, or maybe we visit them more often so the dust doesn't lie so thick, and the memories sit there waiting for us, no different now than the day they happened, good and bad, momentous occasions and those so trivial you can't figure out why you remember them.

But I know this is true: When I was twelve years old, kids my age didn't know as much as they do today. We believed things you couldn't get by most eight-year-olds now. We were ready to believe almost anything. All we required was that it be true—maybe not so much by the rules of the world around us, but at least by the rules of some intuitive inner logic. It wasn't ever anything that got talked out. We just believed. In luck. In wishes. In how a thing will happen, if you stick to the right parade of circumstances.

We were willing to believe in magic.

Here's what you do, Jerry says. You get one of those little pipe tobacco tins and you put stuff in it. Important stuff. A fingernail. Some hair. A scab. Some dirt from a special place. You spit on it and mix it up like a mud pie. Prick your finger and add a drop of blood. Then you wrap it all up in a picture of the thing you like the best.

What if you don't have a picture of the thing you like the best? I ask.

Doesn't have to be a real picture, he says. You can just make a drawing of it. Might be even better that way because then it really belongs to you.

So what do you do with it? Rebecca asks.

I can see her so clearly, the red hairs coming loose from her braids, picking at her knee where she scraped it falling off her bike.

You stick it in that tin, Jerry says, and close it up tight. Dig a hole under your porch and bury it deep.

He leans closer to us, eyes serious, has that look he always gets when he's telling us something we might not believe is true, but he wants us to know that it is.

This means something, he says. You do it right, and you'll always have that thing you like the best. Nothing will ever take it away.

I don't know where he heard about it. Read it in a book, or maybe his grandmother told him. She always had the best stories. It doesn't matter. We knew it was a true magic, and that night each of us snuck out of our house and did it. Buried those tins deep. Made a secret of it to make the magic stronger is how Jerry put it.

I didn't need the magic to be any stronger. I just needed it to be true. We were best friends, the three of us, and I didn't want that to ever change. I really believed in magic, and the idea of the tin seemed to be about the best magic kids like us could make.

Rebecca moved away when we were in ninth grade. Jerry died the last year of high school, hit by a drunk driver.

Years later, this all came back to me. I'd returned to have a look at the old neighborhood, but our houses were gone by then. Those acre lots we grew up on had been subdivided, the roads all turned around on themselves and changed until there was nothing left of the neighborhood's old patterns. They're identical, these new houses, poured out of the same mold, one after the other, row upon row, street after street.

I got out of the car that day and stood where I thought my house used to be, feeling lost, cut off, no longer connected to my own past. I thought of those tins then and wondered whatever had happened to them. I remembered the drawing I made to put in mine. It was so poorly drawn I'd had to write our names under our faces to make sure the magic knew who I meant.

The weird thing is I never felt betrayed by the magic when Rebecca moved away, or when Jerry died. I just . . . lost it. Forgot about it. It went away, or maybe I did. Even that day, standing there in a neighborhood now occupied by strangers, the memory of those tins was only bittersweet. I smiled, remembering what we'd done, sneaking out so late that night, how we'd believed. The tightness in my chest grew from good moments recalled, mixed up with the sadness of remembering friends I'd lost. Of course those tins couldn't have kept us together. Life goes on. People move, relationships alter, people die. That's how the world turns.

There isn't room for magic in it, though you'd never convince Ted of that.

2

Ted and I go back a long way. We met during my first year in college, almost twenty years ago, and we still see each other every second day or so. I don't know why we get along so well unless that old axiom's true and opposites do attract. Ted's about the most outgoing person you could meet; opinionated, I'll be the first to admit, but he also knows how to listen. He's the sort of person other people naturally gravitate to at a party, collecting odd facts and odder rumors the way a magpie does shiny baubles, then jump-starting conversations with them at a later date as though they were hors d'oeuvres.

I'm not nearly so social an animal. If you pressed me, I'd say I like to pick and choose my friends carefully; the truth is, I usually have no idea what to say to people—especially when I first meet them.

Tonight it's only the two of us, holding court in The Half Kaffe. I'm drinking espresso, Ted's got one of those decaf lattés made with skim milk that always has me wonder, what's the point? If you want to drink coffee that weak, you can find it down the street at Bruno's Diner for a quarter of the price. But Ted's gone health-conscious recently. It's all talk about decaf and jogging and macrobiotic this and holistic that, then he lights up a cigarette. Go figure.

"Who's that woman?" I ask when he runs out of things

to say about this *T'ai Chi* course he's just started taking. "The one at the other end of the counter with the long straight hair and the sad eyes?"

I haven't been able to stop looking at her since we got here. I find her attractive, but not in a way I can easily explain. It's more the sum of the parts, because individually things are a little askew. She's tall and angular, eyes almost too wide-set, chin pointed like a cat's, a Picasso nose, very straight and angled down. She has the sort of features that look gorgeous one moment, then almost homely the next. Her posture's not great, but then, considering my own, I don't think I should be making that kind of judgment. Maybe she thinks like I do, that if you slouch a bit, people won't notice you. Doesn't usually work.

I suspect she's waiting for someone since all she's been doing is sitting there, looking out the window. Hasn't ordered anything yet. Or maybe it's because Jonathan's too caught up with the most recent issue of *The Utne Reader* to notice her.

I look away from her when I realize that Ted hasn't answered. I find him giving me a strange look.

"So what've you got in that cup besides coffee?" he asks.

"What's that supposed to mean?"

He laughs. "I'm not sure. All I know is I don't see anyone sitting at this counter, male or female. I see you and me and Jonathan."

I'm sure he's putting me on. "No, seriously. Who is she?"

And he, I realize, thinks I'm putting him on. He makes an exaggerated show of having a look, taking off nonexistent glasses, cleaning them, putting them back on, looks some more, but his attention isn't even on the right stool.

"Okay," he says. "I see her now. I think . . . yes, she's a

princess. Lost a shoe, or a half-dozen feet of hair, or a bag of beans or something. Or maybe turned the wrong key in the wrong lock and got turned out of her bearded husband's apartment, and now she's here killing time between periods of sleep just like the rest of us."

"Enough," I tell him. "I get the picture."

He doesn't see her. And it's beginning to be obvious to me that Jonathan doesn't see her, or he'd have taken her order by now. The group at the table behind us, all black jeans and intense conversation, they probably don't either.

"So what's this all about?" Ted asks.

He looks half-amused, half-intrigued, still unsure if it's a joke or something more intriguing, a piece of normal that's slid off to one side. He has a nose for that sort of thing, from Elvis sightings to nuns impregnated by aliens, and I can almost see it twitching. He doesn't read the tabloids in line at the supermarket; he buys them. Need I say more?

So when he asks me what it's all about, he seems the perfect candidate for me to tell because it's very confusing and way out of my line of experience. I've never been prone to hallucinations before, and, besides, I always thought they'd be more . . . well, surreal, I suppose. Dadaistic. Over the top. This is so ordinary. Just a woman, sitting in a coffee bar, that no one seems to be able to see. Except for me.

"Hello, Andrew," Ted says, holding the first syllable of my name and drawing it out. "You still with us?"

I nod and give him a smile.

"So are you going to fill me in or what?"

"It's nothing," I say. "I was just seeing if you were paying attention."

"Um-hmm."

He doesn't believe me for a moment. All I've managed to do is pique his curiosity more.

"No, really," I tell him.

The woman stands up from the counter, distracting me. I wonder why she came in here in the first place since she can't seem to place an order, but then I think maybe even invisible people need to get out, enjoy a little nightlife, if only vicariously.

Or maybe she's a ghost.

"Did anybody ever die in here?" I ask Ted.

Ted gives me yet another strange look. He leans across the table.

"You're getting seriously weird on me," he says. "What do you want to know that for?"

The woman's on her way to the door now. Portishead is playing on the café's sound system. "Sour Times." Lalo Schifrin and Smokey Brooks samples on a bed of scratchy vinyl sounds and a smoldering, low-key Eurobeat. Beth Gibbons singing about how nobody loves her. At one time we both worked at Gypsy Records, and we're still serious music junkies. It's one of the reasons we like The Half Kaffe so much; Jonathan has impeccable taste.

I pull a ten from my pocket and drop it on the table.

"I'll tell you later," I say as I get up from my stool.

"Andrew," Ted says. "You can't just leave me hanging like this."

"Later."

She's out the door, turning left. Through the café's window, I watch her do a little shuffle to one side as a couple almost walk right into her. They can't see her either. "Sour Times" dissolves into an instrumental, mostly keyboards and a lonesome electric guitar. Ted calls after me. He's starting to get up, too, but I wave him back. Then I'm out the door, jogging after the woman.

"Excuse me!" I call after her. "Excuse me, miss!"

I can't believe I'm doing this. I have no idea what I'll say to her if she stops. But she doesn't turn. Gives no indication she's heard me. I catch up to her and touch her lightly on the elbow. I know a moment of surprise when I can feel the fabric of her sleeve instead of some cool mist. I half expected my fingers to go right through her.

"Excuse me," I say again.

She stops then and looks at me. Up close, her face, those sad eyes . . . they make my pulse quicken until my heartbeat sounds like a deep bass drum playing a march at double time in my chest.

"Yes?"

"I . . ."

There's no surprise in her features. She doesn't ask how come I can see her and nobody else can. What I do see is a hint of fear in her eyes, which shouldn't surprise me. A woman alone on the streets always has to be on her guard. I take a step back to ease the fear, feeling guilty and depressed for having put it there.

"I . . ."

There are a hundred things I want to ask her. About how she did what she did in The Half Kaffe. How come I can see her when other people can't. Why she's not surprised that I can see her. I'd even ask her out for a drink if I had the nerve. But nothing seems appropriate to the moment. Nothing makes sense.

I clear my throat and settle on: "Can you tell me how to get to Battersfield Road?"

The fear recedes in her eyes, but a wariness remains.

"Take a left at the next light," she tells me, "and just go straight. You can't miss it."

"Thanks."

I watch her continue on her way. Two women approach her from the other direction, moving aside to give her room when she comes abreast. So does what appears to be a businessman, suit and tie, briefcase in hand, working late, hurrying home. But the couple behind him don't see her at all; she has to dart to one side, press up against a store window so that they don't collide.

She's invisible again.

I follow her progress all the way to the end of the block as she weaves in and out of near collisions with the other pedestrians. Then she's at the crosswalk, a tall, slouching figure waiting for the light to change. She takes a right where she told me to take a left, and a storefront cuts her from my view.

I almost return to The Half Kaffe, but I don't feel up to being grilled by Ted. I almost go home, but what am I going to do at home on a Friday night? Instead, I run to the corner where she turned, cross against the light, and almost get hit by a cab. The driver salutes me with one stiff finger and shouts something unintelligible at me, but I'm already past him, on the far curb now. I see her ahead of me, almost at the end of the block, and I do something I've never done before in my life. I follow a woman I don't know home.

3

The building she finally enters is one of those old Crowsea brownstones that hasn't been renovated into condos yet— five stories, arches of tapered bricks over the windows, multigabled roof. There'd be at least twenty apartments in the place, crammed up one against the other, shoulder to shoulder like commuters jostling in the subway. She could be living in any one of them. She could just be visiting a friend. She uses a key on the front door, but it could belong to anybody.

I know this. Just as I know she's not about to come

walking out again. As I know she'd be able to see me if her window's facing this way, and she looks out. But I can't help myself. I stand there on the street, looking at the face of the building as if it's the most interesting thing I've ever seen.

"She'll never tell you," a voice says from behind me, a kid's voice.

Here's what it's like, living in the city. The kid can't be more than twelve or thirteen. He's half my size, a scruffy little fellow in baggy jeans, hooded sweatshirt, air-pumped basketball shoes that have seen way better days. His hair is black, short and greasy, face looks as if it hasn't been washed in weeks, half-moons of dark shadow under darker eyes. I look at him and what do I do? Make sure he's alone. Try to figure out if he's carrying a gun or a knife. He's just a kid, and I'm checking out what possible threat he could pose.

I decide he's harmless, or at least means me no harm. He looks amused at the way I've been eyeing him, cocks his head. I look a little closer. There's something familiar about him, but I can't place it. Just the features, not the dirty hair, the grubby skin, the raggedy clothes.

"Who won't tell me what?" I finally ask.

"The invisible. She won't be able to tell you how it works. Half of them don't even know they go invisible. They just figure people treat them that way because that's all their worth. Seriously low self-esteem."

I shake my head and can't stop the smile that comes. "So what are you? A psychiatrist?"

He looks back at me with a steadiness and maturity far belying his years and his appearance. There's a bead of liquid glistening under one nostril. He's a slight, almost frail figure, swamped in clothes that make him seem even smaller. But he carries himself with an assurance that makes me feel inadequate.

"No," he says. "Just someone who's learned to stay visible."

I'd laugh, but there's nothing to laugh about. I saw the woman in the café. I followed her home. If there's a conspiracy at work here, the number of people involved has to be immense, and that doesn't make sense. No one would go through so much trouble over me—what would be the point? It's easier to believe she was invisible.

"So how come I could see her?" I ask.

The boy shrugs. "Maybe you're closer to her than you think."

I don't have to ask him what he means. Self-esteem's never been one of my strong suits.

"Or maybe it's because you believe," he adds.

"Believe in what?"

"Magic."

He says the word, and I can see three small tobacco tins, the children burying them in the dirt under their porches. But I shake my head.

"Maybe I did once," I say. "But I grew out of it. There's nothing magic here. There's simply a . . . a phenomenon that hasn't been explained."

The boy grins, and I lose all sense of his age. It's as if I've strayed into folklore, a fairy tale, tapped an innocent on the shoulder and come face-to-face with a fanged nightmare. I feel I should turn my coat inside out or I'll never find my way back to familiar ground.

"Then explain this," the boy says around that feral grin.

He doesn't turn invisible. That'd be too easy, I guess. Instead it's like a sudden wind comes up, a dust devil, spinning the debris up from the street, candy wrappers, newspapers, things I can't identify. That vague sense of familiarity that's been nagging at me vanishes. There's nothing familiar about this. He's silhouetted against the swirling litter, then his shape loses definition. For one moment I see his dark eyes and that grin in the middle of a shape that vaguely resembles his, then the dust devil moves, comes apart, and all that's left is a trail of debris leading up the sidewalk, away from me.

I stare down at the litter, my gaze slowly drifting toward the invisible woman's building. Explain this?

"I can't," I say aloud, but there's no one there to hear me.

4

I return to my studio, but I'm too restless to sleep, can't concentrate enough to work. I stand in front of the painting on my easel and try to make sense out of what I'm seeing. I can't make sense of the image it once depicted. The colors and values don't seem to relate to each other anymore, the hard edges have all gone soft, there's no definition between the background and the foreground.

I work in watercolor, a highly detailed and realistic style that has me laboring on the same piece for weeks before I'm done. This painting started the same as they always do for me, with a buzz, a wild hum in my head that flares down my arms into my fingertips. My first washes go down fast, the bones of light and color building from abstract glazes until the forms appear and, as Sickert said, the painting begins to "talk back" to me. Everything slows down on me then because the orchestration of value and detail I demand of my medium takes time.

This one was almost completed, a cityscape, a south view of the Kickaha River as seen from the Kelly Street Bridge, derelict warehouses running down to the water on one side, the lawns of Butler U. on the other. Tonight I can't differentiate between the river and the

lawn, the edge of the bridge's railing and the warehouses beyond it. The image that's supposed to be on
the paper is like the woman I followed earlier. It's taken
on a kind of invisibility of its own. I stare at it for a long
time, know that if I stay here in front of it, I'll try to fix
it. Know as well that tonight that's the last thing I
should be doing.

So I close the door on it, walk down the stairs from my
studio to the street. It's only a few blocks to The Half Kaffe
and still early for a Friday night, but when I get there, Ted's
already gone home. Jonathan's behind the counter, but
then Jonathan is always behind the counter. The servers he
has working for him come and go, changing their shifts,
changing their jobs, but Jonathan's always in his place,
viewing the world by what he can see from his limited
vantage point and through an endless supply of magazines.

He's flipping through the glossy pages of a British pop
magazine when I come in. Miles Davis is on the sound system, a cut from his classic "Kind of Blue," Evans's piano
sounding almost Debussian, Davis's trumpet and Coltrane's
tenor contrasting sharply with each other. I order an espresso
from Jonathan and take it to the counter by the front window. The night goes about its business on the other side of
the pane. I study the passersby, wondering if any of them are
invisibles, people only I can see, wonder if there are men and
women walking by that I don't, that are invisible to me.

5

I find Ted at Bruno's Diner the next morning, having his
usual breakfast of late. Granola with two-percent milk and
a freshly squeezed orange juice. All around him are people
digging into plates of eggs and bacon, eggs and sausage,

western omelets, home fries on the side, toast slathered
with butter. But he's happy. There's no esoteric music playing at Bruno's, just a golden oldies station issuing tinnily
from a small portable radio behind the counter. The smell
of toast and bacon makes my stomach rumble.

"So what happened to you last night?" Ted asks when I
slide into his booth.

"Do you believe in magic?" I ask.

Ted pauses with a spoonful of granola halfway to his
mouth. "What, like Houdini?" He puts down the spoon
and smiles. "Man, I loved that stuff when I was a kid. I
wanted to be a magician when I grew up more than just
about anything."

He manages to distract me. Of all the things I can imagine Ted doing, stage magic isn't one of them.

"So what happened?" I ask.

"I found out how hard it is. And besides, you need dexterity, and you know me, I'm the world's biggest klutz."

"But that stuff's all fake," I say. Time to get back on
track. "I'm talking about real magic."

"Who says it's not real?"

"Come on. Everybody knows it's done with mirrors
and smoke. They're illusions."

Ted's not ready to agree. "But that's a kind of magic on
its own, wouldn't you say?"

I shake my head. "I'm talking about the real stuff."

"Give me a for instance."

I don't want to lose my momentum again—it's hard
enough for me to talk about this in the first place. I just
want an answer to the question.

"I know you read all those tabloids," I say, "and you
always let on like you believe the things they print. I want
to know if you really do. Believe in them."

"Maybe we should backtrack a bit here," he says.

So I explain. I don't know which is weirder—the story I tell him, or the fact that he takes me seriously when I tell it.

"Okay," he says. "To start with, all that stuff about Elvis and bigfoot and the like—it's not what I'd call magic. It's entertainment. It might be true and it might not. I don't know. It doesn't even matter. But magic . . ."

His voice trails off and he gets a kind of dreamy look on his face.

"There's a true sense of mystery with magic," he says. "Like you're having a meaningful dialogue with something bigger than you—bigger than anything you can imagine. The tabloids are more like gossip. Something like what's happened to you—that's the real thing. It reaches into what we've all agreed are the workings of the world and stirs them around a little, makes a person sit up and pay attention. Not simply to the experience itself, but to everything around them. That's why the great stage illusions—I don't care if it's a floating woman or someone walking through the Great Wall of China. When they're done properly, you come away questioning everything. Your eyes are opened to all sorts of possibilities."

He smiles then. "Of course, usually it doesn't last. Most people go right back to the reality we've all agreed on. Me, I think it's kind of sad. I *like* the idea that there's more to the world than I can see or understand, and I don't want to ever forget it."

What he's saying reminds me of the feeling I got after I first started to do art. Up until then I'd been the perennial computer nerd, spending all my time in front of a screen because that way I didn't have to take part in any more than the minimum amount of social interaction to get by. Then one day, in my second year at Butler, I was short one course, and for no reason that's made sense before or since, decided to take life drawing, realized I had an aptitude for it, realized I loved it more than anything I'd ever tried before.

After that, I never looked at anything the same again. I watched light, saw everything through an imaginary frame. Clouds didn't just mean a storm was coming; they were an ever-changing picture of the sky, a panorama of movement and light that affected everything around them—the landscape, the people in it. I learned to pay attention and realized that once you do, anything you look at is interesting. Everything has its own glow, its own place in the world that's related to everything else around it. I looked into the connectedness of it all and nothing was the same for me again. I got better at a lot of things. Meeting people. Art. General life skills. Not perfect, but better.

"Have you ever heard of these invisibles?" I ask Ted.

"That's what the practitioners of *voudoun* call their deities. *Les Invisibles.*"

I shake my head. "This kid wasn't speaking French. It wasn't like he was talking about that kind of thing at all. He was referring to ordinary people that go invisible because they just aren't *here* enough anymore." I stop and look across the table at Ted. "Christ, what am I saying? None of this is possible."

Ted nods. "It's easier to pretend it didn't happen."

"What's that supposed to mean?"

But I know exactly what he's talking about. You can either trust your senses and accept that there's more to the world than what you can see, or you can play ostrich. I don't know what to do.

"You had anything to eat yet?" Ted asks.

"Not since last night."

I let him order me breakfast, don't even complain when it's the same as his own.

"See, the thing is," he tells me while we're waiting for

my cereal to arrive, "that you're at the epicenter where two worlds are colliding."

"So now it's an earthquake."

He smiles. "But it's taking place on an interior landscape."

"I saw that woman last night—other people couldn't. That kid turned into a heap of litter right in front of my eyes. It happened here, Ted. In what's supposed to be the real world. Not in my head."

"I know. The 'quake hit you here, but the aftershocks are running through your soul."

I'd argue with him, except that's exactly how it feels.

"Why do you think that kid talked to me?" I ask.

I don't expect Ted to know, but it's part of what's been bothering me. Why'd he pick me to approach?

"I don't know," Ted says. "Next time you see him you should ask him."

"I don't think I want there to be a next time."

"You might not get a choice."

6

Maybe I could pretend to Ted that I didn't want any further involvement with invisible people and kids that turn into litter, but I couldn't lie to myself. I went looking for the boy, for the invisible woman, for things and people out of the ordinary.

There was still a pretense involved. I didn't wander aimlessly, one more lost soul out on the streets, but took a sketchbook and a small paint box, spent my time working on value drawings and color studies, gathering material for future paintings. It's hard for me to work *en plein*. I keep wanting to fuss and fiddle too much, getting lost in detail until the light changes, and then I have to come back another day to get the values right.

A lot of those sketching sessions were spent outside the invisible woman's building, looking for her, expecting the boy to show up. I'd set up my stool, sit there flooding color onto the pages of my sketchbook, work in the detail, too much detail. I don't see the woman. Wind blows the litter around on the street, but it doesn't rise up in the shape of a boy and talk to me.

I find myself thinking of fairy tales—not as stories, but as guideposts. Ted and I share a love of them, but for different reasons. He sees them as early versions of the tabloids, records kept of strange encounters, some real, some imagined, all of them entertaining. I think of them more metaphorically. All those dark forests and trials and trouble. They're the same things we go through in life. Maybe if more of us had the good heart of a Donkeyskin or the youngest son of three, the world would be a better place.

I'm thinking of this in front of the invisible woman's building on a blustery day. I've got the pages of my sketchbook clipped down, but the wind keeps flapping them anyway, making the paint puddle and run. Happy accidents, I've heard them called. Well, they're only happy when you can do something with them, when you don't work tight, every stroke counting. I'm just starting to clean up the latest of these so-called happy accidents when a ponytailed guy carrying a guitar walks right into me, knocking the sketchbook from my lap. I almost lose the paint box as well.

"Jesus," he says. "I'm sorry. I didn't see you sitting there." He picks up my sketchbook and hands it over. "I hope I haven't totally ruined this."

"It's okay," I tell him. It's not, but what would be the point of being unpleasant?

"I'm really sorry."

I look down at the page I was working on. Now there's dirt smeared into the happy accident. Fixable it's not. My gaze lifts to meet his. "Don't worry about it," I tell him. "It happens."

He nods, his relief plain. "I must've been dreaming," he says, "because I just didn't see you at all." He hesitates. "If you're sure it's okay . . ."

"I'm sure."

I watch him leave, think about what he said.

I just didn't see you.

So now what? I've become invisible, too? Then I remember the kid, something he said when I asked why I could see the invisible woman and others couldn't.

Maybe you're closer to her than you think.

Invisible. It comes to me, then. The world's full of invisible people, and our not seeing them's got nothing to do with magic. The homeless. Winos. Hookers. Junkies. And not only on the street. The housewife. The businessman's secretary. Visible only when they're needed for something. The man with AIDS. Famine victims. People displaced by wars or natural disasters. The list is endless, all these people we don't see because we don't want to see them. All these people we don't see because we're too busy paying attention to ourselves. I've felt it myself, my lack of self-confidence and how it translates into my behavior can have people look right through me. Standing in a store, waiting to be served. Sitting in the corner of a couch at a party and I might as well be a pillow.

The kid's face comes back to mind. I look down at my sketchbook, exchange the page smeared with happy accidents for a new one, draw the kid's features as I remember them. Now I know why he looked so familiar.

7

Ted opens his door on the first knock. He's just got off work
and seems surprised to see me. I can smell herb tea steeping,
cigarette smoke. Something classical is playing at low volume on the stereo. Piano. Chopin, I think. The preludes.

"Were we doing a movie or something tonight?" Ted asks.

I shake my head. "I was wondering if I could see that
old photo album of yours again."

He studies me for a moment, then steps aside so that I
can come in. His apartment's as cluttered as ever. You can't
turn for fear of knocking over a stack of books, magazines,
CDs, cassettes. Right by the door there's a box of newspapers and tabloids ready to go out for recycling. The one on
top has a headline that shouts in bold caps: **TEENAGER
GIVES BIRTH TO FISH BOY!!**

"You don't have to look at the album," he tells me. "I'll
'fess up."

Something changes in me when he says those words. I
thought I knew him, like I thought I knew the world, but
now they've both become alien territory. I stand in the
center of the room, the furniture crouched around me like
junkyard dogs. I have a disorienting static in my ears. I feel
as though I'm standing on dangerous ground, stepped into
the fairy tale, but Stephen King wrote it.

"How did you do it?" I ask.

Ted gives me a sheepish look. "How first? Not even
why?"

I give the sofa a nervous look, but it's just a sofa. The vertigo is receding. My ears pop, as though I've dropped alti-
tude, and I can hear the piano music coming from the
speakers on either side of the room. I'm grounded again, but
nothing seems the same. I sit down on the sofa, set my stool
and sketching equipment on the floor between my feet.

"I don't know if I can handle why just yet," I tell him. "I have to know how you did it, how you made a picture of yourself come to life."

"Magic."

"Magic," I repeat. "That's it?"

"It's not enough?" He takes a seat in the well-worn armchair across from me, leans forward, hands on his knees. "Remember this morning, when I told you about wanting to be an illusionist?"

I nod.

"I lied. Well, it was partly a lie. I didn't give up stage magic, I just never got the nerve to go up on a stage and do it."

"So the kid . . . he was an illusion?"

Ted smiles. "Let's say you saw what I wanted you to see."

"Smoke and mirrors."

"Something like that."

"But . . ." I shake my head. He was right earlier. There's no point in asking for details. Right now, how's not as important as . . . "So why?" I ask.

He leans back in the chair. "The invisibles need a spokesperson—someone to remind the rest of the world that they exist. People like that woman you saw in The Half Kaffe last night. If enough people don't see her, she's simply going to fade away. She can't speak up for herself. If she could, she wouldn't be an invisible. And she's at the high end of the scale. There are people living on the streets that—"

"I know," I say, breaking in. "I was just thinking about them this afternoon. But their invisibility is a matter of perception, of people ignoring them. They're not literally invisible like the woman last night. There's nothing *magic* about them."

"You're still missing the point," Ted says. "Magic's all about perception. Things are the way they are because we've agreed that's the way they are. An act of magic is when we're convinced we're experiencing something that doesn't fit into the conceptual reality we've all agreed on."

"So you're saying that magic is being tricked into thinking an illusion is real."

"Or seeing through the illusion, seeing something the way it really is for the first time."

I shake my head, not quite willing to concede the argument for all that it's making uncomfortable sense. "Where does your being a spokesperson fit in?" I ask.

"Not me. You."

"Oh, come on."

But I can tell he's completely serious.

"People have to be reminded about the invisibles," he says, "or they'll vanish."

"Okay" I say. "For argument's sake, let's accept that as a given. I still don't see where I come into it."

"Who's going to listen to me?" Ted asks. "I try to talk about it, but I'm a booking agent. People'd rather just think I'm a little weird."

"And they're not going to think the same of me?"

"No," he says. "And I'll tell you why. It's the difference between art and argument. They're both used to get a point across, but the artist sets up a situation, and, if he's good enough, his audience understands his point on their own, through how they assimilate the information he's given them and the decisions they can then make based on that information. The argument is just someone telling you what you're supposed to think or feel."

"Show, don't tell," I say, repeating an old axiom appropriate to all the arts.

"Exactly. You've got the artistic chops and sensibility to show people, to let them see the invisibles through your art, which will make them see them out there." He waves a hand toward the window. "On the street. In their lives."

He's persuasive, I'll give him that.

"Last night in The Half Kaffe," I begin.

"I didn't see the woman you saw," Ted says. "I didn't see her until you stopped her down the street."

"And after? When she went invisible again?"

"I could still see her. You made me see her."

"That's something anybody could do," I tell him.

"But only if they can see the invisibles in the first place," he says. "And you can't be everywhere. Your paintings can. Reproductions of them can."

I give him a look that manages to be both tired and hold all my skepticism with what he's saying. "You want me to paint portraits of invisible people so that other people can see them."

"You're being deliberately obtuse now, aren't you? You know what I mean."

I nod. I do know exactly what he means.

"Why bring this all up now?" I ask him. "We've known each other for years."

"Because until you saw the invisible woman, you never would have believed me."

"How do I know she's not another illusion—like the boy made of litter that was wearing your twelve-year-old face?"

"You don't."

8

He's wrong about that. I do know. I know in that part of me that he was talking about this morning over breakfast, the part that had a meaningful dialogue with something bigger than me, the part that's willing to accept a momentary glimpse behind the curtain of reality as a valid experience. And I know why he sent the illusion of the boy after me, too. It's the same reason he didn't admit to any of this sooner, played the innocent when I came to him with my story of invisible people. It was to give me my own words to describe the experience. To make me think about the invisibles, to let me form my own opinions about what can be readily seen and what's hidden behind a veil of expectations. Showing, not telling. He's better than he thinks he is.

I stand in my studio, thinking about that. There's a board on my easel with a stretched full-sized piece of three-hundred-pound Arches hot-pressed paper on it. I squeeze pigments into the butcher's tray I use as a palette, pick up a brush. There's a light pencil sketch on the paper. It's a cityscape, a street scene. In one corner, there's a man, sleeping in a doorway, blanketed with newspapers. The buildings and street overwhelm him. He's a small figure, almost lost. But he's not invisible.

I hope to keep him that way.

I dip my brush into my water jar, build up a puddle in the middle of the tray. Yellow ochre and alizarin crimson. I'm starting with the features that can be seen between the knit woolen cap he's wearing and the edge of his newspaper blanket, the gnarled hand that grips the papers, holding them in place. I want him to glow before I add in the buildings, the street, the night that shrouds them.

As I work, I think of the tobacco tins that Rebecca, Jerry, and I buried under our porches all those years ago. Maybe magic doesn't always work. Maybe it's like life, things don't always come through for you. But being disappointed in something doesn't mean you should give up on it. It doesn't mean you should stop trying.

I think of the last thing Ted said to me before I left his apartment.

"It goes back to stage magicians," he told me. "What's so amazing about them isn't so much that they can make things disappear, as that they can bring them back."

I touch the first color to the paper and reach for a taste of that amazement.

A Cascade of Lies

STEVE RASNIC TEM

This dark and angry take on a dysfunctional family, and a father obsessed by death and power, makes me feel both lucky and grateful. My own family life was anything but dysfunctional; as a child, my parents supported me in everything I wanted to do. I loved them dearly then, as I love them still. My father is an extremely nice man. The father in this story is anything but, he is in fact someone whose entire life is "A Cascade of Lies."

—DC

A Cascade of Lies

I WILL SHOW YOU THINGS you thought could happen only in a dream . . .

Alan never had the knack for magic. When his father tried to teach him a science of illusion, Alan saw trickery and lies, and resented the lesson.

He'd believed his father could do anything: saw a woman in half, make an elephant disappear, heal the sick, raise the dead. His father did it nightly, onstage. Alan wanted to believe his father's lies.

When Alan and his brother Billy were seven and eight the boys began touring with their father. Their father—his name was Max back then—had wanted to use them years earlier to play demons in his *Phantasmagoria*, a loose homage to the Belgian E.G. Robertson, but their mother had claimed the doctor told her they were too frail. It was the only trick she'd ever pulled.

But she could not stall Max forever, and the day finally came when the boys were onstage, dressed as girls, midgets, animals, and specters, until Max promoted them to victims: target of the bullet-catching trick, a neck for the Sword of Damocles.

Max had many original illusions in his repertoire: The Palace of Insomniacs, The Missing Child, Tragic Beginnings, A Marriage in Hell. But he was most proud of his versions of old tricks. His linking rings were six feet in diameter, and at the finale the flames consumed them utterly. His three-foot-wide Chinese rice bowls were filled with rats. His cups and balls used brightly colored fezzes and shrunken heads that talked back to the audience.

For the bullet-catching trick—the illusion which killed the great Chung Ling Soo, and which Houdini never performed at Harry Kellar's urging—Max (now The Prodigal Obscure) used a machine gun, and each night either Billy or Alan stood as the new target following the slaughter of several watermelons.

They never had a clue as to how the trick was managed, but they understood part of the Sword of Damocles. It, too, was an homage, a version of the decapitation trick of last century's Professor Josef Vanek. At the end, their father carried the huge sword around the audience, the gory severed head of the son on its broad surface, screaming, begging to be put out of its misery, finally descending into delirium and song. They *knew* that wasn't their head on the sword, even though sometimes they would feel themselves or glance into a backstage mirror to make sure. Max could use either brother in the illusion since they looked so much alike. When Billy assisted, Alan was always relieved that it wasn't his head on the sword screaming. Billy was okay, but Alan always felt guilty because of that relief.

Billy had always accepted the job stoically, arising early and without argument. He might hesitate during an effect, but he always did it, however terrified.

Alan, on the other hand, became a malingerer, spraining a wrist or pulling a muscle, unable to perform. When he could not convince his father he'd convince his brother to take his place. He was too ill. He hurt too much. Billy would nod sadly and go on, and Alan would walk away relieved, yet angry that Billy let himself be tricked so easily.

Sometimes Alan feigned sickness, and his mother kept him off tour, at home for months while Billy went away with Max.

Each time Billy came home he looked worse, and would not speak to Alan for days.

I will show you things . . .

Then Billy died, and Alan refused to tour. Eventually his father stopped trying to persuade him and went away in disgust. Over the years Alan tried to keep in touch. They exchanged phone calls now and then, but Max never saw Alan grow up, never met Ann, never saw them married.

Max used to tell audiences he could raise the dead, but that was a lie. But if he wasn't lying, what had he done with Billy?

The last time Alan talked to him, his father's voice sounded as if it originated beyond the bounds of long-distance. "The baby's two years old now, Dad. She's beautiful. You should see her."

"I'll be there. I'm an old man, but I'll be there. I have some new tricks to show you, boy, things you thought could happen only in a dream. Billy would have loved these." Alan winced at the casual mention of Billy's name. "Kiss her for me," were the last words his father spoke to him. Months passed, years, and The Great Gaspard was somewhere else in the world, entertaining someone else's children. Emily became a toddler, then a young girl, without ever having seen her grandfather.

"He's a jerk," his wife Ann would say. "I don't care what tricks he can do. I wouldn't care if he were Mandrake the Magician. He's no father or grandfather."

"Read me a story, Daddy," Emily used to ask every night, staggering across the room with the massive story-book, then dropping it into his lap.

"A long time ago . . . a very long time ago, there was a

monster," he said, lying, knowing that there were monsters everywhere you looked.

"Daddy . . . Daddy . . ." Alan snapped out of it. Emily had her head against his chest, as if listening for the story to come from there. "You started it wrong."

"What do you mean, sweetheart?"

"You're supposed to say, 'Once upon a time.' Everybody knows stories start 'Once upon a time.' "

A year later Emily still wanted to be read to, and she had begun asking about her grandfather the great magician. She had the knack for magic—Alan could see it in her eyes. And like her grandfather, sometimes she chose magic over the real.

Once upon a time, Daddy, once upon a time . . . as Emily flew from her bedroom window, just out of Alan's desperate grasp, ready to become a bird or a brightly colored scarf, the applause thunderous, but instead falling, falling, a small bundle on the ground below, Alan wailing from the window above her, gone crazy in the suddenness of his grief.

The illusion never ended. At the end of the performance, the child he adored was not returned to him unbroken. Alan, too, was not unbroken. Ann hung on with him for a year before finally leaving. He didn't blame her. Alan called, tried telegrams, left messages at theaters, but his father never responded. His father, the miracle worker.

After a few months one of Alan's uncles gave him his father's last-known address: Franktown, as of twenty years ago, somewhere upstate. The uncle had learned that from Alan's dying mother, sick with cancer and her anger against the man who had reduced them to mere audience members to his ultimate vanishing act.

Alan fell asleep on the train, and would have missed the

early-evening Franktown stop if he hadn't been jarred awake by another dream of the decapitation trick. His own head had shouted a series of unintelligible curses followed by a terse, *it's time to get off!* Then it bled out over the wide silver blade, turned white with the eyes rolled up. As Alan awakened he thought of his body, minus head, still alive and flopping around in some closet somewhere.

He saw the "Franktown Station" sign outside the train window. All the cars were empty. He had to drag his suitcase down the steps; suddenly it seemed intolerably heavy.

No one waited for him. Of course not. But no one waited for anyone. The train glided silently away from the station.

Franktown was the sort of place forgotten more often than remembered, a ghostly circle on the road map. Looking for a hotel, Alan got lost on similar streets with similar buildings. No one returned his stares, or answered his timid inquiries.

He could hear his own footsteps, crossing streets a half inch deep in sand. The clock on the church tower seemed to be running: its hands had passed an hour since he'd left the station, but whenever he stopped moving it did the same. Between buildings was a darkness uncompromised by the slightest gray.

He came to a movie theater and, without a second thought, walked in. The theater was empty, the screen torn. Most of the seats had been pulled up, ripped open. *Must have been a bad show.*

When Alan and Billy were first on the road, with hours between shows, his father would dump them at local movie theaters, retrieving them a scant half hour before curtain. Christopher Lee or Klaus Kinski or some monster became their baby-sitter. They were happy enough, spending their afternoons in a magical world.

In the movies, they learned how to swing through trees, kill vampires, set fire to hidden lairs. But people disappeared at an alarming rate, mostly pretty young women, and the police were at a loss. The man called in at the last minute to save the day always resembled their father, but with a kinder face. He disappeared at the end. Doors were opened, the sound of footsteps everywhere. The trees were more alive than most of the actors.

Sometime during the picture Billy would vanish into a door at the back, ostensibly to find a bathroom, but he always took too long, and when he came back he looked far too old.

When the monster finally did appear, Alan always felt relieved.

"I've been expecting you," said a voice from somewhere near the torn screen.

"Dad?"

"You're a man yourself now. Call me Frank."

Max, now Frank, stepped into the dim light. He hadn't changed. Dark eyebrows, a swarthy face layered in lines, eyes that had no color until he decided on one.

Graffiti surrounded the deeply scarred door: stick figures of gods and goddesses with enlarged sex organs, mouths torn apart by spirals of color and obscenity. Alan's father pushed open the door and slid back the curtains. "I'm making a comeback," he said, "my sixth," and laughed. Lights came on: all his father did was wave his hand. Of course it was a trick; it angered Alan that his father was still performing for him.

"Stay away from the smaller shops," Frank warned. "And if someone asks for the time, walk away as fast as you can."

"Thanks for the advice."

"Oh, and I'm sorry about Emily. I'm sure . . . that was quite difficult for you."

Alan's fear struggled with anger until he swallowed them both. He refused to ask how his father knew. He didn't want to hear the lie.

"There's a hotel above this studio, the entrance around front. I own it. I've arranged for a modest room, but then all the rooms are modest. In Franktown we pride ourselves on simple effects."

His father's new studio was a warehouse of illusion. Alan recognized sets made famous by Robert-Houdin of France, the Scottish magician John Henry Anderson, Alexander Herrmann, Maskelyne and Cooke, Servais Le Roy, Thurston, and Houdini himself. There were props from his father's old acts, and props Alan could not bear to see.

"All this," his father said, "is irrelevant. Mere trickery. It belongs with the jugglers and sword swallowers. It's *events* I'm interested in now, in my old age." Suddenly he shrank and bent into an old man, palsied hands waving. "It's *events* that mesmerize us, history that hypnotizes. The messy business of everyday life, the 'real' world. They cloud our minds and keep us from the important and eternal."

Alan felt a glimmer of hope. "I need your advice, your . . . assistance. My daughter . . ."

"Everyone who gives you advice lives inside a corpse," his father said. "So what do they know?" He drew back a curtain, exposing a wall of corpses. Alan recognized the cast of the Phantasmagoria.

Inside one corpse's mouth—ironically a specter in that earlier performance—the bugs were having a magic show. They kept disappearing into the shadows behind them, only to reappear larger, with things in their jaws.

From another body's empty eye sockets, worms looked at Alan, seeing for the dead man, then running to tell their friends, "At last! Alan is here!"

"Oh, indeed, we'll talk about your daughter later. But now you must rest. Don't wander the streets. Go around to the lobby, my boy."

Alan made his way to the back door, past scenery flats and dummies and things which might have been dummies. And looked up to see the Sword of Damocles dangling from an invisible wire overhead.

The last time he had seen it, Billy had been saying to him, "I don't want to do this, Alan. It's your turn anyway," and trying to give him the black robe. The cloth was stained on one side, ready for the effect. It looked like real blood and gore, it looked like disease, and Alan wouldn't take it. "*You* be the big star tonight." Billy sighed and put the robe on, walked slowly out onstage. Billy was more afraid of their dad than anything. He looked so small Alan felt terrible—after all, Billy was the big brother. Alan almost went after him, almost told him he would do the trick tonight.

The audience gasped as the sword came down. They always did. Some of them screamed as they always did. Someone fainted. Someone always did.

And then there had been his father bearing the fake head that had never before looked fake out into the audience. Maybe it was a trick of memory, but that time the head *had* looked completely fake to Alan, completely unreal. And that time, Billy had not joined him backstage.

Now Alan staggered out into the brilliant light of the alley. The glare brightened the graffiti, making them look fresh, while deepening the shadows to three-dimensional. Two of the shadows, old men, shuffled out of the darkness and began touching him. Alan squirmed but seemed unable to run. "We've waited for you," one said.

With yellow hands the other man fussed with a piece of stained newspaper. He tried to place the object he'd made—a boat, or a crown—on Alan's head. "This is for you."

Alan ran out of the alley and saw the front entrance of the hotel. Despite what his father had advised, he could not bring himself to go back into the building just yet.

People were in the streets now, walking slowly, eyes fixed. He asked a man for the time, but the man ran away.

A woman in a flower-print dress pushed a grocery cart down the walk, pausing to knock at each boarded-up window. Not waiting for responses, she moved her cart intently to the next stop.

A short man in a dark coat came up to him in the street. His breath smelled like old magazines. "Who's the president now?" he asked, but before Alan could answer the man asked, "And what about Joan Crawford? Did she ever die? Sometimes they die, you know."

Alan walked into the lobby of the hotel. Old photographs covered the walls. *So old,* he thought, *all the people in them must be dead.* But they still smiled, played games, ate at picnic tables, kissed one another for the camera. He found himself looking for Emily among the browning figures. *She'd like it there,* he thought.

In the corner a woman nursed her dead baby. Was he the only one who noticed?

Quiet, pale people sat in chairs watching a black-and-white TV. He walked up behind them and looked at the screen. Although voices spoke in the background, the camera never showed the speakers, anchors, or reporters. The screen flickered with sequence after sequence of bombed streets and buildings. Flaming forms with upraised hands of charcoal raced toward the lens. Mile after mile of refugees. Bodies piled by the road. Someone said to stay calm. Someone said it was all a terrible mistake. Someone said this was how we loved each other.

With all those people dying, what turmoil there must be in the spirit world, how it might complicate his daughter's potential rescue.

He got his room key. The boy at the desk couldn't have been over ten. But Alan's father had always liked his assistants young.

The room was as unimpressive as his father had suggested, but cleaner than Alan had expected. Two beds, one bedside table, an old dresser, a closet, and a sink and mirror.

Alan didn't recognize himself in the mirror. *I've sent someone else in my place,* he thought. *I wonder how much I'm being paid?* His reflection smiled, as if the pay were generous, as if he took a perverse enjoyment in the work.

He lay down. He'd suffered from insomnia for years. He knew that the furniture of the night bore little resemblance to the furniture of the day. He immediately fell asleep.

His brother's headless body walked into the room and lay down on the other bed, stretched out its arms as if to relax, kicked off its shoes. The body began to tremble, still afraid of the dark after all these years. The hands fluttered nervously, then reached out as if to grab Alan's head.

I will show you things . . .

Alan said he was sorry. He looked at the clock, turned back to his brother, but by then Billy was gone. He looked at the clock again. In seconds, three hours had passed.

Like the clock in the church tower, this one seemed as timid as Alan himself. He sat up with it awhile, telling it stories of his father, of himself and his brother and their days in magic, of his daughter Emily and how beautiful she had been. The clock recounted time unevenly, but with determination. He finally draped a towel over it to help it sleep, lay on his back, and stared out the window at the moon.

In his dream he was a head crawling through alley trash, pulling himself along with teeth and tongue, eating garbage whenever he passed over it, reading what legible newsprint he could find.

The next day his father sent the young desk clerk to awaken him and show him the staircase down. When Alan got to the bottom he discovered he was in a different part of the studio. Cages lined the walls. Goats and pigs, horses and monkeys, their performing names etched fancifully on plaques mounted to the wall. In one of the cages was a man.

The man in the cage smelled awful. There were bugs in both his ears.

"Please turn out the lights," he begged, "so I won't see him when he comes."

Farther into the studio he found his father sitting at a table reading a book with no words on its cover. Max had once had an extensive library that filled two floors of their home.

"That's the only book in my library now," he said. He was pretending he could read Alan's mind, and Alan was infuriated by the lie. His father hadn't changed at all. "I read it over and over again. And each time something different happens!"

The next room was furnished more sparely, with exhibits on tables, in jars and wooden crates.

"This is Aristotle's poison." His father held up a small vial. "No takers, I'm afraid. And somewhere I have Hitler's alarm clock, the one he had in the bunker, the one he stared at each day, counting down the time. A lot of buyers for that one, but I can't find it—I think it's up in the hotel somewhere. But this . . ." He guided Alan down a narrow corridor where a man wrapped in long hair and the filth of ages was shackled to an iron bar. The man looked up: teeth and one eye gleamed. "This is my friend Jack. Springheel Jack. Jack the Ripper. A corporate executive in New York is mulling over the offer. I think I'm about to become a millionaire."

"I don't believe you," Alan said quietly.

"So what? Maybe it's Jack and maybe it isn't. Maybe it's some geek I modified with electrical shocks and a bottle of booze. No one's going to know any different once he's got a knife in his hand."

"So you faked him. No one comes back. He's just another trick. Another lie."

Frank smiled so widely his face seemed to disappear. "Ah . . . but I didn't say that."

In a bed in another room, Alan's dead mother lay singing softly to herself.

"I keep the worms that infested her body for pets," Frank said. "Sometimes when I feed them I think how much it shows I once loved her."

A puppet show was in progress in another room. Four or five listless youngsters sat on the floor. The puppets— figures of a magician and two young boys—had captured a live mouse.

The puppets tied the mouse to a tiny prop table and began torturing it with needles and razor blades. Alan screamed for his father to stop them, but Frank said, "The show must go on!" The puppets continued their work until the mouse was dead. "And lives, lives must go on as well, my boy."

"Some lives are like unsolved crimes," Alan replied.

"Clever boy," his father said softly, with an angry smile, "but there's one more trick I want to show you, something you thought could happen only in a dream."

The last corridor narrowed sharply until the walls brushed Alan's shoulders, and still it narrowed, until Alan had to turn sideways and shuffle his way through. His father, however, seemed to have no trouble.

At the end was Billy, smiling, the same age as Alan remembered, nine years old forever, smiling forever and laughing with his neck so heavily stitched he couldn't button his collar.

"Presto changeo!" Billy cried, and waved a five-foot wand. "Here she comes, Alan!" But Alan didn't wait.

He ran out of the studio, pushing prop into prop until he could hear a chain reaction of crashes. Finally he ran into the street. No one was out. The wind cut him like a sword. A few lights struggled to illuminate dirty windows. Behind him his father called, "It's *your* trick! I'm *proud* of you, boy—you've got the knack after all! You *made* the place! It's what you expected! But you should have put in an *exit*!"

Not stopping to reply, Alan ran until he found a quiet street.

The street was so small it had only one child, a little girl, and one puppy for the little girl to play with. Only one tree and one pair of lovers. One moon, and it always caught in the same spot in the branches of the tree. And only one grave for all of them to share.

The Goldfish Pool and Other Stories

NEIL GAIMAN

For years, I had an apartment in Hollywood, where "The Goldfish Pool" is set. I found the story, with its view of Hollywood through the eyes of a young Brit writer, to be unutterably charming. I kept thinking about Neil's story, and about his protagonist's experiences. I could not help but agree that Hollywood is an illusion. Taking it seriously is a mistake; enjoying it is not.

—DC

The Goldfish Pool
and Other Stories

IT WAS RAINING when I arrived in LA; and I felt myself surrounded by a hundred old movies.

There was a limo driver in a black uniform waiting for me at the airport, holding a white sheet of cardboard with my name misspelled neatly upon it.

"I'm taking you straight to your hotel, sir," said the driver. He seemed vaguely disappointed that I didn't have any real luggage for him to carry, just a battered overnight bag stuffed with T-shirts, underwear, and socks.

"Is it far?"

He shook his head. "Maybe twenty-five, thirty minutes. You ever been to LA before?"

"No."

"Well, what I always say, LA is a thirty-minute town. Wherever you want to go, it's thirty minutes away. No more."

He hauled my bag into the boot of the car, which he called the trunk, and opened the door for me to climb into the back.

"So where you from?" he asked, as we headed out of the airport into the slick, wet, neon-spattered streets.

"England."

"England, eh?"

"Yes. Have you ever been there?"

"No sir. I've seen movies. You an actor?"

"I'm a writer."

He lost interest. Occasionally he would swear at other drivers, under his breath.

He swerved suddenly, changing lanes. We passed a four-car pileup in the lane we had been in.

"You get a little rain in this city, all of a sudden everybody forgets how to drive," he told me. I burrowed further into the cushions in the back. "You get rain in England, I hear." It was a statement, not a question.

"A little."

"More than a little. Rains every day in England." He laughed. "And thick fog. Real thick, thick fog."

"Not really."

"Whaddaya mean, no?" he asked, puzzled, defensive. "I've seen movies."

We sat in silence then, driving through the Hollywood rain; but after a while he said: "Ask them for the room Belushi died in."

"Pardon?"

"Belushi. John Belushi. It was your hotel he died in. Drugs. You heard about that?"

"Oh. Yes."

"They made a movie about his death. Some fat guy, didn't look anything like him. But nobody tells the real truth about his death. Y'see, he wasn't alone. There were two other guys with him. Studios didn't want any shit. But you're a limo driver, you hear things."

"Really?"

"Robin Williams and Robert De Niro. They were there with him. All of them going doo-doo on the happy dust."

The hotel building was a white mock-gothic château. I said good-bye to the chauffeur, and checked in; I did not ask about the room in which Belushi had died.

I walked out to my chalet, through the rain, my overnight bag in my hand, clutching the set of keys that would, the desk clerk told me, get me through the various doors and gates. The air smelled of wet dust and, curiously enough, cough mixture. It was dusk, almost dark.

Water splashed everywhere. It ran in rills and rivulets across the courtyard. It ran into a fishpond that jutted out from the side of a wall, in the courtyard.

I walked up the stairs into a dank little room. It seemed a poor kind of a place for a star to die.

The bed seemed slightly damp, and the rain drummed a maddening beat on the air-conditioning system.

I watched a little television—the rerun wasteland: *Cheers* segued imperceptibly into *Taxi*, which flickered into black and white and became *The Lucy Show*—then stumbled into sleep.

I dreamed of drummers intermittently drumming, only thirty minutes away.

The phone woke me. "Hey-hey-hey-hey. You made it okay then?"

"Who is this?"

"It's Jacob, at the studio. Are we still on for breakfast, hey-hey?"

"Breakfast. . . ?"

"No problem. I'll pick you up from your hotel in thirty minutes. Reservations are already made. No problems. You got my messages?"

"I . . ."

"Faxed 'em through last night. See you."

The rain had stopped. The sunshine was warm and bright: proper Hollywood light. I walked up to the main building, walking on a carpet of crushed eucalyptus leaves—the cough medicine smell from the night before.

They handed me an envelope with a fax in it—my

schedule for the next few days, with messages of encouragement and faxed handwritten doodles in the margin,
saying things like "*This is gonna be a blockbuster!*" and "*Is
this going to be a great movie or what!*" The fax was signed
by Jacob Klein, obviously the voice on the phone. I had
never before had any dealings with a Jacob Klein.

A small red sports car drew up outside the hotel. The
driver got out and waved at me. I walked over. He had a
trim, pepper-and-salt beard, a smile that was almost bank-
able, and a gold chain around his neck. He showed me a
copy of *Sons of Man*.

He was Jacob. We shook hands.

"Is David around? David Gambol?"

David Gambol was the man I'd spoken to earlier on the
phone, when arranging the trip. He wasn't the producer. I
wasn't certain quite what he was. He described himself as
"attached to the project."

"David's not with the studio anymore. I'm kind of running the project now, and I want you to know I'm really
psyched. Hey-hey."

"That's good?"

We got in the car. "Where's the meeting?" I asked.

He shook his head. "It's not a meeting," he said. "It's a
breakfast." I looked puzzled. He took pity on me. "A kind
of pre-meeting meeting," he explained.

We drove from the hotel to a mall somewhere half an
hour away, while Jacob told me how much he enjoyed my
book, and how delighted he was that he'd become attached
to the project. He said it was his idea to have me put up in
the hotel—"Give you the kind of Hollywood experience
you'd never get at the Four Seasons or Ma Maison,
right?"—and asked me if I was staying in the chalet in which
John Belushi had died. I told him I didn't know, but that I
rather doubted it.

"You know who he was with, when he died? They covered it up, the studios."

"No. Who?"

"Meryl and Dustin."

"This is Meryl Streep and Dustin Hoffman we're talking about?"

"Sure."

"How do you know this?"

"People talk. It's Hollywood. You know?"

I nodded, as if I did know, but I didn't.

People talk about books that write themselves, and it's a lie. Books don't write themselves. It takes thought and research and backache and notes and more time and more work than you'd believe.

Except for *Sons of Man*, and that one pretty much wrote itself.

The irritating question they ask us—us being writers—is "Where do you get your ideas?"

And the answer is, *confluence*. Things come together. The right ingredients and suddenly: *abracadabra!*

It began with a documentary on Charles Manson I was watching more or less by accident (it was on a videotape a friend lent me, after a couple of things I *did* want to watch): there was footage of Manson, back when he was first arrested, when people thought he was innocent and that it was the government picking on the hippies. And, up on the screen was Manson—a charismatic, good-looking, messianic orator. Someone you'd crawl barefoot into Hell for. Someone you could kill for.

The trial started; and, a few weeks into it, the orator was gone, replaced by a shambling, apelike gibberer, with a cross carved into its forehead. Whatever the genius was was no longer there. It was gone. But it had been there.

The documentary continued: a hard-eyed ex-con who had been in prison with Manson, explaining "Charlie Manson? Listen, Charlie was a joke. He was a nothing. We laughed at him. You know? He was a nothing!"

And I nodded. There was a time before Manson was the charisma king, then. I thought of a benediction, something given, that was taken away.

I watched the rest of the documentary obsessively. Then, over a black-and-white still, the narrator said something. I rewound, and he said it again.

I had an idea. I had a book that wrote itself.

The thing the narrator had said was this: that the infant children Manson had fathered on the women of the family were sent to a variety of children's homes for adoption, with court-given surnames that were certainly not Manson.

And I thought of a dozen twenty-five-year-old Mansons. Thought of the charisma-thing descending on all of them at the same time. Twelve young Mansons, in their glory, gradually being pulled toward LA from all over the world. And a Manson daughter trying desperately to stop them from coming together and, as the back cover blurb told us, "realizing their terrifying destiny."

I wrote *Sons of Man* at white heat: it was finished in a month, and I sent it to my agent, who was surprised by it ("Well, it's not like your other stuff, dear," she said, helpfully), and she sold it after an auction, my first, for more money than I had thought possible. (My other books, three collections of elegant, allusive, and elusive ghost stories, had scarcely paid for the computer on which they were written.)

And then it was bought—prepublication—by Hollywood,

again after an auction. There were three or four studios interested: I went with the studio who wanted me to write the script. I knew it would never happen, knew they'd never come through. But then the faxes began to spew out of my machine, late at night—most of them enthusiastically signed by one Dave Gambol; one morning I signed five copies of a contract thick as a brick; a few weeks later my agent reported the first check had cleared and tickets to Hollywood had arrived, for "preliminary talks." It seemed like a dream.

The tickets were business class. It was the moment I saw the tickets were business class that I knew the dream was real.

I went to Hollywood in the bubble bit at the top of the jumbo jet, nibbling smoked salmon and holding a hot-off-the-presses hardback of *Sons of Man*.

So. Breakfast.

They told me how much they loved the book. I didn't quite catch anybody's name. The men had beards or baseball caps or both, the women were astoundingly attractive, in a sanitary sort of way.

Jacob ordered our breakfast, and paid for it. He explained that the meeting coming up was a formality.

"It's your book we love," he said. "Why would we have bought your book if we didn't want to make it? Why would we have hired *you* to write it if we didn't want the specialness you'd bring to the project. The *you-ness*."

I nodded, very seriously, as if literary me-ness was something I had spent many hours pondering.

"An idea like this. A book like this. You're pretty unique."

"One of the uniquest," said a woman named Dina or Tina or possibly Deanna.

I raised an eyebrow. "So what am I meant to do at the meeting?"

"Be receptive," said Jacob. "Be positive."

The drive to the studio took about half an hour in Jacob's little red car. We drove up to the security gate, where Jacob had an argument with the guard. I gathered that he was new at the studio, and had not yet been issued a permanent studio pass.

Nor, it appeared, once we got inside, did he have a permanent parking place. I still do not understand the ramifications of this: from what he said, parking places had as much to do with status at the studio as gifts from the emperor determined one's status in the court of ancient China.

We drove through the streets of an oddly flat New York and parked in front of a huge old bank.

Ten minutes' walk, and I was in a conference room, with Jacob and all the people from breakfast, waiting for someone to come in. In the flurry I'd rather missed who the someone was, and what he or she did. I took out my copy of my book, and put it in front of me, a talisman of sorts.

Someone came in. He was tall, with a pointy nose and a pointy chin, and his hair was too long—he looked like he'd kidnapped someone much younger, and stolen his hair. He was an Australian, which surprised me.

He sat down.

He looked at me.

"Shoot," he said.

I looked at the people from the breakfast, but none of them were looking at me—I couldn't catch anyone's eye. So I began to talk: about the book, about the plot, about the end, the showdown in the LA nightclub, where the good Manson-girl blows the rest of them up. Or thinks she does. About my idea for having one actor play all the Manson boys.

"Do you believe this stuff?" It was the first question from the Someone.

That one was easy. It was one I'd already answered for at least two dozen British journalists.

"Do I believe that a supernatural power possessed Charles Manson for a while, and is even now possessing his many children? No. Do I believe that something strange was happening? I suppose I must do. Perhaps it was simply that, for a brief while, his madness was in step with the madness of the world outside. I don't know."

"Mm. This Manson kid. He could be Keanu Reaves?"

God, no, I thought. Jacob caught my eye and nodded, desperately. "I don't see why not," I said. It was all imagination anyway. None of it was real.

"We're cutting a deal with his people," said the Someone, nodding thoughtfully.

They sent me off to do a treatment for them to approve. And by *them,* I understood they meant the Australian Someone, although I was not entirely sure.

Before I left, someone gave me seven hundred dollars, and made me sign for it: two weeks' *per diem.*

I spent two days doing the treatment. I kept trying to forget the book and structure the story as a film. The work went well. I sat in the little room and typed on a notebook computer the studio had sent down for me, and printed out pages on the bubble-jet printer the studio sent down with it. I ate in my room.

Each afternoon I would go for a short walk down Sunset Boulevard. I would walk as far as the "almost all-nite" bookstore, where I would buy a newspaper. Then I would sit outside in the hotel courtyard for half an hour, reading a newspaper. And then, having had my ration of sun and air, I would go back into the dark, and turn my book back into something else.

There was a very old black man, a hotel employee, who would walk across the courtyard each day, with almost painful slowness, and water the plants and inspect the fish. He'd grin at me as he went past, and I'd nod at him.

On the third day I got up and walked over to him as he stood by the fish pool, picking out bits of rubbish by hand: a couple of coins and a cigarette packet.

"Hello," I said.

"Suh," said the old man.

I thought about asking him not to call me sir, but I couldn't think of a way to put it that might not cause offense. "Nice fish."

He nodded, and grinned. "Ornamental carp. Brought here all the way from China."

We watched them swim around the little pool.

"I wonder if they get bored."

He shook his head. "My grandson, he's an ichthyologist, you know what that is?"

"Studies fishes."

"Uh-huh. He says they only got a memory that's like thirty seconds long. So they swim around the pool, it's always a surprise to them, going 'I never been here before.' They meet another fish they known for a hundred years, they say, 'Who are you, stranger?'"

"Will you ask your grandson something for me?" The old man nodded. "I read once that carp don't have set life spans. They don't age like we do. They die if they're killed by people or predators, or disease, but they don't just get old and die. Theoretically they could live forever."

He nodded. "I'll ask him. It sure sounds good. These three—now, this one, I call him Ghost, he's only four, five years old. But the other two, they came here from China back when I was first here."

"And when was that?"

"That would have been in the Year of Our Lord Nineteen Hundred and Twenty-four. How old do I look to you?"

I couldn't tell. He might have been carved from old wood. Over fifty, and younger than Methuselah. I told him so.

"I was born in 1906. God's truth."

"Were you born here, in LA?"

He shook his head. "When I was born, Los Angeles wasn't nothin' but an orange grove, a long way from New York." He sprinkled fish food on the surface of the water. The three fish bobbed up, pale white silvered ghost-carp, staring at us, or seeming to, the O's of their mouths continually opening and closing, as if they were talking to us in some silent, secret language of their own.

I pointed to the one he had indicated. "So, he's Ghost, yes?"

"He's Ghost. That's right. That one under the lily—you can see his tail, there, see?—he's called Buster, after Buster Keaton. Keaton was staying here, when we got the older two. And this one's our Princess."

Princess was the most recognizable of the white carp. She was a pale cream color, with a blotch of vivid crimson along her back, setting her apart from the other two.

"She's lovely."

"She surely is. She surely is all of that."

He took a deep breath then, and began to cough, a wheezing cough, which shook his thin frame. I was able, then, for the first time, to see him as a man of ninety.

"Are you all right?"

He nodded. "Fine, fine, fine. Old bones," he said. "Old bones."

We shook hands, and I returned to my treatment and the gloom.

I printed out the completed treatment, faxed it off to Jacob at the studio.

The next day, he came over to the chalet. He looked upset.

"Everything okay? Is there a problem with the treatment?"

"Just shit going down. We made this movie with . . ." and he named a well-known actress who had been in a few successful films a couple of years before. "Can't lose, huh? Only she is not as young as she was, and she insists on doing her own nude scenes, and that's not a body anybody wants to see, believe me.

"So the plot is, there's this photographer who is persuading women to take their clothes off for him. Then he *shtups* them. Only no one believes he's doing it. So the chief of police—played by Ms. Lemme Show The World My Naked Butt—realizes that the only way she can arrest him is if she pretends to be one of the women. So she sleeps with him. Now, there's a twist . . ."

"She falls in love with him?"

"Oh. Yeah. And then she realizes that women will always be imprisoned by male images of women, and to prove her love for him, when the police come to arrest the two of them she sets fire to all the photographs and dies in the fire. Her clothes burn off first. How does that sound to you?"

"Dumb."

"That was what we thought when we saw it. So we

fired the director and recut it and did an extra day's shoot. Now she's wearing a wire when they make out. And when she starts to fall in love with him, she finds out that he killed her brother. She has a dream in which her clothes burn off, then she goes out with the SWAT team to try to bring him in. But he gets shot by her little sister, who he's also been *shtupping*."

"Is it any better?"

He shakes his head. "It's junk. If she'd let us use a stand-in for the nude sequences, maybe we'd be in better shape."

"What did you think of the treatment?"

"What?"

"My treatment? The one I sent you?"

"Sure. That treatment. We loved it. We all loved it. It was great. Really terrific. We're all really excited."

"So what's next?"

"Well, as soon as everyone's had a chance to look it over, we'll get together and talk about it."

He patted me on the back and went away, leaving me with nothing to do in Hollywood.

I decided to write a short story. There was an idea I'd had in England, before I'd left. Something about a small theatre, at the end of a pier. Stage magic as the rain came down. An audience who couldn't tell the difference between magic and illusion, and to whom it would make no difference if every illusion were real.

That afternoon, on my walk, I bought a couple of books on stage magic and Victorian illusions in the almost all-nite bookshop. A story, or the seed of it, anyway, was there in my head, and I wanted to explore it. I sat on the bench in the courtyard and browsed through the books. There was, I decided, a specific atmosphere that I was after.

I was reading about the Pockets Men, who had pockets filled with every small object you could imagine, and would produce whatever you asked on request. No illusion—just remarkable feats of organization and memory. A shadow fell across the page. I looked up.

"Hullo again," I said to the old black man.

"Suh," he said.

"Please don't call me that. It makes me feel like I ought to be wearing a suit or something." I told him my name.

He told me his: "Pious Dundas."

"Pious?" I wasn't sure that I'd heard him correctly. He nodded, proudly.

"Sometimes I am, and sometimes I ain't. It's what my mama called me, and it's a good name."

"Yes."

"So what are you doing here, suh?"

"I'm not sure. I'm meant to be writing a film, I think. Or at least, I'm waiting for them to tell me to start writing a film."

He scratched his nose. "All the film people stayed here, if I started to tell you them all now, I could talk till a week next Wednesday and I wouldn't have told you the half of them."

"Who were your favorites?"

"Harry Langdon. He was a gentleman. George Sanders. He was English, like you. He'd say 'Ah, Pious. You must pray for my soul.' And I'd say, 'Your soul's your own affair, Mister Sanders,' but I prayed for him just the same. And June Lincoln."

"June Lincoln?"

His eyes sparkled, and he smiled. "She was the queen of the silver screen. She was finer than any of them, Mary Pickford or Lillian Gish or Theda Bara or Louise Brooks. . . . She was the finest. She had 'it.' You know what 'it' was?"

"Sex appeal."

"More than that. She was everything you ever dreamed of. You'd see a June Lincoln picture, you wanted to . . ." he broke off, waved one hand in small circles, as if he were trying to catch the missing words. "I don't know. Go down on one knee, maybe, like a knight in shinin' armor to the queen. June Lincoln, she was the best of them. I told my grandson about her, he tried to find something for the VCR, but no go. Nothing out there anymore. She only lives in the heads of old men like me." He tapped his forehead.

"She must have been quite something."

He nodded.

"What happened to her?"

"She hung herself. Some folks said it was because she wouldn't have been able to cut the mustard in the talkies, but that ain't true: she had a voice you'd remember if you heard it just once. Smooth and dark, her voice was, like an Irish coffee. Some say she got her heart broken by a man, or by a woman, or that it was gambling, or gangsters, or booze. Who knows? They were wild days."

"I take it that you must have heard her talk."

He grinned. "She said, 'Boy, can you find what they did with my wrap?' and when I come back with it, then she said 'You're a fine one, boy.' And the man who was with her, he said, 'June, don't tease the help,' and she smiled at me and gave me five dollars and said 'He don't mind, do you, boy?' and I just shook my head. Then she made the thing with her lips, you know?"

"A *moue*?"

"Something like that. I felt it here." He tapped his chest. "Those lips. They could take a man apart."

He bit his lower lip for a moment and focused on forever. I wondered where he was, and when. Then he looked at me once more.

"You want to see her lips?"

"How do you mean?"

"You come over here. Follow me."

"What are we . . . ?" I had visions of a lip print in cement, like the handprints outside Grauman's Chinese Theater.

He shook his head, and raised an old finger to his mouth. *Silence.*

I closed the books. We walked across the courtyard. When he reached the little fish pool, he stopped.

"Look at the Princess," he told me.

"The one with the red splotch, yes?"

He nodded. The fish reminded me of a Chinese dragon: wise and pale. A ghost-fish, white as old bone, save for the blotch of scarlet on its back—an inch-long double bow-shape. It hung in the pool, drifting, thinking.

"That's it," he said. "On her back. See?"

"I don't quite follow you."

He paused and stared at the fish.

"Would you like to sit down?" I found myself very conscious of Mister Dundas's age.

"They don't pay me to sit down," he said, very seriously. Then he said, as if he were explaining something to a small child, "It was like there were gods in those days. Today, it's all television: small heroes. Little people in the boxes. I see some of them here. Little people.

"The stars of the old times: they was giants, painted in silver light, big as houses . . . and when you met them, they were *still* huge. People believed in them.

"They'd have parties here. You worked here, you saw what went on. There was liquor, and weed, and goings-on you'd hardly credit. There was this one party . . . the film was called *Hearts of the Desert*. You ever heard of it?"

I shook my head.

"One of the biggest movies of 1926, up there with *What Price Glory?* with Victor McLaglen and Dolores DelRio, and *Ella Cinders* starring Colleen Moore. You heard of them?"

I shook my head again.

"You ever heard of Warren Baxter? Belle Bennett?"

"Who were they?"

"Big, big stars in 1926." He paused for a moment. "*Hearts of the Desert.* They had the party for it here, in the hotel, when it wrapped. There was wine and beer and whiskey and gin—this was Prohibition days, but the studios kind of owned the police force, so they looked the other way; and there was food, and a deal of foolishness; Ronald Colman was there, and Douglas Fairbanks—the father, not the son—and all the cast and the crew; and a jazz band played over there where those chalets are now.

"And June Lincoln was the toast of Hollywood that night. She was the Arab princess in the film. Those days, Arabs meant passion and lust. These days . . . well, things change.

"I don't know what started it all. I heard it was a dare or a bet; maybe she was just drunk. I thought she was drunk. Anyhow, she got up, and the band was playing soft and slow. And she walked over here, where I'm standing right now, and she plunged her hands right into this pool. She was laughing, and laughing, and laughing . . .

"Miss Lincoln picked up the fish—reached in and took it, both hands she took it in,—and she picked it up from the water, and then she held it in front of her face.

"Now, I was worried, because they'd just brought these fish in from China and they cost two hundred dollars apiece. That was before I was looking after the fish, of course. Wasn't me that'd lose it from my wages. But still, two hundred dollars was a whole lot of money in those days.

"Then she smiled at all of us, and she leaned down, and she kissed it, slow like, on its back. It didn't wriggle or nothin', it just lay in her hand, and she kissed it with her lips like red coral, and the people at the party laughed and cheered.

"She put the fish back in the pool, and for a moment it was as if it didn't want to leave her—it stayed by her, nuzzling her fingers. And then the first of the fireworks went off, and it swum away.

"Her lipstick was red as red as red, and she left the shape of her lips on the fish's back.—There. Do you see?"

Princess, the white carp with the coral-red mark on her back, flicked a fin and continued on her eternal series of thirty-second journeys around the pool. The red mark did look like a lip print.

He sprinkled a handful of fish food on the surface, and the three fish bobbed and gulped on the surface.

I walked back into my chalet, carrying my books on old illusions. The phone was ringing: it was someone from the studio. They wanted to talk about the treatment. A car would be there for me in thirty minutes.

"Will Jacob be there?"

But the line was already dead.

The meeting was with the Australian Someone and his assistant, a bespectacled man in a suit. His was the first suit I'd seen so far, and the frames of his spectacles were a vivid blue. He seemed nervous.

"Where are you staying?" asked the Someone.

I told him.

"Isn't that where Belushi . . . ?"

"So I've been told."

He nodded. "He wasn't alone, when he died."

"No?"

He rubbed one finger along the side of his pointy nose. "There were a couple of other people at the party. They were both directors, both as big as you could get at that point. You don't need names. I found out about it when I was making the last Indiana Jones film."

An uneasy silence. We were at a huge round table, just the three of us, and we each had a copy of the treatment I had written in front of us. Finally, I said:

"What did you think of it?"

They both nodded, more or less in unison.

And then they tried, as hard as they could, to tell me they hated it, while never saying anything that might conceivably upset me. It was a very odd conversation.

"We have a problem with the third act," they'd say, implying vaguely that the fault lay neither with me nor with the treatment, nor even with the third act, but with them.

They wanted the people to be more sympathetic. They wanted sharp lights and shadows, not shades of grey. They wanted the heroine to be a hero. And I nodded and took notes.

At the end of the meeting I shook hands with the Someone, and the assistant in the blue-rimmed spectacles took me off through the corridor maze to find the outside world, and my car and my driver.

As we walked, I asked if the studio had a picture anywhere of June Lincoln.

"Who?" His name, it turned out, was Greg. He pulled out a small notebook and wrote something down in it with a pencil.

"She was a silent screen star. Famous in 1926."

"Was she with the studio?"

"I have no idea," I admitted. "But she was famous. Even more famous than Mary Provost."

"Who?"

"*A winner who became a doggie's dinner.* One of the biggest stars of the silent screen. Died in poverty when the talkies came in, and was eaten by her dachshund. Nick Lowe wrote a song about her."

"Who?"

"'I knew the bride when she used to rock and roll.' Anyway: June Lincoln. Can someone find me a photo?"

He wrote something more down on his pad. Stared at it for a moment. Then wrote down something else. Then he nodded.

We had reached the daylight, and my car was waiting.

"By the way," he said. "You should know that he's full of shit."

"I'm sorry?"

"Full of shit. It wasn't Spielberg and Lucas who were with Belushi. It was Bette Midler and Linda Ronstadt. It was a coke orgy. Everybody knows that. He's full of shit. And he was just a junior studio accountant for chrissakes on the Indiana Jones movie. Like it was his movie. Asshole."

We shook hands. I got in the car and went back to the hotel.

The time difference caught up with me that night, and I woke, utterly and irrevocably, at 4:00 A.M.

I got up; peed; then pulled on a pair of jeans (I sleep in a T-shirt) and walked outside.

I wanted to see the stars; but the lights of the city were too bright, the air too dirty. The sky was a dirty, starless yellow, and I thought of all the constellations I could see from the English countryside, and I felt, for the first time, deeply, stupidly homesick.

I missed the stars.

*   *   *

I wanted to work on the short story, or to get on with the film script. Instead I worked on a second draft of the treatment.

I took the number of Junior Mansons down to five from twelve and made it clearer from the start that one of them, who was now male, wasn't a bad guy, and the other four most definitely were.

They sent over a copy of a film magazine. It had the smell of old pulp paper about it, and was stamped in purple with the studio name and with the word ARCHIVES underneath. The cover showed John Barrymore, on a boat.

The article inside was about June Lincoln's death. I found it hard to read and harder still to understand: it hinted at the forbidden vices that led to her death, that much I could tell, but it was as if it were hinting in a cipher to which modern readers lacked any key. Or perhaps, on reflection, the writer of her obituary knew nothing, and was hinting into the void.

More interesting—at any rate more comprehensible— were the photos. A full-page, black-edged photo of a woman with huge eyes and a gentle smile smoking a cigarette (the smoke was airbrushed in, to my way of thinking very clumsily: had people ever been taken in by such clumsy fakes?); another photo of her in a staged clinch with Douglas Fairbanks; a small photograph of her standing on the running board of a car, holding a couple of tiny dogs.

She was, from the photographs, not a contemporary beauty. She lacked the transcendence of a Louise Brooks, the sex appeal of a Marilyn Monroe, the sluttish elegance of a Rita Hayworth. She was a twenties starlet as dull as any other twenties starlet. I saw no mystery in her huge eyes, her bobbed hair. She had perfectly made-up Cupid's-bow lips. I had no idea what she would have looked like if she had been alive and around today.

Still, she was real; she had lived. She had been worshiped and adored by the people in the movie palaces. She had kissed the fish, and walked on the grounds of my hotel seventy years before: no time in England, but an eternity in Hollywood.

I went in to talk about the treatment. None of the people I had spoken to before were there. Instead, I was shown into a small office to see a very young man, who never smiled, and who told me how much he loved the treatment, and how pleased he was that the studio owned the property.

He said he thought the character of Charles Manson was particularly cool, and that maybe—"once he was fully dimensionalized"—Manson could be the next Hannibal Lecter.

"But. Um. Manson. He's real. He's in prison now. His people killed Sharon Tate."

"Sharon Tate?"

"She was an actress. A film star. She was pregnant, and they killed her. She was married to Polanski."

"*Roman* Polanski?"

"The director. Yes."

He frowned. "But we're putting together a deal with Polanski."

"That's good. He's a good director."

"Does he know about this?"

"About what? The book? Our film? Sharon Tate's death?"

He shook his head: none of the above. "It's a three-picture deal. Julia Roberts is semi-attached to it. You say Polanski doesn't know about this treatment?"

"No, what I said was—"

He checked his watch.

"Where are you staying," he asked. "Are we putting you up somewhere good?"

"Yes, thank you," I said. "I'm a couple of chalets away from the room in which Belushi died."

I expected another confidential couple of stars: to be told that John Belushi had kicked the bucket in company with Julie Andrews and Miss Piggy the Muppet. I was wrong.

"Belushi's dead?" he said, his young brow furrowing. "Belushi's not dead. We're doing a picture with Belushi."

"This was the brother," I told him. "The brother died, years ago."

He shrugged. "Sounds like a shithole," he said. "Next time you come out, tell them you want to stay in the Bel Air. You want us to move you out there now?"

"No, thank you," I said. "I'm used to it where I am."

"What about the treatment?" I asked.

"Leave it with us."

I found myself becoming fascinated by two old theatrical illusions I found in my books: The Artist's Dream, and The Enchanted Casement. They were metaphors for something, of that I was certain; but the story that ought to have accompanied them was not yet there. I'd write first sentences that did not make it to first paragraphs, first paragraphs that never made it to first pages. I'd write them on the computer, then exit without saving anything.

I sat outside in the courtyard and stared at the two white

carp and the one scarlet-and-white carp. They looked, I decided, like Escher drawings of fish, which surprised me, as it had never occurred to me there was anything even slightly realistic in Escher's drawings.

Pious Dundas was polishing the leaves of the plants. He had a bottle of polisher and a cloth.

"Hi, Pious."

"Suh."

"Lovely day."

He nodded, and coughed, and banged his chest with his fist, and nodded some more.

I left the fish, sat down on the bench.

"Why haven't they made you retire?" I asked. "Shouldn't you have retired fifteen years ago?"

He continued polishing. "Hell no, I'm a landmark. They can *say* that all the stars in the sky stayed here, but *I* can tell folks what Cary Grant had for breakfast."

"Do you remember?"

"Heck no. But *they* don't know that." He coughed again. "What you writing?"

"Well, last week I wrote a treatment for this film. And then I wrote another treatment. And now I'm waiting for . . . something."

"So, what *are* you writing?"

"A story that won't come right. It's about a Victorian magic trick, called The Artist's Dream. An artist comes onto the stage, carrying a big canvas, which he puts on an easel. It's got a painting of a woman on it. And he looks at the painting and despairs of ever being a real painter. Then he sits down and goes to sleep, and the painting comes to life, steps down from the frame, and tells him not to give up. To keep fighting. He'll be a great painter one day. She climbs back into the frame. The lights dim. Then he wakes up, and it's a painting again . . ."

*   *   *

". . . and the other illusion," I told the woman from the studio, who had made the mistake of feigning interest at the beginning of the meeting, "was called The Enchanted Casement. A window hangs in the air, and faces appear in it, but there's no one around. I think I can get a strange sort of parallel between the enchanted casement and probably television: seems like a natural candidate, after all."

"I like *Seinfeld*," she said. "You watch that show? It's about nothing. I mean they have whole episodes about nothing. And I liked Garry Shandling, before he did the new show and got mean."

"The illusions," I continued, "like all great illusions, make us question the nature of reality. But they also frame—pun, I suppose, intentionalish—the issue of what entertainment would turn into. Films before they had films, telly before there was ever TV."

She frowned. "Is this a movie?"

"I hope not. It's a short story, if I can get it to work."

"So let's talk about the movie." She flicked through a pile of notes. She was in her midtwenties and looked both attractive and sterile. I wondered if she was one of the women who had been at the breakfast, on my first day, a Deanna or a Tina.

She looked puzzled at something, and read: "I Knew the Bride When She Used to Rock and Roll?"

"He wrote that down? That's not this film."

She nodded. "Now, I have to say that some of your treatment is kind of . . . *contentious*. The Manson thing . . . well, we're not sure it's going to fly. Could we take him out?"

"But that's the whole point of the thing. I mean, the book is called *Sons of Man*, it's about Manson's children. If you take him out, you don't have very much, do you? I mean, this is the book you bought." I held it up for her to see—my talisman. "Throwing out Manson is like, I don't know, it's like ordering a pizza, and then complaining when it arrives because it's flat, round, and covered in tomato sauce and cheese."

She gave no indication of having heard anything I had said. She asked: "What do you think about *When We Were Badd* as a title? Two d's in Badd."

"I don't know. For this?"

"We don't want people to think that it's religious. *Sons of Man*. It sounds like it might be kind of anti-Christian."

"Well, I do kind of imply that the power that possesses the Manson children is in some way a kind of demonic power."

"You do?"

"In the book."

She managed a pitying look, of the kind that only people who know that books are, at best, properties on which films can be loosely based, can bestow on the rest of us.

"Well, I don't think the studio would see that as appropriate," she said.

"Do you know who June Lincoln was?" I asked her.

She shook her head.

"David Gambol? Jacob Klein?"

She shook her head once more, a little impatiently. Then she gave me a typed list of things she felt needed fixing, which amounted to pretty much everything. The list was TO: me, and a number of other people, whose names I didn't recognize, and it was FROM: Donna Leary.

I said "Thank you, Donna," and went back to the hotel.

*   *   *

I was gloomy for a day. And then I thought of a way to redo the treatment that would, I thought, deal with all of Donna's list of complaints.

Another day's thinking, a few days' writing, and I faxed the third treatment off to the studio.

Pious Dundas brought his scrapbook over for me to look at, once he felt certain that I was genuinely interested in June Lincoln—named, I discovered, after the month and the president, born Ruth Baumgarten in 1903. It was a leather-bound old scrapbook, the size and weight of a family bible.

She was twenty-four when she died.

"I wish you could've seen her," said Pious Dundas. "I wish some of her films had survived. She was so big. She was the greatest star of all of them."

"Was she a good actress?"

He shook his head decisively: "Nope."

"Was she a great beauty? If she was, I just don't see it."

He shook his head again. "The camera liked her, that's for sure. But that wasn't it. Back row of the chorus had a dozen girls prettier'n her."

"Then what was it?"

"She was a star." He shrugged. "That's what it means to be a star."

I turned the pages: cuttings, reviewing films I'd never heard of—films for which the only negatives and prints had long ago been lost, mislaid, or destroyed by the fire department, nitrate negatives being a notorious fire hazard; other cuttings from film magazines: June Lincoln at play, June Lincoln at rest, June Lincoln on the set of *The Pawnbroker's Shirt*, June Lincoln wearing a huge fur coat—which somehow dated the photograph more than the strange bobbed hair or the ubiquitous cigarettes.

"Did you love her?"

He shook his head. "Not like you would love a woman . . ." he said.

There was a pause. He reached down and turned the pages.

"And my wife would have killed me if she'd heard me say this. . . ."

Another pause.

"But yeah. Skinny dead white woman. I suppose I loved her." He closed the book.

"But she's not dead to you, is she?"

He shook his head. Then he went away. But he left me the book, to look at.

The secret of the illusion of The Artist's Dream was this: it was done by carrying the girl in, holding tight on to the back of the canvas. The canvas was supported by hidden wires, so, while the artist casually, easily, carried in the canvas and placed it on the easel, he was also carrying in the girl. The painting of the girl on the easel was arranged like a roller blind, and it rolled up or down.

The Enchanted Casement, on the other hand, was, literally, done with mirrors: an angled mirror which reflected the faces of people standing out of sight in the wings.

Even today, many magicians use mirrors in their acts to make you think you are seeing something you are not.

It was all easy, when you knew how it was done.

"Before we start," he said, "I should tell you I don't read treatments. I tend to feel it inhibits my creativity. Don't worry, I had a secretary do a précis, so I'm up to speed."

He had a beard and long hair and looked a little like Jesus, although I doubted that Jesus had such perfect teeth. He was, it appeared, the most important person I'd spoken to so far. His name was John Ray, and even I had heard of him, although I was not entirely sure what he did: his name tended to appear at the beginning of films, next to words like "Executive Producer." The voice from the studio that had set up the meeting told me that they, the studio, were most excited about the fact that he had "attached himself to the project."

"Doesn't the précis inhibit your creativity, too?"

He grinned. "Now, we all think you've done an amazing job. Quite stunning. There are just a few things that we have a problem with."

"Such as?"

"Well, the Manson thing. And the idea about these kids growing up. So we've been tossing around a few scenarios in the office: try this for size. There's a guy called, say, Jack Badd—two d's, that was Donna's idea—"

Donna bowed her head modestly.

"They put him away for satanic abuse, fried him in the chair, and as he dies he swears he'll come back and destroy them all.

"Now, it's today, and we see these young boys getting hooked on a video arcade game called Be Badd. His face on it. And as they play the game he, like, starts to possess them. Maybe there could be something strange about his face, a Jason or Freddie thing." He stopped, as if he were seeking approval.

So I said, "So who's making these video games?"

He pointed a finger at me, and said, "You're the writer, sweetheart. You want us to do all your work for you?"

I didn't say anything. I didn't know what to say.

Think movies, I thought. *They understand movies*. I said, "But surely, what you're proposing is like doing *The Boys from Brazil* without Hitler."

He looked puzzled.

"It was a film by Ira Levin," I said. No flicker of

recognition in his eyes. "*Rosemary's Baby.*" He continued to look blank. "*Sliver.*"

He nodded; somewhere a penny had dropped. "Point taken," he said. "You write the Sharon Stone part, we'll move heaven and earth to get her for you. I have an in to her people."

So I went out.

That night it was cold, and it shouldn't have been cold in LA, and the air smelled more of cough drops than ever.

An old girlfriend lived in the LA area, and I resolved to get hold of her. I phoned the number I had for her, and began a quest that took most of the rest of the evening. People gave me numbers and I rang them, and other people gave me numbers and I rang them, too.

Eventually I phoned a number, and I recognized her voice.

"Do you know where I am?" she said.

"No," I said. "I was given this number."

"This is a hospital room," she said. "My mother's. She had a brain hemorrhage."

"I'm sorry. Is she all right?"

"No."

"I'm sorry."

There was an awkward silence.

"How are you?" she asked.

"Pretty bad," I said.

I told her everything that had happened to me so far. I told her how I felt.

"Why is it like this?" I asked her.

"Because they're scared."

"Why are they scared? What are they scared of?"

"Because you're only as good as the last hits you can attach your name to."

"Huh?"

"If you say 'yes' to something, the studio may make a film, and it will cost twenty or thirty million dollars, and if it's a failure, you will have your name attached to it, and will lose status. If you say 'no,' you don't risk losing status."

"Really?"

"Kind of."

"How do you know so much about all this? You're a musician, you're not in films."

She laughed, wearily. "I live out here. Everybody who lives out here knows this stuff. Have you tried asking people about their screenplays?"

"No."

"Try it some time. Ask anyone. The guy in the gas station. Anyone. They've all got them." Then someone said something to her, and she said something back, and she said "Look, I've got to go," and she put down the phone.

I couldn't find the heater, if the room had a heater, and I was freezing, in my little chalet room, like the one Belushi died in, same uninspired framed print on the wall, I had no doubt, same chilly dampness in the air.

I ran a hot bath to warm myself up, but I was even chillier when I got out.

White goldfish sliding to and fro in the water, dodging and darting through the lily pads. One of the goldfish had a crimson mark on its back that might, conceivably, have been perfectly lip-shaped: the miraculous stigmata of an almost-forgotten goddess. The grey early-morning sky was reflected in the pool.

I stared at it, gloomily.

"You okay?"

I turned. Pious Dundas was standing next to me.

"You're up early."

"I slept badly. Too cold."

"You should have called the front desk. They'd've sent you down a heater and extra blankets."

"It never occurred to me."

His breathing sounded awkward, labored.

"You okay?"

"Heck, no. I'm old. You get to my age, boy, you won't be okay either. But I'll be here when you've gone. How's work going?"

"I don't know. I've stopped working on the treatment, and I'm stuck on 'The Artist's Dream'—this story I'm doing about Victorian stage magic. It's set in an English seaside resort, in the rain. With the magician performing magic on the stage, which somehow changes the audience. It touches their hearts."

He nodded, slowly. "The Artist's Dream . . ." he said. "So. You see yourself as the artist, or the magician?"

"I don't know," I said. "I don't think I'm either of them."

I turned to go, and then something occurred to me.

"Mister Dundas," I said. "Have you got a screenplay? One you wrote?"

He shook his head.

"You *never* wrote a screenplay?"

"Not me," he said.

"Promise?"

He grinned. "I promise," he said.

I went back to my room. I thumbed through my UK hardback of *Sons of Man*, and wondered that anything so clumsily written had even been published, wondered why Hollywood had bought it in the first place, why they didn't want it, now that they had bought it.

I tried to write "The Artist's Dream" some more, and failed miserably. The characters were frozen. They seemed unable to breathe, or move, or talk.

I went into the toilet, pissed a vivid yellow stream against the porcelain. A cockroach ran across the silver of the mirror.

I went back into the sitting room, opened a new document, and wrote:

I'm thinking about England in the rain,
a strange theatre on the pier: a trail
of fear and magic, memory and pain.

The fear should be of going bleak insane,
the magic should be like a fairy tale.
I'm thinking about England in the rain.

The loneliness is harder to explain—
an empty place inside me where I fail,
of fear and magic, memory and pain.

I think of a magician, and a skein
of truth disguised as lies. You wear a veil.
I'm thinking about England in the rain . . .

The shapes repeat like some bizarre refrain
and here's a sword, a hand, and there's a grail
of fear and magic, memory and pain.

The wizard waves his wand and we turn pale,
tells us sad truths, but all to no avail.
I'm thinking about England, in the rain
of fear and magic, memory and pain.

I didn't know if it was any good or not, but that didn't matter. I had written something new and fresh I hadn't written before, and it felt wonderful.

I ordered breakfast from room service, and requested a heater and a couple of extra blankets.

*   *   *

The next day, I wrote a six-page treatment for a film called *When We Were Badd*, in which Jack Badd, a serial killer with a huge cross carved into his forehead, was killed in the electric chair and came back in a video game and took over four young men. The fifth young man defeated Badd by burning the original electric chair, which was now on display, I decided, in the Wax Museum where the fifth young man's girlfriend worked during the day. By night she was an exotic dancer.

The hotel desk faxed it off to the studio, and I went to bed.

I went to sleep, hoping that the studio would formally reject it, and that I could go home.

In the theater of my dreams, a man with a beard and a baseball cap carried on a movie screen, and then he walked offstage. The silver screen hung in the air, unsupported.

A flickery silent film began to play upon it: a woman who came out and stared down at me. It was June Lincoln who flickered on the screen, and it was June Lincoln who walked down from the screen and sat on the edge of my bed.

"Are you going to tell me not to give up?" I asked her.

On some level, I knew it was a dream. I remember, dimly, understanding why this woman was a star, remember regretting that none of her films had survived.

She was indeed beautiful, in my dream, despite the livid mark which went all the way around her neck.

"Why on earth would I do that?" she asked. In my dream she smelled of gin and old celluloid, although I do not remember the last dream I had where anyone smelled of anything. She smiled, a perfect black-and-white smile. "I got out, didn't I?"

Then she stood up and walked around the room.

"I can't believe this hotel is still standing," she said. "I used to fuck here." Her voice was filled with crackles and hisses. She came back to the bed and stared at me, as a cat stares at a hole.

"Do you worship me?" she asked.

I shook my head. She walked over to me, and took my flesh hand in her silver one.

"Nobody remembers anything anymore," she said. "It's a thirty-minute town."

There was something I had to ask her. "Where are the stars?" I asked. "I keep looking up in the sky, but they aren't there."

She pointed at the floor of the chalet. "You've been looking in the wrong places," she said. I had never before noticed that the floor of the chalet was a sidewalk; and each paving stone contained a star and a name: names I didn't know—Clara Kimball Young, Linda Arvidson, Vivian Martin, Norma Talmadge, Olive Thomas, Mary Miles Minter, Seena Owen . . .

June Lincoln pointed at the chalet window. "And out there." The window was open, and through it I could see the whole of Hollywood spread out below me—the view from the hills: an infinite spread of twinkling, multicolored lights.

"Now, aren't those better than stars?" she asked.

And they were. I realized I could see constellations in the streetlights and the cars.

I nodded.

Her lips brushed mine.

"Don't forget me," she whispered, but she whispered it sadly, as if she knew that I would.

I woke up with the telephone shrilling. I answered it, growled a mumble into the handpiece.

"This is Gerry Quoint, from the studio. We need you for a lunch meeting."

Mumble something mumble.

"We'll send a car," he said. "The restaurant's about half an hour away."

The restaurant was airy and spacious and green, and they were waiting for me there.

By this point I would have been surprised if I *had* recognized anyone. John Ray, I was told, over hors d'oeuvres, had "split over contract disagreements," and Donna had gone with him, "obviously."

Both of the men had beards; one had bad skin. The woman was thin and seemed pleasant.

They asked where I was staying, and, when I told them, one of the beards told us (first making us all agree that this would go no further), that a politician named Gary Hart and one of the Eagles were both doing drugs with Belushi when he died.

After that they told me that they were looking forward to the story.

I asked the question. "Is this for *Sons of Man* or *When We Were Badd*? Because," I told them, "I have a problem with the latter."

They looked puzzled.

It was, they told me, for *I Knew the Bride When She Used to Rock and Roll*. Which was, they told me, both High Concept and Feel Good. It was also, they added, Very Now, which was important in a town in which an hour ago was Ancient History.

They told me that they thought it would be a good thing

if our hero could rescue the young lady from her loveless marriage, and if they could rock and roll together at the end.

I pointed out that they needed to buy the film rights from Nick Lowe, who wrote the song, and then that, no, I didn't know who his agent was.

They grinned and assured me that that wouldn't be a problem.

They suggested I turn over the project in my mind before I started on the treatment, and each of them mentioned a couple of young stars to bear in mind when I was putting together the story.

And I shook hands with all of them, and told them that I certainly would.

I mentioned that I thought that I could work on it best back in England.

And they said that that would be fine.

Some days before, I'd asked Pious Dundas whether anyone was with Belushi in the chalet, on the night that he died.

If anyone would know, I figured, he would.

"He died alone," said Pious Dundas, old as Methuselah, unblinking. "It don't matter a rat's ass whether there was anyone with him or not. He died alone."

It felt strange to be leaving the hotel.

I went up to the front desk.

"I'll be checking out later this afternoon."

"Very good, sir."

"Would it be possible for you to . . . the, uh, the groundskeeper. Mister Dundas. An elderly gentleman. I don't know. I haven't seen him around for a couple of days. I wanted to say good-bye."

"To one of the groundsmen?"

"Yes."

She stared at me, puzzled. She was very beautiful, and her lipstick was the color of a blackberry bruise. I wondered whether she was waiting to be discovered.

She picked up the phone and spoke into it, quietly.

Then, "I'm sorry, sir. Mister Dundas hasn't been in for the last few days."

"Could you give me his phone number?"

"I'm sorry, sir. That's not our policy." She stared at me, as she said it, letting me know that she *really* was *so* sorry . . .

"How's your screenplay?" I asked her.

"How did you know?" she asked.

"Well—"

"It's on Joel Silver's desk," she said. "My friend Arnie, he's my writing partner, and he's a courier. He dropped it off with Joel Silver's office, like it came from a regular agent or somewhere."

"Best of luck," I told her.

"Thanks," she said, and smiled with her blackberry lips.

Information had two Dundas, P's listed, which I thought was both unlikely and said something about America, or at least Los Angeles.

The first turned out to be a Ms. Persephone Dundas.

At the second number, when I asked for Pious Dundas, a man's voice said, "Who is this?"

I told him my name, that I was staying in the hotel, and that I had something belonging to Mister Dundas.

"Mister. My granfa's dead. He died last night."

Shock makes clichés happen for real: I felt the blood drain from my face; I caught my breath.

"I'm sorry. I liked him."

"Yeah."

"It must have been pretty sudden."

"He was old. He got a cough." Someone asked him who he was talking to, and he said nobody, then he said, "Thanks for calling."

I felt stunned.

"Look, I have his scrapbook. He left it with me."

"That old film stuff?"

"Yes."

A pause.

"Keep it. That stuff's no good to anybody. Listen, Mister, I gotta run."

A click, and the line went silent.

I went to pack the scrapbook in my bag, and was startled, when a tear splashed on the faded leather cover, to discover that I was crying.

I stopped by the pool for the last time, to say good-bye to Pious Dundas, and to Hollywood.

Three ghost-white carp drifted, fins flicking minutely, through the eternal present of the pool.

I remembered their names: Buster, Ghost, and Princess; but there was no longer any way that anyone could have told them apart.

The car was waiting for me, by the hotel lobby. It was a thirty-minute drive to the airport; and already I was starting to forget.

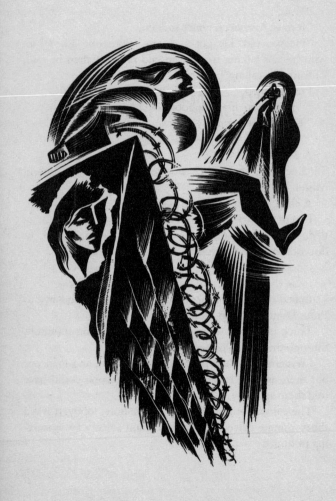

Humpty Dumpty Was a Runner

JANET BERLINER

A few years ago, in one of my television specials, I walked through the Great Wall of China. In my Barclay House piece, I use the effect of restless ghosts from the past. Put the two together, and you approach the dilemma of this story's youthful protagonist. Haunted by the ghosts of young people from the past, she is propelled from her lethargy into awareness, for the ghosts know that the walls which keep people from being free are not built of stone or cement. Rather, their bricks are hatred, and their mortar, apathy. There are none so blind, say the ghosts, as those who will not see.

—DC

Humpty Dumpty
Was a Runner

"Eternal vigilance is
the price of freedom."

—THOMAS JEFFERSON

AT AGE FIFTEEN, the only thing sectarian about Jennie
Abelson was her name. Her father was a banker, living in
Seattle with his ex-secretary; her mother, Susan not Sue,
was an upwardly mobile young exec with an MBA, a live-
in significant other, and a healthy portfolio. Susan jogged
regularly, didn't smoke, and got excited about little except
women's issues—and that only when it suited her. The
only thing political about her was her voter registration
card, which she had used once to vote for a friend of hers
who happened to be running for Congress in her district.

This was all fine with Jennie. She was happy to be a
California girl. In general, she extolled the virtues of
speaking English and driving American cars; in particular,
she had a passion for five-star hotels, admitted to being
secretly in love with Keanu Reeves, and though she had
well-thumbed copies of *The Diary of Anne Frank* and *The
Life of Helen Keller* in her room, she identified most with
Brooke Shields. She'd seen *Casablanca*, but aside from how
beautiful Ingrid Bergman looked, she didn't see what all
the fuss was about. She took German at school as a minor
concession to her heritage, and also because she thought

the German teacher was cute, but none of it really meant much to her because she loved the United States and hoped never to leave its borders. Which she hadn't.

Until now.

She had also never really experienced pain. Until now.

Which probably meant, she thought, that if she had stayed home for spring break, she wouldn't be hurting.

Timing, she decided, was everything. Her Oma had caught her in a weak moment, right after watching that fiftieth anniversary "World War II Victory Special" and seeing those pathetic faces, standing at the docks sometime in the thirties trying to get on a ship to the States. One of them looked up and seemed to stare right at her.

Mouthing the words, *I am Hannelore. Look in the old shoe box, with the other photographs.*

Jennie had found the photo, curled at the edges and faded. A family portrait: mother, father, and four children.

One of them was Hannelore. She looked just like Jennie.

On the back of the photograph was written in fine script: Hannelore. Died Belsen. Age 14.

Jennie remembered the story now, the one her Oma had told her about her nieces and nephews who had died waiting for affidavits from America. From the Denver part of the family, whom Jenny hardly knew. They said there was plenty of time.

There was only time to die.

But it was not their problem, as it was not Jennie's problem. She was not even born.

But Hannelore was born. She was at the docks. Preserved on film. And for a split second, Jennie was looking into a mirror. An epiphany.

"I didn't do it," she said aloud. "It's not my guilt."

She stared out of the window of the L-1011 and shook

her head to clear it. It was no use. The vision of unmarked graves stayed, hovering around the edges of the clouds. And out of the graveyard came ghostly voices. Featureless. Insistent. Holding a dialogue with her each time she dared to glance outside.

This flight seems to be going on forever, she thought, shifting her position. She rubbed her thigh, annoyed at the pain and wondering if being cooped up on the plane had caused it and if so, why, since she had been stretched out most of the way. With two empty seats next to her, why not.

Growing restless, she walked up and down the aisle and stood on line for her turn in the bathroom. When she returned to her seat, the aisle seat was occupied by an elderly woman who was staring fixedly at her lap.

"Excuse me," Jenny said. "I need to get into my seat."

The woman moved slightly, just enough to let Jenny through. She was small and fragile. When she moved, it seemed as if tiny motes of dust floated from her into the dry, ozone-filled air. She was dressed in shades of browns and beiges, and looked to Jenny like one of the old-world photographs she had so recently rummaged through at home. A sepia woman.

Jenny settled back into her seat, buckled her seat belt, and decided there was time for a short nap before touchdown. She closed her eyes, but the sound of quiet sobbing intruded. She opened her eyes and looked sideways. The elderly woman was weeping. Praying. Repeating a long litany of names. Jennie covered her ears. She did not want to know the names or the faces of the dead.

"I'm sorry," the woman said. "It has been so many years since I was here. I never thought I would come back. Berlin was my home before. They tell me I must forgive—"

Let go, Lady, Jennie thought.

"My children want me to live here again," the woman said. "I am old. The compensation money would allow me to live decently. Compensation for what, I asked them. For our children? The flames? Our sorrow? My brother, Jacob, he lives here now, so he put up a stone for our parents. He wants me to join him. Since my Morrie's gone, I'm all alone, but I don't know." She blew her nose and sat up straight, as if actively regaining control of her emotions. "Your first trip to Germany?" she asked.

Jennie nodded.

"Did your family live in Berlin before?"

"Yes." Her great-grandmother. Great-grandfather. Their parents. Survivors who had left in time. Not like the girl, Hannelore. The one on the dock.

The one whose face she *had* seen. The one whose face she *did* know.

"My Oma lives here . . . again. She works for the displaced persons bureau," Jennie told her. "They say a lot of them are going back."

"Them?" The woman shrank from her.

"Us," Jennie said.

"Could it happen again, do you think?"

The plane was circling Berlin, and she stared out of the window into the sun, letting it blind her. This is insanity, she told herself as the plane landed. It's over. Forget it—or at least let it be a part of the past.

"I don't know," Jennie said. She looked away. If there was anti-Semitism in Germany, she didn't want to know about it. If there was misery here or anywhere else, like last year in Bosnia, when Clinton sent in troops and everyone was arguing about it, she hadn't wanted to know about that either. Now there was trouble in Liberia. She didn't even know where those places were on the map, fer

Godssakes. "I keep seeing . . . I don't really want to think about it. It was all so long ago."

"It was yesterday," the woman said quietly. "It is today."

Jennie turned to answer, but the woman was gone.

Jennie lay on the old sofa in her Oma's small Niebuhrstrasse Senioren flat and listened to the U-Bahn, cursing the overhead railroad and blaming it and the heavy food for her insomnia. When she did, finally, fall asleep, it was to dream of being lost in a city filled with brooding images and the sound of lamenting.

She woke to the smell of strong coffee. A small wooden table in the center of the room had been covered with a handmade, lace-edged cloth. On it stood an old-fashioned percolator, a thin china coffee cup, and a plate of her favorite pumpernickel and liverwurst.

"You'll have to roll me out of here, Oma," she said, stretching. "Oma?"

A car outside skidded on the wet sidewalk; a neighbor yelled at an errant dog. Jennie stumbled out of bed, poured herself a cup of coffee, and saw the note propped against the sugar bowl.

The note was dated 1986. Her great-grandmother was getting real old, Jennie thought, reading the note.

"Good morning, Sleeping Beauty," it said. "I had some things *zum einkaufen.*" Jenny wondered if her Oma was aware that she mixed languages on paper more than she did verbally. "Meet me at the Jewish Community Center at twelve o'clock, opposite where we had coffee yesterday afternoon. Here is a kind of map. Be sure you are there on time. There is to be a ceremony and speeches. We must all be there, all the generations."

Again speeches, Jennie thought. Did they never get

tired of talking about the past? And why the devil did anyone think she wanted to be there? She loved and admired
the old lady, but all of that stuff had nothing to do with
her. She couldn't relate, any more than she could relate to
South Africa and her grandmother's memories of that.

Her family kept trying to involve her—giving her a
ticket to come here.

Her Oma was in her twenties when all that stuff was
happening. She was thirty and living in South Africa when
WWII broke out. That was the year her grandmother was
born, the immigrant child of immigrant parents. She was
nineteen when she came to America, and twenty when
she gave birth to Jennie's mother.

She, Jennie, was born in America in 1981. A blond,
blue-eyed California baby, now fifteen and counting the
days until she could get her learner's permit.

That meant something to her.

All this stuff that they kept rehashing was ancient history: the pogroms; the ghettos; the concentration camps
fifty years ago; the erection of the Wall. It was even longer
ago than the Beatles and Marilyn Monroe and Vietnam
and Elvis Presley—before Internet fer Chrissakes.

She was no more responsible for any of that than she
was for the IRA or Mau Maus. Might as well tell her that
the Israel–Palestine mess was her fault, too.

She had overheard a bunch of Midddle Eastern and
German foreign exchange students talking about this one
day in the school cafeteria. They were resentful as hell, as if
they were supposed to feel responsible for what had happened. Guilty for what a completely different generation
had done. It was not their concern. They didn't do it.
They couldn't relate. They didn't want to hear about it
anymore. And nor did she.

She didn't care about any of it. But the others did, her

Oma and her grandmother. And they seemed to need her to care, as if she were their great white hope or something. If only they would stop already and understand that it had nothing to do with her.

So maybe she just wouldn't go today, and they could do their damn speechifying without her.

Jennie smeared liverwurst on a slice of bread and poured herself a second cup of coffee, happy not to have to drink her mother's decaf. Much as she enjoyed seeing and handling the beautiful china, with its long history, there was something to be said for the practicality, impersonality, disposability of a big old American mug, she thought.

After a long, hot soak in the prewar cast-iron tub, Jennie dressed and left the small apartment. Strolling along cobblestoned streets, past rebuilt shells of once-ruined buildings, she made her way to the Kurfürstendamm. Window-shopping made her feel better. It always did. The anonymity of exquisite stores and movie houses advertising familiar names like Woody Allen and Muhammad Ali calmed her. She wondered in passing why the movie theaters were all playing ten-year-old films instead of the latest thing, but she felt benign enough that it no longer seemed to be such a big deal to please her Oma and go to the Community Center after all. It took her about half an hour to walk to the Kempinski Hotel, which was, as her great-grandmother had said, a block away from the Jewish Community Center.

Her Oma was waiting. Next to her stood a guard with a rifle. He was not much older than Jennie, twenty maybe. He was very handsome, Ethiopian or something.

"Did something happen?" Jennie asked.

"He is here so that nothing does," her Oma said matter-of-factly.

"I don't get it," Jennie said. "I mean I just don't get it.

Why do you people always have to anticipate trouble? Leave it alone already. And while you're about it, leave me alone, too."

"*You people?*" The guard gripped her arm. "Are you not a Jew?" he asked. "We are the new generation. We must keep everything in active memory. For all of us. For all of the world. So that the hating will stop—"

"But I was not there. I am not responsible for what happened." She was shouting now. "It is not my problem."

"We are responsible for carrying the memory, or the walls can never come down. Walls aren't built of brick and mortar. They're built of layers of hatred. You have to carry the memories forward in your active, conscious memory. Yes, there are photographs, books, but the feelings can only be transferred from generation to generation. Your Oma's generation is the carrier of the collective unconscious, but you and I, the new generation, we are the carriers of the collective consciousness."

Bullshit, Jennie thought, biting her tongue. She concentrated on the building's architecture, a strange juxtaposition of prewar brick and postwar concrete and glass.

"I'm sorry, I didn't mean to upset you," she said. "It's just that I can't take myself that seriously." She walked indoors, past an ancient scroll that someone had donated to the Center and into an atrium where a stone wall commemorated Jews who had died in the camps. The foot of the wall was alive with fresh flowers. Her Oma bent to pick off a dead bloom. For a moment, in Jennie's eyes, it became a bow, like the one she had seen in Hannelore's hair on the faded, sepia photograph.

Jennie saw her Oma's eyes cloud with tears, and she almost cried with her as she witnessed the pain.

But it was not her pain, and she could not cry. She was a witness to the pain, but felt nothing.

Except in her leg, which ached mercilessly.

Be a tourist, Jen, she told herself. *Go with the flow.*

Jennifer. The voice was soft and sweet. Jennie looked around for the source but could see no one to whom it could possibly belong. *It's not about being a Jew, or about being a Catholic or a Buddhist. It's not about being white or black, or a communist or a capitalist.*

Oh shit, I'm definitely losing it, Jennie thought.

It's about Freedom, Jennifer.

Not about my freedom. I am an American. Freedom is my inalienable right. None of this means anything to me. Who cares. Nothing that ever happened in Germany—or anywhere else—has anything to do with me. It never will.

Heart pounding, she ran into the tiled foyer of the Community Center and opened the entrance door. The building was filled suddenly with the unlikely sound of trumpets.

"It's coming from across the street," the guard said, recognizing her as she stepped outside and pointing at a British band playing oompah-pah behind a horse-drawn carriage advertising beer.

Bullet-marked buildings displayed flower boxes with geraniums; corner stands sold Dutch gladioli, carnations, and roses. The horses had stopped to defecate next to a barber pole which advertised an American-made Hitler documentary.

Jennie had been forced to see it a long time ago at school. She had not been able to relate.

Now, in the gloom of this sunless afternoon, Jennie stood rooted to the ground. Silent. Chilled. Hugging herself like a homeless child as she stared at the collage across the street, at the massive barber pole that said HITLER. Nothing else. Just HITLER, in a constantly repeating pattern, shouting the word at her to the tune of oompah-pah and a wailing police car parked somewhere out of sight.

"I'm just a tourist," she said. As if to prove it, she let her Oma, who had followed her out of the building, lead her into the closest restaurant. There she willed herself to absorb some Berlin *gemütlichkeit* by actually eating the calves liver her Oma ordered for her.

Later, her Oma led her to the cosmetic counter at Wertheim's Department Store, where the international language of Revlon and Rubenstein made her feel a whole lot better, except that everything she tried to buy they'd never heard of, like her favorite color lipstick and the anti-acne stuff that had come onto the market last year.

That night, Jennie gaped at the jeweled and begowned balletomanes who filled the Berlin Opera House to watch Diane Bell dance "Daphnis" and "Bolero," and wrote home saying that doing it as an erotic study in black and white was a stroke of genius, an analysis which made her feel very grown-up and quite the woman of the world.

The following day, encouraged by a returning sense of normalcy, she walked alone through the streets, ate too many rich cakes, and sent home postcards—one of each— of the world's biggest delicatessen and the nude bathers at Freibad Hallensee.

Immersed in the city's kaleidoscope, she took in the smell of the dogs in central Berlin; the Salvation Army playing marches to Jesus in German; Americans playing guitars in the Kudamm. There was the young couple walking a creature that was half cat, half cheetah; the young man drawing a Madonna and child next to a trestle table covered with wire jewelry. And there was Jenny learning the art of avoiding the dog droppings without having to keep her eyes glued to the ground.

Happy to be playing tourist, she took a bus to the Reichstag. The bus drove past the congress, with its ultra-modern structure and sculptures, its flags and fountains, kind of like Disneyland German-style, she thought, almost getting off to wander around. But instead she continued on to the end of the line, to Hitler's headquarters.

Since she didn't really have a clue as to what she was looking at, she picked up a tour guide. It was dated 1986.

"Don't you have a more recent one?" she asked the woman who was handing them out.

The woman shook her head and looked at Jenny strangely. "It is a new one," she said.

They're all crazy, Jennie thought, turning to the English translation. The building had apparently been rebuilt by masters; other than its missing central dome, it was exactly as it had been in Hitler's day. The main hall housed an exhibition—a photographic history of Berlin. It also housed a life-size portrait of John F. Kennedy captioned: "*Ich bin ein Berliner.*" I am a Berliner.

Outside the Reichstag, Jennie approached the banks of the Spree. Across the river was what looked like the Wall, though of course it had to be a mirage caused by the encroaching fog, and through the drizzle she could see the top of the Charlottenburger Turm. On her side of the river stood a row of stone monuments dedicated to the men and women who had tried to cross the Wall—and failed.

Jennie took photographs in the grey dusk, and cried because the photographs would not show what she was beginning to see. What she did not want to see.

That night, in her journal, which she was comforted to see was still dated 1996, she noted the weather, the cost of souvenirs at the Reichstag Gift Shop, what time the Egypt Museum opened and closed. She did not record the tears, or write about how weird she'd felt later that day, drinking coffee with her Oma and the wife of a German Jewish millionaire. Trying not to stare at the woman's tattooed arm; listening to her talk of her work in the Jewish community and of the new rise in anti-Semitism in one breath and of rising property values in Berlin in another.

She did not write about the pain in her thigh. Or about the dreams. Night after night. Of being lost in a city filled with strange, brooding images and the sound of lamenting.

"I want to marry a prince and live in a castle like this," Jennie said, staring at the Schloss Charlottenburg.

"I don't know about living in one," her Oma said, "but we can eat in one."

Jennie was so enchanted at the idea that her Oma made reservations at the Schloss Gerhus in the Grunewald—the green forest where the rich people lived, she said. There, the cobbled streets were lined with trees, and there was a remarkable absence of the dog droppings that punctuated the streets of the city proper.

"Who lived here?" Jennie asked, limping into the reception area.

"Kaiser Wilhelm's attorney," her Oma said, looking around at the wealthy patrons dining in riding habits on antique chairs and under crystal chandeliers. "They say the Kennedys stayed here when they came to Berlin. Come, Jen, let's sneak into the ballroom."

A rock band blared through the radio speakers. *Hardly Strauss*, Jennie thought, rubbing her leg, which was aching badly today. Her Oma danced alone on the parquet floor, watching herself in the mirrors that lined the walls. She danced lightly at first, as if she were eighteen again and not eighty. Then her feet seemed suddenly to grow heavy. "They aren't crazy about Jews here," she said softly. "Nothing definite. Just a rumor. Sort of like the NJA business that still goes on here and there in the States."

"NJA?"

"No Jews Allowed."

"Oma! Don't you ever let go?" Rubbing her thigh, Jennie fled down the stairs toward the dining room.

Freedom, Jennifer.

The words echoed in the stairwell, pushing into the crowd of diners. They did not seem to hear a thing above the clatter of dishes, the loud music, the wine-driven conversation.

She wanted to be of them, with them.

"Leave me alone," she whispered, pushing at the words as if they had taken on a tangible form. "Find someone else to bug. I'm no one important. I'm just a tourist."

"You wanted to be a tourist," Jennie's Oma said, "so all right, be a tourist. Today we go to the East."

"You mean what used to be the East, don't you?"

Jennie's grandmother looked at her as strangely as the woman at the Reichstag had done. "I mean the East," she said.

Jennie decided not to argue. She had not seen a newspaper or, since her grandmother did not own a set, watched television since her arrival, but she wasn't crazy. She knew what day it was, what year, even if no one else did.

It was one of Berlin's monochromatic days, drizzling and damp, hardly more than a mist, really, but enough for the cold to penetrate Jennie's jacket. She was limping badly, using her Oma's umbrella as a walking stick, and straining to think of some reason she could opt out of this excursion. "Do I really have to do this?" she asked.

"Yes, Jennie. This you must do. There is someone over there who wants . . . needs . . . to meet you."

"Who?"

"Your great-grandfather's best friend."

"Oh please!"

"I know, Jen. That kind of stuff bores you. But I promised I'd take you over there to meet him, and he's coming all the way from Dresden. He's a very old man and ... his granddaughter was a champion runner," she said, "long before running was 'in' as you children say. I think it will help him to meet you. . . ."

"*Was* a runner?"

"She was training for a special kind of race," her Oma said slowly. "From East to West."

Jennie felt the blood drain from her face. "All right, I'll fall for it. What happened to her?" she asked.

"She was shot in the leg going over the Wall," her Oma said. "They say she stopped for a moment to look back in the direction of Dresden."

"Was that when . . . ?"

"Yes, Jen. She tumbled to the ground on the Western side."

"Humpty Dumpty sat on a wall . . ." Jennie murmured, kneading the pain in her leg. She did not want to know that she was crying again.

The train left from Bahnhof Friedrichstrasse. Jennie dozed and tried not to think.

"Where are we, Oma?" she asked when she awoke.

"At the border."

"What border?"

"The border between the East and the West," her grandmother said. "What other border would it be?"

"There is no border anymore, Oma," Jennie said, trying not to shout and wondering why her mother hadn't warned her that the old lady was suffering from incipient Alzheimer's. As a matter of fact, she was about ready to believe that all of Berlin was infected by the same disease. "There is no more Wall. That was ages ago."

"*It was yesterday,*" a woman's voice said quietly. "*It is today.*"

Jennie turned quickly in the direction of the voice and caught a fleeting image of the elderly sepia woman before the image became a dust mote and was absorbed into the mist.

It is 1996, there is no Wall, Jennie told herself, as she and her Oma relinquished their passports and a handful of coins into the hands of Communist officials who gave them each a declaration form and a number. As at a deli, except that they were not calling out numbers in sequence, Jennie thought, deciding that she might as well keep her promise to herself and go with the flow—a wise decision, she reckoned, since policemen with machine guns outnumbered the motley assortment of people in the waiting room, where they sat on a wooden bench beneath party-line banners and slogans.

"Abelson. Number seventy."

Big Mac, large fries, and a Coke would be nice, Jennie thought. *Fat chance.*

"Abelson. Number seventy."

"Better hurry before they change their minds," her Oma said.

"What minds?" Jennie murmured irreverently, and was promptly sorry when she went to the wrong window and was reprimanded for her stupidity. She figured someone had understood her flip comment, and was pleased when her tactlessness did not lead to a denied entry. She really did not want to explain that one to her Oma, who had missed the small battle.

At the next checkpoint, money again changed hands; at the third and last, they were given East marks and strict instructions to spend it all. After one more close comparison with their photographs, the formalities were over, and they found themselves on the other side of the Wall.

The wide streets of East Berlin were immaculate. There were few cars and fewer people. As they walked along the main boulevard, Jennie peopled it with the images her Oma has passed on to her. Mentally, she reunited Berlin. She conjured up Opera-going throngs, women in chiffon, carved walking sticks, and taxicabs lined up and waiting for the call of the elegant. But there was no way to avoid the feeling of antisepsis. The avenue was bare, the taxi ranks deserted. Only Unter den Linden, the tourist hotel, had a flower garden. Reconstructed buildings hid burned-out shells; miniature parks grew where famous buildings once stood; and everything was dominated by the lookout towers, which observed the West around the clock. There were very few stores, and of those many had H.O. signs, which apparently meant that they were government-owned businesses. One, without the sign, had a note attached to the door: "We have permission to close for our annual vacation."

"Permission from whom?"

"The DDR. Deutsche Demokratische Republik . . . the government."

They passed a motorbike, for sale at the price of what Jennie was told was half of a man's yearly salary, and went into a bookstore. There was not one piece of fiction available—not even Danielle Steel—nothing but propaganda, art books, and posters extolling the virtues of the Communist Youth Movement.

"I couldn't live here," Jennie said.

"What would you do?"

"Run away."

Do you think it's that easy, Jennifer?

Jennie hadn't heard the voice since the train. Now here it was again, loud and clear and insistent. She shivered and put her hands over her ears. Her Oma seemed not to notice.

"We have just enough time to go to the Brandenburger Turm before lunch," she said.

"What's the Br . . . whatever?"

"It's where tourists like you go to see the Wall from this side."

Again, Jennie started to argue about the Wall's existence; again she did not do so. "Can't we see it from any old place?"

"There are land mines and guards and policemen even there, where the tourists are allowed," the old lady said.

"Let's skip it. My leg hurts, and I'm hungry," Jennie said. "Besides, I saw it all yesterday from the Reichstag."

"You should see Checkpoint Charlie from this side," her Oma said.

"Who cares?" Jennie asked.

You must care, Jennifer, the voice said.

Her Oma did not hear it. She did not need to hear it. She already cared. Too much.

The old man, Max, was waiting for Jennie and her Oma outside the Unter den Linden. He was wearing a silk paisley scarf, one he said Jennie's great-grandfather had given him. He embraced both of them and cried when he looked at Jennie, saying she reminded him so much of the grandchild he had lost.

The meal cost a dollar a head; the waitress, a government employee who couldn't be fired, ignored their orders and brought them kitchen surplus. Her service, or lack of it, constituted the only similarity thus far, Jennie thought, between East and West.

After the meal, Jennie needed to go to the bathroom. Had she not been convinced already, she said, the toilet paper would have been enough to make her a capitalist. She made a mental note to send a carton of Charmin to Max when she got back to the States.

"Max wants to buy you a present," her Oma said.

They went to the Alexanderplatz, the center of reconstruction for East Berlin. It was a shopping mall, designed in imitation of the architecture of Frank Lloyd Wright, her Oma said. The mall's hub was a department store where, because prices were low, too many people fought for too few pieces of merchandise.

Max bought Jennie a small jewelry box. He led her to a bench in the center of the mall and insisted upon handing it to her ceremoniously, using her Oma as his translator.

"If I were a young man," he said, "this would be considered a betrothal gift." Though his back was bent, his eyes were vital and alive. "I will tell my friends in Dresden that I am betrothed to the most beautiful girl in the world. You won't mind, will you?"

Jennie leaned over and hugged him.

"It's been too long since I felt young arms around my neck," he said, weeping openly. He was looking at Jennie, but she could see that he was thinking about another young girl, also not quite into womanhood. "She wouldn't give up," he went on. "I told her not to, but she said she had to try. She said it was easier than pretending to be what she was not." He wiped his tears on a large white handkerchief and stood up.

"Would you and your Oma do me the honor of riding the train with me back to Dresden?"

"How far away is it?" Jennie asked.

"Three hours," Max said, "but it requires a visa."

The red tape, however, turned out to be inordinate. Several hours later, the three of them decided they had set themselves an impossible task.

"You could simply ride with me as my guests," Max said. "If the authorities question you, plead ignorance."

Her Oma translated.

"They'll put us in a camp," Jennie wailed.

The old man understood. "No, young lady," he said, pronouncing the English words with difficulty. "For there, too, you would need a visa."

Not knowing how to respond to such a statement, Jennie said, "Well, if we're not doing Dresden, you two will want to enjoy each other for a while longer. Why don't you sit on the bench in the Alexanderplatz and chat. Oma says I must see Checkpoint Charlie from this side before we leave. I'll go take a look and come back here in an hour or so."

"It's getting late. Don't bother with going all the way to the Brandenburger Turm," her Oma said. "You can see part of the *Mauer*—the Wall—at the bottom of this road."

Yeah, sure, the Wall, Jennie thought. What she needed was a walk, by herself, away from all of these people who had lost touch with reality.

Once again using her Oma's umbrella as a cane, Jennie limped toward the far end of the street. Rounding a curve in the road, she took her camera out of its case and held it up to one eye.

She could see nothing through the lens except a wall, *the* Wall, its top decorated by a spiral of barbed concertina wire.

"I give up," Jennie said aloud, and focused on a car that was winding its way from East to West over a series of hazards, metal spikes set backward into the road like teeth in the jaws of a shark.

Can you see the obstacle course, Jennifer? It was built after several people escaped by strapping themselves under cars.

"I think that guard's trying to get my attention," Jennie said, speaking out loud because she felt spooked and somehow the sound of her own voice comforted her.

The man waved at her from the ramp of a tower. *See,* she thought, waving back, *they're perfectly human. It's probably just lonely up there. . . .*

She moved closer. The guard appeared to be saying something to her, but she was just out of earshot.

He moved off the ramp and down a ladder, and suddenly he was near enough for his voice to reach her. She could hear his words. See his machine gun.

"*Weg!*" he shouted. Away.

There was no mistaking the menace in his voice.

You have done nothing wrong, Jennifer. If humanity keeps running from oppression instead of trying to change it, freedom will become an empty word.

"Don't tell me, tell the dude with the gun," Jennie said. "I know I haven't done anything wrong. All I have to do is convince him."

The guard lowered his weapon slightly and gestured at her. Shaking his head, he pantomimed replacing a camera over his shoulder, his machine gun tucked under one arm and held loosely, like a bag of groceries. He was close enough to her now that Jennie could feel his tension; he didn't want to shoot her, she thought, but he would if he had to.

The guard lowered his weapon. Waiting.

Lights! Camera! Action! Jennie thought, psyching herself up. "I am not involved," she yelled. "I'm innocent." She lowered her voice. "Cry your eyes out, Brooke Baby," she whispered. "The Award is mine. Mine, I say."

The guard nodded, but didn't move.

Jennie had no idea what she was supposed to do next. "No need to get upset," she said, choosing the direct approach. "I'm leaving."

For California, where they would never believe any of this.

And which she hoped never to leave again.

Then she glanced at the Wall and pictured Max's granddaughter sitting astride it. "All the king's horses, and all the king's men," she said softly.

She looked back at the guard. He had come close enough now that she could see his face. He reminded her of the guard at the Community Center; not black, but young, handsome, a little older than she.

"We are the new generation," she called out to him, in English, but using the words that the other guard had said to her. "We are not accountable for the past, but the future is our responsibility."

He smiled at her, and turned away. She wasn't sure if he spoke English or not, but she knew it didn't matter; he understood. What surprised her even more was that *she* understood.

She remembered the sweet young voice, who spoke for all of the dead, and, for at least that moment, she knew that she, Jennie, must listen for all of the living.

It's not about being a Jew, or about being a Catholic or a Buddhist. It's not about being white or black, or a communist or a capitalist.

"You are right, my friend," she whispered, her voice barely audible against the receding tromp of the guard's boots as he returned to his lonely vigil. "It's about Freedom."

She turned to face the Alexanderplatz. She could see shapes, now, in the twilight, ones she had not seen before: modern hotels; tourists; businessmen in well-cut suits and students with overstuffed backpacks. Closer to her, crossing her path and moving through the curves where moments ago the Wall had stood, she could make out the shape of a sepia woman, and, flying into the wind, the ghostly shape of a runner—long legs striding easily, blond hair streaming outward like a victory banner.

"It's a beginning," Jennie shouted out, walking without a limp along the path where, ten years before, bricks and mortar and hatred had separated East from West. "They may never believe me in California, but it's a beginning."

Author Biographies

Kevin J. Anderson has written over twenty-five books, including five *New York Times* bestsellers. He has also edited the anthologies *War of the Worlds: Global Dispatches*, *Tales from the STAR WARS Cantina*, and *Tales from Jabba's Palace*.

In 1994, Anderson's novel *Assemblers of Infinity*—written with Doug Beason—was nominated for the Nebula Award for best science fiction novel. Also that year his solo novel, *Climbing Olympus*, launched a new paperback line from Warner Books and has been published in a fine leatherbound edition from Easton Press and will be produced unabridged by Books on Tape. Other major novels include *Ill Wind* (also with Beason) and *Blindfold*, both published in 1995. More recently, *Ignition*, a high-adventure novel cowritten with Beason, was bought by Universal for film.

Peter S. Beagle was born in New York City in 1939. He has been a professional freelance writer since graduating from the University of Pittsburgh in 1959. His novels include *A Fine and Private Place*, *The Last Unicorn*, *The Folk of the Air*, and *The Innkeeper's Song*. His short fiction has appeared in such varied places as *Seventeen*, *Ladies Home Journal*, *Atlantic Monthly*, *The Saturday Evening Post*, and *New Worlds of Fantasy*, and his fiction to 1977 was collected in the book *The Fantasy Worlds of Peter S. Beagle*. Peter is also the coeditor (with Janet Berliner) of Peter S.

Beagle's *Immortal Unicorn* (HarperPrism, 1995), and most recently he wrote *The Unicorn Sonata* (Turner Publishing, 1996) which he co-created with Janet Berliner.

His film work includes screenplays for Ralph Bakshi's animated film *The Lord of the Rings*, *The Last Unicorn*, *Dove*, and an episode of *Star Trek: The Next Generation*. He has also written a stage adaptation of *The Last Unicorn*, and the libretto of an opera, *The Midnight Angel*.

Peter currently lives in Davis, California with his wife, the Indian writer Padma Hejmadi.

Greg Bear is regarded by many as the premiere author of hard science fiction. He has published over fifteen novels, among them the classic *Blood Music* and the best-sellers *Eon, Eternity, The Forge of God, Anvil of Stars, Queen of Angels, Moving Mars*, and *Legacy*. His works have won the Hugo and Nebula awards, have been translated into twelve languages, and have been adapted for television and radio.

Bear has acted as a technical and speculations advisor for the Spielberg/Amblin Productions TV series, *Earth 2*, and has consulted with Microsoft and others on multimedia, interactive television, and future forms of fiction and nonfiction.

Present works-in-progress include a new novel, *The Country of the Mind*. He has recently edited a major anthology of original science fiction, *New Legends*.

Janet Berliner is the creative force behind, among other things, *Peter S. Beagle's Immortal Unicorn* (HarperPrism, 1995), which she coedited with Peter, and *The Unicorn Sonata* (Turner Publishing, 1996), which Peter wrote. More recently, Janet has been asked to develop several projects for television, film, and Broadway.

Her recent novels include the first two volumes of the Madagascar Manifesto series, *Child of the Light* and *Child of the Journey*, cowritten with George Guthridge and published by White Wolf Books. The third volume, *Children of the Dusk*, will be released in January 1997. The next novel she hopes to write is *Dance of the Python*, a novel of treachery and witchcraft in modern tribal South Africa, written in the tradition of H. Rider Haggard.

Edward Bryant, though born in White Plains, New York, grew up on a cattle ranch in southeastern Wyoming. He began writing professionally in 1968 and has published more than a dozen books, starting with *Among the Dead* in 1973. Some of his titles have included *Cinnabar* (1975), *Phoenix Without Ashes* (with Harlan Ellison, 1975), *Wyoming Sun* (1980), *Particle Theory* (1981), and *Fetish* (1991). *Flirting with Death*, a major collection of his suspense and horror stories, appeared in late 1996, simultaneously with a new edition of *Particle Theory*.

Bryant's short stories have appeared in all manner of magazines and anthologies, including the prestigious *Norton Book of Science Fiction*. He's won two Nebula Awards, and in 1984 made it onto the map—literally—when he was placed on the Wyoming Literary Map by the Wyoming Association of Teachers of English.

He has worked as a guest lecturer, speaker, writer-in-residence. He frequently conducts classes and workshops. He occasionally works in film and television, as a writer and as an actor; in 1994, he played the Bard's parody of himself-as-opportunist-writer, Peter Quince, in *A Midsummer Night's Dream*. He has been a radio talk show host, a substitute motel manager, and a stirrup buckle maker, as well as holding other jobs. These days he lives with two Feline-Americans in a century-old house in North Denver along with many, many books. Presently he's working on a feature film script, a start-up comic book, and trying to finish a novel.

Robyn Carr, the author of fourteen novels, has established herself as a versatile writer, having published in a variety of genres. Her seventh novel, *By Right of Arms*, a historical romance, was the winner of the Romance Writers of America's Golden Medallion Award for the best historical novel. Her eleventh novel, *Woman's Own*, was awarded best multigenerational saga in 1990 by *Romantic Times*. Carr has recently concentrated on suspense, making her debut with *Mind Tryst*, a psychological thriller published by St. Martin's Press. She also contributes regularly to *Writer's Digest Magazine* and is the author of *Practical Tips for Writing Popular Fiction*, a how-to aid for would-be novelists, published by Writer's Digest Books.

Robyn Carr lives in Arizona with one husband, two children, three dogs, and no living houseplants.

David Copperfield was born in 1956 in Metuchen, New Jersey. His first television special, *The Magic of ABC*, aired in 1977. From then until now, between his yearly CBS specials, and his 500 live performances per year, he has been seen worldwide by more people than any other illusionist in history, including Houdini.

His celebrated feats and sense of theater have won him numerous Emmys, and have led him to be twice named "Entertainer of the Year." Six times he has performed for the president of the United States.

Performing professionally at the ripe age of twelve, David became the youngest person ever admitted into the Society of American Magicians. By the age of sixteen, he was teaching magic at New York University. While still in college, David was cast as the lead in a Chicago musical *The Magic Man*, in which he sang, danced, acted, and created all the magic in the show, which became the longest-running musical in Chicago's history.

David writes all of his own material, for his stage shows and his TV specials. Having already rewritten the book on magic, he is turning his hand to the writing of fiction.

Charles de Lint was born in the Netherlands and is presently a citizen of Canada. His father's job with a surveying company allowed him to grow up in places as diverse as the Yukon, Turkey, Lebanon, and the province of Quebec. A full-time writer and musician, he currently makes his home in Ottawa, Ontario, with his wife MaryAnn Harris, an artist and musician.

He is the proprietor/editor of Triskell Press, a small publishing house that prints occasional fantasy chapbooks and magazines. His writing includes novels, short stories, comic-book scripts, poetry and nonfiction, as well as reviews and columns for many magazines and newspapers. His short fiction has appeared in hardcover and paperback anthologies as well as in numerous magazines. He is the recipient of multiple awards, has served on many Awards Committees and Juries, and is an ongoing reviewer: "Books to Look For" for *The Magazine of Fantasy and Science Fiction*.

His most recent books are *The Ivory and the Horn* and *Memory and Dream*, both published by Tor Books.

Katherine Dunn's novels include: *Attic* and *Truck* (Harper & Row, hardcover; Warner Books, paperback), and the highly acclaimed *Geek Love*, (Alfred A. Knopf, hardcover; Warner Books, paperback). *Geek Love* was one of five finalists for the 1989 National Book Award and for the Bram Stoker Award. Her in-progress novel, *Cut-Man*, is under contract to Alfred A. Knopf.

Raymond E. Feist is the international best-selling author of the Riftwar Saga, *Faerie Tale*, and the Empire Trilogy. His books have been translated into more than a dozen languages, and he presently has over fifteen million books in print. His newest book, *Rise of a Merchant Prince*, is the second volume of the Serpentwar Saga, and was published in the fall of 1995. He lives in Rancho Santa Fe, California, with his wife, novelist Kathlyn S. Starbuck, their two children, several horses, cats, and assorted wildlife. Feist's hobbies include collecting wine, movies, and art.

Karen Joy Fowler was born in Bloomington, Indiana. She now lives in Davis, California, with her husband and two children. Her novel, *Sarah Canary*, won the Commonwealth Book Award for best first novel by a Californian. It has been compared to E.L. Doctorow's *Ragtime*. The *New York Times Book Review* said of it, "Ms. Fowler's prose is beautifully simple and evocative, and the narrative conception itself is a *tour de force*." She has also published *Artificial Things*, a collection of short stories. She has written many short stories which have been published in all manner of magazines and anthologies.

Fowler's latest novel is *The Sweetheart Season* (Henry Holt).

Neil Gaiman is creator/writer of the monthly cult DC Comics horror-weird series, Sandman, which has won

Neil the Will Eisner Comic Industry Awards for best writer (1991–1994), best continuing series (1991–1993), best graphic album—reprint (1991), and the Best Graphic Album—New (1993); the Harvey Award for best writer (1990, 1991) and best continuing series (1992). "Sandman #19" took the 1991 World Fantasy Award for best short story (the first comic ever to earn a literary award).

Angels and Visitations (DreamHaven 1993), a hardcover small press collection of his short fiction, prose, and journalism, issued to celebrate ten years as a professional writer, won the 1994 International Horror Critics' Guild Award as Best Collection. His stories have appeared for the last four years' running in the annual Year's Best Fantasy and Horror collection. His journalism has appeared in *The Sunday Times*, *Punch*, and many other places, and he recently finished his first book for children. *The Sandman: Book of Dreams*, which Gaiman edited along with Edward E. Kramer, was recently published by HarperPrism. Gaiman has also written for television and film, both in the States and in the U.K.

In 1982, **George Guthridge** accepted a teaching position in a Siberian-Yupik Eskimo village on a storm-swept island in the Bering Sea, in a school so troubled it was under threat of closure. Two years later his students made educational history by winning two national academic championships in one year—a feat that earned him the description as "Alaska's Jaime [*Stand and Deliver*] Escalante" and resulted in his being named one of seventy-eight top educators in the nation. Essays on his teaching techniques have been included in such books as *SuperLearning 2000*.

As a writer, he has authored or coauthored four

novels, including the Madagascar Manifesto series (with Janet Berliner, from White Wolf Books) and the Western *Bloodletter* (Northwest Books, 1994) and has been a finalist for the Nebula and Hugo awards. He currently teaches English and Eskimo education at the University of Alaska Fairbanks, Bristol Bay.

Eric Lustbader was born and raised in New York City. He graduated from Columbia University in 1969. Before becoming the author of such bestselling novels as *The Ninja*, *Angel Eyes*, *Black Blade*, and others, he had a successful career in the music industry. In his fifteen years of work in that field, he wrote about and worked with such artists as Elton John, who later asked Lustbader to write the liner notes for his 1991 box set *To Be Continued* . . . He was also the first person in the United States to predict the success of such stars as Jimi Hendrix, David Bowie, and Santana.

He has also taught in the All-Day Neighborhood School Division of the N.Y.C. Public School System, developing curriculum enrichment for third- and fourth-grade children. He currently lives in Southampton, New York, with his wife Victoria, who works for the Nature Conservancy.

Lustbader is currently hard at work on his next novel and playing with his new computer.

Anne McCaffrey's first novel was created in Latin class and might have brought her instant fame, as well as an A, had she written in that ancient language. Much chastened, she turned to the stage and became a character actress, appearing in the first successful summer music circus in Lambertsville, New Jersey. She studied voice for nine years and, during that time, became intensely interested in the stage direction of opera and operetta, ending that phase of her experience with the stage direction of the American premiere of Carl Orff's *Ludus de Nato Infante Mirificus*, in which she also played a witch.

By the time the three children of her marriage were comfortably in school most of the day, she had already achieved enough success with short stories to devote full time to writing. Her first novel, *Restoree*, was written as a protest against the absurd and unrealistic portrayals of women in the science fiction novels of the fifties. It is, however, in the handling of broader themes and the worlds of her imagination, particularly the two series (Helva, *The Ship Who Sang*, and the twelve novels about the Dragonriders of Pern) that Ms. McCaffrey's talents as a storyteller are best displayed.

Ms. McCaffrey graduated *cum laude* from Radcliffe College, majoring in the Slavonic languages and literatures. She presently lives in a house of her own design, Dragonhold-Underhill in Wicklow County, Ireland. Of herself, she warns: "My eyes are green, my hair is silver, and I freckle; the rest is still subject to change without notice."

Robert Silverberg's many novels include the best-selling Lord Valentine trilogy, the Nebula-winning *A Time of Changes*, the critically acclaimed *Hot Sky at Midnight*, *Kingdoms of the Wall*, and *The Face of the Waters*. He is also the coauthor, with Isaac Asimov, of *The Positronic Man*, as well as the coeditor of the recent Universe series of short-fiction anthologies. He has won numerous awards for his fiction, including five Nebulas, four Hugo Awards, a Jupiter Award, and the Prix Apollo. He lives near San Francisco with his wife, Karen Haber.

Steve Rasnic Tem has published over two hundred short stories to date in such publications as Robert Bloch's *Psycho Paths*, *Asimov's Science Fiction*, *Year's Best Fantasy & Horror*, *Metahorror*, *The Ultimate Dracula*, *Cutting Edge*, *Best New Horror*, *Love in Vein*, *It Came from the Drive-In*, *Sisters of the Night*, *Tales of the Great Turtle*, *Forbidden Acts*, and *Xanadu 3*. He's been nominated for the Bram Stoker Award, the World Fantasy Award, and the Philip K. Dick Award, and is a past winner of the British Fantasy Award.

He lives in Colorado with his wife, the Bram Stoker–winning novelist Melanie Tem, and their children.

Tad Williams is the author of the internationally acclaimed *Memory, Sorrow and Thorn* trilogy (New York Times and London Sunday Times best-sellers), *Caliban's Hour*, *Tailchaser's Song*, and with Nina Kiriki Hoffman, *Child of an Ancient City*. For a decade he hosted a syndicated radio show, *One Step Beyond*. He has also worked in theater and television production, taught grade-school and college classes, and worked in multimedia for Apple Computers. He is co-founder of an interactive television company, and is also writing film and television scripts. His graphic novel, *MirrorWorld*, and his latest novel, *OTHERLAND*, were published in the autumn of 1996. He and his wife Deborah Beale live in London and the San Francisco Bay Area.

Copyrights